Every Little Thing

D1446824

A.M. Myers

Every Little Thing
Bayou Devils MC
Book Seven

A.M. Myers

A.M. Myers

Every Little Thing

Cover Design by Jay Aheer
Proofreading by Julie Deaton

A.M. Myers

Every Little Thing

Chapter One
Wyatt

My eyes burn as I scan over the file in front of me again. It doesn't matter that I have read this same information a hundred times in the past week, I still search for more. There has to be more, something I missed along the way that will finally make all of this make sense. Sighing, I run a calloused hand over my face and grab my beer off the table as I lean back in my seat and take a sip. It's warm now but I don't give a shit. To be honest, I can't even taste it because I'm consumed with these cases. When I wake up in the morning, I look over the files. Before I go to bed at night, I look over the files and anytime I find a spare moment in my day, I look over these goddamn files. It's become my obsession and I know there is something here. I just need to see it. The rest of the Bayou Devils MC might like to believe that this is all just bad luck but I refuse. Three girls are dead, girls that we helped, girls that we were responsible for and there is no way in hell their deaths are simply a coincidence. No matter what my brothers think.

Leaning forward, I slam the bottle of beer back onto the table with too much force before scooping up the top file and scanning it again. Girl number one was Dina. She came to us for help to escape her piece of shit husband who liked to talk with his fists instead of his words. When she ended up in the hospital with bruises all over her body, a nurse slipped her our card and she gave us a call. We couldn't let her go back home to him so the nurse agreed to shelter her until we could get her to safety. Chance and Storm were on that run and shit went bad when her husband, Mitch, showed up at the nurse's house and tried to take her back by force. In the end, it all worked out and we took her to a hotel to keep her safe but almost two weeks later, we got the news that she was dead. At the time, we all assumed it was her husband but now... I just don't know.

Flipping the page, I read over the crime scene report Detective Rodriguez was able to give me and blow out a breath. A maid at the hotel where she was staying found her when she came to clean the room and called an ambulance. When paramedics arrived, she was barely breathing and they rushed her to the hospital. The doctors ran numerous tests before it was determined that there was no brain activity and her mother decided to turn off life support. She slipped away a few hours later. We were all hit hard by her death but we understood that it was a part of what we did, a sad reality of helping women and children in these volatile situations.

The Bayou Devils MC used to be a real outlaw club, running guns and drugs, just out to make a quick buck but after one of our members, Henn, was sent to jail and our

Every Little Thing

President, Blaze, was shot, things started to change and when a frantic woman crashed into Blaze at a gas station, everything changed. We started helping people and we opened up a legitimate business. This is all secondhand information, of course, since I didn't join until after the club started down the straight and narrow but I have heard enough stories from the guys who have been around longer than I have to know how chaotic things used to be. For me, joining the club after years of aimless wandering was like finally finding the place where I belonged and I loved being able to use my skills to help people without the restrictions that held me back in the past. Although, I can't help but feel like I am failing them now.

Barely holding back a growl, I toss the file down on the table and grab the next one before flipping it open. The second girl was Detective Rodriguez's girlfriend, Laney. We first met Diego Rodriguez a few years back when Blaze's son, Nix, and his girlfriend, Emma, needed our help and ever since then, he has helped us out on cases when he could and we return the favor. When he called us in to help on Laney's case, he had just started digging into it and all we knew was that she had been getting weird phone calls from a man. At first, all he did was breathe on the other end of the line to scare her and when that wasn't enough anymore, he escalated to commenting on her outfit that day or the errands she had run - anything to let her know that he was watching her. Just before we were called in to help watch over her, he told her it would be such a shame when he had to kill her. While Rodriguez dug into the case, we kept an eye on her and made sure she was safe until he tracked down Owen, the man responsible for harassing her.

But just a couple of weeks after he was locked up, Rodriguez came home and found Laney in a pool of blood. After that, he kind of lost it and our main focus was to keep him from spiraling out of control.

As I scan through the facts of the case, I notice a note scribbled at the top of the page about a man that Smith saw at Laney's funeral and scowl. It would be incredibly moronic for the killer to show up there but that doesn't mean he didn't do it. Then again, it could have just been someone visiting a dead relative. I read over the note again and me knee bounces underneath the table as I sigh.

Average white guy, kind of tall, brown hair, slim.

Shaking my head, I flip through the file and pull out the dark, grainy photo Rodriguez got off of a surveillance camera near the pay phone this guy used to call Laney when he was stalking her. You can't see his face, but he matches Smith's description from the funeral to a T which is the biggest problem. He's perfectly average, the kind of guy you don't even notice, the one who can slip through a crowd without a single person remembering the features of his face. The kind of guy that can get away with murder. Shaking my head, I toss the file down on the table and grab my beer before finishing it off.

"You need another one, Fuzz?" Cleo, our bartender, asks and I nod. She flashes me a coy smile as she fishes another bottle of beer out of the fridge and opens it. Her hips sway back and forth as she walks over to me and normally, I might be interested in what she's offering up tonight but with the cases on my mind, there is no way in hell I can focus on anything else. She sets the beer down in front of me and I nod as I scoop the third file off of the table.

"Thanks, Cleo."

She winks. "Anytime, babe."

I watch her as she sashays back behind the bar before taking a sip of my beer and flipping the third file open. Girl number three, Sammy, was just killed a little over a month ago and her death was the catalyst for my newfound obsession. In the first case, it was safe to assume that Dina's husband came back to finish the job and for Laney, I suppose we were all too busy looking out for Rodriguez to put the pieces together but with Sammy... it was different.

The club first got into contact with Sammy through her sister, who asked us to help her break Sammy away from her insane boyfriend. We later realized that her boyfriend was Biche, the guy who was responsible for Henn going to jail, but before we could do anything, we lost contact with her. She resurfaced a couple of years later, called us and we swooped in to get her away from him. The plan went off without a hitch and Sammy was starting a new life on her own when we got the call that she had been killed. Normally, we would assume that Biche got to her again but with him not in the picture anymore, it's just not possible. Which left me wondering if there was more going on here than any of us realized and started my trip down this demented rabbit hole.

"Church!" Blaze calls from the door to the war room and I release a breath as I close the file and toss it on the table. Grabbing my beer, I run my hand over my face and stand up, taking a sip before I follow the rest of the guys into the room. We all file around the table to our regular seat before Blaze grabs the gavel and bangs it on the table, nodding to Streak. Streak stands up and passes a sheet of paper to each of us.

"First up this week, we have Marina who hired us to investigate the man her father went into business with. Her father has run a very successful Italian restaurant for many years and took on a partner last year to lighten his workload but Marina is concerned that Mr. Girouard is taking advantage of her father. Fuzz and Smith, this case is yours."

I glance over at Smith and nod.

"Second up is a security detail for Mikayla Silva. She's a witness to a murder and Rodriguez has requested our assistance in keeping her safe through the trial."

"Storm, Chance, Kodiak, and Henn, y'all will rotate shifts round the clock to keep her safe," Blaze says and they all nod in agreement. "Anything else we need to go over?"

Nodding, I sit forward and meet Blaze's eyes. "We need to talk about the cases I've been looking into."

Kodiak sighs from his spot two seats down and I flick an annoyed glance in his direction before focusing back on Blaze. From the very beginning, Kodiak has been adamant that there is nothing going on and I'm afraid that other people are starting to believe him but I know there is something here. Call it experience or intuition but either way, I'm convinced that the death of these three girls aren't just coincidence.

"What about them?" Blaze asks, his brows furrowed. "Have you found anymore evidence?"

I drop my gaze to the table and shake my head. "No."

"That's because there's nothing to find," Kodiak snaps, slamming his hand on the table and my head jerks up.

"Look, if you want to bury your head in the damn sand

like a coward, that's your business but if we ignore this and I'm right, the next one to die could be someone important to all of us. Y'all have wives and families now that you have to think about and you can't afford to dismiss this."

Kodiak growls. "Leave Tate out of this."

"Or what?" I snarl as I square my shoulders and meet his gaze. He stands, his hands balled into fists but before I can jump out of my chair, Blaze slams the gavel down on the table, drawing the attention of everyone in the room.

"Enough." The roar of his voice echoes through the room as his gaze flicks between the two of us, anger lighting up his eyes. "It will be a cold day in hell before I let you all turn on each other. That's not the way this club works."

I deflate as I nod my head and Kodiak murmurs his agreement as Blaze turns to me.

"Listen, Fuzz… unless you can show me some new evidence, I'm inclined to side with Kodiak…"

"Hell, no," I say, cutting him off. "I know I'm right about this."

"And what proof do you have?"

"Since this club turned things around eight years ago, we've lost five girls total and three of those girls have been in the last two years and the other two, we *know,* beyond a shadow of a doubt, were killed by their exes. Also, all three of the girls who were killed in the last couple of years had our card with them when they died."

"Of course they had our card, we helped all of them," Kodiak mutters.

"But they *all* had them when they died. Are you gonna tell me they just carried our card around all the time with them?"

He nods. "It's fucking possible."

"For the sake of argument here," Streak says, leaning back in his chair. "Why would they need the card? Wouldn't they have put the numbers in their phone?"

"Exactly and what about Sammy? Our card was *laying* on top of her body when they found her."

"Not to mention, Biche couldn't have done it," Henn adds and I nod. Holy shit, are they actually saying I might be onto something? Finally?

"I'll admit that Sammy's case is weird but it's also entirely possible that it was a fluke. Dina was murdered by her ex, Mitch. Rodriguez locked up the wrong guy and Laney was killed by the guy who was really stalking her and Sammy could have just been random."

I squeeze my eyes shut. "And this random killer found our card and decided to place it on top of her dead body?"

"Maybe."

"Jesus Christ," I growl, shaking my head. "Why can't you open your damn eyes and see what's right in front of you?"

"If there was something to see, I'd see it but there isn't."

"And what if I'm right and the next time someone gets hurt, it's one of your old ladies? Or your sister? Or someone's mom?"

"I fucking told you not to talk about my wife and maybe if you stopped obsessing over this shit, you'd finally be able to find a woman willing to put up with you." His comment stings more than I'd like to admit but I push it down. It's not important right now. He shoves his chair away from the table like he's going to storm out but Blaze holds his hand up to stop him.

"Enough!" he bellows and the room is painfully silent as he shakes his head in disappointment. "Fuzz, there isn't enough evidence to move on this yet and I can't spare anymore people to look into it right now but if you want to keep investigating, you can."

I scoff as I cross my arms over my chest and lean back in my seat. As if he could stop me from digging into this more. I know I'm right and I won't stop until I find the truth.

"And the two of you," he says, motioning between Kodiak and me. "Need to sort this shit out now. If Fuzz is right and there is more to these cases than we can see, we cannot be divided. Is that understood?"

I nod. "Yeah, boss."

"Fine," Kodiak growls, sparing a glance in my direction. Blaze rolls his eyes before turning to look around the table at the rest of the guys.

"If there's nothing else…"

When no one says anything, he nods and slams the gavel on the table to dismiss us. I grab my beer off the table and follow everyone else out of the room before going back to the table with the files on it and sinking into the chair.

"Holy shit!" Chance yells from the bar, a wide smile on his face as he slaps Smith on the shoulder. I arch a brow as he turns to the rest of us and holds up his beer. "Quinn's knocked up!"

The room explodes with cheers and shouts of congratulations as they all drift toward Chance and Smith to give him the old "atta boy" shoulder pat. I force a smile to my face before lifting my bottle of beer to my lips and draining half of it, my stomach churning. I don't mean to be an asshole and I certainly don't want to be but each time one of my brothers falls in love and starts his own family, I can't help but think of all the plans I had for my life that haven't come to fruition. I'm happy for all of them, especially Smith and his wife, Quinn, after everything they went through but it still doesn't stop the onslaught of memories of pain that I usually keep under lock and key.

Shaking my head, I try to force my mind to turn off as I finish off my beer and set the bottle on the table. Cleo holds up another bottle in question from behind the bar and I shake my head. In the mood I'm in, if I keep drinking, I'll end up too drunk to drive home and I can't stay here tonight with the celebration that is sure to follow an announcement like that. Sparing a glance at the group, I gather up my files and slip away from the bar without anyone noticing before stepping outside. It's still muggy as hell even though the sun went down hours ago and I sigh as I slip the files into my saddlebag, looking forward to the ride home. Maybe it's just what I need to clear my mind.

After climbing on the bike, I back it out of the parking spot and turn the key, my heart kicking in my chest as the engine rumbles to life. God, I love that sound. After I got back from my first deployment, I needed something to take my mind off of all the shit in my life and jumping on the back of a bike gave me the peace and quiet I so desperately craved. The roar of the motor drowned out the sounds of war and the vibrations of the bike beneath me distracted me from the hollow, persistent ache in my chest. Just thinking of that time in my life brings back awful memories and I try to clear them as I peel out of the parking lot. For a solid two years, I was a miserable, cranky bastard and even now, ten years later, it still kills me to think about that time and my traitorous bitch of a wife. I guess I assumed that, in time, the throbbing ache in my chest would disperse and if I'm thoroughly distracted, it's easier to ignore but it never really goes away.

I try to relax as downtown Baton Rouge blurs past me, fighting back memories both good and bad. Thinking back to the last time I saw her, the day I deployed, that damn ache returns and I rev the bike's engine like maybe if I go fast enough, I'll finally be able to outrun it. Man, how fucking pathetic am I? Piper threw away everything we had and everything we could have built together and here I am, still thinking about her when it's clear, she doesn't give a damn about me or the plans we made. And they were grand fucking plans, too - a cute little house, some kids running around in the backyard with the dogs and my woman by my side until the end. Thing is… I still want all that. Not with Piper, of course. She can rot in hell for what she did to me but the wife, the kids, the house, and the dogs… I've never given up on that dream and hearing Smith's news tonight just reminded me how badly I want it.

Pulling my bike into my parking spot in front of my building and climbing off, I run through my options as I grab my files out of the saddlebag and turn toward my door. I've spent years working my ass off to avoid thinking about Piper and what she did to me and it's left me without options. I mean, occasionally I'll hook up with Cleo when the need gets to be too much but it's never been anything more than mindless fucking and I can't see that woman being the mother of my children. So, what else is there? I could go out to a bar and try to pick someone up but the odds of finding someone that is looking for the same things I am seems unlikely at best. Sighing, I unlock my door and slip into my place before dropping the files onto the table with a thump and flipping the light on.

My gaze flicks around my one thousand square foot townhouse and I sigh again, rubbing my hand over my face. It's a quintessential bachelor pad complete with the signature black leather couch and it's even more depressing than Smith's announcement. I peel my jacket off and toss it on one of the dining room chairs before turning to the fridge and grabbing a beer. As I sink into the couch, I grab the remote and kick my boots off before flipping through the channels. A baseball game catches my eye and I toss the remote to the cushion next to me and take a sip of my beer. My vision blurs. I drop my head back and close my eyes, rubbing them as I yawn. An image of Piper fills my mind almost immediately. Growling, my eyes snap open and I down half my beer as a commercial for a dating site flashes across the TV. I snort.

"There's no way in hell," I mutter, shaking my head. I'm not too proud to admit that I'm desperate for my dream to become a reality but I'm not that desperate. Finishing off my beer, I stand up and trudge back into the kitchen to grab another one before plopping down on the couch again. The game helps me turn my brain off and I drink three more beers before glancing at the stairs and telling myself I should go to sleep. The commercial for the dating site comes on again and I turn back to the TV. Maybe it's the five beers making my brain fuzzy but I don't have the same reaction to it that I did last time. Instead, I'm left wondering... why not? My brows draw together and before I know what I'm doing, I have my phone in my hand and I'm typing in the website.

"Jesus Christ," I whisper to myself as I click the sign-up button and the application flashes across my screen. "I'm not really doing this."

Glancing up at the TV, a gorgeous brunette models shampoo but in my head, all I can see is Piper - her pale skin, rosy cheeks, smokey green eyes, and long dark red hair as she straddles my lap and takes my cock inside her.

"Fuck."

I chug my beer and set the bottle down on the coffee table before holding my phone in front of my face and start filling in my information before uploading a photo of myself. When I'm finished, my thumb hovers over the submit button and I suck in a breath. I blow it out as my stomach flips and I press the button. The page refreshes and my profile stares back at me as I shake my head.

Fuck it.

What's the worst that could happen?

Chapter Two
Piper

The familiar chords of Canon in D by Pachelbel begin to play, drifting across the manicured grounds of the plantation, twisting between the sprawling branches of the massive oak trees scattered around the plantation and float across the gleaming water as every guest in attendance stands and turns toward the back of the house, waiting for the bride to make her first appearance. Ignoring her, I focus my lens on the man waiting for her at the other end of the aisle and start snapping photos, one right after the other in rapid succession and the moment he sees her, his eyes widen and his jaw drops. Tears well up in his eyes and I grin as warmth radiates through my body and I continue snapping photos. Most people like to watch the bride walk down the aisle when they come to a wedding and Eden, my business partner and best friend, will make sure we get plenty of shots of her but my favorite part of any wedding we're hired to photograph is to watch the groom's expression as soon as he sees his bride for the first time. Whether he smiles, stares at her in awe, fights back tears, or bawls like a baby, it's always magical and it reminds me of a time in my life when I had the same thing.

Pushing away those memories, I continue photographing her walk down the aisle and when she reaches the altar, I move to the middle of the aisle and creep forward to continue capturing their ceremony. I glance over to my side as Eden works her way around the outside of the guests to get an even better angle of the groom's face as the preacher begins speaking. Staring up at the couple, I notice their hands intertwined and snap a couple shots of that before moving the camera up to their faces. The dress our bride chose embodies classic southern elegance and it's molded to her body like a second skin, showing off her curves as she stares up at her groom, her eyes shining with unshed tears. It would be a killer shot if I could just find the right vantage spot... scanning the outskirts of the property, I notice a tree that would give me the perfect angle and I rush back to my equipment, swapping out my lens for a longer one before motioning to Eden. She glances over to where I'm pointing and smiles with a nod.

After securing my camera around my neck with the strap and kicking off my heels, I jog around the outside of the seating area, ignoring the disapproving looks from the older guests as I loop my hands around the lowest branch and pull myself up as discreetly as possible. Wedding photography is a delicate balance because each couple wants that perfect shot that they will proudly hang in their home for the rest of their lives but I also have to be careful not to be a distraction and sometimes, that's easier said than done. Especially when I'm doing something crazy like climbing a tree to get the right angle but if it works… it will be glorious.

With my heart thundering in my chest, I climb the tree as quickly and quietly as possible before situating myself on one of the branches and bringing my camera to my eye and grinning. Just over the groom's shoulder, I can see the bride's face as he begins reciting his vows and I start snapping, capturing each and every emotion that flits across her face as a few tears spill down her cheeks and her smile nearly splits her face. Love shines in her eyes and it smacks me in the chest. I suck in a breath as pain blossoms where my heart should be and branches out through my body like a virus. Fighting back tears of my own, I keep shooting, trying frantically to focus on the job at hand instead of the source of the agony ripping through my body.

As the bride begins reciting her vows, Eden crouches down on the other side of them and I climb back down the tree as quickly as possible so I can get set up for their first kiss. Once I'm on the ground again, I jog around the crowd to the back of the aisle and creep forward before dropping to my knees and training my lens up at the happy couple.

"I now pronounce you husband and wife," the preacher declares. "You may kiss your bride."

The groom flashes his new wife a wide smile as he hooks an arm around her waist and pulls her onto his lips before dipping her and the crowd whoops and hollers around me. Grinning, I snap several photos and an image of Wyatt smiling at me flashes through my mind before I can stop it. God, I love his smile. When we were married, it was one of my favorite things in the world but now it only serves as a reminder of everything I've lost... everything I walked away from. Shaking my head, I push the emotions down as I start backing up, snapping photos constantly, as the bride and groom clasp hands and begin walking down the aisle toward me, beaming at their guests and each other before turning to me to flash me a grin. When they get to the end of the aisle, they turn to each other and kiss again and I snap a couple more photos before moving to the table Eden and I set up to organize all our equipment.

"Wait until you see the photo I snapped of you climbing that damn tree," Eden says as she walks up to me and I scoff as I shake my head.

"Whatever. As long as the client is happy."

She nods. "Did you get a good shot?"

"You think I climbed a tree and missed the shot?" I ask, clicking over to the photos I took today and flipping to the one I snapped up in the tree before showing it to her. Her lips part in a silent gasp.

"Okay. That's gorgeous. Totally worth climbing a tree over. Although, Teresa's grandma looked like she wanted to murder you."

I glance over at the bride's grandma and she meets my gaze before narrowing her eyes in disgust. I shrug as I turn back to Eden. "Again, whatever."

"What are you thinking for the official wedding photos?" she asks as she turns to scan the property. I secure the flash on top of my camera and turn to do the same, pursing my lips. The afternoon sun is bouncing off the water and in about an hour, the light will be absolutely perfect.

"Let's get all the family shots and then we can get the

bride and groom down by the water and also by one of these oak trees."

She nods and holds out several strings of mini paper lanterns. "You want to string these through the branches while I round the family up?"

"You got it."

As she heads into the crowd to collect everyone, I go back to the tree I climbed earlier and inspect it before looking around the property. Other trees have better branches on them but this tree has a perfect view of the lake in the background that will look gorgeous with the lights as the sun starts to go down. I quickly hang the strings of lights off the branches before plugging them into one of our extension cords to make sure they are all still working. The soft light they emit is so romantic and I can practically see the photos in my head as I smile and unplug them until we're ready for them.

"Piper," Eden calls and I glance over my shoulder as she waves me over to a shady spot where the family is waiting for us to begin. Nodding, I jog over to the table and grab my camera and a reflector before joining them. As Eden gets the bride's extended family set up for their first shot, I loop the camera strap over my neck and move the reflector around until it casts a golden glow on the group. Eden snaps a few photos before reorganizing the group to include the bride and her parents. Once she has enough shots, she pulls the groom in and snaps a couple more photos before replacing the bride's parents with the groom's and going through the whole process again. After we grab a big group photo with everyone in it, she sends everyone on their way except for the bride, groom, and the wedding party.

"How are you guys holding up?" Eden asks Teresa as we make our way down to the lake. Maybe it sounds like a weird question to ask someone on what is supposed to be the happiest day of their lives but after doing a couple of these, we figured out that weddings are as exhausting as they are exciting. Teresa beams, clasping her new husband's hand in between both of hers as she glances up at him and he grins down at her.

"It's been magical."

More images from my past hit me in the gut as we reach the edge of the lake and I resist the urge to squeeze my eyes shut. Eden glances over at me with a concerned expression but I just shake my head. When I first met Eden in a photography class a little over six years ago, I put on one hell of a good show but I was still a shell of a person, struggling to figure out how to just be but Eden always saw through the bullshit and she never pushed me to open up before I was ready. As we both continued studying photography, our friendship grew and I spilled the truth of my ugly past to her one drunken night. She never once judged me for it and she's never used it against me. By the time the class ended, we both knew we wanted to pursue doing photography full-time and we were practically like sisters so it only made sense for us to go into this together.

"You okay?" she whispers under her breath and I nod my head. Eden knows how hard weddings can be for me which is why we don't take all that many but they are good money so every once in a while, I have to bite the bullet. She sighs, her brows still knitted in concern. "I've got your back if you need to bounce."

"Thank you."

As she sets the wedding party up for their first photo, I stare out across the water. My issues with weddings are so layered and so complicated that I don't even know how to begin to explain it. My own wedding day was one of the happiest days of my life and if I close my eyes, I can still see Wyatt smiling down at me as he told me that he was going to love me with his whole heart until the day he took his last breath but everything that happened after that day… I turn away from the group as I blink away tears and suck in a breath.

"You know, I think I'm going to go get some shots of the reception while you finish this up," I say just loud enough for Eden to hear me and she places her hand on my arm, drawing my gaze back to her as she nods.

"Go. I got this."

Nodding, I mouth a thank you to her before hiking back up the hill with my camera in my hand, grateful to be away from all the love, happiness, and wedded bliss. Not that I'm bitter or anything… When I go to my appointment with Dr. Brewer next week, she's going to be disappointed that I ran away instead of confronting my feelings in the moment and as much as she's helped me, sometimes her advice isn't all that practical. I mean, hell, I can't exactly have a mental breakdown in the middle of someone's special day. That's just about the tackiest thing I've ever heard. Besides, these couples hire Eden and I to capture every moment of one of the most important days of their life, not blubber on about the mistakes I've made in my life.

Once I get back up to the house, I take my time as I grab the equipment I'll need for shooting indoors and slip in the back door, wandering around the lavish house before following the sound of music. The party isn't really in full swing yet since everyone is still waiting for the happy couple to show up but I lift my camera to my face and snap a few photos of the flower girl, the ring bearer, and their friends dancing to the pop song playing around the ballroom before scanning the crowd and getting a great shot of the groom's grandma laughing at something the gentleman next to her said. Sighing, I glance over at the door, guilt eating away at me that I'm not out there doing my job with Eden before shoving the feeling down and gazing around the room again. I wouldn't mind being able to sit down for a second either. Eden and I have been here, photographing everything since noon when the bride started getting ready and my feet are starting to ache.

"Ladies and Gentlemen, Mr. and Mrs. Stewart," the DJ booms and everyone stands and cheers as the bride and groom walk into the room, hand in hand. I raise my camera and snap a couple of shots before feeling a nudge at my side.

"Feeling better?" Eden asks.

"Yeah. Get some good shots?"

She nods, surveying the crowd. "The sunset was incredible and those little lanterns you hung in the tree worked perfectly."

"I can't wait to see them," I tell her with a smile. My stomach flips, the guilt eating away at me again. It's really not fair to Eden that she has to take on the bulk of work sometimes because of my issues but I also don't know what else I can do about it. She nudges me again and I glance over at her.

"I know what that look on your face means and you need to knock that shit off right now."

I scowl as I turn away from her. "I don't know what you're talking about."

"Mmhmm. Wanna talk about it?"

"Not particularly," I mutter.

"I thought maybe this wedding wouldn't be so hard since you have James now."

I flinch at the mention of my boyfriend... or ex-boyfriend now, technically. "I ended things with James."

"Why?" She doesn't sound all that surprised by my news and even I have to admit, I'm not even a little upset by the fact that we broke up so maybe she saw this coming before I did. I glance back at her.

"We didn't want the same things."

She arches a brow. "Which means what? That he wasn't Wy…"

"Don't finish that statement," I warn her, shaking my head. There are some things I like about Eden knowing everything about my past and then there are things that I really hate like her calling me on my shit each and every time. "He didn't want to have kids."

"Oh," she whispers. "Are you okay? With the breakup, I mean?"

I nod. "Yeah. Honestly, I'm not even upset about it. More relieved than anything else… I don't know. I guess I only started dating again to try and move on with my life but I'm starting to wonder if it's a lost cause."

"You're not a lost cause, Piper. Don't talk about yourself like that."

"I just mean… maybe I'm not meant to have all this," I

answer, motioning to the reception surrounding us. "Maybe I had my shot at love and a family and I screwed it all up."

Wrapping her arm around my shoulders, she pulls me into a hug with a sigh. "People don't just get one shot at love, babe. That I'm sure of and if you're serious about wanting a family, you don't need a man for that."

"Uh, technically you do need a man. That's like one of the two main ingredients."

She laughs. "Don't be a smart ass. You know what I meant. You could get a sperm donor and get inseminated or whatever."

"Do it myself? Seriously?"

"Why not?" she answers with a shrug. "It's two thousand nineteen and you are a strong, independent woman. If you want to have a baby, find a way to make it happen."

Staring out at the newly married couple as they dance, I chew on my bottom lip and raise my camera to my eye to snap a couple photos as the thoughts bounce around in my mind. Could I really do it all myself? I mean, anytime I thought about the family I wanted to have, Wyatt was always a part of that picture and no matter how hard I tried, the image never changed. That's probably why none of my other relationships worked out - not that there were all that many - but still, there is no room in my life and my heart for anyone else because Wyatt is always there. Having a baby, though... it has always been one of my greatest dreams.

"Just think about it, okay? Don't sell yourself short because this is the kind of thing that you'll come to regret if you don't go for it."

Pulling the camera away from my face, I meet her eyes and nod. "Okay. I'll think about it."

"That's all I ask," she answers, grinning at me and I snort out a laugh.

"It's a pretty big ask. We're talking about a baby here and me being a single mother."

She shrugs. "Just imagine how happy you'll be when you have that little baby in your arms."

"Hold up. I thought I was just thinking about it and now I'm picturing my fictional future baby?"

Looping her arm through mine, she guides me to the corner of the ballroom where we can stay out of the way while we talk and snap candid photos. "Yes. Visualization is an essential part of destiny manifestation."

"I said I'll think about it, Edie. Don't push your luck."

"Okay, fine." She laughs. "But in all seriousness, I don't want you to think you're doing this alone. If you decide to go down this road, you'll have Lillian and me in your corner. Always."

I nod, my chest aching at the thought of having a baby on my own. Not because I think I couldn't do it or because I know it will be hard but because anytime I ever pictured my baby in the past, he always had Wyatt's hazel eyes and I'm not sure if that is an image I can let go of.

Every Little Thing

Chapter Three
Wyatt

"How many?" the cute blonde hostess asks as Smith and I walk into the homey little Italian restaurant that our client's father owns and I hold up two fingers as I scan what I can see of the dining room. She grabs the menus and instructs us to follow her as she turns and walks further into the restaurant. After leading us to a table situated along the front windows that gives us a perfect view into the bustling kitchen, I flash her a smile of thanks as I slide into my seat and Smith sits across from me. She briefly runs over the day's specials as she lays our menus in front of us.

"Can I get you two started with a drink? A beer, maybe?"

I shake my head. "Just water."

"I'll take a beer," Smith answers and she nods.

"Okay. I'll be right back with those and your waitress will be with you in just a moment."

As she turns and leaves, I scan the dining room, searching for the subject of our investigation but he is nowhere to be found. Sighing, I turn toward my menu and flip it open. When our client, Marina, came to us a couple weeks ago to ask for our help, she told us that her father has owned this restaurant for damn near forty years but as he got older, it was harder for him to keep up so he took on a partner to ease the workload. The only problem is, Marina has been hearing from the other staff that the partner, Ben, is a sleaze ball and running this place into the ground but she needs rock solid proof to try and force Ben out which is where we come in.

"I'll tell ya, brother," Smith says, engrossed in his menu. "I've definitely been on worse stakeouts."

I snort out a half laugh. "Yeah, I suppose."

"What's your deal lately?" he asks, glancing up from his menu with a knitted brow. I shake my head.

"I don't have a deal."

"Bullshit. I mean, you're usually pretty serious but you're not this damn grouchy. What the hell is going on?"

I run my hand through my hair. "Just worried about the club and the girls."

"Ah," he whispers, nodding his head before he turns to look out at the dining room. "I don't know, man. I don't want to believe that you're right but I'm not ready to proclaim that you're wrong either. Plus, that shit you said at church about it being someone we love next, well... I can't get that shit out of my head and with Quinn pregnant..."

"I never got a chance to say congratulations, by the way."

He nods, studying me. "Yeah, you bailed pretty quick after my announcement..."

"Yeah, I did."

"That's all I'm going to get?" he asks, irritation creeping into his tone. "I mean, you know that I know that it's bullshit, right?"

I arch a brow. "That your new favorite word?"

"Bullshit?" he questions and I nod. "Only when I smell the overwhelming scent of bullshit like right now."

"You can't smell anything but lasagna and garlic bread."

His stomach growls and his gaze flicks to the kitchen before he turns back to me. "I really wish I could smell that cause it sounds amazing but I'm like drowning in bullshit right now so…"

"Jesus Christ, you're not going to stop, are you?"

Grinning, he shakes his head. "Nope."

"Fine," I growl before my body deflates and I sigh. "I've just been thinking a lot lately with all of you settling down and starting families."

"You want the same?"

I nod. "Yeah, I do."

"So, do it. What the hell is holding you back?"

An image of Piper pops into my mind, her smokey green eyes boring into mine and asking me the same damn question.

"Shit…" Smith breathes and I meet his gaze as he looks up at me. "What's her name?"

"What?"

He rolls his eyes. "Oh, don't give me that, Fuzz. Your fucking face says it all. There's a woman and she's got you by the balls."

"No, she doesn't."

"Yeah, okay," he murmurs, flashing me a look that

makes it clear he doesn't believe a word coming out of my mouth. "You know what… I'm picking up on that scent again."

"Fuck off," I grumble as a petite little thing stops by our table with a pen and pad in her hand.

"Hey, boys. I'm Kenzie and I'll be your waitress today. What can I get you to drink?"

"Uh," I mutter, glancing back at the hostess who is playing on her phone by the front door. "We ordered a water and a beer already."

She follows my gaze and whispers a curse. "I'm so sorry. I'll be right back with those, okay?"

"Sure."

As she stomps off, I turn back to Smith who flashes me an expectant look. "So, what's her name?"

"Go fuck yourself, that's her name. Why don't you focus less on me and more on the case?"

"The way I see it," he replies, leaning back in his chair. "I can do both. Now, what's her name?"

"Anyone ever tell you that you're a goddamn pain in the ass?" I ask and he laughs.

"Yeah, it's part of my appeal."

I shake my head. "I doubt it."

"Name, please," he repeats with a shrug and my irritation grows. It's clear that he is not going to let this go and I would much rather get it out there and move on with my damn life.

"For fuck's sake. It's Piper, my ex-wife."

"Oh," he whispers, nodding. "The one who cheated on you when you were deployed and then left you?"

Gritting my teeth, I nod. "That's the one."

"Hold up," he demands, holding his hand up in front of him. "Why the hell does your ex-wife still have you by the balls?"

"Just forget about it, Smith."

He studies me for a second before his eyes widen. "Are you still in love with her?"

"Absolutely fucking not," I snap as the waitress stops at our table with our drinks and I am thankful for the interruption.

"Here you guys go. I'm so sorry about the mix-up. Who had the beer?"

Smith raises his hand and she sets the bottle down in front of him before setting my glass of water on the table by me and wiping her hands on her apron. She pulls the pen and pad out again and flashes us a bright smile.

"Okay. Y'all know what you want to order?"

Smith nods. "Yeah, I'll get the lasagna."

"Okay," she answers, scribbling his order down before turning to me. "And you, sir?"

"Chicken Alfredo."

Smiling, she writes my order down on her notepad before scooping up our menus and turning toward the kitchen. When I turn back to Smith, he looks like he wants to delve deeper into our conversation but I shoot him a warning look and he rolls his eyes as he pulls his phone out of his pocket. Relieved, I scan the dining room again, searching for our subject as I try to push thoughts of my least favorite person in the world out of my mind but even after all these years, she's fucking relentless. Like a parasite that no amount of medicine can kill.

"So…" Smith starts and I shake my head, flashing him

a look that makes it clear I'm done talking about this. He sighs as he leans back in his chair. "Dude, come on. How long has it been since she left?"

"This conversation is over." I don't want to think about how long it's been since Piper destroyed everything we had and walked away from me or how empty my life has felt in the years since. She doesn't matter to me anymore. Someone walks out of the kitchen and I glance over before nudging Smith's foot with mine. "Look who finally decided to show up."

Ben Girouard walks toward the register and smacks our waitress on the ass as he passes by her. Hatred burns in her eyes as she glares at him and I shake my head.

"What a pig," Smith growls and I nod.

"I know but we need something concrete."

Smith nods and pulls his phone out of his pocket, pretending to be playing a game as he begins recording Ben. We both watch him as he strolls right up to the register and opens it before pulling a couple of twenties out and shoving them in his pocket.

"Did Marina say anything about missing money?" Smith asks and I shake my head, disgust twisting my stomach as Ben shuts the register and starts walking toward the hostess who seated us.

"No, but she may not know."

He nods. "We need to get Streak to dig into the restaurant's finances."

"Not that there will be much to dig into," I reply, scanning the almost empty dining room. "My parents used to come here for their anniversary every year and they had to make a reservation like a month in advance. They said it had gone downhill but I didn't realize it was this bad."

The waitress walks out of the kitchen with a tray in her hand and Smith sits forward, tucking his phone away.

"Well, let's see how the food is."

"Here you boys go," the waitress says as she stops at our table and sets a plate in front of each of us. "Can I get y'all anything else?"

Smith smiles up at her. "I think we're good for now, darlin'."

"Just holler if you need me," she replies with a blush staining her cheeks and I nod as she turns and walks back to the counter. By the time I glance back at Smith, he's already shoving a huge piece of lasagna into his mouth and I sit back with an arched brow to see his reaction. He chews for a second before his face contorts with disgust and I laugh. To his credit, he doesn't spit it out but once he has forced the first bite down, he doesn't take a second.

"That's fucking terrible," he whispers and I nod, combing through the noodles on my plate that look like they were cooked a week ago.

"Yeah, we should get pictures of this shit, too."

He nods as he pulls his phone out again and starts snapping pictures of the food. "I gotta tell ya…"

His words are cut off by a crash from the kitchen and we both turn as Ben slaps one of the waitresses across the face. I'm out of my chair before I even realize what I'm doing but I don't get far before Smith grabs my arm.

"Sit down, brother," he hisses, his gaze flicking around the room and I do the same, deflating when I see the two other tables brave enough to risk lunch here, watching me. "We have to keep a low profile."

I stare at him for a second before shaking him off. Everything he says is true but I also can't let something like that just happen and not do anything. After charging across the dining room, I step into the kitchen and Ben turns to look at me. The man is a little pissant and I mean that literally since he just barely reaches the top of my chest as I glare at him. My gaze flicks to the blonde he hit.

"You okay, darlin'?"

She nods. "Yes."

"You feel safe enough to stay here?"

"I…" Her gaze flicks to Ben and I notice her hands shaking before she turns back to me with resolve in her gaze. "Yes, I'm okay."

"Guess what…" I say, turning back to Ben with my skin on fire and my fingers itching to wrap around his throat. I pretend to glance down at his name tag. "…Ben. You just made a new best friend."

"What the fuck is that supposed to mean?"

I take a step forward and flash him a menacing smile. "It means I'm going to be back here every goddamn day and if I ever see you put your hands on another woman, I'll show you how it feels. Are we clear?"

"You think I'm afraid of you?" he sneers, crossing his arms and I glance around the kitchen as the three cooks and dishwasher look on with a mixture of amusement and trepidation. Fuck this little shit, thinking he's a badass and hitting the women who work for him. Before he even realizes what's happening, I sweep his legs out from under him, flip him on his stomach, and shove my knee against his spine as he screams.

"What was that, Ben?"

"Okay, okay. It won't happen again."

"You're fucking right, it won't." I release him and stand back as he lumbers to his feet. As he backs away from me, I wave and flash him another grin. "See you tomorrow, Benjamin."

"Jesus, dude," Smith says as I get back to the table and sink into my seat. I shrug.

"What? I couldn't let him get away with that. Besides, I just gave us the perfect cover for coming back here every day."

He shakes his head. "Where the hell did you learn that move and can you show me how to do it?"

"The Marines and no," I answer with a laugh, feeling lighter than I did when we first arrived. My phone pings from my pocket and I pull it out, frowning when I see the notification from the dating app I signed up for.

"Everything okay?"

I glance up and nod before shoving the phone back in my pocket. I can't believe I actually signed up for that stupid thing and that I still haven't deleted it. "Yeah."

"You sure?" he asks, his face knitted in concern. I sigh.

"I drank too much the other night and signed up for a goddamn dating site."

He grins and leans forward. "Did you now? Any luck?"

"No," I lie, thinking of the message from a woman named Shiloh I just got. He laughs.

"You fucking liar."

I shake my head. "It doesn't matter cause it was a dumbass idea and I'm not going to go through with it."

"Why not?"

"'Cause like I said, it was just a dumb idea that sounded

good after a few too many beers."

"Yeah," he agrees, leaning back again. "But you just said you wanted the wife and the family and all that, right?"

I nod.

"So, you're never going to find it if you don't try."

I roll my eyes. "Like you tried? Or Storm? Or Kodiak? You all met your wives because of luck."

"Dude, just give it a shot. There's a coffee shop literally right across the street," he says, pointing out the window and I glance over my shoulder, eyeing the little cafe. "Just pop over there and get coffee with her. It's like thirty minutes out of your day."

I flash him a glare. "Just let it go."

"No. I'm serious. Give it a shot. Maybe she's the one."

"You sound like a goddamn girl right now, you know that?"

He shrugs. "All I hear you saying is that you're scared and maybe you should shut up and listen to me cause I know how good it is on the other side of that mountain you're too afraid to cross."

Motherfucker.

I want to come back with a snappy remark but his words hit a target I didn't even realize I'd put up and I sigh as I lean back in my chair and fiddle with the silverware next to my plate. Jesus Christ, what the hell am I doing? I'm thirty years old and I've been single for the last ten goddamn years because of one dishonest woman.

"You're an asshole," I growl as I pull my phone out of my pocket and he laughs.

"I'm okay with that."

Ignoring him, I pull up the message from Shiloh.

Shiloh062:
Hey, handsome ;)
I'd love to get to know you more.
Are you free soon to go out?

WyattL23:
I'm free right now, actually.
Want to grab a cup of coffee?

"So…" Smith asks, leaning across the table to try and see my phone as I move it away from his gaze. "What did she say?"

"None of your damn business."

"Aw, come on. Let me see the fruits of my labor."

My phone buzzes with a notification and I scoop it up as I shake my head. There's no way in hell I'm giving him the satisfaction of this. "No."

Shiloh062:
I'd love to.
Just tell me where.

I send her the name and address of the cafe across the street and she replies back right away, telling me she'll be there in fifteen minutes. Setting my phone back down on

41

the table, I run my hands through my hair as my knee bounces. Smith smirks.

"Jesus, dude. You look like you're about to shit a brick."

I pin him with a glare. "Shut the fuck up. I'm going on this damn date, aren't I?"

"When is she going to be here?" he asks, grabbing his fork and cutting off another piece of lasagna. I watch in fascination as he shoves the bite in his mouth and chews for a second before making a face and spitting it out on his plate. "Fuck! I forgot how bad that was."

"You're an idiot."

"It's not my fault, man. It's sitting in front of me, looking and smelling like lasagna and I'm so fucking hungry that my brain blocked out how bad it is. Now, answer the question."

I scowl. "What question are you talking about?"

"You know damn well what question I'm talking about. When is she going to be here?"

Rolling my eyes, I glance down at my watch. "Ten minutes."

"And just to give me an idea of how screwed you are, when was the last time you went on an actual date?"

"Fuck you," I spit, crossing my arms over my chest as I turn to look out the window. It pisses me the fuck off but he's right. The last time I went on a real life date was when I was married to Piper, before I deployed and my whole world collapsed. Since then, if I did hook up with a girl, it was always casual, something just to fulfill a need and dating was never required.

"Holy shit, please tell me you've been on a date since

she left you…"

"I said shut up, Smith," I snap, interrupting him and he blows out a breath.

"Oh, this is such a bad idea."

My gaze flicks to his and I glare. "Now you tell me this. Five minutes ago, you were calling me a pussy and egging me on."

"Five minutes ago I didn't know how fucked you were."

"Thanks, asshole."

He shakes his head. "It's okay. We can fix this. Just ask her questions about herself and don't delve into religion, politics, or shit like that. Keep it fun."

"I'm not a goddamn idiot."

"I have to cover all my bases," he answers, picking up his fork again before remembering how terrible the food is and dropping it onto the table with a sigh. He looks at his phone and nods to the coffee shop. "You should get going."

"I hate you," I tell him and he laughs.

"No, you don't. Oh, if they have pastries, please bring me one. I'm so fucking hungry and this food is inedible."

I shake my head. "Not a fucking chance."

"Come on, Fuzz," he pleads as he stands up and I laugh, shaking my head again.

"Nope. Enjoy your stakeout."

He continues to plead as I walk away from the table and I feel a little bit of satisfaction over the fact that he'll have to sit there hungry while I get this stupid date over with. Then again, maybe I'd prefer to sit there hungry. When I step outside, I suck in a breath and lean back against the brick wall of the restaurant to relax. I already know I'm a moody fucking bastard and if I go into that date pissed off, the poor girl will be miserable. As I glance up at the cafe, I release a breath. It hadn't occurred to me until Smith said something that I haven't actually been on a date in ten damn years and I don't know how I let so much of my life get away from me. Jesus, I've pissed away so much time being angry at Piper that I haven't lived but that just infuriates me more.

How did it all come to this?

Dropping my head back, I run my hand through my hair and blow out a breath. I can still remember the first time I laid eyes on Piper Robichaud like it was yesterday even though it's been twenty damn years since that day. She had just come to live with her aunt Myra who was my next-door neighbor and even at ten years old, when I looked at her, I felt something I never had before. The look in her eyes... it hit me right in the chest and I just knew, with the innocence of a boy, that she was different than any other girl I'd ever looked at before. We hit it off like a house on fire and I rarely spent more than the eight hours my parents required me to sleep away from her. Three years later, I asked her to be my girlfriend and the rest is history.

That girl, she fucking owned me, heart, soul, and body and even though I was still too young to fully grasp the magnitude of our feelings for each other, I still knew that she was it for me so the night we graduated from high school, we drove out to the river and under the full moon, I dropped down on one knee and asked her to marry me. Right after that, I joined the Marines and we got married down at the courthouse with my parents and a couple of our friends watching on before I shipped off to boot camp.

Every Little Thing

They stationed me in North Carolina and shortly after we arrived, I had to break the news to her that I was deploying. Leaving her was hands down one of the hardest things I'd ever done and as terrified as I was, I knew I would make it back to her safely. I had to. With Piper in my life, I had too damn much to live for to die in the desert and I would never leave her like that. Too bad I never saw the real threat coming.

Shoving off the wall, I shove my hands in my pockets, pushing thoughts of my ex-wife out of my mind as I start crossing the street for my date but her memory is fucking persistent. It always is and thoughts of her always leave me feeling the way I did ten years ago when she walked out of my life. What the hell is wrong with me? I was supposed to be relaxing so I could go on my damn date but I feel more agitated now than I did before I stepped outside and I am already feeling sorry for poor Shiloh. Any woman I want in my life deserves a hell of a lot better than a messed up man with trust issues.

Jesus Christ, Landry.

Get your shit together.

"Wyatt?" a sweet voice calls and I turn, taking in the curvy blonde walking toward me. Damn, her pictures didn't do her justice and the way her jeans hug her hips flips a switch in me. She smiles and I straighten my shoulders as I pull my hands out of my pockets.

"Shiloh?"

She nods as she reaches me and I extend my hand at the same time that she goes in for a hug. I awkwardly wrap my arms around her and pat her back like she's a fucking child before rolling my eyes at myself.

45

For fuck's sake.

I can almost hear Smith laughing his ass off at me from across the street.

"Nice to meet you," I tell her as I pull away and her smile widens.

"You, too. Are you ready? I'm dying for some caffeine." She motions to the cafe and I nod before gesturing for her to go first before placing my hand against the small of her back and leading her inside. I don't know how I look but everything I do, every movement, every word I utter, feels so goddamn forced and awkward and I barely resist the urge to apologize to her for what is sure to be a terrible date. As she steps up to the counter and orders her latte, she reaches into her purse for her wallet and I shake my head, stepping forward to lay a twenty-dollar bill on the counter.

"I got this."

She shakes her head. "Oh, you don't have to do that."

"I insist," I assure her with a smile. I may be a little rusty at this dating thing but I still know that my mother would kick my ass black and blue if she found out I didn't pay for a date. Shiloh flashes me a grin as she moves off to the side for me to order. The barista, a teenage kid with big, bug glasses, looks up at me expectantly as I scan the counter, my stomach growling at the sight of the donuts and muffins. "Cup of coffee, black, and a blueberry muffin."

Once I pay and we both have our orders, I let her lead me to a table along the back wall and sit across from her as she stares out the window for a second before laughing.

"So, I have a small confession."

I nod. "Okay. Let's hear it."

Every Little Thing

"This is my first date after signing up on the site and I'm so nervous." Color rushes to her cheeks and I smile as she ducks her head. Fuck, she's cute. Okay, so maybe I haven't dated in a long time but I've got this. Shaking off some of my nerves, I reach across the table and grab her hand.

"If it makes you feel any better, this is my first date, too."

"Really?" she asks, her gaze flicking up to mine and I nod. Tension seeps out of her shoulders and she takes a deep breath before taking a sip of her coffee. "Okay. Now I feel a little bit better."

I pull my hand back. "Glad I could help."

"So, Wyatt... tell me about yourself."

"What would you like to know?"

She tilts her head to the side as she studies me for a second before leaning forward and meeting my eyes. "Actually, there is one very important question I have for you."

"Shoot," I answer with a nod.

"What are you looking for out of this?"

I arch a brow. "Our date?"

"Yeah, 'cause I've talked to a couple other guys on the site who were looking for something different than I was and I don't want to waste my time, ya know?"

My stomach sinks as I nod. "And what is it that you're looking for?"

"A good time. I mean, I'm only twenty-four and I'm certainly not ready to settle down anytime soon."

"Oh," I mutter, trying not to grimace as my mood plummets. "Unfortunately, we are looking for different

47

things."

She purses her lips. "I was afraid of that… but that doesn't mean we can't have a good time together until you find what you're looking for, does it?"

"Actually, it does. I'm sorry and I hope you find what you need," I say as I stand and grab my coffee and muffin from the table. Between my sour mood earlier and the disappointment coursing through me now, I don't have the patience for anymore of this. I nod at her, ignoring the shocked expression on her face, before turning and walking out of the cafe. After tossing my stuff in a trash posted right outside the door, I pull my phone out of my pocket and open the dating app. This was a bad idea from the jump and I never should have let Smith talk me into going on this date. In the settings menu, my thumb hovers over the delete account button as a message pops up on the screen from a woman named Violet and I pause, studying her photo.

Again, what the hell is wrong with me?

Apparently, I am a glutton for punishment because instead of deleting the account like I damn well know I should, I open her message and reply.

Every Little Thing

Chapter Four
Piper

"Pip-Squeak!" Eden calls as the door to my apartment opens. "You home?"

I poke my head out of my bedroom on the second level and glare at her as she pulls her keys out of the lock and shuts the door behind her before turning to me. "How many times have I asked you not to call me that?"

"Dunno. Why don't you try a few more?" She shrugs as she walks into my apartment and sets her purse down on the kitchen table before waving the thick folder in her hand. "Come down. I have something to show you."

"Fine," I grumble. She drops the file onto the table with a thud as I walk down the stairs and I arch a brow. What the hell is in that file? She turns and walks into the kitchen, grabbing a bottle of water from the fridge. Since the day we met, we've always had an open door policy with each other when it came to our apartments and most days, I absolutely love it but I didn't sleep well last night, haunted by nightmares, and my patience is wearing thin today.

"What's with the briefcase?" I ask, nodding to the file as we meet at the kitchen table. She takes a sip of her water before grinning at me.

"Sit down and I'll show you."

"You're so damn bossy," I grumble as I pull the chair closest to me out and plop down in it. She sits across from me, flips the file open, folds her hands together, and flashes me a look that honestly terrifies me a little.

"What the hell are you up to?"

She grins. "Do you remember last week when we talked about you having a baby?"

"Um... I remember saying I would *think* about it."

"Perfect," she replies, slapping her hand on the table in front of me before grabbing the top paper off of the stack and placing it in front of me. "We're thinking about it."

Arching a brow, I pick up the paper and roll my eyes. The title is "Your Reproductive Health and Your Growing Family" and I don't need to read anymore. "Are you kidding me? Is that whole folder about having a baby?"

"Yes. I found lots of good information on the internet."

Jesus take the wheel...

"Edie... I think this is a little premature. I haven't even decided if I'm going to do this yet."

She scowls at me as she slaps another paper down in front of me. "But how can you decide without all the information?"

"With my heart?" I ask, squinting because I know that is never going to fly and she scoffs before slapping another paper down in front of me.

"Read."

"You're not going to let this go, are you?"

51

She shakes her head and I sigh as I grab the latest paper she put in front of me. Scanning the headline, I turn to her with narrowed eyes.

"I am not over thirty," I say, shaking the paper all about how fertility starts declining after thirty. "I'm twenty-nine, Eden."

Shrugging, she takes a sip of her water. "Close enough. Your birthday is next month and you can't be too prepared."

"I'm not doing this." I drop the paper on the table and scoot my chair back, ready to get up and go back to what I was doing before Eden barged in but she reaches out and grabs my hand, stopping me. I meet her gaze. "What?"

"Just read the information, Piper. You need to know this stuff before you make your decision."

I shake my head. "Why? Why do I need to know all this stuff?"

"What if you decide you want to have a baby and then start researching only to realize you can't for one reason or another? Then your heart is going to be broken and I don't want to see you get hurt so read," she orders, pointing to the paper in front of me and I scoop it up.

"I can't believe I let you talk me into this shit," I whisper, thumbing through the papers Eden shoved in my hands. I eye the large stack of papers still in the file as I blow out a breath. She may claim that she wants me to consider the possibility but considering the massive amount of information on alternative ways to get pregnant in this folder, I would say she has moved past the "let's think about this" phase. I read through the three pieces of paper and just before I finish the final one, she sets a stack down

Every Little Thing

in front of me. Looking up at her, I sigh. Am I really going to let Eden talk me into this? This is insane and without the husband and the family, is this really what I want? Closing my eyes, an image of a baby pops into my mind and warmth spreads through my chest and a smile crosses my face. No, I definitely do want to have a baby but doing it alone isn't exactly the dream I had for myself.

On the night of our wedding, Wyatt and I drove out to the river where he proposed and talked for hours about everything we wanted, the life we wanted to build together, and our dreams for the future. Having a couple kids running around the house was at the top of that list and even though we're not together, even thinking about doing this without him feels a little bit like I'm betraying him. Back when we were together, I used to dream about the day I could finally tell him that I was pregnant, that we were starting a family together. Now, as I think about doing this by myself, his absence in my life and in this whole process is immense. I suppose that's nothing new though. Since the day I left, I've carried around this huge gaping hole where my heart used to be but it's just something I have to live with now. I made so many mistakes and I can't ever take them back.

"Hello?! Earth to Piper!" Eden says and I blink as I meet her eyes.

"Huh?"

Her eyes roll back in her head. "I asked you what you thought."

I glance down at the paper in my hand and shake my head before looking through some of the other papers. After flipping through page after page on reproductive health, pregnancy statistics, and other options for starting a family,

53

A.M. Myers

I sigh.

"I can't focus on this much information at once, Eden. It's like gibberish and my mind is running at a hundred miles an hour."

She nods and pulls a notepad out of her purse before tossing it onto the table in front of me. "I thought you might say that so I made bullet points."

"You had this the whole time and you're just now giving it to me?" I ask, picking up the notepad and waving it around. She nods.

"I wanted you to have everything you might need to make this decision."

I do a quick scan of the information printed on the front page of the notepad before looking up at her. "Can I ask you a question?"

"Of course."

"Why is this so important to you?"

Her eyes shine with unshed tears as she looks down at the table. "Because I love you and you have this tendency to live in fear. You let it paralyze you and until someone pushes you, you don't grow or move forward. I know how badly you want to have a family and so I'm going to push you because I think, in the end, you'll thank me for it."

"Eden," I whisper as a tear streaks down my face. I wish she wasn't one hundred percent correct but I know she is. After everything that I've been through, it's the way I protect myself but I know I need people like her in my life to push me past what feels safe. "Okay. Lay this out for me?"

She nods as she grabs the notepad and sets it on the table between the two of us. "So, as far as I can tell, your options to have a family without a man in your life is to use a sperm donor or adoption."

"I figured as much but the real question is what is the cost?"

Wincing, she flips to the second page of the notebook and slides it across the table to me.

Adoption:
$35,000 - $50,000

"Jesus Christ," I snap, glancing up at her with wide eyes as she nods, looking guilty.

"I know. When I saw that number I about passed out."

My heart drops and glance back down at the paper. "There is no way in hell I can afford that, Eden. Like ever."

How does that make any kind of sense? There are children who desperately need homes and I want to give them that and all the love they can handle but I still can't adopt a child unless I take out so many loans I'll never recover or win a small lottery.

"Just keep reading," she instructs and I take a deep breath as I move to the next line.

Sperm Bank & IUI:
$4,000

Well, I guess it's not impossible but it's still a large

amount of money for me. Eden and I do well with our studio but we're not rich by any means. Wringing my hands together, I shake my head.

"Maybe I could squeeze that. I'd have to save up for a little while, though."

"Well…" Eden squeaks and my head jerks up.

"What?"

She winces again. "That number is per cycle of IUI and the chances that you'll get pregnant are only about twenty percent, at best."

It's fucking impossible.

"Are there any other options?"

"Um… yes… there is IVF, which has a higher success rate but… it's way more expensive."

I nod as my chest aches. "How expensive?"

"Like fifteen thousand dollars per cycle," she whispers and I gasp before leaning back in my chair and dropping my head back as tears sting my eyes.

"So, it's hopeless, then?"

"No," she whispers, reaching across the table and grabbing my hand. Sitting up, I look at her. "You could… I don't know… join a dating site or something. Ooh, or maybe an ad on craigslist."

"For what?" I hiss, shaking my head as a tear falls down my cheek. "A baby daddy? I'm sure that will go over well as long as I don't get murdered first."

She shakes her head as tears fill her eyes again. "I'm so sorry, Piper. I didn't know how expensive all this stuff was when I suggested it to you. Who knows? Maybe you'll meet someone and all of this will be a moot point."

"Yeah, right," I scoff, shaking my head as more tears

fall down my cheeks. Pulling my hand out of her grasp, I prop my elbows up on the table and hide my face as a sob overwhelms me. God, I'm such an idiot. Why the hell did I ever walk away from everything? Closing my eyes, I can picture the life I could have had with Wyatt and it kills me to know that I was stupid enough to lose all that. I can imagine our boys who would have looked just like him and our girls who would have thought their daddy hung the moon and stars. I can imagine Friday movie night on the couch and Sunday dinners around the table and so much love that the void of it in my life, even if it is fictional, is soul crushing.

Eden's arms wrap around me from behind but I can't stop the aching sobs coming out of my mouth now as images of a life I left behind flash through my mind. It's not something I do often, as a means of self-preservation, but as the tears fall, I imagine what Wyatt is doing now. The last time I saw him, he seemed happy and I can't help but wonder if he went out and found everything he wanted out of life. Maybe, in the end, his life got better when I walked out of it. As much as it hurts, as much as I want to scream into the void to release some of this agony, I hope that is the case. I hope he met someone new, fell in love, and started the family he always wanted.

"Oh, God, I'm so sorry," I say as I sit up and wipe at my eyes even though tears are still dripping down my cheeks. "It's just been one of those days, you know?"

She hugs me tighter. "Sweetie, you don't have to apologize to me. I understand and we're not giving up, okay? We'll find a way."

Before I can respond to her, the alarm on my phone

goes off and I whisper a curse as I remember my support group is tonight. I wiggle out of Eden's arms and run to the kitchen to grab it off the counter. As I turn the alarm off, I wipe the tears from my face and pull a shaky breath into my lungs as I try to rein in my tears and turn toward her.

"I'm so sorry. I totally forgot my group is tonight."

"Don't even worry about it," she says, brushing off my concern with a wave of her hand. "Say hi to Lillian for me and tell her we need to make plans for all three of us to get together soon."

I nod as I close the distance between us and give her a hug. "I will."

After I release her, she grabs her purse off of the table and waves good-bye before leaving. As soon as she's gone, I rush upstairs and wash my face to try and combat some of the redness from crying before I put some mascara on and rush out of the apartment. I don't particularly feel like going to my support group tonight but I've learned that nights like this one are when I need the group the most so I force myself to go. Truthfully, I'd much rather crawl under a blanket and eat a pint of chocolate ice cream but I know that's not healthy.

Traffic isn't bad as I make my way across town and my mind wanders to everything I learned today about having a baby and tears sting my eyes again but I force them back. I am not going to start crying again. I refuse. Shaking my head, I run through the figures Eden had written down and sigh. When I checked my bank account this afternoon, I had four hundred dollars in checking and twelve hundred in savings - not even half of what it would run me to try a cycle of IUI. It would take me, at least, six months to save up enough for the first round and there is still an eighty percent chance it wouldn't even work and I don't even want to think about how long I'd have to save for the IVF. Maybe, I just have to accept the fact that when I left Wyatt, I was walking away from more than just my husband.

I pull into the parking lot of the building where the support group is held and park in the front before staring up at the building. My chest aches and every cell in my body wants desperately to turn around and just go home. I can't do this today - not when it feels like my entire body is a giant open wound and I have to walk through a salt mine - but maybe it will be better tomorrow. Or not. Who fucking knows anyway? Dr. Brewer always tells me that things will get easier with time and yeah, most days, I am okay but days like today when the magnitude of mistakes comes crashing down on me and the pain is so intense that I feel like I can't breathe, it sure as hell doesn't feel like it's getting any better.

"Piper!" a voice calls and I take a deep breath as I turn to look at my friend, Lillian, forcing a smile to my face. Her face falls as she studies mine. "What's wrong?"

"I can't go in there today."

"What happened?"

I shake my head because I do not want to talk about it but I already know that this is not going to slide with Lillian. We met at one of the worst times in my life and she has always had my back. Between her and Eden, I built myself a little family to lean on during the bad days and I am always so grateful for their presence in my life.

"You know what? I'm fucking starving. You wanna go grab some food?" she asks and I nod as relief rushes through me.

"I could eat."

Grinning, she rounds the back of the car and slides into the passenger seat before buckling her seat belt. I back out of the parking space and glance back at the building to see Dr. Brewer frowning at me, her arms crossed over her chest, and her glasses slipping down her nose. She is going to chew me out when I go in for my next appointment but this feels right. I'm not in the right head space to go share all this fresh pain with the group but talking to one of my best friends about it is still better than hiding under the covers and wishing the rest of the world would go away.

"So, where are we going?"

I smile as I pull out onto the street. "I'm feeling nostalgic. How does Sunrise Diner sound?"

"Perfect. We haven't been back there since…"

"I know," I say, cutting her off with a nod. With the state I'm in, I'd rather not think about the last time I was at Sunrise Diner and instead focus on the security I always felt there.

"So… we gonna talk about what's bugging you so much today?"

Sighing, I nod. "Eden suggested that I look into having a baby on my own last week and today, she brought over a bunch of information about my options."

"Oh. It didn't go well."

"It did not," I confirm, shaking my head. "Everything is so expensive that I would have to save for years and by then, who knows if I could even get pregnant."

"Aw, babe. I'm so sorry. I know this isn't any sort of consolation but you'll always have me, no matter what happens."

I smile as I glance over at her. "You know, that's exactly what Eden said."

"You know why?" she asks, her lips stretching into a smile that I know all too well and I laugh as I shake my head.

"Oh, no. Don't you dare do it."

She pats out a little beat on her thighs. "'Cause we're the three best friends that anybody could have… Come on, Pippy. Sing it with me."

"Hell, no," I say, giggling as she pats her legs harder and continues singing.

"We're the three best friends that anyone could have. Wolfpack howl, Piper! Do it with me!"

She throws her head back and lets out a howl. Laughing, I tip my head back as I copy her, most of my stress melting away as we pull into the parking lot of the Sunrise Diner. As I park the car, I turn to her and smile.

"Thanks, Lil. This is exactly what I needed."

She smiles. "Anytime, girl. You know that."

A.M. Myers

Every Little Thing

Chapter Five
Wyatt

"She's fucking haunting me," I whisper to myself, staring down at the divorce papers on top of my desk as they taunt me with their presence. Last I checked, those papers were stuffed into the bottom drawer of my desk so I wouldn't have to look at them or think about them and yet, here they are, tormenting me and I can't force myself to look away as an all too familiar pain pierces my chest and a memory from the day these showed up in the mail assaults me. I hadn't heard from Piper in six years and I thought I was moving on with my life when a scrawny kid knocked on my door and told me I was served. The rest of that week is a blur because I don't think I stopped drinking long enough to even begin to sober up until Storm came over and told me to get my shit together. I threw the papers in the desk and told myself I would deal with them later but later never came.

Staring at her signature at the bottom of the page, I blow out a breath and shake my head. How? Even after all these years, I don't understand how could she take everything we had, everything we were starting to build together and just throw it all away on some fucking guy. I sink into the chair and lean my head back, running my hand over my face before I unlock my phone and pull up the email she sent me during that deployment that shook my world and ruined everything.

Wyatt,
This isn't working for me anymore and I met someone new.
Take care of yourself.
Piper

I barely resist the urge to chuck my phone across the room and toss it onto the desk instead. Why the fuck do I even still have it? When I first got that email, I thought it was a joke and sent her an email back telling her she wasn't funny but the next day, there was no reply and the day after that, still nothing. I lost my shit and three other guys had to drag me back to my rack where I spent the night imagining all sorts of scenarios where my wife had been kidnapped or something. The next day, I called my dad and asked him to go check in on her. He drove all night and when he got to our house in North Carolina, he found it empty and all her stuff gone. Truthfully, I still didn't believe it. I *knew* there had to be some kind of explanation but when I came home from deployment six months later and walked into that house, it hit me like a ton of fucking bricks. At first glance, it looked almost exactly like I left it but when I started going through things and noticed her clothes missing along with the few mementos that were most important to her, it really drove home the fact that she was gone. The thing that really took it over the top for me, though, was her wedding ring sitting on the kitchen table with a note that just said, "I'm sorry."

As I stare at the papers, I swear I can feel her here with me, like she is just in the next room or standing over my shoulder with that sweet smile on her face and I shake my head. She is a ghost in my heart, pieces of her embedded in my soul that I'll never be able to get rid of, and I have to wonder if all this dating I'm doing is pointless. Could I ever really find the kind of connection I had with Piper? Do people get more than one of those in a lifetime?

Glancing at my watch, I whisper a curse. My dinner date with Violet is in fifteen minutes and I was already running late when these damn papers caught my attention and now I'm stuck here, unable to pull myself away from her.

How fitting…

Can someone who is still alive even haunt you? She sure as hell feels like a ghost in this house and in my life but she is still very much alive. At least, I think she is. She sure as fuck was four years ago when she sent these papers. Shaking my head, I run my hand through my hair and drop my gaze to the bottom of the paper where I'm supposed to sign.

Jesus Christ.
What the hell is wrong with me?
Why haven't I ever gotten around to signing these damn

things?

Standing up, I grab a pen off of the desk and position it above the dotted line as I read over the first page. My gaze gets stuck on *Petition for Divorce* printed at the top and I suck in a breath, my mind going back to the same question I've been asking for ten years. Why?

Just sign the goddamn papers, Landry.

Get this shit over with… finally.

My heart races as I lower the pen to the paper but before I can sign my name, my phone pings with an incoming text and I drop the pen like it's on fire before grabbing my phone with a sigh.

Violet:
Running a little late but
on my way now

"Shit," I hiss as I turn away from the papers and grab my keys off of the counter before turning back to glance at them one more time.

Whatever.

The goddamn papers are just going to have to wait until I get back.

As I leave the apartment and walk out to my bike, I try to push thoughts of Piper and our divorce out of my mind. It would be nice if I could go on one motherfucking date without thinking about my ex-wife first. Is that too much to ask?

Climbing on my bike, I start it and some of my stress

melts away as the engine rumbles to life beneath me and I check the address of the steakhouse Violet wanted to meet at before pulling away from the curb. I don't know much about Violet since we only talked long enough to realize that we both wanted to go out and get to know each other better but she seems cool and she's fucking gorgeous, based on the photos she had on her profile. Hopefully, this one goes better than the last or I really will just delete that damn account and say "fuck it" on the whole wife and family thing. Like I said, maybe people don't get more than one soul mate in their life and despite it all, I still believe Piper was that for me. But that doesn't mean that everything will work out and you get the happily ever after. And it sure as hell doesn't mean that I have to be miserable for the rest of my life... right?

Driving through the streets of downtown Baton Rouge with the wind in my hair, I imagine what my life might have been like if I'd never married Piper, if we had just drifted apart after graduation but the more I try to picture it, the harder and harder it is to see. What she and I had... there was no way we would have just drifted apart. Which leaves me wondering yet again, what the hell happened in that six months I was gone to make her throw everything away but I know I'll never get the answers to those questions. She made damn sure of that when she walked out of my life with nothing more than a half explanation and a shitty ass apology.

As I pull into the parking lot of the steakhouse, I pull into a spot near the back of the lot away from other cars and push my ex-wife out of my mind once and for all. Or, at least, try to. Like I said, she's fucking persistent and if I haven't been able to accomplish it in the last ten years, I don't know what it will take to finish the job. But I can attempt to forget about her for the next couple hours, at least, so I don't ruin this date. Shoving my hands in my pockets, I walk across the lot and stop next to the front door of the steakhouse, leaning back against the building where Violet and I agreed to meet. As I wait, my mind drifts back to my last date and I blow out a breath as I shake my head. Maybe I should have taken a page out of Shiloh's book and asked Violet what she was looking for before we ever agreed to meet. The last thing I want to do is have an amazing date and see a future with someone only to find out they aren't looking for a relationship.

Sighing, my gaze wanders around the parking lot and when I still don't see her or the red dress she told me she would be wearing, I pull my phone out of my pocket and check for another message from her but there are no notifications.

"Wyatt?"

My head jerks up and I blink in surprise as a leggy brunette walks toward me, her red sundress swishing back and forth with the sway of her hips and her dark hair tumbling over her shoulder. The red lipstick she's wearing conjures up images of her on her knees in front of me and she flashes me a smile.

Fuck.

She's gorgeous.

"You are Wyatt, aren't you?" she asks, her voice a mixture of nerves and playfulness and I nod dumbly as I push off the wall and scoff at how completely hopeless I am.

"Yeah, I am. It's really nice to meet you."

"You, too," she answers, her gaze raking over me slowly before she glances over at the door to the restaurant. "Shall we?"

Nodding, I close the distance between us and place my hand at the small of her back before leading her inside. We stop at the hostess stand and a teenage girl with braces smiles up at us.

"Name?"

"Landry," I answer and she glances down, scanning her list for my reservation before nodding and grabbing two menus from the shelf behind her.

"Follow me, please."

Violet peeks over her shoulder, a coy smile on her face and our eyes meet. A blush creeps up her cheeks as she turns away from me and my dick takes notice immediately. Okay, this is definitely going better than the last time. The hostess leads us to an intimate little table in the back and I smile, pulling Violet's chair out for her before taking my own seat. After the hostess hands us the menus and promises to be back in a minute with a pitcher of water, I turn to Violet.

"So…" I mutter, my brain shorting out as I try to come up with something to say. She giggles and glances down at her menu before meeting my gaze again.

"I have this theory. You want to hear it?"

I nod. "Absolutely."

"I think if something is awkward, like first dates," she continues, motioning between us. "Then if you just say it's awkward, you steal its power."

"Ah, I see. So if I just say, 'goddamn, first dates are

awkward as hell'…"

She nods. "Then, viola, no more awkwardness."

"You know what? I think it's working," I tell her with a laugh, feeling my body release some tension and she smiles as she leans forward and props her elbow on the table and resting her chin in her hand.

"See? Like magic."

"I'm impressed."

The hostess interrupts us before she can say anything else, dropping off a basket of rolls and a pitcher of water before assuring us our waitress will be by in a minute. Once she's gone, Violet flashes me an expectant look.

"Give me one random fact about you, Wyatt."

I arch a brow as my mind goes blank. "Uh, like what?"

"Too vague?" she asks and I nod. "Okay. How about this, what do you do for a living?"

"I'm a private investigator and a member of the Bayou Devils MC."

"Oh, I've heard of you guys! You help women in domestic violence situations, right?"

I nod, grabbing a roll from the basket and slathering it in butter. "Yeah. What about you? What do you do for a living?"

"I'm a cosmetologist but I don't really consider it work since I love it so much."

I nod as a waitress stops at our table and flashes us a smile. "Good evening, you two. I'm Kelly and I'll be taking care of you tonight. Can I get you started with a beer or glass of wine, maybe?"

"I'll take a glass of red wine," Violet says and Kelly turns to me.

"A beer, please."

She nods, slipping her pen and notepad back into her pocket. "I'll be right back with those."

"So," Violet says as soon as she leaves. "We've covered what you do but what else can I ask you? Hmm…"

Leaning back in my seat, I cross my arms over my chest and watch her run through all the questions she's been thinking of all damn day with a smile on my face. Finally, she meets my gaze.

"How old are you?"

I arch a brow. "Is it important?"

"No," she answers with a shrug, a lighthearted smile on her face. "Just curious but now that you won't answer, I'm a little concerned."

"Well, there's no big mystery. It's just a number."

She narrows her eyes but they still dance with playfulness. "If it's just a number, why won't you tell me?"

"Because you're so damn cute when you're suspicious."

Her lips part and a blush stains her cheeks as she pulls her gaze away from me. "Oh."

"But, to answer your question, I'm thirty. Now it's your turn."

"Oh, Wyatt," she whispers, shaking her head as her eyes connect with mine. "Don't you know it's rude to ask a woman's age?"

I shrug. "So I'm rude, then. And see, now I'm concerned since you won't tell me."

"I'm younger than you," she answers and I lean forward, narrowing my eyes and pretending to study her.

"Please tell me you're at least eighteen."

71

A laugh bubbles out of her. "Flattery will get you everywhere, sir."

The waitress stops next to the table, interrupting our banter and after passing both of us our drinks, she pulls the notepad and pen out of her apron again.

"Y'all ready to order?"

Shit.

I haven't even glanced at the menu.

"I'll just get the steak," I tell her, guessing it is a pretty safe bet for a steakhouse and she nods as she jots it down in her notepad.

"How would you like that cooked?"

"Rare."

She nods. "And your sides?"

"Potatoes and whatever vegetable you've got."

Kelly turns to Violet, who slaps her menu shut. "I'll get a half rack of ribs with a salad and mac and cheese."

Once Kelly leaves to give our orders to the kitchen, Violet leans back in her seat and studies me as her fingers drum against the table top.

"Come on now, darlin'. I know you've got more questions brewing in your pretty little head."

She nods. "Okay, but remember you asked for it… Have you ever been married?"

"Yes," I answer, nodding my head as Piper's face pops into my mind. She nods, looking a little more apprehensive than she was a moment ago. Shit. I knew Piper was going to ruin this damn date.

"How long ago?"

I scrub my hand over my jaw. "Ten years ago."

"Oh, wow," she says as her eyes widen. "You were

young."

"I was."

"High school sweethearts?" she asks and I nod, that all too familiar pain reaching back into my chest and constricting my heart.

"Yep."

She studies me for a moment before letting out a sigh. "Are you still in love with her?"

"No," I scoff, shaking my head. "Definitely not."

"Look, Wyatt… I'm not going to be mad if you are but I'm also not willing to invest myself into a relationship with someone who is still hanging onto feelings for someone else so just be upfront with me."

"My wife left me for another man when I was deployed," I tell her, pain ripping itself through my body as those memories come rushing back. "So the subject is not one of my favorites but I haven't seen her in ten years."

She breathes a sigh of relief. "Thank God."

"Now it's my turn to ask you an uncomfortable question."

"Shoot," she answers, nodding her head. Shit… do I really want to ask her this and potentially ruin this when it's going so well? Then again, I certainly don't want to get to the end of the date only to realize she's just looking to head back to my place for a one-night stand.

"What are you looking for? 'Cause I gotta be honest, I'm kind of over casual."

Nodding, she lifts her wine glass and takes a sip before setting it back on the table. "I'm not looking for something casual either. I had my fun but I'm ready to settle down with someone special."

"Since you asked about my past," I prompt, toying with the beer bottle in front of me. "I have to pass the same question off to you."

"Have I ever been married?" she asks and I nod. She shakes her head. "No. Came close once but things didn't work out."

"I'm sorry," I tell her because it seems like the right thing to say. She smiles.

"Don't be. I was heartbroken at the time but I realized that it was for the best. He and I wanted different things from life and it wouldn't have been fair to either of us to go through with the wedding."

I nod. "How long has it been?"

"Eighteen months."

Sucking in a breath, I lift my beer bottle off of the table and take a sip as thoughts race through my mind. What the hell does it say about me that, after ten years, I'm still reliving my breakup with Piper and asking myself "what-if" when she split from her fiancé only eighteen months ago and she has already come through the other side?

"Okay, so what else should I know about you?" she asks, pulling my focus back to her as she arches a brow and takes a sip of her wine. "Do you have any kids?"

I shake my head as my chest aches. "No. I can't wait to have a couple rug rats, though."

"Oh," she whispers, her smile falling away as pain streaks across her face for a second before she gets it under control. "Well, shit."

"What is it?"

Sighing, she sets her wine glass down on the table. "That's the reason my ex and I split. He wanted to have kids and I… don't."

Well, shit.

"And this was going so well," she says, pain in her voice and when I meet her eyes, she blinks away tears. I drop my head as my stomach tightens and my limbs feel heavy. "I'm so sorry. I have to go."

Without another word, she grabs her bag and stands up, not even sparing me a glance as she marches toward the front door with determination in every step. I shake my head and scrub my hand over my face before grabbing my bottle of beer and chugging half of it.

"Oh," someone says and I glance up. The waitress stands next to our table with a tray in her hand.

"Could you just throw those in boxes and I'll take it to go?"

She flashes me a sympathetic look. "Sure, sweetie."

While she hurries off to fulfill my request, I lean back in my seat and finish off my beer before gazing out at the rest of the dining room. The couple at the table across from me keep looking over at me with sympathy on their faces but I ignore them as I start picking at the label on my beer bottle.

God, this is so fucking stupid.

My mind goes back to earlier when I promised myself if this date didn't work out, I would delete my account and I pull my phone out of my pocket to do just that when I see the message from a woman named Eden.

Jesus Christ.

Apparently I'm a complete idiot because as I read her cute little introductory message, I can't help but wonder if I should keep trying. I mean, yeah, dates one and two didn't end well but I was really starting to like Violet and I think there could have been *something* there if the whole kids thing hadn't gotten in the way.

Shit...

Am I really going to keep doing this?

Isn't this the goddamn definition of insanity?

Staring at her message, I shake my head and click reply as every cell in my body screams that it's a bad idea but I can't stop now. Not when it feels like maybe I was finally getting somewhere.

Besides, third time's the charm, right?

Every Little Thing

Chapter Six
Piper

"Good morning," Eden practically sings as she breezes into the office and I turn in my chair, arching a brow as I raise my coffee cup to my lips and take a sip. What the hell is she so cheery about this morning? Eden usually isn't much of a morning person. She points to the steaming mug in my hand. "Please tell me there's more of that."

I nod as I study her. "In the back."

"Thank God!" she exclaims, dumping her stuff on her desk before slipping behind the curtain that hides things like our microwave, fridge, and coffee maker.

"Late night?"

She steps back into the office with a grin on her face that completely gives her away as she leans back against the door frame and lifts the steaming mug of coffee to her lips. "Yeah... I saw this commercial for a dating site last night and decided to sign up."

"And that's why you have that stupid grin on your face?" I ask, narrowing my eyes. A blush creeps up her cheeks and I shake my head. "Oh my God, you already met a guy, didn't you?"

She nods. "Yeah, I did. God, Pipes. He's just…" She struggles to find an adequate word and finally just clenches her fist in front of her as she makes a noise of frustration.

"Yeah?" I ask, forcing a smile to my face as I try to ignore the pang in my chest. It's certainly not Eden's fault that my life has turned out this way and I'm not going to do anything to bring down her stellar mood. Even if I have been in a funk since I realized how much having a baby was going to cost me.

"Oh, by the way…" Eden says and I glance up at her. "I was thinking about your baby issue…"

Sometimes, I swear this girl can read my mind. I nod and take another sip of my coffee. "And?"

"And I really think you should just find a guy, tell him you're on the pill, have some meaningless fun, and when you get pregnant, you can just break things off."

I scrunch my nose up. "That's… dishonest and also a really good way to end up with an STD, Edie."

"I know," she sighs, her body deflating. "I've just been trying to come up with any other options for you. I still think you should try signing up for this site I found last night. You never know, babe. You could meet your soul mate."

Turning back to my computer, my chest aches something fierce at her words. I've already met my damn soul mate and I fucked it all up. God, I wish I could go back to that day and make a different choice. Shaking my head, I push the thoughts from my mind and turn back to her.

"I'm not looking for a soul mate. I already had one of

those."

"Who says you just get one?" she asks and I have to stop my body from recoiling as I imagine another man filling Wyatt's place. It's... just not possible.

"Me."

"But you could finally be happy again, babe."

I shake my head. "I just don't see it happening. Wyatt was... is still..."

She shakes her head as she sets her cup of coffee down on her desk and grabs her phone. "Forget about him. You have to see this guy I was talking to last night. I'm telling you, he's the complete package and oh so very yummy. Wouldn't that be better than being alone and miserable?"

I roll my eyes as she rolls her chair across the hardwood floor to my desk and thrusts her phone in my face. I scoop it up and glance down at the screen, sucking in a breath as my stomach flips and a fist grips my heart and squeezes. My head spins and each breath I take rings in my ears.

"Eden," I breathe, my voice barely audible as a couple tears slip down my cheeks. I glance up at her and her eyes widen as she reaches for me.

"What is it?"

I glance back down at the screen. "It's Wyatt."

"Yeah, I know his name," she says, rolling her eyes at me like I'm the world's biggest idiot. "I can read."

I shake my head. "No, Edie... that's *my* Wyatt."

"What?" she hisses, grabbing her phone and looking at his photo before looking back up at me as my heart thunders out of control in my chest. He looks even better than the last time I saw him... God, how long has it been? Four years ago? I shake my head again, unable to believe it hasn't been longer. Each day without him feels like an eternity and I have carried this gnawing ache around with me since the moment I walked away from him.

My mind drifts back to the first time I met him after I went to live with my Aunt Myra. I was in a bad place then, walking around in a fog of pain and fear and then he was there, shining through the darkness like a beacon. He became my savior, my best friend, and the absolute love of my life.

"Piper?" Eden whispers and I glance up. Her look of concern grabs my attention and I look down at my lap only to realize that I'm trembling as more memories from my childhood come rushing back. There was once, just after I moved in with Aunt Myra, that Wyatt took me down to the pond behind our houses to go swimming. Back then, I was afraid of everything, even my own damn shadow, so when he jumped off the dock without me, I stood there frozen and shaking as I stared down at the calm water beneath me, fear gripping my heart. Wyatt circled back around to see where I was and when he saw me standing up on that dock, he raced back to me and held my hand as we jumped in together. That's always the way it was between us - I was scared of everything and he was my white knight - but that's always where our biggest problem lied. When he deployed, I didn't know how to just exist without him and...

Shaking my head, I push the memories of those days from my mind as I glance up at Eden again. "Please, Edie. Please don't go out with him."

"Of course I'm not going to go out with him," she snaps, looking all sorts of offended as she sets her phone on my desk. "What the hell kind of friend do you think I am?

This isn't just some high school fling that you dated years ago. This is your Wyatt…"

Her words trail off as a slow smile stretches across her face.

"What the hell is that look? I don't like that look."

Her grin widens as she grabs her phone again. "I was just thinking… what if I message him again and set up a date…"

"Eden!" I scream, betrayal ripping through me as I stare at her with wide eyes but she just giggles.

"But instead of me, you'll show up."

I shake my head as she continues grinning at me like this is the best damn plan in the world. "What? That's insane!"

"No," she insists, shaking her head as she grabs my arm. "Hear me out. For years, I've heard about this incredible, epic love you and Wyatt had…"

"And?" I growl, cutting her off. "It didn't matter in the end, did it?"

"Those were extenuating circumstances, Pip-Squeak! That's what I'm saying. I'm willing to bet that if your love was as strong as you claim then he never got over you either."

I shake my head, unable to take my eyes off of her. Oh, God, she's finally lost it. "I… that's… No way, Eden. I saw him… He was happy… He was moving on with his life."

"You saw him for all of what? Five minutes? And besides, that was four damn years ago. You have no idea what's really going on in his life."

"But," I utter, motioning to her phone. "To just ambush him like that… I mean, what the hell would I even say?"

She grins. "Hey, Wyatt. Wanna have a baby?"

"Oh my God, you've officially lost your mind if you think this is a good idea!" I yell, rolling my eyes and ripping myself out of my chair as I grab my coffee mug and slip behind the curtain. Grabbing the pot out of the machine, I pour myself another cup as her idea starts to nag at me.

No, it's absolutely insane.

I can't.

But the thought of seeing Wyatt again after all these years, it makes my heart race and my stomach flutter with the good kind of nerves.

"Just listen," she says as I walk back into the office, holding her hands up in front of her like I have a loaded weapon in my hands. I glance down at the hot cup of coffee in my hand and shrug. I suppose it would do in a pinch. "I know, right now it sounds crazy and admittedly, it is a little out there but what if you don't? What if we just let this go and you spend the rest of your life alone, with no babies and wondering what would have happened if you had just gotten the courage to meet him?"

"Stop making sense," I mutter, bringing the cup of coffee to my lips as her words bounce around in my head. Eden grins.

"I can't. Come on, you know it's a good idea."

I pin her with a glare. "It's an idea, I'll give it that but I haven't said a word to him in over ten years, Edie…There is no way in hell he's still hung up on me."

"Then answer me this, why hasn't he signed the divorce papers in the four years since you sent them to him?"

I freeze with the coffee cup halfway to my lips,

flabbergasted that her crazy plan is sounding better and better the more she talks.

Could it really be possible?

Could he still have feelings for me?

Shaking my head, I blow out a breath.

No, that's too much to hope for.

"What did you guys talk about last night?" I ask her and she unlocks her phone before handing it to me with a smirk.

"Read it for yourself."

Setting my coffee down on the desk, I take her phone and take a deep breath as I start reading through their messages. The first few messages are standard getting to know you questions but when I get further down, my hands start to shake.

WyattL23:
Are you looking for something casual or more?

WyattL23:
Also, sorry if that's too forward.
I've had a couple bad dates and don't want to make the same mistake again.

EdiePB09:
No, it's fine. :)
I guess I'm open to either.
It's got to feel right, you know?
What about you?

WyattL23:
Yeah, I do know.
I'm ready to settle down and start a family.
Are you opposed to the idea?

EdiePB09:
Not at all ;)

"You sent him winky faces, Edie?" I hiss as jealousy burns through my chest. She holds her hands up in surrender as she shakes her head.

"I didn't know!"

Dropping my head, I release a breath and take another deep breath as I try to calm myself down. It's not Eden's fault, I know that but seeing it and knowing that he's been talking to other girls kills me which is bullshit since I don't have a claim to him anymore but my stupid, irrational heart doesn't give a damn. Wyatt is mine and he always will be.

"Did you read the messages, Piper? He's looking for the same thing you are. You have to give this a shot."

I lift my head, meet her eyes, and sigh. "It's crazy, Eden. He's going to be…"

"Pissed?" she supplies and I nod. "Maybe at first but I really think I'm on to something here. I mean, why not sign the papers if he truly wanted to be done with you?"

"I don't know. Why didn't he ever come looking for me if he wanted to keep me?" I ask and she scoffs.

"Oh, that's an easy one. His damn pride. Plus, the pain and betrayal was fresh."

The word betrayal rings in my ears and I suck in a breath as my heart seizes in my chest. "Oh, God... he thinks I cheated on him! He's never going to forgive me."

"Maybe," Eden says, her voice softer than before. "It's time to tell him the truth."

"I don't know," I whisper, shaking my head and she leans forward, grabbing her phone out of my hand.

"Well, I do." She starts typing out a message and my eyes widen as I lunge for the phone but she dodges me.

"What the hell are you doing?"

She bolts out of her chair and runs into the studio, calling out over her shoulder, "Pushing you out of your comfort zone!"

"Eden!" I scream as I run after her, my stomach flipping as I imagine seeing him again. "Please don't do this!"

She skids to a stop and turns to face me. "You really don't want me to?"

"I really don't," I assure her, shaking my head as my heart thunders in my chest. There is so much crap between Wyatt and me at this point that I don't even know what I would say to him. What could I say? I lied to him and betrayed him and Wyatt is not the type of man to forgive so easily.

"Okay... on one condition."

I take a deep breath, trying to get my nerves under control. "What?"

"You let me find you a different cute guy and set up a date."

"Eden…" I say, shaking my head and she holds her phone up, arching a brow in challenge as a smile tugs at her lips.

"It's either that or I set up a date for you with Wyatt."

Turning, I march back into the office and sink into my chair, trying to ignore the ultimatum she just threw down at my feet.

"Which one is it going to be?"

"How about neither?" I growl, moving the mouse to wake up my computer as she stands behind me. In the reflection on the screen, I watch her as she crosses her arms over her chest and fixes me with a look.

"You have to pick one. I'm not going to stand by and watch you waste your life away and not going after what you want because you're too damn scared."

I spin around to face her and level a glare in her direction, opening my mouth to fire back a retort but she holds her hand up to stop me.

"Save it. We both know that's the real reason you don't want to make a decision and what kind of friend would I be if I allowed you to wallow in your fear?"

"A good one," I grumble, glancing away from her.

"Uh, no. A terrible one. So, pick your poison, Pippy. Am I messaging Wyatt? Or are we looking for a new guy for you?"

Turning back to her, I sigh. There is no way in hell she's going to let me off the hook, this I'm sure of so it's better to just get it over with. "Let's look at guys, I guess."

"Excellent," she chirps with a grin as she grabs her chair and pulls it closer to mine so I can see her phone's screen as she starts flicking through photos of men on the site. My stomach rolls as the possibility of going on a date with one of them crashes down on me.

Oh, God, I'm going to be sick...

A.M. Myers

Every Little Thing

Chapter Seven
Wyatt

What the hell am I missing here?

Slapping the file in my hand down on the table in front of me, I release a groan and lean back in my chair as I scrub my hand along my jaw, the two day old stubble scratching my palm. In an effort to relax, I close my eyes and blow out a breath. The frustration slowly seeps out of my body and I take another breath before opening my eyes again and leaning forward to skim Dina's file. I don't know why I keep hoping that each time I read it, something will click for me and it will crack the whole case wide open because, at this point, I am losing faith that it's ever going to happen. The thing is, there's just too many options for who could be behind the deaths of these three girls and virtually no evidence besides our business cards at each scene.

Maybe Kodiak is right.

Maybe I'm just being paranoid and seeing things that aren't really there but I just can't shake this feeling - the gnawing sensation deep in my gut that is screaming at me to pay attention to what is obviously right in front of my face. But if that were true, I would have seen something by now, right? I would have found something to back up my theory. I read through Rodriguez's notes and grit my teeth when I get to the part about Dina clutching our business card as she died, almost like she was desperately trying to call us for help.

I just wish we could have been there for her.

With a sigh, I flip to the next page in her file and study the autopsy report again for the tenth time today. She had blunt force trauma to the head which is to be expected since they couldn't find any brain activity when she was rushed to the hospital but she had defensive wounds all over her body as well. Whoever attacked her, she gave them hell and she didn't go down without a fight. Of course there was no DNA found under her fingernails that could make this case real simple but she also had five broken ribs and a lot of internal bleeding. Reading over the information, I can see how we jumped to the conclusion we did with her husband's history but when you add in the other girls, it doesn't make sense anymore. Unless...

Holy shit.

What if Mitch is behind all of this? After he killed Dina, he could have continued killing girls we helped in an act of revenge for our role in helping her escape his abuse.

Jesus Christ...

It actually makes a whole lot of fucking sense and I can honestly say it's the first viable lead I've come up with since I started digging into this. Besides, it takes a hell of a lot of rage to beat someone to death - something Mitch has in spades. The last time we ran into him, he punched Storm in the face and Chance had to pull a gun on him to get him to back down. I'm sure that hurt his pride quite a bit and to a man like Mitch, it's enough to make him feel justified in his actions. Grabbing Laney's file off of the table, I flip it open and turn to her autopsy report, hoping that maybe I'm onto something.

Fuck.

It's a completely different MO.

In Laney's case, it looks like her attacker surprised her and she didn't have time to defend herself before the killer sank a knife into her chest. Why would Mitch change the way he was doing things? To throw us off his track? Or maybe I'm not onto anything at all. Shaking my head, I toss the file down and look up toward the stairs as my mind races with possibilities. If I'm going to truly pursue Mitch as a suspect, I need more information on him.

Nodding, I gather up the files and head upstairs, dropping them off in my room before I walk down to the end of the hall where Streak's lair is. Streak is our resident tech expert so if anyone is going to dig up information on Mitch for me, it's him.

"What?" he calls after I knock on the door and I open it. He flicks an annoyed glance over his shoulder before turning back to his computer screens. "I didn't say come in, asshole."

I shrug as I step into the room and close the door behind me. "Get over it, buttercup. I have a question for you."

"Buttercup," he mutters, shaking his head before he turns to face me and crosses his arms over his chest. "What's your question?"

"You've been looking into the girls' cases, too, right?"

He nods. "Yeah."

"Have you looked into Mitch at all?"

"Mitch?" he asks, scowling. "Dina's Mitch?"

I nod, grabbing a chair and dragging it next to his desk before I sink into it. "Yep. I was just going through the cases downstairs…"

"As per usual," he interrupts, rolling his eyes.

"Yes, as usual. Anyway, I was thinking how when you add in the death of Laney and Sammy, Mitch killing Dina doesn't make sense…"

"Right. And?"

"But what if it makes perfect sense?"

His head jerks back as he looks at me like I've lost my mind. "What the hell are you talking about?"

"I'm saying," I shoot back. "What if Mitch was so pissed that we took Dina from him and pissed at Chance for pulling a gun on him that he started coming after us?"

He studies me for a second before shaking his head and turning back to his computer. "Well, shit."

"Exactly."

"So," he starts, turning to face me again. "You think Mitch has been behind all of this as a way to get revenge against the club?"

"I don't think anything right now but it's a possibility and that's better than anything else I've come up with."

Nodding, he stares at a spot on the wall and I can practically see his wheels turning. "Or it could be the husband slash boyfriend of any girl we've helped since we started doing this."

"But why not start with Dina?"

"Okay," he agrees, nodding as he turns back to his

computer as he starts typing. "I'll start looking into him. What all do you want?"

"Everything you can find."

He glances at me with an arched brow. "Everything? Like... *everything?*"

"Maybe everything from six months before Dina died until now."

"You got it."

He starts typing furiously and I know that's my cue to get the fuck out. I close his door behind me as I step back into the hallway and check my watch as I head back downstairs. I still have a little time before my date this afternoon and I'm feeling damn good after what feels like my first major break in this case. Sure, it might still be nothing but, at least, I'm doing something other than staring at those damn files and floundering. Which is especially irritating because this is what I did for almost a year before joining the club. My mind drifts back to my time as a Baton Rouge police officer and I shake my head. God, what a shitty time that was in my life. I had just gotten out of the Marines and I was looking for a fresh start but joining a department that had more dirty cops than legit ones made it hard to achieve that. Once I found out about the Devils and the work they had started doing, I got out of there as fast as I could.

Back downstairs, I slip behind the bar and grab a beer from the fridge before slipping onto a bar stool and popping the cap off as I turn my focus to my plans for the rest of the day. It's weird but I'm actually looking forward to this date. Eden has been easy as hell to talk to and she seems sweet and carefree. Plus, we've already gotten all the important questions out of the way so hopefully I won't be blindsided again. Although, I'm serious this time when I say if this date doesn't go well, I'm deleting my profile and throwing in the towel.

The door to the clubhouse opens and sunlight streams into the room. I glance over my shoulder to see who just walked in and as soon as the door closes again and my eyes adjust, I almost fall off my bar stool. Every eye in the room turns to look at the woman standing in the doorway as a hush falls over the room.

What in the fuck is she doing here?

"Uh... is Moose here?" Tawny asks, shifting from one foot to the other before going back again as her gaze shifts between Chance, Storm, and me as we all stare back at her. The nerve of this bitch...

I shake my head in disbelief. A while back, Tawny and Moose were seeing each other but it was casual as hell and when Tawny pushed him for more, he ended things with her. Not that she took the rejection well. She kept coming around, trying to get him back and when that didn't work, she went down to the police with a mysterious black eye and claimed that Moose hit her. It's a load of shit. Especially in this club. I mean, you don't join a club that helps women being abused if you're secretly smacking them around on the side. In the end, she dropped the charges and Moose was able to get back to his life and his new woman but she still isn't welcome here.

"Please?" she pleads, her hand shaking as her gaze lands on me. I take a step toward her and shake my head.

"Nope. He's not here."

She flicks imploring eyes to me. "I saw his bike

outside. Please. I just need to talk to him."

"Hell, no. You can turn right the fuck around and walk back out that door."

Tears fill her eyes but she blinks them away. "Look, I know what I did was fucked up… and I know I'm not welcome here but I need to talk to…"

"Tawny?" Moose growls from behind me as he walks into the room and she sucks in a breath as her gaze snaps to his. He stops next to me and crosses his arms over his chest, anger radiating off him in waves. "What the fuck are you doing here?"

"Can we talk?"

"Fuck, no. I don't have shit to say to you."

He releases a breath, her gaze falling to the floor before meeting his eyes again. "Please, Moose? I really need to talk to you. It's important…"

Moose stares at her for a second before his gaze flicks to me. I shrug my shoulders as I take a sip of my beer and he turns back to her.

"Fine. Talk."

"Uh," she whispers, looking at the rest of us watching on. "Could we go somewhere more private?"

"No. Apparently I need witnesses around you."

She flinches and nods. "That's actually what I wanted to talk to you about."

"Get on with it, then," he snaps, raising a brow as he waits for whatever she feels she needs to say to him. She sucks in a breath as she takes another step into the room.

"I… uh, when you ended things between us, I was really pissed and I went out drinking for a couple of nights…"

His head jerks back. "I don't give a shit what you did."

"Just… listen," she mutters, shaking her head as she draws a breath into her lungs. "I met this guy there and we got to talking. I told him all about us and how you had ended things with me. He was sympathetic and the more we drank, the more he started suggesting that I find a way to get back at you."

"And you thought pretending that he had abused you was the way to go?" I ask, disgust rolling through me. "How the hell did you even get that black eye? Did you punch yourself?"

She shakes her head. "No, actually… that was his idea. He knew who you guys were and the work you do and said it would be hilarious if one of you got arrested for hitting a woman…"

Chance stands and kicks his chair back as he shakes his head in disgust. "Yeah? Did you two get a good laugh out of it?"

"No," she whispers, shaking her head. "After I sobered up and I woke up with a giant black eye, it didn't seem like such a good idea anymore."

Moose glances at me before turning back to Tawny. "You never answered Fuzz's question. How did you get the black eye?"

"He did it… After we were completely wasted, he talked me into going out behind the bar and he…" Tears sting her eyes again as she looks up at the ceiling. "He punched me in the face a couple times."

"So, this guy hit you, " Moose starts, tilting his head to the side, studying her as he tries to understand her flawed logic. "And you decided to take advantage of a bad situation by going to the police?"

"I wasn't going to go through with it but then my roommate saw me and asked what happened… I didn't know what else to say so I just told her the story we came up with and she made me go to the police."

"Great," Moose snarls, turning away from her. "Thanks for the fucking explanation."

"Wait!"

He turns back around, arching a brow and she straightens her shoulder as she meets his eyes.

"I wanted to tell you how sorry I am, Moose. It was a lot of stupid decisions fueled by your rejection and my anger, not to mention alcohol but I wish I could take them all back."

He stares at her for a second before nodding. "Is that all?"

"Yes," she whispers, dropping her gaze to the floor. Blaze walks out of the office and as soon as he sees Tawny, his eyes narrow into a glare.

"What the fuck did I tell you would happen if I ever saw you in my clubhouse again?"

Tawny takes a step back, holding her hands up in surrender. "I'm leaving."

"Get, then. And don't let me catch you around here again. You are not welcome."

She turns and practically runs from the building and when the door shuts behind her, everyone lets out a breath. Blaze sighs as he turns to Moose and slaps his shoulder.

"You all right?"

"Yeah," Moose says with a nod before nodding his head to the closed door Tawny just disappeared behind.

"Ready to finally put that mistake behind me though."

"You have, brother," Chance tells him as he slides back into his chair and crosses his legs. "You got your old lady now."

Moose nods, fighting back a smile. "Yeah, I do."

"You fuckers disgust me," I growl, rolling my eyes as I turn toward the bar and down half of my beer, jealousy ripping through my gut.

"Speaking of which," Moose continues, ignoring me. "I have some news. Juliette is pregnant."

A huge grin splits his face as Chance and Storm jump up to run over and congratulate him as bitterness twists through me and I finish off the rest of my beer. Shit, I've got to be the worst fucking brother to these guys because all their good news only reminds me of everything I don't have and no matter how hard I try, I can't force the jealousy down. As everyone disperses after giving Moose a slap on the back, I slip into a bar stool and grit my teeth. Moose sits down next to me and looks up at the TV as a rerun of a football game plays on the screen.

"You all right, brother?" he asks and I nod, reaching over the bar to throw my beer bottle away.

"I'm good."

He nods for a minute before turning to me. "You know we're not fucking idiots, right? We can all see that you're going through something."

"Don't worry. I really am working on it," I tell him, my mind drifting to my date in a couple hours before going back to Tawny's confession and apology. Something about it nags at me but I can't figure out what it is. "Hey, let me ask you something…"

"What?"

"Who do you think that guy was that Tawny met at the bar?"

Moose stares up at the TV for a second before shrugging and glancing over at me. "Who fucking knows? If I had to guess, I would say it was Gavin but, at this point, I've got better things to focus on."

"Yeah, I suppose you do. Congrats, by the way," I tell him and he nods.

"Thanks. I'm just glad Juliette wasn't here when Tawny walked in," he replies, his eyes widening as he blows out a breath and I laugh.

"Your girl got a jealous streak?"

He scoffs. "No, more like protective and someone would have had to hold her back."

"Sounds like a good problem to have."

"I suppose," he answers with a laugh. "Just not while she's got my baby in her belly."

I nod, my gaze drifting back to the TV. "Good point."

"How are the cases looking?"

"Good," I answer, nodding my head as I continue staring up at the TV, my mind consumed with thoughts of what it would be like to finally have all the things in my life that I've been looking for. The guys in this club have always been good men, the kind of guys you know you can always count on but after they each met their women, there was this peace that settled over them and I feel like a caged tiger every damn day as I watch their happiness play out in front of me.

"You got any leads?"

I nod. "Maybe. I've got Streak looking something for

me so we'll see."

"Fuzz… are you really okay?" he asks and when I turn back to him, he's studying me with concern on his face. I release a breath as I nod and slip off my bar stool, slapping him on his shoulder.

"Yeah, brother. I'm good."

I can feel his eyes on me as I walk out of the clubhouse and into the parking lot where my bike is waiting for me. I swing my leg over and brace my hands on my thighs, thinking about my date this afternoon. Jesus, I need this to go better than the last two and I hope like hell, the next time I tell someone I'm good, I'll really mean it.

Chapter Eight
Piper

Drawing a nervous breath into my lungs, I yank down the visor and check my reflection in the mirror before climbing out of my car. As I look up at the restaurant, I smooth my hands over the short little skirt Eden forced me to wear to my date and mentally prep myself for this. It's not like I haven't dated since leaving Wyatt but I still don't have a ton of experience and when you add in the fact that I have no idea who I'm meeting, it makes it even more nerve-wracking.

I can't believe I agreed to this.

After Eden agreed to not contact Wyatt, she sat next to me for nearly two hours flicking through endless guys on her dating app and forced me to choose three that I could see myself going on a date with. Then, she skipped off to the back of the studio and told me not to stress my pretty little head, that she would handle everything. I spent all morning peppering her with questions but all she would tell me is that my date would meet me at our favorite table at

Mama Adele's - a cute little comfort place that Eden and I absolutely love - and the mischievous little smirk on her face as she sent me off an hour ago only made my nerves worse.

Shaking my head, I push off the car and hold my head up high as I walk through the parking lot toward the front door. You know, it's not even whatever guy is waiting for me on that other side of the door that I have a problem with. It's that I'm almost thirty damn years old and I don't want to date anymore. This isn't what was supposed to happen with my life and even from the time I was a little girl, I always knew what I wanted and then… one night changed everything and I still haven't recovered. Sighing, I reach up and run the tips of my fingers over the raised skin of the scar running down the side of my neck as a shiver works its way down my spine. I shake my head, pushing the unpleasant memories from my mind. *That* is the very last thing I need to be thinking about before I go on a date with a man I've never met before.

As I walk alongside the building, I turn my head and gaze in the big picture windows, trying to get a look at our table and my mystery guest. I stumble as my gaze lands on the man sitting there. I press a shaking hand to my chest as my heart starts racing and my stomach flips. Every thought in my head screeches to a halt and all I can see is *him*.

Oh, God.

She didn't…

"No," I hiss as he turns in my direction and hoping to everything that is holy that he won't see me as I race back to my car as fast as I can in the four inch heels Eden insisted I wear.

I'm going to kill her.

Pulling my phone out of my purse, I slip behind the wheel and slam the door shut before dialing her number and putting it on speakerphone. My heart thunders out of control and I can't keep my eyes off of the restaurant as the phone rings. Jesus Christ. What the hell was Eden thinking? My body is in chaos, conflicting emotions waging war in my chest and tears sting my eyes as I lean my head back against the headrest and suck in a stuttered breath.

"Yes?" she answers, her voice bright and cheery and I clench my fist. Oh, she's been waiting for this damn call since I left the studio. I swear to God, I could strangle her with my bare hands right now.

"What have you done?!"

"I don't know what you're talking about, Pip-Squeak."

"The hell you don't," I growl, glancing up at the restaurant again. "What kind of game are you playing? What happened to the three other guys I picked?"

"You were never going to go out with any of them," she scoffs like it was obvious and I should have known better. "You and Wyatt belong together but the two of you just needed a little push so... I pushed."

"This isn't a game, Eden," I snap, pinching the bridge of my nose as I try to slow my heart rate. How could she think this was a good idea? She knows about everything that happened between Wyatt and me so I just can't understand why she would think that her plan would work. She scoffs.

"I never said it was."

"What the hell am I supposed to do?"

She sighs. "Go on the date, Piper. It's not that hard to

figure out."

"I can't go in there!" I screech, gesturing wildly to the restaurant. A few people walk by my car and flash me a look before looking away.

"Are you really going to stand your husband up?" she asks, her voice full of faux shock and I grit my teeth. This is insane. She has lost her ever-lovin' mind if she thinks I'm going to go in there and have a date with Wyatt.

"What would I even say to him, Eden? The last time he saw me was before he was deployed and now I'm just supposed to show up and go 'hey' like the last ten years didn't happen?"

As she scoffs again, I can almost picture her rolling her eyes at me. "Oh, I'm sure you guys will have *lots* to talk about and then, you know, ask him if he wants to have a baby with you."

"What? No!"

"Oh my God, stop with the dramatics and trust me when I say that I have a good feeling about this."

I shake my head. "You went too far this time, Eden."

"No," she murmurs. "I think I went just far enough and look, if this doesn't work out, if the two of you don't end up in wedded bliss again, I'll never push you to go on another date."

"Really?"

"Yep. Now, get your butt out of the car and into the restaurant. You don't want to leave your man waiting."

I scowl as I glance up at the restaurant. "I just want you to know that I'm still really pissed at you."

"I can live with that. Bye, now." She hangs up before I can say another word and my stomach flips as I turn to the restaurant. I hide my face in my hand and let out a little growl. I can't believe I am about to march in there and come face-to-face with Wyatt for the first time in ten years.

Oh, God, I'm going to throw up.

My hands shake as I reach for the door and open it, stepping out into the dense Louisiana heat. Closing the door behind me, I lean back against the car and press my hand to my chest as I stare up at the restaurant, trying to come up with something to say to him that won't sound callous or flippant after everything we've been through. I mean, I can't just walk up to him and say "hi", can I? There is so much to say, so much to apologize for but I'm not sure that I'm ready to tell him any of it. The things that happened back then... I don't want him to know any of it. I don't want him to see me that way but what else can I say?

When I left him, I told him that I had found someone new but that couldn't have been further from the truth. There's never been anyone else for me and even the few guys I've dated since leaving him haven't been able to breach the barrier around my heart that is Wyatt Landry. He has owned me since we were two little kids, too naive to know how special and meaningful our love was. Truth be told, it took leaving Wyatt and spending the last ten years without him to truly understand the magnitude of our relationship and the love I have for him. I wish I could say I had a plan when I left but I didn't. At that point, I wasn't thinking clearly and by the time things did become clear, too much time had passed for me to just run back to him. The damage was done and I had to live with it. Pushing off the car, my heart thunders against my ribs and my legs feel like Jell-O as I make my way across the parking lot.

"You can do this," I whisper to myself as tears sting my eyes and a memory from the first time I met Wyatt flashes through my mind. Aunt Myra was guiding me up the steps to her house after picking me up in Shreveport and Wyatt was running through his yard next door with one of his friends. Right in the middle of their game, he stopped and stared at me before flashing me a half smile and waving. It was such a simple gesture but after all of the horror I had just been through, it was... everything and I can't help but picture what it's going to be like when I get in that restaurant and he sees me again. Anger, maybe? Shock? I can't imagine that any part of him will be happy to come face-to-face with me again but ever since Eden brought it up, I've been wondering why the hell he never signed the divorce papers I sent him. At the time, I thought I was doing him a favor but now, I don't know.

When I reach the front door, I pull it open with trembling hands and step inside as my head screams at me to turn and run back to the safety of my car. But it's not really safety, is it? It's cowardliness. And weakness because every cell in my body is urging me forward, pushing me to close the distance between Wyatt and me like it knows where it belongs even if my head can't get on board. I glance up from the entryway and suck in a breath. Oh, God, there he is... He's looking down at his phone with a scowl and my belly flips as my heart races and the memory of his kiss tingles on my lips. It's been so long since I have seen him and the years have certainly been kind but guys always get all the luck with that kind of thing. His hair is longer, falling into his face and he brushes it back. My fingers itch to run my fingers through it like I used to when we were younger and my chest aches as memories flood my mind, barely giving me a chance to recognize one before the next is invading my thoughts.

Gulping in air and trying my best not to throw up as I start walking through the dining room, my heart beating so fast that I'm afraid I might pass out. A memory of the first time he kissed me pops into my mind and I shake my head, remembering how awkward it was since we were only thirteen but also, how special it was in spite of all that. We were back behind Aunt Myra's house, hiding in the oak trees and when I looked over Wyatt was staring at me with this look on his face that I had never seen before. The next thing I knew, his lips were pressed to mine and my heart was thumping. When we pulled apart, he smiled at me and I couldn't stop the giggle from bubbling out of my lips. The next day he asked me to be his girlfriend and that was it for us. We were no longer two separate people. We were *Wyatt and Piper*, one solid unit.

Something on his phone makes him smile and his full lips quirk up on one side as warmth floods my body and I fight back a smile of my own.

Oh, that smile…

It's one of my favorite things on this earth and I forgot how much I missed it, or blocked it out in an effort to survive without him. His smile widens and he shakes his head before typing out a message and I have to force myself to keep my eyes open as the memory of those lips dragging along my skin burns its way into my memories. My skin tingles with awareness and my belly flutters with nerves as I close in on the table and will him to look up at me so I don't have to be the first one to speak. Just as I stop by the seat across from him, he sets his phone down and glances up. Recognition flickers across his face and his eyes widen as he falls back against his chair and his lips part.

"Piper," he breathes, staring at me like I'm a ghost or a figment of his imagination and I force a smile to my face but it feels shaky, at best, and my heart pounds in my ears.

"Hi, Wyatt."

Every Little Thing

Chapter Nine
Wyatt

"Hi, Wyatt." Her voice washes over me like a thunderstorm, electricity racing across my skin and my heart thundering in my chest as I stare up at her, trying to find the right words to say. One part of me wants to stand up, pull her into my arms, and kiss her until neither one of us can breathe, until I get every single second of affection I'm owed for the past ten years and the other part of me is fucking pissed, raging out of control and demanding answers to the questions that have been dogging me day and night since she left. And I have no clue which side to give into. How the fuck can she make me want to fuck her senseless and scream at her at the same time?

Fuck, she looks incredible, too.

Her dark red hair is longer now, hanging down her back as she stands in front of me, trying to put on a brave face but looking nervous as hell. My gaze drops down her body slowly, taking her in as I try to collect myself again and I swallow hard when I catch a glimpse of her long legs and the pink heels she's wearing. They remind me of the lingerie she wore on our wedding night and my cock strains against my zipper as I shift in my seat and meet her gaze again. She arches a brow and I realize she's still waiting for me to say something.

Shit.

What the hell do I say to her?

I mean, there is so much I want to say, so many fucking questions to ask her but what am I supposed to do? Just blurt them out in a crowded restaurant? When I still don't open my dumb mouth and force words out, she pulls out the chair across from me and sits down. I remember my date with Eden and I shake my head as I glance around the restaurant. Well, this is awkward.

"I'm… uh, I'm actually meeting someone, Piper, so you can't stay here."

She nods as she sets her purse on the floor. "I know. You're meeting me."

"No," I answer, shaking my head. "I'm meeting someone named Eden."

"Eden is my best friend and she set this up. I didn't even know until I got here."

Well, fuck.

I scowl as I study her face and my gaze falls to the scar on her neck and she subtly covers it with her hand. "And why would she do that?"

"Because…" she sighs, her tongue darting out to run along her bottom lip and I bite back a groan. Fuck her for still being able to get to me like this. "Because she thinks we need to talk."

"What could we possibly have to talk about, *wife*?" I

growl, pissed at Eden for blindsiding both of us and hurt creeping back into my chest as the shock of seeing Piper again wears off. My memory of reading her email in that Godforsaken desert pops into my mind and pain floods my body. I remember the pain of coming home to an empty house and her wedding ring on the table, the pain of getting the divorce papers in the mail and I clench my fist on top of the table. Shit. I wish I could punch something. Her gaze flicks to my hand and she sucks in a breath before meeting my eyes again.

"I don't want to fight with you, Wyatt. I know that I hurt you and I don't have any excuses for you but I do want to tell you how sorry I am… losing you… leaving you is my biggest regret."

I consider coming back with a snappy remark, something designed to hurt her in return but as she looks up at me from across the table, I can see the truth in her eyes which only leaves me with more questions. Shaking my head, I suck in a breath.

"So, what do you want, then?"

Her teeth sink into her full bottom lip. "I don't want anything."

"Liar."

"I didn't even know I was meeting you here today so truly, I don't want anything from you."

I tilt my head to the side, studying her. "You could have just left, stood me up."

"Well… I didn't want to do that, either."

"So you're just here to torture me then?" I ask and she flinches, unshed tears shining in her eyes. Fuck. I always hated it when she cried. Her hand shakes as she presses it flat against the table and I can see her warring with herself before she looks at me with a determined expression on her face.

"I want you to help me have a baby."

Blinking, I stare at her as my lips part in shock. "What?!"

"I want you to help me have a baby," she repeats, her gaze unwavering and strength reflected in her gaze.

Holy shit.

That's new.

Where the hell is the scared girl I grew up with? The one that would jump out of her skin and start crying if you snuck up on her, the one who never made it through a week without, at least, three nightmares that woke us both up and the one that I loved so fucking much in spite of all that. Watching her, I can't help but wonder who she is now and how much I would like to get to know her again before I shut that thought down and press my lips into a line.

"Is this why Eden set this whole thing up?" I fucking hate feeling like I'm being played right now and I don't know how she thinks the two of us having a baby together is a good fucking idea. It's insane. At best, she and I are a mess of pain and resentment and she wants to bring a child into this? She shakes her head.

"I've been looking into how to have a baby on my own lately and when I realized how expensive it was, she joked that I should ask you but it was never something I seriously considered until I walked in and saw you."

"Oh, good," I snap, crossing my arms over my chest. "'Cause here I thought you had thought this all through and still thought it was a good idea. What was Eden's plan then

112

when she messaged me?"

She sucks in a breath and her nerves flash through her eyes for just a second before she shuts it down. "No... She seems to think that there is still something between us."

"Did you tell her she's fucking insane?" I ask with what I know is a condescending laugh but my chest aches as I force the words out of my mouth. Sitting here across from her, staring at the face of the woman I fell in love with at thirteen years old, I'm not so sure that's true anymore. She lets out a breath and shakes her head, sadness creeping into her green eyes and I'm back to a teenage kid who just wanted to make her smile.

Fuck.

I have to get out of here.

"The answer is no," I force out through gritted teeth as I grab my phone off of the table and stand up. She reaches out and grabs my arm as I try to pass her and I swear to God, my heart stops for a second as I look down at her. His gaze pleads with me and my gut turns as the ache in my chest grows.

"Please just think about it, Wyatt. I don't ever expect you to forgive me for what I did but I think you might be my last hope." Her eyes hold me prisoner, wrapping chains around my heart and my anger drains away, forcing me to confront what lies beneath.

I can't do this.

I can't let myself go there.

I can't even let myself think about it because up until this moment, I didn't realize that I was balancing on the edge of the cliff overlooking a ravine but now I've looked down and seen the jagged rocks on the bottom and if I reach for her, I know it will destroy me.

"Good-bye, Piper," I say, pulling my arm from her grasp and walking away from her. Fuck, it hurts like hell. I'm halfway to the door when I hear her hushed sob and it takes every ounce of strength I possess to keep on walking but I know better than to turn back. The only thing waiting for me back there is more betrayal, more pain, and more lies. I am supposed to be moving on with my life, finally, and I can't let her pull me back.

By the time I get to my bike, my anger is returning full force and I almost slam my fist into the seat before shaking my head and swinging my leg over. It rumbles to life beneath me and I try to ignore the pain in my chest as I pull out of the parking lot. It's fucking baffling to me why she thought any of what just went down was a good idea.

Her and I have a baby together?

I scoff and shake my head as I weave through traffic. It's moronic. Plus, I'm still trying to figure out how I feel about her just wanting me to be her sperm donor after everything we've been through. That is the cherry on top of the pain sundae courtesy of Piper Robichaud… or Landry?? Fuck, I don't even know if she ever changed her name. No, it doesn't matter. It doesn't mean anything if she still has my last name. Then again, I have to wonder what happened to the "someone new" she found if she is coming to me to give her a baby. Why the hell doesn't she go to that fucker and beg him to knock her up?

Just the thought of someone else's hands on her body makes me see red. Fuck. She's not mine, I know that, but goddamn it if she doesn't still feel like mine. Especially with the feeling of her hand still imprinted on my arm. My stomach twists with the rival emotions battling inside my chest. I want to turn this bike around and pull her out of her chair, throw her on the floor, and fuck her so hard that she'll realize everything she's been missing and never think of leaving me ever again.

Wait, what?

What the fuck is wrong with me?

I don't want Piper back.

A red Fiat cuts me off and I slam on the brakes as my body tenses and flushes with heat. Grinding my teeth together, I speed up and slip into the other lane before riding right up next to his little piece of shit and smacking my hand on the window. He looks over at me with wide eyes and rolls the down the window. Big mistake, fucker.

"Why don't you learn how to drive, motherfucker?" I bellow at him before punching the door frame and pulling ahead. Once I've merged over in front of him, I hit the brakes just enough to make his heart stop for a second before racing away from him. The speedometer hits one hundred before I feel calm enough to slow down and I sigh as my townhouse comes into view.

After parking in my spot, I climb off my bike and clench my fists as I march up to my place, trying to push all the thoughts from my mind. Fuck. I need something... a beer? Maybe. To punch a hole through a wall? Possibly. I'm still undecided. Hell, maybe I'll make a real night out of it and do both. Once inside, I toss my keys onto the kitchen counter and throw myself into the seat in front of my desk as I lean my head back against the headrest and cover my face with my hands.

"Fuck," I groan, dragging them down over my jaw

before dropping them into my lap as someone knocks on the door. "What?"

The door opens and Cleo steps in with a sly smile on her face. "Hey, Fuzz."

"Cleo," I answer with a nod as she walks over to me and braces her hands on the arms of the chair, leaning over me just enough that I can see down her shirt. "What are you doing here?"

"Oh, come on, Fuzz. Don't play games. You know why I'm here."

I shake my head. "I'm not in the mood tonight."

"I think we can get you there, big guy," she whispers, leaning forward and pressing her lips to the side of my neck. My eyes close and in my head, it's Piper in front of me, her cherry lips against my neck and I moan. Her hand strokes my cock over my jeans and I groan again as it hardens and presses against my zipper, the teeth biting into my skin. "That's what I thought."

"Stop talking," I growl as I slip my hand into her hair and give it a tug. Cleo laughs as she drops to her knees in front of me but behind my eyes, all I can see is Piper. She unbuttons my jeans and I lift my hips on the chair so she can pull them down. A sexy little hum slips out of her lips as she wraps her fingers around my length and I groan, massaging the back of her head as she takes the tip into her mouth.

Oh, fuck.

That's fucking perfect.

I open my eyes and my mood sours instantly when I look down and Cleo meets my eyes, grinning around the length of my dick in her mouth. Piper's face flashes through

116

my mind again, her pleading look in the restaurant as she begged me to help her have a baby and the strength that flashed in her eyes - so goddamn sexy. God, as much as I loved her even when she was broken and damaged, seeing her hold her own and be strong makes my heart swell no matter how much I don't want it to and the image of a baby in her arms pops into my head. Turning my head, I catch sight of the damn divorce papers again and clench my teeth as I shove Cleo away from me, feeling all kinds of wrong as I stare at Piper's name signed at the bottom of the page. My mind screams, rage and a desperate need for relief ripping their way through me as I try to make sense of the last ninety minutes.

"Are you okay?" Cleo asks and I look down at her. She arches a brow in question as she releases me and I shake my head as I stand up and pull my jeans up.

"No. You need to go."

She balks. "What?"

"You heard me. You need to leave. Now."

"Oh my God," she hisses as she stands up and shoves my shoulder. "You're a real fucking asshole, Fuzz."

I nod, watching her as she walks to the door. "Yeah, you'll get over it."

As the door slams behind her, I sink back into the chair and grab the papers off of the desk. My mind churns as I think about our date and Piper's request but when I look down at the papers in my hand, I shake my head. What's that old saying? Fool me once, shame on you. Fool me twice, shame on me and I'm sure as hell not letting Piper pull me into her shit storm ever again.

Chapter Ten
Piper

"Piper," Dr. Brewer calls as she pokes her head out of her office and I look up from my magazine, returning her smile as I set it down on the table next to me and standing up. She stands back to allow me to walk into the room before shutting the door behind me. Her smile is kind as she sits across from me and places her notebook on her lap. "How are you today?"

I nod. "I'm good."

"We missed you at group last week," she muses, studying me in that way she does as her pen hovers over the paper, ready to write any notes she feels are important. I nod.

"Yeah, I had a rough day and I couldn't deal with the whole group so Lillian and I went to get some food and talk."

"And that helped?"

I think back over that night and how bad my belly hurt from laughing so much as I nod. As unconventional as Dr.

Brewer might think it is, it was exactly what I needed. "Yeah."

"Do you want to talk about what put you in a bad headspace that day?" she asks, jotting down some notes before glancing up at me again.

"Sure."

She nods for me to continue and I take a deep breath before nodding to myself. "I've been thinking a lot about what I want out of my life, you know… all the things I had planned before everything fell apart."

"Mmhmm," she hums, writing down some more notes as I take another deep breath. It doesn't matter that I've been seeing Dr. Brewer for seven years, I still find it difficult to open up and talk about my feelings, especially from that time in my life.

"So Eden was encouraging me to go after the things I want…"

Dr. Brewer holds her hand up to interrupt me. "What exactly are we talking about here? Love?"

"No," I whisper, shaking my head. "Love is… complicated and not my focus. I do still want the family, though and she's been encouraging me to look into ways I could make that happen without a man in my life."

"I see," she answers with a nod, writing some more notes.

"Anyway, that day she came over with information and I realized how expensive it all was and I just felt so defeated. It wasn't something I was ready to talk about in front of the whole group, though."

Dr. Brewer finishes her notes and leans back in her chair, narrowing her eyes as she studies me. "You seem less defeated today, though. Has something changed?"

"Um," I whisper, my mind slamming me back into a memory of seeing Wyatt yesterday as I shake my head. "I'm not sure."

"Care to elaborate?"

Sucking in a breath, I nod. "I saw Wyatt yesterday."

"Oh," she breathes, dropping her gaze to her notepad as her pen scratches furiously across the paper. "Did you just run into him?"

I shake my head. "No. Eden found him on a dating site and she started talking to him. When she realized who he was, she set up a date but sent me instead."

"And were you in on this deception?"

"No," I scoff. "I didn't know who I was meeting until I showed up and he was sitting at the table."

She peeks up from her notes. "That must have been…"

"Yeah," I answer, interrupting her. Whatever word she was going to use, seeing Wyatt again with no warning was exactly that. "It was a lot to deal with and I almost stood him up."

"But you didn't?"

I shake my head.

"Why not?" she asks and I shrug. Truthfully, maybe it would have been the smart thing to do but I just couldn't force myself to get back in my car and drive away from him. Not again.

"I don't know. I just… couldn't."

She hums to herself as she scribbles some more notes onto her notepad. "So you spoke to him for the first time in ten years?"

I nod.

"How did that go?"

"It was tense," I admit, remembering the blanket of pain and anger that draped over us as we sat across from each other in that restaurant. I knew he would be hurt. I knew he would be angry but I still wasn't prepared for it to smack me in the face as soon as I sat down. Closing my eyes, an image of him pops into my head and my chest aches.

"What are you thinking right now?" Dr. Brewer asks and my eyes open as I wipe away a sneaky tear and shake my head.

"Nothing."

She holds up her finger in warning. "Remember, you're not allowed to do that. If you don't feel like talking about it, that's fine but quit calling your emotions in this moment nothing."

"Okay," I whisper as I nod. One of Dr. Brewer's biggest rules is not invalidating my feelings in any way and something I always struggle with but after a lifetime of telling everyone around me I was fine when I had chaos raging through me every day, it's almost second nature. It's one of the biggest things that got me in trouble in the past and something I always have to be careful about. "I just... I miss him so much and every day that I have to continue without him, feels impossible. I hate the mistakes I made and I wish, more than anything, that I could take them back. I want him back in my life."

By the time I'm done, tears are streaming down my face and Dr. Brewer nods as she passes me a box of Kleenex with a sympathetic expression on her face.

"Did you tell him that?"

I shake my head. "No. He wouldn't want to hear that.

Not after what I did."

"You mean what he thinks you did," she points out, jotting down some more notes and I nod as I wipe my nose with the tissue.

"I don't know that it matters that I never cheated on him now. He's lived with that for ten years and it's almost like it's become a part of him."

She glances up, tilting her head to the side. "Why do you say that?"

"It was obvious as soon as we started talking. He's angrier now, rougher in a way he never used to be, and maybe it's just because he was talking to me but I don't think so. It feels like I ruined his life."

"And you don't think that is your own guilt talking?" She jots more notes down, glancing up at me as she writes as I think through my response. I know all too well the way your emotions can influence the way you see the world but something about the look on Wyatt's face revealed to me the damage I'd done when I walked away from him. I could practically see the walls being erected around his heart as we talked...

I shake my head. "Yes and no. Maybe my guilt amplified it but he's definitely closed himself off from the world and that blame lies with me."

"So," she muses as she finishes up some more notes and looks up at me. "If you didn't talk about any of that, what did you talk about with him?"

"Oh, that..." My eyes widen as I drop them to my hands and fiddle with my thumbs as my mind drifts back to what I blurted out at the restaurant yesterday. I didn't mean to ask him to help me have a baby but when he insisted I tell him what I wanted and the only thing screaming through my head was the word, "You", I panicked. Sucking in a breath, I look up. "I asked him to help me have a baby."

She jerks in her seat and her gaze snaps to mine. "What?"

"I asked him to help me have a baby," I repeat, refusing to meet her eyes. I don't have to see her look of disapproval to know it's there. She's quiet for a few seconds and my heart pounds as I glance up. With her mouth slack in shock, she stares back at me before shaking her head.

"Piper, it's been a hell of a long time since someone shocked me but I honestly don't know what to say…"

I nod. "I know… I don't even know why I did it except that when he asked me what I wanted, I panicked and blurted it out."

"I see…" she muses, jotting down a few more notes before looking at me again. "But it's not entirely a lie, is it?"

"Oh, God," I groan, burying my face in my hands before shaking my head and leaning back into the couch. "I don't know. It was just something Eden said when we were talking about the options for me to have a baby and then when he asked me what I wanted…"

"You had to tell him anything other than the truth?" she supplies and I nod. Sighing, she folds her hands over her notepad and pins me with a look.

"Okay, I have a couple of things."

I nod.

"First off, I think you need to have a discussion with Eden about her over-stepping. While it's good that you have someone who will push you out of your comfort zones and force you to grow, I'm concerned with the choices she's making for you and the choices you're making with her influence."

"She means well," I object, feeling the need to defend my friend. "She thinks there is still something between Wyatt and me…"

"She and I would agree on that point, at least from your perspective but it still doesn't absolve her of tricking both of you into confronting each other again. Her methods are… irresponsible."

I nod. As much as I love Eden, I am still upset over what she did. "I know."

"And as far as having a baby with Wyatt, I hope I don't have to tell you that it is a *very* bad idea. Especially considering that he still doesn't know the truth. If the two of you reconciled and you told him everything, I would be happy to see you moving forward in your life but not like this. *This* isn't a healthy way of dealing with things and I don't want to see you slip back to where you were seven years ago."

A shiver runs down my spine and I nod. "I don't want that either."

"I'm glad we're in agreement, then," she answers with a nod, tension seeping out of her shoulders as she leans back in her chair and looks over her notes. "Actually, before we close this topic of discussion, I would just urge you, again, to tell Wyatt the truth."

"I can't."

She frowns. "Piper, if you truly want to move on with your life, whether that is with Wyatt or without him, this is an essential step. Those secrets you're holding under lock and key, they're keeping you prisoner and I worry that you'll never be happy as long as you cling to them."

"I can't tell him," I insist, shaking my head as I picture spilling my secrets to Wyatt in my head. God, he can never know. She sighs.

"I'll drop this… for now." She pins me with a look and I nod. I know we'll be talking about this again but I just can't ever imagine telling Wyatt the things that happened before I left him. I can't let him see me that way. "Now, tell me, how have the nightmares been? The same or better lately?"

My head jerks up and I meet her eyes. "Better."

"Good," she answers with a smile, jotting down some more notes. The rest of the appointment goes by quickly as we go over the plan we have to help me deal when things get hard and she reinforces the fact that I can call her whenever I need her. She's been having the same conversation with me once a week for seven years so I doubt I would forget it now but she always makes sure to end our sessions with those words. I suppose they do bring me a bit of comfort to know that she's always there, standing behind me and ready to reach out if I start to fall.

My phone rings as I walk out of the office and I smile when I see Lillian's name on the screen. "Hey, girl. What's up?"

"Eden and I are out for drinks, come meet us!" she yells into the phone over the sound of music blaring in the background. I crinkle my nose as I step outside. Eden and I haven't spoken since my date with Wyatt and I don't know if I'm ready to face her yet.

"Oh, I don't know, Lil…"

"Please, Pippy? It's been so long since we've had a girls' night," she pleads and I blow out a breath as I stop next to my car and unlock the door before slipping behind the wheel.

"All right." I flip down the visor and check my reflection in the mirror. Sometimes when I come out of Dr. Brewer's office, I look like some kind of swamp thing but today, it is not so bad. "Send me the address and I'll meet you guys over there in a few."

"Yay!" she squeals before promising to send me the address and while I wait for her text, I pull out my compact and touch up my makeup before nodding and flipping the visor closed. As much as I'm not ready to face Eden, I suppose it is better to just get it over with. We will have it out and then we can move on because as angry as I am with her, I do know she was only trying to help in her unique Eden way.

My phone pings with a text and I plug the address into my GPS before pulling out of the parking lot and following the instructions to the little bar downtown that is a favorite of ours. After finding a place to park, I climb out of the car and step inside, weaving my way through the crowd and searching for their faces near the table we usually sit at. Eden and Lillian wave at me through the mass of bodies and I smile as I wave back at them and push through the cluster of people surrounding me.

"We got you a glass of wine," Lillian says as I reach them, pushing the glass toward the empty seat at the table. Eden flashes me a nervous smile and I sit down, grabbing my glass and taking a sip.

"Thanks."

"I know you're mad," Eden says, looking appropriately contrite and I lean back against my chair, crossing my arms over my chest.

"I am."

"Did it not go well?"

I scoff, shaking my head. "No, it didn't go well but even if it had, doing that to both Wyatt and me was not cool."

"I know," she whispers with a nod. "Wyatt messaged me, too, and chewed me out last night. I really didn't mean any harm though. It's just… the two of you…"

"Your heart was in the right place," I say, reaching across the table and placing my hand on hers. "I know that but you did cross a line. The issues between Wyatt and me… they're complicated and painful and not something that can be fixed during one lunch date."

"Speaking of…" Lillian cuts in, leaning forward with a gleam in her eyes that makes me laugh. "How did the lunch date go?"

"Terrible."

She rolls her eyes. "I know but I need details, woman!"

I glance over at Eden and flash her a small smile to let her know that she's forgiven and her body deflates for a second before she sits up straighter, almost back to the Eden I'm used to as I launch into my story about my date with Wyatt. Lillian is enthralled, watching me with an arched brow as she sips her drink and Eden studies me closely.

"So, when he asked me what I wanted, I panicked and told him I wanted him to help me have a baby."

Eden's mouth pops open. "You did not."

"I did," I answer with a nod and she shakes her head as she buries her face in her hands.

"Oh my God."

Lillian's gaze bounces between the two of us before she turns back to me, her eyes wide and she's practically hanging off of the edge of her seat. "Well, what did he say?"

"He told me I was insane, rightly so I might add, and stormed out."

"And you didn't tell him the truth about anything?" Eden asks and I shake my head. I just can't imagine ever telling Wyatt the real reason why I walked away from him. He wouldn't understand and he certainly wouldn't see me the same ever again. Although, at this point, I don't know what it matters. "Well, he sure was fired up when he messaged me last night."

"What did he say?" I ask, my heart pounding.

Shit.

Maybe I don't want to know what he said...

She grabs her phone off of the table and unlocks it before handing it to me and my hands tremble as I start reading through his messages from last night.

WyattL23:
I don't know what kind of fucking game you think you're playing but
ambushing me with my whore of an ex-wife is fucking low.
Which is a shame since you seemed like such a cool

girl.

Tears well up in my eyes and I flinch as I read the message again, the words "my whore of an ex-wife" echoing through my head.

EdiePB09:
I know. I'm so sorry…
I just thought it would help.

WyattL23:
Help what?

EdiePB09:
All I can say is that you don't know everything about why
Piper left you and she still loves you.

"Eden," I hiss, staring at her last message in horror before I look up at her and she sheepishly flashes me a smile.

"I'm sorry…"

My muscles tense as anger pulses through me and I don't even know what to say to her right now so I glance

129

back at the phone and continue reading.

WyattL23:
What the hell is that supposed to mean?

EdiePB09:
I can't say anything else. I'm sorry.
If you want to know the truth, ask Piper.

I stare at the message, reading it three times as my heart pounds in my ears and anger races through my veins. My head snaps up and I lock eyes with Eden as she holds her hands up in surrender.

"I know, Pip, I know and I'm sorry. I was just still trying to help."

"This is help?" I ask through clenched teeth, whipping the phone around to show her the same messages I just read as the reality of the situation crashes down on me.

Holy fuck.

What has she done?

Every Little Thing

Chapter Eleven
Wyatt

If you want to know the truth, ask Piper.

Eden's words run through my mind again, just like they have on repeat for the last two days, tormenting me and making me question everything I thought I knew. And when they're not running through my head, I'm reading those damn messages, trying to find a clue hidden in her responses to tell me what the hell to expect but there's nothing. I've spent more hours than I care to admit trying to remember everything that went down ten years ago, searching for a clue there that might provide me with an insight for what Eden meant when she said I didn't know everything but I'm officially stumped. If I want answers, I have to talk to Piper again and I just don't know if I can. Sighing, I run my hands through my hair and resist the urge to rip it out.

Goddamn it.

What are these girls trying to do to me? Piper left because she cheated on me and fell in love with someone else. There isn't much else to the story so I have to wonder if this is all just another game dreamt up by Eden and possibly Piper, just like the surprise reunion a couple of days ago. Shaking my head, I blow out a breath. As much as I'd like to believe the worst of Piper, I don't think she had any clue until she showed up to the date because just like me, she looked shell-shocked and for all of her faults when we were together, I never would have accused Piper of being manipulative or someone who liked to play games. Which leaves Eden... God, this is fucking insane. I'm officially losing my mind over a single message from a woman who has already crossed a line when it comes to Piper and me. She clearly has boundary issues and likes to play games with people so why can't I stop obsessing over her words?

What is the truth?

What is Piper hiding from me?

Why do I even fucking care?

Suppressing a groan, I scrub my hand over my jaw and stare out at the parking lot as everyone else sets up for the barbecue Blaze decided to throw tonight. Everyone is coupled up except for Streak, who is probably still locked away in his room, and me and seeing them all together, displaying their love and happiness for the world to see makes me feels like drowning myself in a vat of whiskey. My chest aches and my mind spins. I have been off balance since I saw her in that restaurant, looking better than even my best fantasy could remember, and as much as I want to drop this and move on with my life, I can't figure out how. Goddamn it. I was so fucking close and then just one look from her and she embedded herself under my skin like a goddamn parasite. The worst part is I'm afraid there is no way to get rid of her.

"Hey," Streak says, slipping into the seat next to me as he holds out a cold bottle of beer and I grab it, nodding in return before turning to stare out at all of the couples milling around as they set everything up. "Makes you sick, doesn't it?"

I glance over at him before shaking my head. The last thing I need is my brothers knowing just how tormented I am by all of their happiness. Not to mention, it's not fair to them. "Whatever. They seem happy."

"Sure, I guess," he scoffs before taking a sip of his own beer. "But you won't ever see me looking like these assholes."

"Famous last words, Streaky boy," I tease and he shakes his head, making a face as he leans back in his chair.

"Hell, naw, not gonna happen."

Turning, I study him for a second before taking a sip of my beer as I fight back a smile. "Gotta be honest, I never really saw you as the type to go for dudes but if that's what you're into, man…"

"Fuck you, douchebag. I don't swear off women in general, I just swear off relationships. They don't vibe with my lifestyle."

"What the hell does that mean?" I ask with a laugh and he sighs.

"It's like this, I'm up all hours of the night in front of three computer screens digging up shit for y'all and I rarely even leave this goddamn clubhouse all of which isn't conducive to developing or maintaining a relationship. Believe me when I say, everyone is better off if I don't ever fall in love."

I shrug as I turn back to the rest of the group and take a sip of my beer. "Maybe you just haven't met the right one."

"You're one to talk," he fires back and Piper's face pops into my mind again, her smile blinding me as the ache in my chest grows. I shake my head and blow out a breath as I try to shove her from my thoughts. As much as I need answers, I can't obsess over her anymore tonight.

"By the way, have you come up with anything on Mitch?" I ask in an effort to distract myself and he groans, slamming his forehead against his open palm.

"No. Dude is a goddamn ghost." He glances up at me. "I'm honestly impressed with how low of a profile he has online and if I had to guess, I would say he's into some heavily illegal shit."

"Hmph."

Well, shit.

There goes that idea.

"Rodriguez did bring him in for questioning once, though. Right after Dina died."

I nod. "But he didn't find anything?"

"Don't know," he answers with a shrug. "You'll have to go talk to Diego. I promised not to hack into his files anymore."

"That something you did often?" I ask, glancing over at him with a smirk and he shrugs again. That's about as much of an answer as I'm going to get out of him. Streak got his road name for being the luckiest son of a bitch any of us had ever met but he is also really fucking smart and careful. He won't ever say anything that would incriminate himself or that someone could use against him and his main goal is to be the smartest guy in the room and to be holding all the cards. I suppose that is also another point against him in a relationship, though.

"Ugh, just look at them," he grumbles as I turn as Storm pulls his old lady, Ali, into his arms and kisses her before taking their baby girl, Magnolia, from her. My chest burns and I shake my head as I look away.

Fuck.

Streak is right.

Being around these guys and their never-ending happiness is fucking torture even on the best days but when all I can think about is this big secret that Piper has been keeping from me for God only knows how long, it's unbearable. Someone turns some music on and "I Knew I Loved You" by Savage Garden starts playing.

"Aw, fuck," Streak growls as Moose pulls Juliette out of her chair and into his arms. She laughs as they begin swaying back and forth and it feels like someone dropped a boulder in my stomach. "What is it with those two and that damn song?"

I shrug, remembering the winter formal I took Piper to our freshman year of high school where we danced to this song and my arms ache with the memory of holding her.

"You know, it's not even a good song. At least pick a decent fucking song, right?" Streak continues and I just nod, my mind consumed with the memory of Piper in her black dress and her red curls falling down her back. Closing my eyes, I remember the way she leaned into me and the smile she flashed me all night long, like she was keeping a secret except that time, we were both in on it. I can still remember the way she looked up at me as we swayed

135

together under twinkle lights and multi-colored streamers like we were the only people there. Her honeysuckle perfume fills my nose almost like I'm right back there with her in that gym and my heart thuds in my chest.

"Savage fucking Garden," Streak hisses and I open my eyes, glancing over at him. He shakes his head, disgust rolling off of him as he finishes off his beer before standing up and turning back to me, pointing to my bottle. "You want another one?"

I shake my head. "Naw, I'm good."

He heads back into the clubhouse and I lean back in my chair as I stare out at the rest of the club and their old ladies. A few of the girls have talked their men into dancing with them as well while Blaze fires up the grill and that damn ache in my chest only gets stronger. Pulling my phone out of my pocket, I open the dating app that I haven't gotten around to deleting yet and scroll through some of the girls on the site but no one snags my interest when all I can see is Piper.

Fuck.

She ruined me.

She ruined us.

Shaking my head, I cross my arms over my chest and do my best to steel myself against thoughts of her but it only works for a second before another memory slips through the cracks. I squeeze my eyes closed and suck in a breath as pain fills my chest and images flash through my head. Since she and I just went down to the courthouse to get married, we didn't plan a reception or anything but my parents surprised us with a little get-together in their backyard with my family and some of our closest friends. It was a lot like the parties Blaze is so fond of throwing with good barbecue, good music, family, and lots of laughs. Before she left me, I considered that night one of the best of my life.

Hell, maybe it still is…

Maybe that is the whole fucking point. I can't ever move on with my life because Piper still owns a piece of me that I'll never be able to get back. She used to say that we were destined for each other and that after all of the bad that she had been through and all the pain she had endured, I was her reward. So then why the hell did she throw all of it away?

"Fuzz."

Opening my eyes, I arch a brow as Blaze sits in Streak's vacated chair and nods a greeting at me before he glances out at everyone dancing and laughing.

"Blaze," I reply, following his gaze as my stomach clenches and jealousy rages through me.

Fuck.

How amazing would it be to be out there with all of them, Piper in my arms again…

Wait… What?

With a sigh, Blaze crosses his arms over his chest, mirroring my posture before glancing over at me. I wait for him to say something but he just stares like he's waiting for me to start the conversation and I squirm in my seat.

What the hell?

"What?"

He shakes his head. "Nothing."

Okay, then…

"Something I can help you with?" I ask when he still

doesn't tear his eyes from me and he shakes his head again, trying like hell to appear casual but I can see the wheels turning in his mind. That man is up to something.

"Uh… you need something?"

"Nope," he answers, shaking his head as he turns to stare out at my brothers again as a smile tugs at his lips. "Sure is a nice picture, isn't it?"

I follow his gaze to the couples out in the parking lot and nod half-heartedly. "Yep."

"Let me ask you something…"

Oh, here we go.

"What?"

He turns back to me and pins me with a stare that radiates power and Blaze's signature no-nonsense attitude. "You planning on pulling your head out of your ass anytime soon?"

"Excuse me?" I ask, jerking back as my eyes widen. "What the fuck are you talking about?"

"Do you think you joined this club without me doing my research on you?"

I arch a brow, still unsure about where this is going. "No, I suppose not."

"So, then you know that I know about your wife."

"Ex-wife," I growl, sinking into my chair as I glare at the pavement and tightening my arms across my chest. He sighs.

"You haven't signed the papers."

I flick my eyes in his direction.

How in the fuck does he know that?

"What's your goddamn point?"

"Look, I don't know exactly what went on between

y'all but I do know that you've been moping around this clubhouse for years, missing that woman, so throw your pride out of the window and go find her."

"I am not missing her," I snap, dropping my gaze to the ground as the pain in my chest seems to throb in agreement with Blaze's words.

"Oh, save the bullshit."

"I'm not bull…"

He holds his hand up, interrupting me as he rolls his eyes. "Save it. I know the look on your face too damn well. The only difference is, in your case, you can do something to change it but you're just too stubborn to try."

"You don't know what you're talking about," I growl. Blaze's story is a sad one for sure and there were things that were out of his control that kept him away from the woman he loved but it doesn't mean our situations are the same. Piper cheated on me. Am I just supposed to let that go? He shrugs as he stands up.

"Fine. Do whatever you want. Just didn't realize we patched in a little bitch."

He walks away before I can say anything else and I stare at him as he goes back to the grill and takes over for Storm, anger eating away at me. Fuck him and his goddamn assumptions. What Piper and I had, when we had it, was fucking everything and there is no way in hell I can go back after what she did. Things would never be the same and what the hell would it make me if I just forgave her for her betrayal?

As I stare out at everyone else, laughing and having a good time, my mind drifts back to right before I left for my first deployment. I took Piper out as often as I could then, trying to pack as many memories into as little time as possible and we had an amazing month together before I left. Despite the fact that we'd be apart for almost a year, we still had such grand plans for our life and we were happy… at least, I thought we were. Maybe I didn't know anything at all, though. Piper's face pops into my mind, all red hair, freckles, and her green eyes shining with happiness and I shake my head.

No.
We were happy.
I know we were.
So why the hell did she leave?

God, I hate all the fucking questions I still have but the truth is, I don't even know if the answers would make me feel better at this point. Piper leaving me was the start of a downward trend in my life. I started drinking and fighting. Anyone that even looked at me funny was liable to get a fist to the face and I didn't care about what would happen to me. I mean, my girl was gone so what did it matter if I got my ass kicked, kicked out of the Marines, or arrested for assault?

Without her, I had nothing to lose.

The thought echoes through my head and I release a heavy breath as I sit forward and scrub a hand down my face. Shit. Here I am, talking about how fucking epic our love was and how lost I was without her but I never even went looking for her. I didn't even try.

Why the hell not?
Why didn't I fight for her, for us?

Maybe if I had, I would have the life that I want so goddamn badly.

Every Little Thing

Turning my gaze back to all of the couples milling around the clubhouse, I shake my head. No matter how hard I fight it, Piper is still the only woman I can see spending the rest of my life with and as I think about her betrayal, I can't even find the energy to care anymore. I loved her since I was a fucking kid and if I'm honest with myself, that never went away. There are still a whole lot of answers I need before she and I can begin to fix this but Blaze is right.

It's time to get my woman back.

Every Little Thing

Chapter Twelve
Piper

I take a sip of my wine as I walk out of the kitchen and cuddle into the comfy armchair by the window that I found in a little thrift shop a couple of blocks away from my apartment. Raindrops streak down the window and I stare out at the dreary sky, the gray ominous clouds perfectly reflecting my mood for the past two days. My phone rattles with an incoming call and falls off the windowsill, crashing to the floor and I lean down and pick it up. Eden's smiling face mocks me from the screen and I sneer as I decline the call and set the phone back on the sill. I don't care how many times she tells me she is sorry or she was just trying to help because the damage is done and there is nothing she can do about that. Wyatt knows I'm keeping secrets from him and I've spent the past forty-eight hours waiting for his next move.

Then again...

Maybe I will luck out and he'll just let it go. Shaking my head, I sigh as I take another sip of my wine. No, I know better than that. Now that he knows that I didn't tell him the truth, it will eat away at him until he decides to finally confront me for answers. God, walking into the restaurant was such a stupid idea and I can't believe I let Eden talk me into it. Things were good... okay, well, maybe not good but I was okay before I came face-to-face with him again and now, all I feel is turmoil. The worst part is seeing him, right in front of me, full of rage and looking better than he has a right to, reminded me just how much I love him. Not that I ever truly forgot but most days, it was easier to ignore than it is now. Closing my eyes, I lay my head back against the chair and let out a groan. I can't believe I asked him to help me have a baby, too. Of all the stupid things I could have said, I definitely picked the worst.

He must think I'm insane.

Hell, maybe I am.

Knocking pulls me out of my thoughts and my head snaps forward before turning to look at my apartment door with a scowl. I would bet that Eden decided to drop by personally since I haven't taken any of her calls since our "girls' night" and I shake my head before turning back to my window. It's not like this is it for Eden and me. She is one of my very best friends in the world, something I didn't really have until I met her, and I'm not ready to throw all that away but she can certainly sweat this out a little. It serves her right for sticking her nose in my business and crossing more damn lines than I can count.

"Piper!"

Oh, fuck...

Wyatt's voice bounces off the walls in the apartment

144

and it feels like I'm moving in slow motion as I turn to stare at my front door.

This is exactly what I was afraid of and now that it is happening, I don't know what to do. I am not anywhere near ready to tell Wyatt the truth about what tore our marriage apart and I don't know if I ever will be but I know I can't avoid him forever. The Wyatt I knew ten years ago was *persistent* and I can't imagine that particular quality has mellowed out in the years since.

"Goddamn it, Piper! I know you're in there."

Sucking in a nervous breath, I down the rest of my glass of wine and set it on the windowsill before climbing out of the chair with shaky legs. I press my hand to my stomach and take another deep breath as I start slowly moving toward the door. Wyatt's fist pounds against the other side, making the wood crack and I shake my head.

"You got this, girl," I whisper to myself, hoping like hell I'm lying as I reach the door and pull it open. Wyatt's hazel eyes slam into mine as he towers over me with both hands gripping the door frame around him. He's breathing heavily and the determination steeling his gaze terrifies me.

"We need to talk."

I shake my head. "No… I don't think we do."

"Well, you're wrong," he says as he releases the frame and gently moves me to the side so he can let himself into my apartment.

Fuck.

Shit.

Damn.

Blowing out a breath, I close the door and turn to him as he paces through my living room, his gaze taking in the decor before he freezes and I squeeze my eyes closed.

Shit.

He just saw the framed photo from our wedding that is sitting on my bookshelf.

"Look at me."

My eyes snap open, almost like I have no choice but to obey him, and I meet his gaze as my heart thunders in my ears and my hands shake. Questions fill his stare and my body tenses, waiting for him to make the first move but he doesn't say anything. In the closed space of my apartment, I can feel his body calling out to me, demanding that I close the distance between us and let him wrap his arms around me. A shiver runs down my spine. I swear I can almost feel it despite the five feet separating us and I resist the urge to close my eyes and soak it up.

Fuck.

It's been ten years but absolutely nothing about how much he affects me has changed. He takes a step forward and my heart skips a beat. Sighing, he seems to shake off whatever just happened between us and he takes two steps back before running his fingers through his hair.

"Eden told me the truth," he finally says, crossing his arms over his chest and I can't help but admire the way his arms stretch the sleeves of his t-shirt.

Whoa, those are new...

Yanking my gaze away, I walk around him and grab my wine glass off of the windowsill before turning toward the kitchen. "The truth about what?"

I figure playing innocent is my best bet since I'm sure as hell not telling him anything and informing him of that would only push him harder to uncover the secrets I have

146

kept locked away for years.

Setting my wine glass on the counter, I turn back to him and arch a brow in question. He narrows his eyes. I fight back a nervous smile.

Shit.

I never was very good at lying to him.

"I've been thinking about what you asked me," he says, his body relaxing as he changes tactics and the hair on my arm stands on end as I watch him walk into the kitchen and sit down at the table. Crap. I completely forgot about my epic brain to mouth filter malfunction while I was stressing about his reaction to Eden spilling the beans. I wish I could face palm myself right now because I never should have asked him that.

"Huh?" I ask, sticking to my innocent facade. He smirks and I can't tell if it's because he knows I'm lying my ass off or something else.

"The baby."

"Oh, that…"

He nods. "Yeah… that."

"Listen, you can just forget about that. I don't know what I was thinking asking you with our history and everything. It was a terrible idea," I tell him, leaning back against the counter as I shake my head. His face falls and he scowls.

"I was going to say yes."

My heart kicks in my chest. "What?"

"Yeah, I thought about it and I think we should do it."

"I… uh… what?" I stutter, staring at him with what I'm sure is a bewildered look. What the hell kind of game is he playing right now? There is no way in hell he is serious about having a baby with me but even knowing that… can I really pass up the opportunity? He nods again.

"Look, at first, I thought it was completely crazy but the more I thought about it, the more it made sense. We always talked about having kids together and sure, this isn't exactly how we planned it but, let's be honest, neither one of us has been able to find anything better."

I wince before I can stop myself. It's not fair of me but it hurts like hell to hear him say that I'm an okay consolation prize. What did I expect though?

"No… Wyatt, we can't do this…"

He scowls as he stands up and takes a couple steps toward me. My heart races. "This was your idea."

"I know," I breathe, my mind consumed with how close he is to me right now. There aren't many things I wouldn't give up to feel him wrap his arms around me again. "But like I said, it was a bad one."

Closing the distance between us, he props his hands on the countertop and cages me in. His breath warms my cheek as his gaze holds me prisoner and I struggle to draw air into my lungs.

What the hell is he doing?

"Don't you want a baby, Pip?"

I shake my head as tears sting my eyes at the nickname he used to call me when we were kids. "Don't call me that."

"Answer my question," he whispers, leaning in closer and I try to take a breath as the blood rushes in my ears and my fingers ache to reach out and touch him. God, he smells so damn good and having him this close again is like everything I've wanted for the past ten years. "Do you want a baby?"

"Yes."

His lips brush against mine and a breathy moan slips out. Pulling back slightly, his gaze meets mine again, desire pooling in his eyes and my belly clenches with need.

He looks like he wants to devour me.

"So, you want a baby and I want a baby… there's just one thing I need first."

"What?" I whisper, ready to agree to anything he wants if he will just lean in and press his lips to mine.

"Tell me what happened when you left me."

Except that…

Shaking my head, I duck beneath his arms and cross to the other side of the kitchen as I suck air into my lungs and my head becomes clearer. "No."

"Yes," he growls as he spins around, leans back against the counter, and crosses his arms over his chest. "Don't you think you owe me that much, at least?"

"Why rehash it?" I ask, twisting my gaze away from his as I mirror his pose, crossing my arms. "You already know why I left."

He shoves off the counter. "That's not what your friend, Eden, says."

"Eden doesn't know what she's talking about," I snap, reciting the urge to curl my lip in disgust. Gah, I can't believe she did this to me. He takes another step toward me and I step back, my butt hitting the edge of the kitchen table as I gasp.

"You're lying."

I shake my head. "No, I'm not."

"Yes," he growls, closing the distance between us and grabbing my face to force my gaze to his. "You are. Why did you leave me?"

"You know why," I whisper, unable to make the lie sound anymore convincing as his eyes fight to pry the truth from my lips. His gaze hardens.

"Before I came over here, I wasn't sure if Eden was telling the truth or not but now I know she was. You've been keeping secrets from me, Pip."

I rip my face from his grip. "Stop calling me that."

"Tell me why you left me."

"No," I repeat, leveling a glare at him as I feel some of my strength slipping away. It doesn't matter how much he begs, demands, or asks, I can't tell him the truth. The way he sees me now, as a cold callous bitch, who ripped his heart apart, is better than the way he would look at me if I told him what really went down. This is for the best.

"Goddamn it, you're so fucking stubborn," he seethes, taking a step back as he takes a deep breath. I arch a brow.

"Look who's talking."

He shakes his head, staring down at my kitchen floor for a second before he looks up and meets my gaze, his eyes blazing. "If you want me to help you have a baby, you have to tell me. That's the only way I'll agree to it."

My head spins as I try to work through his train of thought.

Is this all about my request to have a baby?

Or is there more to it?

Is he just here playing games with me?

If he is, I'm fucking done going along with it. Shaking my head, I turn away from him.

"Forget about it. Like I said, it was a bad idea and I never should have asked you. I'm sorry."

He grabs my arm, spinning me back to him and pulling me into his arms. I suck in a breath as I look up and meet his eyes. "What if I don't want to forget about it? What if I don't want to try and forget about you anymore?"

"What are you saying?" I whisper, searching his gaze but he doesn't give anything away. My heart hammers in my chest as my body wants to melt into his as he presses himself against me, his arms locked tight around my waist.

He opens his mouth like he's going to say something before clamping it shut again and his eyes search my face but before I get the chance to say anything else, he slips his hand into my hair and slams his lips down on mine. We move on instinct, coming together like we were never apart and my body sings as I wrap my arms around his neck and arch into him. His kiss is rough, demanding, and full of the pain of the last ten years but it's exactly what I need, what I've craved since the moment I walked away from him. Gone is the boy who treated me with kid gloves but I can't say that I mind all that much. He sinks his teeth into my bottom lip and I cry out. My nipples tighten as I rub my chest against him, needing more and he growls against my lips.

Gripping my hair, he pulls my head back and drags his lips down the side of my neck, ripping another moan from my mouth as he kisses, licks, and bites at my skin. My belly clenches and tears form in my eyes as he works his way back up to my kiss, claiming me, consuming me. Fisting his shirt in my hands, I cling to him as a delicious shudder racks my body and I whimper for relief.

God, I missed him.

"Piper," he groans, grabbing my hips and pulling me

closer as he thrusts forward, pressing his hard length into my hip. I moan again, desperate for all of him. "Fuck. I want you…"

I nod frantically. "Yes."

With a sexy little growl, he lifts me off the floor and spins around before setting me on the counter. His hands roam all over my body, touching me everywhere he can reach as his mouth plants possessive kisses all down my neck and lips. My pussy clenches with need. Moaning, I slip my hands under his shirt, my fingertips dancing over the ridges of his muscles and he grips my hair again, pulling my head to one side as he kisses up my neck and releases a rough breath in my ear. I shudder.

"Wyatt."

"Aw, fuck," he whispers, his breath heating my skin before he drops his head back. "I missed that sound, baby."

Pressing my lips to his neck, I start dragging his shirt up his body and he leans back to pull it over his head before grabbing my hips and slamming our bodies together again. Warmth floods my body and our heavy breaths fill the kitchen. He nips at my jaw as his hands slip under my tank top and he wastes no time ripping it over my head before reaching behind me and unhooking my bra. Cupping my breast in his hand, his groan rattles against my skin as he drags his mouth down to my chest and swirls his tongue over my nipple. My eyes close and I drop my head back and my fingers find their way into his hair.

"Oh, God… Wyatt."

"Say my name again, Pip. Who do you belong to?"

I moan as my skin tingles. "You, Wyatt."

"Damn fucking right you do," he growls, slipping back

up my body and claiming my lips again. Oh, fuck, I *love* possessive Wyatt. His hand slips into the back of my shorts and he grips my ass, pulling me into him as he thrusts forward. "Tell me why you left me?"

I shake my head. "No."

His growl is more intense as he reaches between us and unbuttons my shorts before thrusting his hips against me again.

"Tell me."

"No," I snap, grabbing the back of his head and shoving his lips to my neck. He kisses and bites a line down to my shoulder and I gasp as he growls, biting me a little harder than before. Yanking me off the counter, he still manages to be gentle as he sets me back on my feet but as soon as I'm steady, he shoves my shorts down my legs and spins me around. My body throbs with need stronger than I've ever felt and my heart flutters as he grabs my wrists and plants my hands on the counter in front of me.

"Why did you leave me?" he growls in my ear. I hear the sound of his belt coming undone and my heart thunders against my ribs as my entire body tightens in anticipation. I shake my head again in response and his frustrated groan reaches me at the same time that he pulls my panties to the side and I feel the head of his cock press against my entrance.

"Tell me," he demands and I shake my head again, squeezing my eyes closed and mentally begging for him to thrust forward.

"No."

With a roar, he slams into me and I cry out, my fingertips gripping the counter in front of me as he grabs my hips and squeezes them to the point of pain. He pulls back and drives home again, his pace punishing and rough but it's exactly what I needed. Leaning over me, he reaches around my body and wraps his hand around my throat, pulling me back to him and I moan. If this were any other man, the move would terrify me but not Wyatt. He's always been my solace, my port in the storm and even in his righteous anger, I know without a shadow of a doubt that he would never hurt me. His fingertips trace the scar along my neck and he presses a soft, loving kiss to it. It's such a contrast to the aggressive way he's taking me that tears spring to my eyes again.

"Wyatt," I whisper, pain swamping my chest as I feel his love, buried underneath years of hurt and anger, and my body tightens with my impending release.

"You wait for me."

I shake my head. "I can't."

"Figure it out. You'll wait for me just like you should have done ten years ago."

Between the mention of our past and the demanding tone of his voice, I can't hold it back any longer and I cry out as my orgasm tears through me. His grip on my throat tightens as he thrusts into me a few more times before tensing and groaning loudly in my ear. We both struggle to catch our breaths as the silence of the apartment becomes louder and louder, my mind racing with what we just did and wondering if he thinks it was a mistake.

Oh, God…

Please say something…

My heart races for a whole other reason as he pulls out of me and I hear his belt clink. When I spin around, he is pulling his jeans up and he refuses to meet my eyes, an unreadable expression on his face. Finally, after what feels like an eternity, he leans down and scoops up his t-shirt before meeting my gaze with a sigh. We stare at each other for a second before he shakes his head and walks out of my apartment. The door slams behind him and I stare at it for a second before the tears start falling.

Every Little Thing

Chapter Thirteen
Wyatt

A heavy sigh slips past my lips and I close my eyes and I run my hand through my hair before opening them again and staring up at the same spot on the ceiling that I've been staring at for hours. I've been here, thinking and making myself crazy since three this morning when I was woken up by a very vivid dream of Piper and me, with just one thought running through my head.

I fucked up.

The plan when I went over to her house last night was simple enough. Step one, find out if Eden was telling the truth about Piper lying to me and if she was, get Piper to open up and tell me whatever this big secret is. Step two, find a way to get my woman back. I'm not naive enough to think that it will be easy but after my little revelation at the barbecue last night, it is the only option.

See?

Simple.

Except, as soon as I walked through the door of her

apartment and saw the ridiculous little shorts she was wearing that showed off her toned legs and I remembered what it felt like for them to be wrapped around my waist, I knew I was I trouble. When the smell of her honeysuckle perfume, the same stuff she used to wear when we were kids, surrounded me and I saw the framed photo of us on our wedding day proudly displayed on her bookshelf, I was fucking doomed. My head was swimming and I couldn't ignore the way she makes me feel. It's fucking insane that even after ten years apart, and all the pain and anger between us, that she can still do that to me but every cell in my body was screaming at me to pull her into my arms and never let her go again. I was going to use our connection and the insane chemistry between us to try and trip her up, forcing her into revealing something she didn't intend to but I got careless and I was right there with her. Next thing I know, I'm balls deep inside my wife for the first time in ten years and demanding answers that she refused to give. Now, all I can fucking think about is doing it again. Groaning, I throw the covers off of my legs and sit up on the edge of the bed as I drop my head into my hands.

Fuck.

What a goddamn mess.

At least the night wasn't a total waste, though. One thing I know for sure now is that Eden was telling the truth when she told me Piper is keeping secrets from me. Not that I know what those secrets are yet but as soon as I looked into Piper's eyes, I knew she was lying. I honestly can't believe I didn't see it before and the other thing that became very clear to me last night is that Piper still loves me just as much as I love her.

Every Little Thing

So, why did she leave?

Shaking my head, I stand up and toss my covers back so the bed looks like I at least made an attempt to make it before I throw on some clothes and head downstairs. I don't want to say that why she left me doesn't matter anymore because I still want to know but it also has lost some significance after what happened last night. Whatever took her away from me ten years ago didn't do anything to the love we share or our connection and if anything, I'm more determined to get my wife back than I was before. I've been a goddamn idiot for a decade and that ends now but first... I have to know what happened to make her leave me. It's clear to me now that there never was anyone else if the look in her eyes and our wedding photo on her bookshelf is any indication but I am more confused now than I was before she walked back into my life.

What the hell made her leave?

Maybe I should just ask Streak to dig into her past but I want her to be the one to tell me. How could we truly move forward if she wasn't?

Trudging into the kitchen, I sigh and after turning on the coffee maker, I sit down at the table and stare down at the files in a neat little stack before flipping open the first one. Laney's picture stares back at me and I remember what Streak told me about Mitch last night. Sighing, I lean back in my chair and cross my arms over my chest as I stare at the file, my mind working through the new information... or lack of information, really. The fact that Streak can't find any information on the man makes him even more suspicious but what can I do without hard evidence? God, maybe I'm barking up the wrong tree here. It takes a hell of a lot of brutality to commit these murders and if Mitch had that, shouldn't we have seen it? Because there is a big difference between being a narcissistic asshole that hits your wife and the kind of psychopath that puts together a whole revenge plan that includes murdering three women.

The rich scent of coffee fills the air just before the machine beeps, letting me know it's ready and I sigh as I stand up to grab a cup. I check my watch and glance over at the front door. After I got home last night, I tried to distract myself from how badly I had messed up and all the damn questions that have only gotten louder in the last twenty-four hours by reading through the files but I still couldn't focus so I called Rodriguez to follow up on what Streak shared with me. He didn't answer but maybe I can try him again now. I don't know how much information he has to give me but truthfully, I'll take anything at this point. It feels like I've been studying these damn files for years even though it's only been a few months and I need to catch a break soon if I'm going to convince my brothers that we need to be looking into this. Stream billows around me as I pour myself a cup and turn, leaning back against the countertop as I sigh.

Pulling my phone out of my pocket, I dial his number and walk back over to the table, setting my coffee cup down before I slump in my chair. My gaze locks onto Laney's picture again and I shake my head.

"Hello?"

"Hey, Diego. It's Fuzz. You got a minute?" I ask, leaning forward and flipping the file closed. I can't stand to look at her face anymore. It's like she is mocking me with my inability to solve this or find any sort of evidence to back up my theory.

"Yeah, a couple. What's up?"

"It's about the cases."

He sighs. "I don't have anything new to give you, Fuzz. I really fucking wish I did but even I'm beginning to think I'm going crazy over here."

"Yeah," I mumble, running my hand through my hair. "Streak mentioned that you brought Dina's husband, Mitch, in after she was killed…"

"That son of a bitch," he hisses and I bite back a laugh. "He promised me he wouldn't go through my files anymore."

I chuckle, shaking my head. "Naw, he didn't. He was looking into Mitch for me and saw that you brought him in for questioning."

"Ah, okay…"

"He didn't dig any further than that," I assure him. "Out of respect for you, of course."

He scoffs. "Respect, my ass. He won't dig into my shit anymore because I told him I'd haul him into the station next time he did it."

"Shit," I reply, laughing as I shake my head and picture the look on Streak's face if Rodriguez stormed the clubhouse and put him in cuffs. Rodriguez chuckles.

"Yeah. So, what do you need to know about Mitch?"

"Did you get anything out of him?"

He sighs again. "Not really. I asked him where he was when Dina was killed and he had an alibi…"

"How solid of an alibi?"

"Not super solid," he answers, frustration lacing his tone. "But solid enough that I couldn't justify keeping him any longer. His friends vouched for him but you know how that goes…"

I nod, running my hand through my hair. "Yeah. They've got his back whether they actually saw him or not."

"Exactly. Why are you looking into him? You think he had something to do with this?"

"I don't know," I sigh, leaning back in my chair and shaking my head. "It's a theory but I'm not getting anywhere with it."

"Run it by me," he instructs.

"Well, the killing started with Dina, right? So, yeah, technically, it could be anyone connected to the girls we've helped but why start with Dina? Not to mention, that when Storm and Chance went to pick her up, they got into a fight with Mitch and Chance pulled a gun on him…"

Rodriguez sucks in a breath. "I didn't know that part."

"I mean, nothing happened but seems to me a guy like Mitch wouldn't take that embarrassment very well."

"Yeah, you're right."

My mind drifts back to what Streak said last night and I lean forward, flipping open Laney's file. "Have you been able to find anything else on him? Streak said the guy is pretty non-existent online."

"Naw, man. He lives his life like he's got something to fucking hide but he does it well enough that I can't find anything."

Staring down at Laney's photo, I nod. "You think he's capable of this?"

"Shit, Fuzz," he sighs. "You never know what someone is really capable of… but if you told me he was the guy, I wouldn't be too surprised. He's got serious anger issues and I get the feeling that is just the tip of the iceberg so yeah, I guess I think he's capable."

"You ever get anywhere on Laney or Sammy's cases?"

"No," he answers, pain lacing his voice and a pit forms in my stomach. I know he hasn't been coping with Laney's death very well but when you add in the fact that he still hasn't found her killer, it only makes it worse.

"All right. Well… if you find anything, will you let me know?"

He sighs again. "Yeah, you got it."

We say good-bye and after I hang up, I lean back in my chair and sigh. My mind drifts from the cases to the other huge problem in my life right now.

Piper.

What in the hell do I do about her?

Scrubbing my hand down my face, I close my eyes and the image of her looking up at me last night pops into my head, her green eyes boring into my flesh and I suck in a breath. My eyes pop open and I check my watch again, contemplating driving over to her place and demanding answers again before I stop myself.

Shit.

Should I really be doing this?

Maybe I have just finally lost my mind and this whole plan to get Piper back is a delusion, fueled by my insanity. Then again, I haven't felt this good in fucking years and even the frustration of the cases is not enough to damper my mood. Not when I can still feel her skin under my fingertips and her lips pressed against my neck. Fighting back a smile, I shake my head.

163

There are a few things I'm absolutely certain of - one, Piper never cheated on me. There is no possible way that is how things went down ten years ago because more than once I've caught her giving me the same damn look she used to give me when we were kids, like I'm her whole damn world. And yeah, she is still keeping secrets from me but that brings me to number two. Whatever she is hiding, whatever she has kept locked up for a decade doesn't matter. We'll get through it together. Last and most important, I'm not going to stop until I get my wife back.

If Piper thinks she's seen me determined before, she's got a whole other thing coming.

Letting my smile break through, I stand up and swipe my keys and phone off of the table before heading toward the door, ready to do whatever it takes to win her over. As I climb on my bike and it rumbles to life beneath me, I try to imagine what happened back then to make her leave. Since working with the club, my mind is full of awful scenarios but none of them really explain why she would leave. Did something happen to her? Did someone hurt her? The thought makes my blood boil and I swear I'll hunt down whoever it is and make them pay. But it still doesn't explain her disappearance...

I shake my head and steer my thoughts toward how I can convince her to open up to me as I pull out of my driveway. Clearly, I can't use our connection because we'll just end up in the same spot we were in last night, naked and all over each other, and if I try to push her, it will only make her lock up. I definitely need to drop the baby thing, though. As much as I want that for us, it's not the only thing I want or even the most important and getting her to open up to me is going to be hard enough without adding that little element into the mix.

Fuck.

It scares the shit out of me to think about giving her the ability to crush me again but what else can I do? If the last week has proven anything to me, it's that I have to get her back. The pulsing ache that has been a constant in my life since she left is fading each time I'm around her again and for the first time in a long time, I can see my future, painted so clearly in my mind. Before now, I was walking around in a fog, only able to plan the next step but blind when I tried to gaze further ahead until she walked back into my life. So, she can fight me as long and as hard as she wants but I won't stop.

Her front door opens as I pull up in front of her apartment and she looks up, her eyes widening as we stare at each other and I can see the moment she shuts down, locking away her feelings for me in an attempt to protect herself. Why the hell does she feel like she needs to protect herself from me, though? After climbing off my bike, I walk up the sidewalk to her front door as she turns away from me to lock it.

"Pip," I say as I come to a stop a couple feet from her. She takes a deep breath as she turns around and meets my gaze.

Aw, hell.

She's pissed.

"What are you doing here?"

I shrug since it should be pretty fucking obvious. "I'm here to see you."

"Why?" she hisses, trying to push past me but I block

her path. "Didn't get enough last night? I hate to burst your bubble but I'm on my way to work and I think the neighbors would have an issue with you bending me over the bushes."

Yeah…

Walking out without a word after I fucked her up against the counter was probably not my smartest move.

"I'm sorry about last night, Pip." I place my hand over my heart. "Honest."

She glares up at me, her gaze dropping to my hand before meeting my eyes again and I swear I can see a trace of pain shining back at me. "Well, at least we both agree it was a damn mistake."

"Hold up. I didn't say that. I'm apologizing for just walking out on you afterward… *that* was the mistake. Not us, never us."

"Stop saying us like that's a thing," she sighs, trying to push past me again but I pull her into my arms.

Fuck.

She fits against me like she was made for me and it only hardens my resolve to work things out with her. She is the only woman in the world for me and I can't believe it took me this long to figure it out.

"It is a thing. It's always been a thing and you know it."

Shaking her head, she looks up at me and defeat slips into her gaze. "What is it that you want, Wyatt? I don't have the energy to play this game with you anymore."

For the first time I notice the dark circles under her eyes and I can't help but wonder if she was up all night thinking about us just like I was or if the nightmares of her past still haunt her. Reaching up, I brush my thumb along her cheek

166

and she leans into my touch for just a second before jerking back.

"What's keeping you up at night, baby?"

She sucks in a breath. "Don't call me that."

"Why not?"

"You know why, Wyatt," she breathes, her voice full of pain as she looks away from me. "I haven't been your baby in a long damn time."

I nod, tucking a stray lock of red hair behind her ear. "Yeah, about that…"

Her gaze snaps to mine.

"I've been thinking lately that maybe we should revisit things, you know… re-evaluate."

She jerks out of my arms and stares up at me like I'm insane. "What does that even mean?"

"It means I want my wife back."

"But," she whispers, her eyes wide and her mouth agape. "I cheated on you…"

I shake my head. "No, you didn't."

"Yes, I did."

"Pip," I scold as I reach out and pull her back into my arms. She struggles for just a second before her body practically melts into mine and she meets my gaze. "*You* know you're lying. *I* know you're lying. So let's just stop and you tell me the real reason you left me back then."

She shakes her head. "No."

"I'm getting real damn tired of that word," I growl, remembering how much it annoyed me last night as she refused to give me what I wanted. Scoffing, she slips out of my hands again and tries to push past me. With a sigh, I stop her and she glares up at me.

"Let me go. I have to get to work."

"As soon as you tell me why you left."

She rolls her eyes in mock annoyance but I can see the fear underneath the attitude. "What does it matter now?"

"Fine," I snap, her words grating on my nerves. What does it matter? It's fucking everything and I don't know why she can't see that. "I'll make you a deal. You look me in the eye and tell me you don't love me anymore and I'll never bother you again."

Her gaze slams into mine and she doesn't need to say anything. The nineteen-year-old girl I left behind when I deployed is staring back at me, love shining in her eyes as she shakes her head again.

"Just stop, Wyatt. The rocks you're poking under are not pretty."

I scoff as I pull her back into my arms. She can run as many times as she likes because I'm never going to make the same mistake I did ten years ago. This time and all the times in the future when she runs, I'll be right behind her.

"I didn't sign up for pretty, Pip. I signed up for forever, for better or worse. So, one way or another, you are going to tell me what happened back then and when you do, we are going to figure out how we can move forward from here."

"It's not that easy, Wyatt," she whispers and I get the feeling that she is talking about more than just us. Whatever split us up ten years ago, whatever drove her away from me, is big and our biggest hurdle is going to be getting Piper to open up to me again.

"No one said it was going to be easy but I'll be damned if I let you walk away from me again."

Every Little Thing

A.M. Myers

Every Little Thing

Chapter Fourteen
Piper

"You almost here?" Lillian asks as I pull into the parking space outside of the restaurant and I sigh, putting the car in park as I lean my head back against the headrest. It's been one hell of a day and somehow I let Lillian talk me into going out to dinner when I should have just stayed home with a big glass of wine and my comfiest clothes.

"I just parked."

"Oh, the waitress is here. Do you want me to order you a drink?"

I nod as I turn the car off and grab my purse out of the passenger seat. "Yeah, a berry sangria and make it a large if you can."

"It's been one of those days, huh?" she asks before relaying my order to the waitress and I nod to myself as I step out of the car.

"Yes, it has."

"Well, get your butt in here so you can tell me all about it. I gave them your name at the hostess stand."

We hang up and I'm just about to slip my phone into my bag when it starts ringing again. I let out a groan. Between dodging Eden and Wyatt's calls today, I'm about ready to just shut this damn thing off and be done with everyone. Glancing down, I roll my eyes at Wyatt's name on the screen before declining the call and slipping the phone into my bag.

I honestly don't know how to take my conversation with him this morning. For so long, all I knew was that I ruined us and anything we could have had so to have him show up and declare that he wants me back just as soon as I tell him what made me leave has me… off balance. Not to mention, that anytime he pulls me into his arms, I want to beg him to never let me go again but I have to force myself to close off around him and push him away. Although, now that he *knows* I didn't cheat on him, I don't see that happening. Telling him the truth, though… I just don't know if I can. I've run it through in my head a hundred times and each time, all I can see is the look on his face - the one that says I'm weak, the one that will be full of disgust once he knows everything.

Shaking my head, I step into the restaurant and a young brunette looks up from the hostess stand with a smile. "Hi. Just one?"

Party of one?

That's me.

I resist the urge to scoff… or burst into tears.

"No. I'm meeting someone. My name is Piper."

"Oh, yes," she replies with a nod. "Follow me, please."

She turns and I follow her as she walks away from the entrance and into the dining room. The smell of tomato

172

sauce and garlic bread hits my nose and my stomach growls. I press my hand to my stomach as my mouth waters. Oh, God, I've been so consumed with what Wyatt said before he left this morning that I forgot to eat anything. At least I didn't have any in-studio shoots scheduled for the day so I didn't have to be around Eden and keep up the silent treatment.

"They're in the back corner," the hostess says, pointing toward one of the tables and I scowl. *They?* I follow her outstretched hand and stumble when my gaze lands on Eden, sitting across from Lillian and looking guilty as hell. I grit my teeth as I close the distance between us and cross my arms over my chest.

"What the hell, Lil?"

She holds her hands up in surrender. "Listen, you guys need to talk and I knew you would never hear her out unless I forced you to."

"I would have… eventually."

"Well," she replies with a shrug. "Eventually is now. Have a seat."

With a huff, I sit next to Lillian and take a sip of the large sangria in front of my plate before leaning back in my chair, arching a brow and pinning Eden with a look. "Well?"

"Pippy, I'm so so sorry, okay? You know I love you like a freaking sister and I just hated seeing you in pain all the time so I thought if I put you guys together, things would… you know?"

I nod my head. "Oh, yeah… I know and guess what, your little plan worked. Wyatt knows I didn't cheat on him and he wants me back just as soon as I tell him all the ugly, nasty details about what happened ten years ago so thanks for that."

"Wait, what? It worked? You guys are getting back together?" she asks, barely resisting the urge to clap her hands in glee and I level a glare across the table.

"No! Yes... I don't know. Did you miss the part where I have to bare my soul to him?"

She shrugs. "So do it, Piper. All I've heard for the last six years is how much you love this man. Why would you let him go again?"

"You know what," I snap. "Not the point right now. I'm still really mad at you and it doesn't matter that it worked because you went too far. I've trusted you with some very deep secrets and you almost lost that trust."

"Only almost?"

I keep my glare on her for another second before sighing. "Yes, almost... just don't do it ever again and I suppose I can accept your apology."

"Done," she answers with a nod. "Now, can we go back to why you won't just tell him?"

Lillian raises her hand. "Back up. We're going to start with what happened after the texts Eden sent because I feel like I'm missing a whole chunk of information here."

Sighing, I launch into the whole story, telling them about Wyatt coming over to my apartment and demanding answers before we both got caught up in our feelings and we ended up sleeping together. Eden slams her hand on the table, her eyes shining with interest as she stares at me.

"You slept together?" A slow grin spreads across her face. "This is even better than I imagined. How was it?"

I scoff. "Not the point, Edie."

"Oh, I disagree," Lillian adds, smiling. "I think it's exactly the point."

They both look at me expectantly and I roll my eyes as I take a big sip of my drink before leaning back in my chair. My thoughts drift back to last night and the way Wyatt pressed me up against the counter and demanded every ounce of pleasure from my body. I drop my gaze to the table, my cheeks heating as I shrug.

"I mean... it was all right."

"All right, my ass," Eden says with a laugh, smacking her hand on the table again. "That look on your face tells me everything I need to know."

"Oh, yeah," Lillian agrees and I glance up at them as she starts fanning her face.

"Stop it," I growl, the back of my neck feeling like it is on fire. The waitress stops by our table, saving me from further embarrassment and I chug half my drink as Eden and Lillian order their dinner. When she gets to me, I order the lasagna and another sangria before finishing off my first. She takes the glass from me and as soon as she is gone, Eden whips her head in my direction again.

"Okay, so you guys had super hot sex in... wait, where did it happen?"

I cover my face with my hand. "In the kitchen."

"Oooh, kitchen sex, even better. What happened afterward?"

"We just stared at each other and then he stormed out of my house without a word," I answer, meeting her gaze with a glare. It may be a good story for her but it hurt like hell for me and I'm not nearly as giddy about it as she is. Her lips part.

"Oh…"

"Yeah. It was a ton of fun."

She sighs. "Please tell me he called you today, at least."

"Nope," I answer, shaking my head. "He showed up as I was leaving for my first session today and demanded that I tell him the truth since he *knows* I didn't cheat on him."

"And what did you say?" Lillian asks and I shrug.

"I don't know. I was mostly trying to not give into him but I think I said something about the past not being pretty and he should stop poking around."

Eden nods, leaning forward like she can't get enough. "Then he said?"

Sighing, I replay the rest of the conversation for her, word for word, and by the end, she is practically bouncing in her seat and clapping her hands.

"Oh, this is excellent."

I roll my eyes. "Can you please stop acting like a cartoon villain as you plan out my love life?"

"No, I can't. Honestly, I was hoping you guys would talk and maybe, just maybe, you would work things out but this is even better than I imagined."

"Hold on," Lillian says, ever the voice of reason. "Let's go back to why you can't just tell him what happened when you left him."

I sigh, shaking my head as I fiddle with my silverware. "Because it's dark and ugly…"

"Yeah, but… he's your husband, Pippy. This isn't just some man you met and or some guy you've been dating."

"Don't you see, Edie. That just makes it worse. This would be so much easier if I was trying to tell some guy that I just met or some guy I was dating but it's not. It's

Wyatt and I don't know how to tell him…"

She reaches across the table and grabs my hand. "Well, maybe a little more tactfully than you told me."

"Eden," I cry out, my eyes widening as she starts giggling and releases my hand. Shaking my head, I remember my drunken rambling as I tried to explain it all to her and start laughing right along with her. "God, you're no help sometimes."

"But other times, I'm loads of help. I mean, look at you and Wyatt now."

I shake my head again. "Don't say that like things are magically fixed. Even if I told him everything and we tried to work through things, it wouldn't be easy or simple."

"True," Lillian says, studying me. "But from what you've told us, he's willing to do whatever it takes to fix your relationship."

"Pipes, you could have everything you've ever wanted from your life," Eden says, reaching across the table again and grabbing my hand with an encouraging look on her face. "All you have to do is be a little brave and tell Wyatt the truth."

"I'm scared."

Lillian nods, wrapping her arm around my shoulder. "I know but everything will be okay."

"And if it's not," Eden adds, giving my hand a squeeze. "We'll go kick that idiot's ass for hurting our girl."

"I'll think about it," I tell them and they both nod in approval. Lillian releases me and I lean back in my chair, fingering the scar along my neck as I think about what I need to tell Wyatt. I'm terrified of his reaction but I'm also terrified of living the rest of my life without him which leaves me in a pretty shitty spot. I've never been all that good at pushing myself out of my comfort zones which is why Dr. Brewer says I gravitate toward people like Eden and Wyatt who will force me to do the things that I don't want to do but it still doesn't make it easy for me.

"Piper?"

My head jerks up and I blink as James, my ex, stops next to our table and smiles down at me. "Uh… hi."

"How are you?" he asks and I scowl as my mind struggles to catch up. Nodding, I sit forward and try to paste a pleasant smile on my face but it's a struggle. James and I broke up because we didn't want the same things and if I'm being honest with myself, I was never really that into him. I was just into the idea of him, of finding someone and finally starting a family like I've always wanted.

"Uh, good. How are you?"

"Really good," he answers with a nod before his gaze flicks down to my chest. He lingers there for a moment and I resist the urge to cover myself as he meets my eyes again. Seriously? How did I not notice how sleazy he was when we were dating? "You look amazing."

"Thanks," I mutter, shooting a confused glance in Eden's direction. She rolls her eyes and shrugs. I peek over at Lillian who just shakes her head, looking almost embarrassed for James. Someone calls his name from a couple tables over and he glances back at them before turning back to me with a grin.

"Listen, I've got to go right now but maybe we can grab lunch sometime. I'll call you."

I force a smile to my face but he doesn't even wait for my nod before he turns and heads over to the leggy blonde waiting for him. Arching a brow, I watch him sit down before turning back to the girls and shaking my head.

"Quick, block him on your phone," Eden says, jabbing her pointer finger into the table. "Right now. I'm not letting that clown ruin all my hard work."

I scoff as I dig my phone out of my bag. "Yes,, ma'am. And what the hell do you mean all your hard work?"

"Listen, I did not risk life, limb, and best friend just so this douchebag can come swinging his dick around and mess it all up. I am determined to be photographing your wedding with Wyatt someday."

Scoffing, I shake my head as I block James on my phone. "We're already married, Edie. Even if we get back together, there won't be a wedding."

"Well, then a vow renewal or whatever," she says, waving her hand through the air to dismiss my comment. "You mark my words. I will document your happily ever after."

"You need a hobby."

She grins at me. "I have one and you're looking at it."

"Have you ever thought about crochet or something?" I ask, leaning back and crossing my arms over my chest. She shakes her head as she grabs her drink and takes a sip.

"No. Maybe I'll look into it when this mission is finished."

I roll my eyes at her but the waitress returns to our table to drop off our dinners before I can say anything else and I decide to let it go. Hopefully Eden has developed some boundaries since her last little meddling episode but I'm not holding my breath.

Chapter Fifteen
Piper

An early autumn wind ruffles my hair as I smile and wave at Eden and Lillian parked on the curb, watching me carefully. Eden arches a brow and I roll my eyes as I turn to my front door. She always has this thing where she has to see me, at least, open the front door before she feels comfortable leaving me and while it's sweet, sometimes I would prefer not to have an audience while I fumble with my keys. The rest of the dinner passed quickly with *a lot* of sangrias for me and plenty of laughs between the three of us and it was nice to forget about my problems for a while. Or forget about them as much as I can. Anytime there was a lull in the conversation or I was bored with the current topic, my mind would wander back to my new issues with Wyatt. Although, tonight I had the added bonus of painful memories from the past waiting in the wings to ambush me as soon as I let my guard down. Shaking my head, I push those thoughts from my mind as I finally find the right key and shove it into the lock.

Once I get the door open, I turn back to them and wave again. Eden flashes me a satisfied smile as they return the gesture and she pulls away from the curb. I wouldn't say I'm super drunk right now but I'm definitely in no shape to drive myself home either. I was just going to take a cab but Eden insisted that she was giving me a ride home while Lillian followed behind us in my car so I would be able to get myself to work in the morning. Glancing over at my car in the driveway, I smile. You know… when she's not being too nosy for her own damn good, I'm really glad I have Eden in my life. And Lillian, too. Honestly, I don't know where I would be without the two of them. They know when I just need some space and when I need them to push me and as angry as I was with Eden for going behind my back and talking to Wyatt, I'm not entirely convinced that it was a mistake.

Stumbling through the front door, I toss my keys onto the table next to me and shut the door before making sure it's locked three times as the damn memories threaten to bombard me again. Shaking my head, I check the lock one last time and promise myself that I'm not going to let them beat me today.

As I walk into the living room, I kick off my heels and breathe a sigh of relief. My thoughts turn to Wyatt as I peel my jacket off and toss it on the floor before heading for the stairs. I didn't want to admit it to her or even myself but Eden was right when she said everything I've been dreaming of for the past ten years is staring me in the face and I just have to be brave enough to reach out and grab it. I just wish it was that easy. God, I don't know how to tell Wyatt the truth… It's not a time in my life I'm particularly proud of and I can't imagine how painful it will be to see him react with disgust to the news. Not that he will, *for sure*, but… he might. And that kills me.

When I reach the bottom of the stairs, I pull my t-shirt over my head and toss it onto the floor before looking back. I'm usually pretty neat when it comes to my home and my things but I have just enough alcohol flowing through my system that all I want is to put on my oldest, comfiest t-shirt and fall into my bed. Staring at the mess, I release a breath and shrug.

Whatever.

I'll deal with it in the morning.

Turning back to the stairs, I reach for the button of my jeans and grab my phone out of the back pocket before I start shoving them down my legs and by the time I get to the top, I'm kicking them off behind me. The last thing off is my bra and I smile as I step into my bedroom and grab the old Marines t-shirt I stole from Wyatt off of the bed and slip it over my head. The moon shines through the large window, casting a blue glow on the entire room as I set my phone on the bedside table and fall back into the mattress, a content sigh slipping through my lips.

Oh, this is exactly what I needed.

I close my eyes but as soon as I do, those damn memories that have been stalking me all night are right there in the front of my mind and my heart starts to beat a little faster. I reach up and trace the scar along my neck. Tears well up in my eyes as the memory pushes forward, demanding my attention and I know it's going to be a rough night.

No.

No.

No.

Shaking my head, I open my eyes and stare up at the ceiling fan above me but it doesn't matter if my eyes are closed or not, the pain of my past will not be ignored tonight. Closing my eyes again, I see my childhood home, just the way it always was before a dark cloud drowned out the light and a tear streaks down the side of my face and I suck in a stuttered breath. Every moment of that night is seared into my memory, so much so that it's become part of my identity, a piece of my very DNA and it seems I have no choice but to relive it now. My eyes snap open and I stop fighting, letting the memory and the pain that always accompanies it, wash over me.

Crash!

My eyes pop open and I squint into the darkness, confusion filling me as I try to place the sound. Someone screams from downstairs and it takes me a second to realize it's my mother. My heart kicks in my chest and my tummy twists as I shove the covers off my legs and hug my teddy bear to my chest.

"Mama?" I call out as I slip from the bed, my legs shaking like crazy. The silence is dominating and tears fill my eyes as I tiptoe across my room and pull the door open just enough to peek out into the hallway. "Mama?"

Something doesn't feel right...

Sucking in a breath, I remember Daddy telling me that sometimes it's important to be brave and I open the door further, clutching my bear as I step out into the hallway and glance toward the faint glow coming from downstairs.

"It's probably nothing," I tell myself as I walk to the

top of the stairs, careful not to step on the board that creaks as my heart beats faster, crashing into my rib cage. As I start down the stairs, I want to call out for my mom again but something tells me not to and I decide to listen to that little voice in my head.

"Please!" Mama screams and I freeze halfway down the steps, each breath punching out of me. "Don't do this! Take whatever you want."

Squeezing my eyes shut, I bury my face in my teddy bear's tummy and wait. My imagination takes over, dreaming up all kinds of monsters that could be lurking downstairs. Mama screams again but it sounds different this time and when she stops, the house is quiet again. Too quiet. Opening my eyes, I take a deep breath, trying so hard to be brave as I start down the stairs again. When I reach the bottom, I turn toward the living room and a gasp catches in my throat. The giant figure standing next to chunks of wood that I think used to be the coffee table turns and his gaze lands on me. I can hear my heart in my ears and it's hard to breathe as I stare up at him, my body going cold as his blue eyes roam over my body.

Oh, God.

I need to run.

I want to run but my legs won't move.

They're stuck to the floor.

Moonlight glints off the piece of metal and my eyes widen at the sight of the bloody knife in his hand. A scream bubbles up but gets stuck in my throat as my entire body shakes and little black spots dot my vision. He takes a step toward me and before my mind even has a chance to catch up, I spin and take off running as a scream trails off behind me.

"HELP!"

I run into my daddy's study and turn toward the dining room but I don't have time to stop because I can hear his loud, clumping steps as he chases after me.

"Mama! Daddy! Help!" I scream, tears streaking down my face and my chest feeling tight like my heart is about to burst. His footsteps are louder on the hardwood floor of the dining room and I whimper and beg my legs to go faster as I turn toward the kitchen and freeze. Mama is lying on the floor next to Daddy and her eyes are wide open, staring at me, but she can't see me. A large pool of blood surrounds them and I shake my head as more tears fall and I run to them, dropping to my knees.

I don't even care that I'm getting blood all over me.

I have to help them.

Grabbing Mama by the shoulders, I give her a little shake but nothing happens and a sob bubbles out of my chest as I shake her again.

"Mama," I whisper through my tears, shaking my head. When I was six, my grandpa died and at his funeral, they brought him into the church in a big wooden box so everyone could see him but all I could think was that he didn't look right. Mama looks the same now and even if I don't want to admit it, I know, deep down in my heart, that she's gone. Tears pour down my face in torrents as I shake my head again. "Mama."

"Gotcha."

I scream as the man grabs my arm and rips me away from my parents. With the blood, it's hard for him to keep his grip on me and I fight back as hard as I can, hitting and

185

kicking at him with all my strength. I land a kick between his legs and he grunts as his grip on me falters, allowing me to slip my arm free. As I turn to run again, he slices the knife through the air. A burning sensation scrapes down the side of my neck but I don't stop to see what it is as I start running again. The pain follows and I press my hand to my neck, hissing as it stings and blood trickles through my fingers. Pulling my hand away, I stare down at my palm and shudder. My blood mixes with my parents' and a sense of dread washes over me.

I'm going to die tonight.

"Come here, you little bitch," the man growls from the kitchen and it's the kick in the butt that I need. My gaze flies from the stairs to the front door to the living room.

Where do I go?

When the sound of his boots smacking against the kitchen tile fills the house, I bolt toward the front door with my hand pressed to my neck. I need to keep running but it's getting so hard to make my feet work and all I want to do is close my eyes and go back to sleep. Shaking my head, I push myself forward and unlock the front door before ripping it open as red and blue lights fill the night.

Tears pour down my face and I suck in a stuttered breath before a sob overtakes me. I remember crashing into the police officer that was walking up my sidewalk that night and begging him to please help me. I run my fingers over the scar on my neck again. The doctors said that I was incredibly lucky since the attacker just barely nicked my artery and if the knife had gone any deeper, I would have joined my parents in the ground. I don't feel lucky though. That man and that horrid night have haunted my life ever since. I was only nine years old but as soon as I was woken up, I could tell there was something different, that something was very, very wrong. The air was thicker, more ominous, and it almost felt like the very thing that I needed to sustain my life was slowly choking me to death and still to this day, I can feel that dread pushing down on me when I think about the events of that night.

I can still hear the sound of my mother's gurgled scream as the man plunged the knife into her chest and the eerie silence that followed. They are both still so loud in my mind and my stomach rolls. I spent two weeks in the hospital, first for the cut on my neck and then for my mental health before I was moved to a group home to wait for any family to step forward to claim me. It took a year for them to locate and convince my great Aunt Myra to take me in. I had only met her once before and she wasn't a huge fan of kids so I suppose that I should just be grateful she took me in at all.

Closing my eyes, the image of my parents lying on that kitchen floor floods my mind and I suck in a stuttered breath as I remember sinking to my knees and the slippery feeling of their blood against my skin as I grabbed them and tried to wake them up. The rich scent of iron fills my nose and I open my eyes again, shaking my head to clear the memory. The man, who I later learned was named Clinton Wood, was arrested that night and charged with two counts of murder in the first degree, one count of attempted murder, and one count of breaking and entering. At his trial, his lawyer painted a story of a good man who got addicted to drugs and lost his way but I'll never forget the evil in his blue eyes as he stared down at me with that bloody knife in his hand. Despite my fragile state, I gave a compelling testimony about what happened that night and although I couldn't meet his gaze, it felt good to know that I had a part in putting him away for the rest of his life. He was convicted and sentenced to three life sentences so I never have to worry about him getting released and being out in the world but it doesn't really help when he's free to run rampant through my mind and torment me.

The tears fall, unchecked, down my cheeks and into the pillow as the memory replays in my head again and my chest aches. It's been so long that I can't even remember what my parents' voices sound like and if I didn't have photos of them everywhere, their faces would be fuzzy in my mind. I never got to go prom dress shopping with my mama or have my daddy walk me down the aisle when I married Wyatt. No one stood up and cheered for me at my high school graduation and when my life fell apart, I didn't have anyone to help me pick up the pieces. The ache of missing them and the void they left behind in my life never really goes away. It's just one more thing that became part of who I am. I fell apart that night and I didn't have the love of my family to put me back together. All I had was pain and fear and that is what I became.

And then I met Wyatt.

My phone rattles across the bedside table with an incoming call and I scoop it up, not even bothering to check the caller ID as I frantically swipe tears off my face.

"Hello?"

"Hey, Pip."

I release a breath as my body melts back into the mattress. "Wyatt."

"You okay?" he asks, genuine concern lacing his voice and I whisper a curse as I sit up and clear my throat while I try to dry my tears.

"Yeah, I'm fine." I clear my throat again. "What do you want?"

He chuckles. "Back to business as usual, I see."

"What do you want, Wyatt?" I repeat, rolling my eyes and he sighs. I can picture him running his hand through his hair and I wish I could do the same. Back before I left, Wyatt always had to keep his hair short because of the Marines but I love how it looks now, long enough to fall into his eyes and a little unkempt. It just makes me want to run my fingers through it again and again.

"Can I come in?"

I blink and turn toward the window before climbing out of bed. "You're here?"

"Yeah," he says as I reach the window and look down. He waves up at me and I shake my head. Any other night, I would try to resist but I just don't have the energy for it after my little trip down memory lane. Besides, the thought of Wyatt wrapping his arms around me and kissing the top of my head like he used to anytime I woke up from a nightmare sounds way too good to pass up.

"Okay… there's a key taped to the underside of the mailbox."

He frowns as he glances at the little black box next to the front door. "That's not safe, Pip."

"Do you want to scold me or do you want to come in?"

"You just told me where the damn key is, baby," he says, looking up and meeting my eyes through the window as he fights back a grin that makes a shiver run down my spine. Good Lord, I always thought Wyatt was the cutest boy I'd ever met but now… he is all man and he can reduce me to a puddle with just a simple look. "Do you really think you could stop me?"

I roll my eyes. "Just get up here."

"Yes, ma'am." His grin makes my heart melt and I blink, fighting back tears again. God, I missed that man so

189

much these past ten years and it's a wonder how I ever survived. Now that he's back in my life, or sort of back, I don't know how I ever went one day without him. But the bigger problem is, I don't know how to keep resisting him. I watch him as he walks up to the front door and peels the key from under the mailbox before I turn back to the bed and hang up, tossing my phone on the bedside table. As I climb on the mattress and pull the blankets around me, I hear the front door open and my heart kicks in my chest.

I'm so stupid.

I've known him for twenty damn years and I still get butterflies in my belly at the thought of seeing him. Just the sound of his name is enough to have me fighting back a grin and when he steps in close to me, my heart beats a little bit faster. Shaking my head, I close my eyes. I seriously need to get ahold of myself if I'm going to face him. I still don't know which way I'm going to go when he asks the inevitable question - keep my secrets or tell him everything - but either way, I'll need all the strength I can muster. When I open them again, he's standing in the doorway, his brow arched as he grins down at me.

"Nice shirt."

I glance down and nod as I meet his gaze again. "Yeah. It is."

"I like the little trail you left for me," he says and I scowl.

"Huh?"

He motions over his shoulder. "The clothes leading up to your bedroom."

"Oh. That."

"You okay?" he asks again, tilting his head slightly as he studies me. The genuine concern filling his eyes kills me. If I tell him the truth… he may never look at me like that again. I nod as my lip trembles.

Shit.

"I'm fine."

"No," he whispers, taking another step into the room. "You're not."

Biting the inside of my cheek, I rip my eyes from him. "Stop acting like you still know me, Wyatt. It's been ten years."

"And whose fault is that?" he growls and I shake my head as my heart sinks. I look up at him and hope he can see how truly sorry I am for the state of our relationship. Not that it really matters at this point, I suppose. We are where we are and we can't go back.

"I wasn't trying to pass off any blame. We're not together now because of me, I know that."

"Yeah, about that…" He steps further into the room and shoves his hands in his pockets. "You ready to talk?"

"No."

He shrugs. "Do it anyway."

"Stop telling me what to do," I snap, ripping the covers up my body as I cross my arms over my chest and scowl at him. He shakes his head.

"No."

"You're so fucking stubborn."

He barks out a laugh. "Me? Are you serious?"

"Yes, you." I narrow my eyes and he laughs again. The sound sends heat radiating through my chest and I fight back a smile. Wyatt's laugh was always one of my favorite sounds and I used to do the silliest things just to hear it or see him smile at me.

"Did you just tell me to come up here so you could fight with me?"

I'm about to tell him that is exactly why I let him come in but I stop myself as I let out a sigh, Eden's words from dinner run through my mind and I bite my lip as I go over my options. As much as I hate it, it is time to decide for good. Am I going to continue pushing him away and spend the rest of my life with my secrets or can I really let him in again? Finally, I shake my head. "No. That's not why."

"Then why?"

"I don't know…" I admit, my voice weak as tears sting my eyes again. It's a total fucking lie and we both know it. I let him come in because staying away from him, missing him is torture. I've lived with it for ten years and I just don't have the strength to keep going. His gaze softens and he walks around the side of the bed before sitting next to me.

"What happened back then, Pip? Just tell me. Whatever it is, I can handle it." His voice is kind, full of empathy, and I avoid his gaze as tears well up in my eyes. As soon as I tell him the truth, that kind, caring voice will be gone. I just know it. Shaking my head, I pull my hand back.

"I can't."

He rakes his hand through his hair. "You can. I'm telling you, baby, I'm here for you. Whatever it is."

"You won't see me the same way," I whisper as a tear streaks down my cheek and I meet his gaze. He reaches forward and cups my cheek, the desperation and love in his eyes is too much to bear. He brushes his thumb over my cheek, wiping away the tear.

"I promise you that I will. You're my Pip, you always have been, and you always will be. Just tell me the truth."

I shake my head again. "No."

"Goddamn it," he snaps, releasing me and jumping up from the bed as he starts pacing across my bedroom floor and running his hand through his hair again. I'm not trying to cause him any pain but I can see that this is killing him and it's not fair to keep dragging this on. But neither one of us know what the truth will do to him and I'm terrified once he learns everything that he will wish I had kept my mouth shut. He turns to me, fire and determination dancing in his eyes, and his lips set into a firm line.

"Why did you leave me?"

I shake my head and drop my gaze to the bed. He growls.

"Why did you leave me?" he yells and another tear slips down my cheek as I shake my head again.

I can't tell him.

I can't...

"Why did you leave me?!"

A sob tears through me as his roar echoes around the room and I meet his eyes as I scream, "I don't know!"

Silence descends on us and time seems to stand still as we stare at each other. Both of us stunned by my sudden admission. I didn't intend to say anything but hearing the hurt in his voice as he demanded the truth again pulled it out of me. More questions fill his eyes and he shakes his head as he takes a step toward me, his brows knitting together.

"What do you mean you don't know?"

Sucking in a breath, I play with a loose thread on my blanket.

Fuck.

I guess we're doing this now...

"It's complicated, Wyatt."

"So explain it," he demands and I look up, my heart pounding in my chest as the words I need to say roll around in my brain. I open my mouth to speak before snapping it shut again.

God, I don't even know where to start.

193

"I…"

I snap my mouth closed again as the words stick in my throat. He closes the distance between us and grabs both of my hands between his. "Just start somewhere, babe. I don't even care if it makes sense at first. Just start talking."

"I…" I whisper, my mind screaming the words that I can't seem to force through my lips. I suck in a breath and squeeze my eyes shut. "I had an episode…"

"What does that mean, Pip? What kind of episode?" The worry and pain in his voice breaks my heart all over again and I blow out a breath, trying to find a piece of my soul that might still have a little bit of the bravery I need to tell him everything.

"Technically, it was called a psychotic break…"

Silence.

Just like the night my parents were killed, the silence steals the air from my lungs, choking me as I wait for his reply and more tears fall down my cheeks.

I can't open my eyes.

I can't see the disgust on his face.

The one time he needed me to be strong for him, I couldn't and living with the shame of that for the past ten years is just as bad as the pain of missing him. He went to war for God's sake and I couldn't even handle being without him for a year. It's pitiful and I don't blame him one bit for being appalled by my weakness.

"Piper," he whispers and my lip trembles.

Please don't hate me…

"Piper, look at me," he says, his voice soft and my eyes snap open immediately, meeting his gaze as my heart beats so hard I think it might explode. His eyes are filled with love and sympathy instead of the disgust and anger I expected and a sob bubbles out of my mouth. "Tell me what happened, baby."

Oh, God...

Nodding, I grip his hands and give them a squeeze as a newfound strength rolls through me but it's always been that way for us. Wyatt is my support system and he makes me feel strong enough to take on the world around me which was exactly the problem that led to the end of our marriage.

"After you deployed, I felt pretty good, at first. I thought I could handle the stress of everything and I knew that you would be back with me soon enough..."

He nods.

"But then there was this news story about a troop that was killed over where you were and I remember sitting on the couch for an entire day with my eyes glued to the screen as I waited to hear from you."

His brows draw together. "But I was okay, baby."

"I know," I whisper, nodding. "But after that, my mind was consumed with thoughts of you never making it home to me. I was still able to deal with it, though. I mean, I wasn't taking good care of myself but I hadn't completely lost it yet and then four months into your tour, I was bringing in some groceries and I saw one of those black town cars pulling down our street."

Closing my eyes, I still remember that day like it was yesterday and the fear that I was about to lose everything, again, as the Casualty Assistance Officers rolled up to our house and then the pure relief that flooded my body when they kept going.

"After that, I was paralyzed by the fear that you weren't going to come back to me. I stopped eating. I stopped sleeping and I didn't leave the house for two months. Anytime someone rang the doorbell, I would cower in the corner of the living room and wait for them to leave. Some days, I didn't even get out of bed, too scared to face the possibility and things just devolved from there. By the time I left, I can't even tell you what was real and what wasn't. I was seeing the man that killed my parents and I was seeing you... dead with bullet holes all over your body... lying in our bed... sitting on our couch. No where was safe anymore."

"My God, baby," he breathes, releasing my hands and pulling me into his arms. Another sob tears through me as he crushes me to his body and buries his nose in my hair before pressing his lips to the top of my head. It's even better than I remember and for the first time in ten years, I feel safe enough to let myself fall apart because Wyatt has always loved me enough to put me back together. Pulling away, he shakes his head. "But why didn't you come back?"

I meet his eyes. "My next clear memory was waking up in the psychiatric wing of the hospital a year later."

"What?" He blinks, confusion all over his face as he waits for an explanation.

"My doctor said that the psychotic episode was compounded by PTSD from the night my parents were murdered and I spent a year living in my car and running from the demons that had become very real for me. When I didn't think the man who killed my parents was after me again, I thought you were dead and I was completely alone in the world."

He stumbles off the bed and backs up a few steps before slowly shaking his head and running both hands through his hair, gripping it and tugging. "Why wasn't I contacted? I'm your goddamn husband! I should have been notified that you were in the hospital."

"I asked them not to," I whisper, shaking my head as my stomach rolls. I don't want to hurt him but if I'm going to tell him this, I have to tell him all of it. "I was so ashamed of what had happened while you were gone and I didn't want you to know how weak I had been. Plus, Dr. Brewer thought I used you as a crutch instead of dealing with my issues and that I needed to learn how to cope on my own."

"That's bullshit."

"No, Wyatt. It isn't… I've learned a lot in the years we've been apart and Dr. Brewer was right. I leaned on you to right my world after my parents were killed so when you were gone, I didn't know how to stand up on my own two feet."

I can see him working through everything I've told him before he sighs and nods, turning back to me. "And now?"

"Now, I have better ways to cope with the trauma I went through and when I struggle, I call Dr. Brewer or I go to my support group."

"Why didn't you just tell me all that? Why did you feel like you couldn't trust me?" he asks, pain etches across his face as he closes the distance between us and sits down on the bed. I drop my gaze to the blanket as a tingling sensation rushes up the back of my neck and my cheeks heat. I shake my head as my chest tightens.

"I'm not proud of what happened back then, Wyatt. I was so incredibly weak and I didn't want you to…"

He cups my cheek and slams his lips to mine, silencing my fears with a kiss hot enough to burn the room down around us. It consumes us, wrapping us up in its flames and transporting us to my favorite place in the world - the one where only Wyatt and I exist. His kiss still holds the intimate details of our love and with his lips pressed against mine, it's like the past ten years didn't happen. It's like we were never apart. Whimpering, I climb in his lap and wrap my arms around his neck. He kisses me hard, commanding my body with an expert touch and when he pulls away, we're both gasping for breath.

"Whatever you were going to say, I don't want to hear it, Pip. You are not weak and what happened wasn't your fault. I'm so fucking sorry I wasn't there for you when you needed me but this right here..." He pulls me closer, molding my body to his. "This is where you belong."

"I don't want to hear you apologize either, then. You didn't do anything wrong and as painful as it was... I think I needed to be away from you or I never would have learned how to handle my issues on my own."

He blows out a breath. "I should have come looking for you when I got back... I just let my damn pride get in the way and it cost us everything."

"It's not..."

He silences me with another kiss and I melt into him, my entire body rejoicing as his hand slips under my t-shirt and presses against my back. My skin tingles with need and I slip my fingers into his hair and grip a chunk of it just like I've been dying to do since he got here. Growling, he trails kisses down my neck and I drop my head back, releasing a moan. I can't believe I ever thought this feeling, this connection between us was gone and dead.

"Fuck," he rumbles, his hands all over my body and he pulls me into him, clinging to me like he can't get me close enough. "I missed you so much, baby."

I nod as a few tears slip down my cheeks. "I missed you, too, Wyatt. So, so much."

"I'm never letting you go again. We'll do whatever we have to do to fix this but I refuse to live another second without my wife," he vows and a few more tears slip from my eyes as I nod. I don't want to lose him either. I'm scared as hell to try again and I know we've both changed over the past ten years but I'm ready to give this relationship a real shot. I just hope it doesn't break me.

Chapter Sixteen
Wyatt

An alarm pierces the silence followed by a groan and a slapping sound that I can only assume is Piper smashing the offending object into a thousand pieces as the noise cuts off and I reluctantly peel open my eyes. A mass of red hair fills my vision and I smile as my gaze trails down the curve of her naked body as it calls to me, tempting me from the other side of the bed. Images of the hours we spent wrapped up in each other last night, making up for lost time, fill my mind and I bite back another groan. Scooting across the mattress, I pull her closer and press the front of my body against her back. She wiggles, rubbing her ass against my cock before she finds a comfortable spot and lets out a contented sigh. It's the most glorious fucking sound in the world and I want to hear it again.

Immediately.

As I'm sinking into her...

Shaking my head, I blow out a breath and push the thoughts from my mind. As much as I would like that, I also can't bring myself to wake her up just yet. She looks so damn peaceful like this, something I don't think I'm used to yet. In a lot of ways, my woman is the same that she has always been - fun, sexy, sweet, and a whole lot of sassy - but in the past, there were always ghosts in her eyes and a struggle on her face like surviving each day was a challenge. When she looks at me now, I see this newfound strength shining in her eyes and not only do I find it sexy as hell but it also makes me so damn proud of her. She lived through hell but she came out stronger on the other side.

She's a goddamn phoenix.

It still kills me to think about how hard it must have been for her when I deployed, though and I shake my head as guilt crashes down on me. I close my eyes as I press my lips to her shoulder, breathing in her scent. War is brutal - a kind of ugly that I can't even begin to describe but Piper was at home, fighting a war of her own and I hate that it never even occurred to me. I knew about her issues but I was a stupid kid and too wrapped up in my own fears for our time apart to realize what she would be dealing with. I can picture her in that little house on base, seeing the man who killed her parents and seeing me dead, scared out of her ever-lovin' mind and all alone. My chest aches and I shake my head again like I can somehow deny the pain. From the moment we met, I was her protector. When she was with me, she never had to be scared of anything because I always had her back and I hate myself for just walking away from her.

The morning after we got married, I woke up before she did and I laid in bed with her in my arms as the realization crashed down on me that I had to find a way to take care of her. Not only that but I knew Piper deserved the moon and stars so I had to find a way to give it to her. I didn't have the money for college so when I saw an ad for the military, it seemed perfect. It guaranteed me a regular paycheck, health insurance, and a house for the two of us. I thought it was perfect but if I had known what it would do to her and everything it would cost me, I never would have enlisted. Piper was and always will be the most important thing in my life.

Opening my eyes, I prop myself up on one arm and stare down at her face, thinking over everything she told me last night and the pain in my chest grows. Over the past week, I've gone through a hundred scenarios of what happened back then to make her leave but I never considered that I was the one at fault. The last time I walked away from her, most would consider what I did noble and brave but it was just a means to an end. It was about Piper and giving her the whole world which is what she deserves but now, I can't help but think that maybe I don't deserve her. How could I when I just abandoned her without considering that it might be too hard for her to handle?

I imagine her living in her car - dirty, hungry, scared, and I grit my teeth as I fall back to the bed and roll to my back. Fisting my hair, I close my eyes and drag a breath into my lungs. Why the fuck did I leave her? It was such a dumb shit move and it doesn't matter what my motives were because I almost lost her forever. Hell, I don't even know that we're really back together but like I told her last night, I'll do whatever it takes. There was always one thing I was sure about in my life and that was Piper so I can't let her walk away from me again.

Releasing my hair, I ball both of my fists and pound them into the mattress at my sides, wishing I could put one of them through a wall. Maybe then I would feel better. A knot forms in my throat and I try to swallow it down but it refuses to budge as my mind wanders to what happened the night Piper's parents died. Years ago, she told me the basics - a man broke into her house, looking to rob them and instead he killed her parents but she has never revealed any of the details to me. It didn't matter how many times she woke up screaming in the middle of the night or how often I caught her stroking the scar down the side of her neck, she still wouldn't tell me. Thinking over everything she shared last night, I can't help but wonder if that led to her breakdown when I left. She mentioned that she never learned how to deal with the trauma of that night and as I roll my head to look at her, I wonder if she's able to talk about it now. Hell, I wonder if *I* would be able to handle the details of that night. Seeing the scar on her neck is enough to send me into a rage if I think about that man hurting her.

Scrubbing my hand down my face, I blow out a breath. There is still so much we have to talk about and I still have a few questions about what happened when she left me but all of that can wait. Right now, my only mission is to convince Piper to go all in with me again. Last night, when I told her I wasn't ever going to let her go again, behind the happiness shining in her eyes was a little bit of fear, a slice of hesitation, and it killed me. I will do whatever it takes to erase those feelings. It doesn't matter if I deserve her or not because if the last ten years has taught me anything, it's that losing her is not a fucking option. With renewed determination, I roll to my side and slip my arm around her waist, pulling her back into my body and she sighs again, a soft smile stretching across her face. I press my lips to her shoulder before moving up her neck and drawing a moan out of her as I kiss behind her ear.

"Wake up, darlin'," I whisper and she groans, shaking her head as she reaches down and pulls the covers further up our bodies. Chuckling, I shake my head and pull the blanket back down before kissing her neck down to her shoulder. Playfully, I nip at her skin and she gasps, spinning to her back as she glares up at me.

It's fucking adorable.

"It's too early."

I kiss her cheek. "Too bad. Your alarm went off five minutes ago."

"Just five more minutes," she groans, rolling back to her side and wiggling her ass against me. I grit my teeth as I grip her hip and lower my mouth to her ear.

"You keep doing that and your 'just five minutes' are going to be spent with my cock inside you, baby."

She fights back a grin and shakes her ass again but before I can do anything about it, her phone starts ringing and she lets out a long exaggerated groan as she reaches up and grabs it off the bedside table. As soon as she accepts the call, she puts it on speakerphone and tosses it onto the mattress next to her.

"What?"

"Good morning, Pip-Squeak! It's time to wake up," a female voice calls through the phone and I grin as I glance down at Piper.

Pip-Squeak.

Why didn't I think of that one?

She peeks open one eye and glares at the phone. "I'm awake."

"Liar."

I bite my lip to hold back my laughter as Piper rolls to her back and opens her eyes. "I'm awake, Edie. I promise."

Ah…

So this is the infamous Eden.

"Uh-huh, that's what you always say and somehow, you're usually ten minutes late."

"I'm awake," Piper repeats, rolling her eyes and she pins me with a glare as I start laughing.

"Either get out of bed right now or I'll be forced to come over there and drag you to work myself."

Piper shakes her head. "You live on the other side of town and do you hear this thing I'm doing right now? It's called talking and it means I'm fucking awake."

"She's telling the truth," I add, laughing, and Piper's gaze flies to me as her lips part as silence hangs heavy on the other side of the phone. Her eyes are wide as she gives me a "what the hell did you just do" look and I shrug. Isn't this exactly what Eden wanted when she set us up on our little reunion tour?

"Who is that, Pip? Please tell me that's not James… Please tell me you didn't do something massively stupid and fuck up the whole Wyatt…"

Piper scrambles for the phone and takes it off speakerphone before Eden can say anything else and presses it to her ear.

"I will talk to you about this later," she growls through gritted teeth but my focus is on that name Eden dropped as my mind spins. I clench my teeth as my chest burns and lights flash in my vision.

Who the *fuck* is James and what does he have to do with *my* wife?

Piper hangs up and sets the phone back on the bedside table before peeking over at me. I arch a brow, pinning her with a look.

"Who the hell is James?"

She sighs. "My ex…"

The burning in my chest intensifies and a knot forms in my stomach. It's not fair of me to act like this to news that she has an ex when I haven't been a saint over the last ten years either but the thought of another man with his hands on her body makes me want to kill someone.

"How recent?"

"We broke up a couple of weeks ago."

Nodding, I fling the covers off of my legs and climb out of bed.

"Wyatt? Please don't be mad… You know how complicated this situation is and I didn't think we would ever be…" She motions between the two of us. "Here."

"I know," I snap as I run my hand through my hair and start pacing at the end of the bed. It's not fair but no matter how many times I say that to myself, it doesn't ease the ache.

"It was never anything… I was just trying to fill the void… Trying not to feel so broken without you…"

My gaze snaps to hers. "You broke up with him or he broke up with you?"

"Does it matter?" she asks with a scowl and I narrow my eyes as I nod.

"Yeah, it fuckin' matters. Did you break up with him?"
She nods.

"And why would Eden think you were with him?"

"We ran into each other when I was out with the girls last night. He said he wanted to grab lunch sometime and talk but I blocked him on my phone after he left. I'll show you."

I stare at her for a second before releasing a breath and squeezing my eyes shut. I have to remind myself repeatedly that she never really cheated on me, there was never another man and I have no reason to not trust her before the tension slowly seeps out of my shoulders. Nodding my head, I open my eyes and hold my hand out for her, needing her touch to feel right again. She climbs up onto her knees and walks across the bed until she reaches me and wraps her arms around my neck. Peace settles over me and I release a breath.

"I'm sorry," I say, my voice soft as I brush my thumb over her cheek and she nods.

"I don't like thinking of you with other people either, Wyatt, but if we're really going to make this work, we have to find a way to deal with it."

I nod and slip my hand into her hair as I lean down, pressing my lips to her. She makes that perfect little sigh again and I want to beat my chest. I bet that James fucker never got her to make that sound. I bet he never knew that kissing her behind her ear will make goose bumps pop up all over her body and I know he never owned her heart.

It's mine, all mine.
Just like she has always been.

Pulling away, I smile and press another quick kiss to

her forehead. "Come on. Let's get dressed and go get some breakfast. I saw a little cafe a couple blocks over on my way here last night."

"How about we stay in? I have bacon and eggs downstairs. I'll cook for you."

"I don't think so, Pip. Today is all about you," I tell her, picturing her perfect naked body in my lap as she eats and my dick hardens. She arches a brow and glances down before shaking her head and meeting my gaze again.

"Didn't you get enough last night?"

I tweak her nipple and she gasps. "Did you?"

"No," she breathes and I grin as I lean in for another kiss and grab her ass. A moan slips past her lips just before I claim them and she melts into me. My tongue tangles with hers, teasing and urging each other on as she leans into me further, trying to get as close as she can. Her phone pings from the bedside table and she pulls away, glancing back at it.

"That'll be Eden."

I arch a brow. "Checking to make sure you didn't go back to sleep?"

"Something like that," she answers, rolling her eyes and I laugh as I nudge her chin and guide her gaze back to me. I plant a quick kiss before pulling away.

"Come on. I'm getting hungry."

She flashes me a grin as desire pools in her eyes and she grabs my old Marines t-shirt off the bed before pulling it over her head and hopping off of the bed. I turn, watching her as she walks out of the room. My t-shirt stops halfway down her ass and it sways back and forth with each step, teasing me.

Shit.

I should have made her stay in bed.

"You keep swinging that ass at me, baby, and *you* are going to be breakfast," I call and she laughs as she shakes her hips and continues on down the stairs.

"God," she fires back but I can hear the smile in her voice and in my head, I can see her rolling her eyes at me. "I forgot what an ass man you are."

"I'll show you ass man," I grumble as I scoop my jeans off the floor and pull them on as I chase after her. She squeals and takes off running. When I get to the bottom of the stairs, I grab her and toss her over my shoulder with her ass in the air as I smack it. She gasps and pounds her little fists against my back. I spot the counter where I bent her over and took her a couple of nights ago and grin. "You teasing me cause you're looking for a repeat performance?"

"I suppose that depends."

"On what?" I ask, setting her down in the kitchen. Heat pools in her eyes and I lick my lips, picturing lifting her up and setting her on the counter before spreading her legs and dropping down between them to devour her.

"You going to walk out without a word again?"

I shake my head as I wrap my arms around her waist and pull her closer. "Didn't you hear me last night, baby? I'm never walking away from you again."

She smiles but that damn fear flicks through her gaze again, so quick that I would miss it if I wasn't paying attention, and it fucking kills me.

Why the fuck is she so scared of being with me again?

God, I have to fix this.

"I have a really important question for you, Pip," I tell

her and she smiles up at me as she nods.

"Shoot."

"You still like your eggs over easy?"

She laughs and nods. "Yes. You still hate eggs?"

"Yes!" I exclaim with a mock shudder as I back away from her and open the fridge. "The road trip of nineteen-ninety-six ruined eggs for me forever. You know this."

Her sweet laugh is music to my fucking ears. As I open the fridge, she pushes off the counter and steps up behind me, wrapping her arms around my waist and splaying her hands across my chest as she presses a kiss to the center of my back. In the simple touch, I can feel everything she is not saying and I smile as I grab the carton of eggs and turn back to her. Wrapping my free arm around her back, I press a kiss to her head and she sighs before she pulls away with a soft smile on her face.

"Hey, you know what I dreamed about last night?" she asks as she grabs a mug off of the shelf and fills it with coffee.

"When in the hell did you make coffee?"

She grins, shaking her head at me. "It's set on a timer so I don't have to deal with bullshit in the morning."

"Shit, I forgot how grumpy you get in the A.M.," I shoot back with a laugh and she shakes her head again. With the steaming cup in her hands, she walks across the kitchen and sits cross legged on one of the dining room chairs. I arch a brow as I start opening cupboards, looking for a pan to cook in. She points one out. "Next to the stove."

I open the cupboard she mentioned and grab the pan. "Thanks."

She nods in response and I grin as I set the pan on the stove.

"Now, what were you saying about a sex dream?"

Laughing, she rolls her eyes. "I didn't have a sex dream, you pervert. I had a dream about that little vacation we took to South Carolina right before you deployed. Do you remember it?"

About two weeks before I deployed, I took leave and Piper and I went down to Charleston for a little getaway, something to remember during the year we were going to be apart and we spent five days on the beach or in bed, loving on each other and wishing we didn't have to go back. I glance over at her and nod.

"Yeah, I do."

She smiles. "We should do it again someday."

"Yeah," I agree as I open the carton and grab an egg. That trip was amazing and by the time we got back, Piper and I were so connected that I had no doubt in my mind that we were going to make it. Too bad I never saw the storm coming until it was too late. Just as I'm about to crack the egg over the pan, I turn to her.

"We should do it."

She rolls her eyes. "I know. I just said that. Geez, pay attention, Landry."

"I was paying attention, Pip." I glare at her playfully as I set the egg back down in the carton and walk over to her. As I sink into the chair next to her, I grab her hands. "I'm saying let's go back now."

"We can't just go back now."

"Why not?"

Her gaze flicks up to the clock above the sink. "Because

I have to be at work in an hour."

"Yeah, but, do you, though?" I ask. "You are your own boss and I think Eden would understand if you bailed for a few days to spend time with your husband."

"Don't you dare use Eden's obsession with getting us back together to your advantage," she grumbles, her eyes betraying her mood. As much as she wants to be a responsible business owner and partner to Eden, she knows this sounds like a damn good idea. We can get to know each other again and really talk about everything. By the time we get back, we'll be unbreakable.

"Come on, baby," I urge, squeezing her hands between mine before leaning forward and cupping her cheek. "We need this."

She sighs.

"Okay. Only because you look so pitiful when you beg." She leans forward and kisses me before standing up. "I'll call Eden and get her to cover or reschedule my shoots for the next three days if you'll find us a house on the beach to rent."

I nod. "Deal."

Flashing me a huge grin, she jumps up to go grab her phone and as I watch her walk away, a feeling of peace settles inside me. This trip is going to be perfect and by the time we get back, that fear I see in her eyes will be gone, banished from our lives forever.

Every Little Thing

Chapter Seventeen
Piper

"I can't believe you still have this thing," I say as I run my fingertips over the multicolored stitching on the bench seat of his old Ford Bronco and take a deep breath. It smells exactly the same as I remember. I can't identify it or compare it to anything but to me, it has always brought me a sense of peace because the scent is burned into my brain and forever associated with Wyatt. Peeking over my shoulder, I smile as my gaze lands on the back where Wyatt and I would cuddle up and make out down by the river on Friday nights.

When he was fifteen, his dad pulled into the driveway with this thing on a trailer. It looked like shit and it hadn't ran in years but the two of them spent the next seven months fixing it up. I would go over to their house every single day and sit in a lawn chair, tanning, while they cranked on the engine and made it like new again and on his sixteenth birthday, his dad tossed him the keys and told him it was his. I'll never forget the look on his face as he stared up at the truck he'd been working on for so long or the way he pulled me into his side and threw his arm over my shoulders as we took it for that first drive.

He scoffs and I turn back to him as he shoots me a look that makes me giggle. "Of course I still have it."

Patting the steering wheel like he has to reassure the truck of his love, he shakes his head and I giggle again as I lean my head back against the seat and turn to stare out of my window as the endless ocean crashes against the shore. Butterflies flutter around in my belly and I can't wipe the smile off of my face. I'm living in a level of happiness I honestly forgot existed today and I pray that I'm not going to wake up anytime soon. So many times over the past ten years, I've had dreams just like this one where Wyatt and I are together and back in Charleston, reliving the best time in our lives and I've had to pinch myself several times during our drive up here to remind myself that this is real.

Last night was incredible. After our talk and Wyatt's little declaration, we reconnected and it was everything I could have wanted and more. Overnight, everything changed and sometimes it is easy to forget that we were ever apart but I know it is not always going to be that way. Right now, I'm happy and so fucking in love with my husband but I'm not foolish enough to think it will be this easy. There are still things we need to talk about and we need to learn to be with each other again, which will take time and patience.

I just hope I can handle it.

To be honest, I'm scared shitless. The last time Wyatt and I were together, I was so codependent that when he had to leave, I couldn't even function without him and I don't want to fall back into those same bad habits. He makes me feel so safe but I can't rely on that anymore or I'll be right back where I was before. We need to take things slow but that's easier said than done... especially with Wyatt. He was never the guy to tread lightly or be cautious. He runs into things full-on with no plan and no fear at all. It's so different from me that you have to wonder how we ever got together but even if I can't explain it, it works. We work and I'm so fucking happy to have him back. Just the simple fact that I'm sitting next to him in his truck and we're not yelling and screaming at each other and he doesn't hate me anymore... I never thought this would happen. And when Eden forced us back into each other's lives, I couldn't even hope for this when the issues between us seemed so big and impossible to overcome.

"I think this is us," Wyatt says as he slows down and pulls into the gravel driveway in front of little blue cottage with a bright pink door that might be the cutest thing I've ever seen. Each window is framed by white shutters and it's private... or as private as you can get right on the beach in Isle of Palms. There is an empty lot on both sides of the house and our closest neighbors only have one car in the driveway so we don't have to worry about crazy parties going on all night. I grin as I peek over at him and slap my hand on his thigh.

"Damn, you did good, babe."

He nods with a smirk on his face like he already knows he did good and reaches across the seat, unclipping my belt and pulling me toward him as hunger fills his eyes.

"Wait, you're gonna crush the food!" I yell, placing my hand on his chest to stop him and he sighs, glancing down at the bag of chicken and sides we picked up on the way over here as he releases me.

"I'm not hungry." His stomach growls, betraying him and I laugh as I back away from him and grab the food.

"Sure, but let's go eat anyway."

His smile widens and he flashes me a predatory look before he turns and opens his door. "Fine. I'll eat dinner and then I'm eating you."

"Wyatt," I gasp and he laughs as he slams the door behind him and walks around to the back to grab our bags. I hop down with the bag of food in my hand and meet him at the front door as he punches a code into the little box attached to the door. It beeps and a secret compartment pops out, revealing a key.

"Fancy," I mutter and he glances back at me with a smirk as he unlocks the door. It swings open to a bright, airy, all white color scheme that has a quintessential beauty feel to it and memories from our first trip here rush back to me. We stayed in a hotel that time but it was right on the beach and if we weren't playing in the ocean, we were in bed or in the hot tub just trying to soak up as many moments together as we could. Hell, I don't even think we showered separately that entire trip.

"Come on. Let's take a tour," he says, grabbing my hand and heat settles in my chest at the feeling of his touch and I nod, fighting back a smile as he leads me into the kitchen before turning down a hallway. At one end is a bedroom and a bathroom with a large walk-in shower and at the other end is a screened in back porch that leads out to a yard and a pool. I point to the little round table next to the pool.

"Let's eat here."

He nods and releases my hand. "Sure. I'll go see if I can find some plates and stuff."

As he turns and walks back into the house, I sit down and set the food on the table before looking out at the water and sighing. The sun is sinking into the ocean, fire red merging with cool blue as intense purples, pinks, and oranges streak across the sky. A light breeze ruffles my hair and the sound of the waves crashing onto the beach soothe my soul as I take a deep breath. I can't remember the last time I was this relaxed. Then again, I also can't remember the last time I took a vacation. When I called Eden this morning, she was ready to rip me a new one but when she found out who I was with she was all too happy to cover some of my shoots and reschedule the others for me. Her only stipulation was that I spill all the details as soon as I got home but I would expect nothing else. Honestly, it is a miracle she let me leave *without* a full rundown of events. Giggling, I imagine how much it has to be driving her crazy as I shake my head.

"What are you giggling about out here?" Wyatt asks, walking up behind me with two plates, silverware, and a couple beers. I shake my head again as he sets them down.

"I was just thinking about how crazy it has to be making Eden that I didn't tell her everything that happened before we left."

He scoffs as he sits down and passes me a plate. "She a good friend to you, baby? Or can I keep being mad at her?"

"You can do whatever you want but she is my best friend and she really did mean well."

"Yeah," he answers, meeting my gaze with a smile. "I

217

suppose it worked out all right in the end but that girl has got boundary issues."

I nod. Truthfully, I can't argue with him but I know Eden and I know her heart was in the right place when she put this whole little plan into motion. "She's working on it."

"Mmhmm," he hums, his gaze full of doubt as he peeks over at me and I laugh as he puts a big piece of fried chicken on my plate before holding up one of the sides. "Mashed potatoes or mac and cheese?"

I roll my eyes as I lift up my plate and hold it out to him. "Both. And a biscuit, please."

He chuckles as he scoops some potatoes onto my plate and pours a little bit of gravy over the top before grabbing the mac and cheese. Once he plops the biscuit next to everything else, I set my plate back down and take one of the beers from him.

"Sorry it's so small," he says, glancing around as he finishes loading up his plate. "It was all I could find at the last minute. Apparently whoever originally rented this place out for the next five days cancelled last night."

I shake my head as I look up at the little cottage. "I think it's perfect. We have everything we need and if this trip is about us reconnecting, I wouldn't want to be in a hotel or some big house with tons of neighbors around."

"Yeah?" he asks, his lips twitching with a hidden grin as he arches a brow. "There something specific you need privacy for, Pip?"

"Maybe... I've kind of always wanted to have sex in a pool," I say, my gaze flicking to the pool next to us and he sucks in a breath as his gaze drops down to my chest and he licks his lips. Goddamn, the man is going to kill me. He grabs his fork and nods to my plate.

"You better hurry up and eat."

I lean back in my seat and cross my arms over my chest. "Oh? And why is that?"

"Because you started talking about getting fucked in that pool and now my cock is hard as a rock."

"Oh," I whisper, a shiver working its way down my spine as my eyes flick to the pool before snapping back to him. His hazel eyes are molten, staring at me like a man possessed and my hand shakes as I lean forward and grab my fork but nothing on my plate looks good anymore. Without a word, he stands up and walks over to me.

"Wyatt!" I scream as he lifts my chair up with me still in it and carries me over next to his chair before setting me down again. I watch him as he goes back around the table, grabs my plate, and sets it down in front of me before returning to his chair. "What was that for?"

He grabs my hand, laces his fingers through mine, and lifts it to his lips, pressing a kiss against my skin. "You were too far away."

"Across this tiny ass table?" I ask and he just shrugs.

"I don't make the rules, baby."

"I see," I whisper as I reach over and press my hand against his chest. "And what if I don't feel like eating anymore?"

He glances over at me and grins. "You're going to need your energy."

"You're talkin' a big game, Landry."

"Try me," he growls, tucking his finger under my chin and turning me to him before slamming his lips down on mine. His kiss is demanding, full of need and I whimper as I wrap one arm around his neck and straddle his lap. Fingertips dig into my back as he groans and trails kisses down my neck.

"Wyatt."

"Fuck it," he snaps, lifting me out of his lap and setting me back in my chair. "You don't move. I'm gonna go put these plates in the fridge and we can eat afterward."

I nod, the air punching out of my lungs as I cross my legs and watch him pick up our dishes and walk into the house. As soon as he's gone, I glance in both directions before stripping my shirt over my head. Thank God, we both decided to wear our swimming suits in the car or the few neighbors we have on this vacation would be getting a full-on show. Standing up, I bend over and shove my shorts down my legs as the screen door creaks behind me.

"Goddamn," he breathes as I stand up, kicking my shorts off as I peek over my shoulder at him. His lips part and his tongue darts out, trailing along his bottom lip in a way that makes me imagine it trailing up my body and I shudder as a grin stretches across my face as I take a step toward the pool.

"Come and get me."

He starts toward me, yanking his shirt over his head as he goes and I squeal and take off running for the pool. When I reach the edge, I plop down on my butt and slide in before kicking away from the wall and moving to the middle of the pool. There is a huge splash as he jumps in after me and I spin around to watch him. When he surfaces again, he brushes his hair back and stares me down like he wants to devour me. My belly twists with need and I smile as I kick my feet, still swimming away from him but he's gaining on me quickly.

"Where are you going, sweetheart?"

I cock my head to the side. "I told you to catch me. Did you think I was kidding?"

He growls and dives under the water in my direction and I dart to the side to try and escape but he wraps his hand around my ankle and drags me back to him as he pops out of the water and flashes me a hungry smile.

"Gotcha."

"Oh, no," I whisper with mock shock and fear, shaking my head as I flash him wide, damsel in distress eyes. "What will I do now?"

He drags his hand down the side of my body, leaving a trail of heat as he goes that contrasts with the cold water and I gasp as he grabs my thigh and lifts it to his hip, his fingers digging into my skin. "I can think of a few things."

"Yeah? Like what?"

"For starters," he whispers back, his breath heating my skin as he leans in and lets his lips hover just above mine. My heart hammers in my chest and my body aches for his touch. "You could kiss your husband."

"Mmm," I moan with a nod before pressing my lips to his and wrapping my arms around his neck. He hooks my other leg around his waist and moves us to the edge of the pool as his tongue tangles with mine, teasing me with the promise of more as my back presses against the tile on the wall of the pool. His hands roam over my body, giving me what I thought I wanted but it's still not enough and I whimper as I rock my hips into him, feeling the steel of his erection against my entrance.

"Baby, please."

He chuckles. "Naw, you're not ready yet."

"I am," I argue, nodding frantically and he shakes his head again as he pulls the string on one side of the bikini bottoms, untying the knot, before moving to the other side. When it's free, he pulls the fabric away and I watch as it floats up to the surface behind him. His lips press to my neck and I close my eyes, moaning as his fingers find my clit and circle it gently, teasing me to the point of madness. Just when I think he might finally give me what I want, he pulls his hand away. I try to protest but before I can, he pulls the triangle of my bathing suit top to the side and sucks my nipple into his mouth.

"Wyatt," I breathe out as goose bumps race across my flesh. I slide my fingers into his hair and he rumbles against my skin as he thrusts his hips against me. It's still not enough. I need to feel him, all of him, against me with nothing between us. "Take your shorts off."

Nodding, he releases my tit with a pop but refuses to let me go as he switches arms back and forth to wrestle his trunks off and when he's finally free of them, I wrap my hand around his cock and slam my lips back to his as I stroke him. He groans, grabbing a chunk of my hair and the bite of pain only spurs me on as I press my free hand to his chest. His heart hammers against my palm and I don't stop moving my hand. More than my own release, I want to watch him fall apart because of me. I want to know that no other girl in the ten years we've been apart has ever affected him the way that I do. For the first time in a really long time, I want to feel like his everything again.

I continue to stroke him as I kiss down his neck,

nipping along the way and the closer he gets to his release, the tighter his hold on me becomes. He reaches up with his free hand and twists my nipple between his thumb and finger as he groans in my ear. I kiss back up his neck, making sure that I'm teasing him as much as I possibly can before pressing my lips to his again. He releases my hair and slips me down his body slightly, shoving his leg between mine and I moan into his kiss as I rub my pussy against his thigh.

"Wyatt," I moan before sealing our lips together again and he abandons my nipple to slip his hand under the water, gripping my waist and guiding my hips against his leg. Pressure builds in my belly and I try to move faster but he stops me, prolonging my pleasure as he shudders with his impending orgasm. Ripping his lips from mine, he drops his head back and groans as he squeezes his eyes shut.

"Pip… you gotta stop…" he whispers in between frantic breaths and I shake my head. I won't stop. I need this. His hands on my hips get more forceful, moving me faster and faster until I feel like I'm going to explode. "Stop, Piper. I'm gonna come."

"No." I shake my head and bite his neck, pulling another groan from his lips as he releases my hips and pulls me toward him, driving into me in one fluid thrust. I cry out, gripping his shoulders as he groans through gritted teeth and throw his head back.

"Aw, fuck," he groans again. "I'm not gonna last. I've been thinking about getting inside you all goddamn day and it's too fucking good."

I press my lips to his neck, just under his ear and his grip on my ass tightens as he moves me back and forth, fucking me to the point of desperation. "I'm almost there. Besides, we've got all night, baby."

"Fuck, Piper," he growls, his muscles tightening as he slams into me again before he releases a breath and his shaft throbs inside me with his release. He grits his teeth and groans again, shuddering as the orgasm rolls through him. "Jesus Christ."

"Mm," I hum, kissing his neck again and he slips a hand into my hair and pulls, dragging a gasp from my lips as he opens his eyes and flashes me a grin.

"Now it's your turn."

"Have at it, baby," I whisper as my heart kicks in my chest and my teeth sink into my bottom lip. He pins me to the wall of the pool again and thrusts into me, stealing the breath from my lungs as he claims my lips once more. It doesn't take much - a few well placed drives, a scorching hot kiss, and his thumb brushing over my clit - and I'm falling apart. Dropping my head back, my body trembles and I moan as stars explode in my vision and pleasure consumes me. When I finally drift back to earth, I let out a sigh and open my eyes. Wyatt's wide grin greets me and he turns, carrying me in his arms across the pool with one thing on his mind.

Shit…

This is going to be a *very* good night.

Every Little Thing

Chapter Eighteen
Wyatt

"Wyatt," Piper moans, fisting her hands into her hair as she rides me, eyes closed as pleasure overwhelms her. I groan, gripping her hips as I thrust off the bed, so fucking close.

"Fuck, baby…"

She grins down at me and rolls her hips again. "Squawk!"

"What?" I ask, scowling up at her as she begins to fade away. She opens her mouth to respond but the only sound I hear is another squawk. Shaking my head, I try to reach for her but she disappears…

"Squawk!"

I groan as I rub the sleep from my eyes before peeling them open. The cottage's white bead board ceiling stares back at me and I flick a glance to the open window where the seagulls like to sing us their daily morning song.

"Squawk!"

"Fucking useless birds," I hiss. I turn, ready to pull

Every Little Thing

Piper into my arms and catch a few more hours of sleep but the only thing waiting for me is cold sheets. Shooting up in bed, I listen for sounds of her moving around the house but silence greets me and my heart thuds in my chest as I throw the covers off of my legs and jump out of bed. Walking to the doorway, I try to push my fears down but they don't want to go quietly.

"Pip?"

When I still don't get an answer, I grab a pair of mesh shorts out of my bag and pull them on before wandering out into the kitchen.

Fuck.

Where is she?

Glancing over at the living room, I frown before I see the large lemon poppyseed muffin and steaming cup of coffee sitting on the island. I scoop the little note next to the food and run my hand through my hair as I read it.

> *I didn't want to wake you so I ran*
> *out and grabbed us some breakfast.*
> *Come find me in the backyard when you're ready to*
> *face the world.*

She signed the note with a cute little heart and I smile as I set it down and pick up my muffin, slowly unwrapping it from the cling wrap surrounding it. Piper and I spent yesterday morning down at the beach, playing in the ocean like we were two kids again before coming back up to the house and spending damn near an hour in the shower together. We spent the rest of the day vegging out in front of the TV, eating junk food, and watching Netflix in practically nothing, which was perfect after the drive up here the day before and another long night of catching up but now, it's time to talk. I feel like I've put this off for long enough and with us going home tomorrow, I want to ask all my questions now so we can truly have a fresh start.

With my muffin and coffee in hand, I walk out to the screened in porch and smile when I see her sitting on one of the chairs with her knees pulled up to her chest, watching the sunrise. Her red hair is pulled up into a messy bun but a few pieces are falling down, brushing against the strap of her tank top as she grabs a cup off of the table and brings it to her lips. She looks gorgeous down there, so damn peaceful and I hope she is feeling as good about things as I am.

There is only one way to find out, I suppose.

"Morning, baby," I call as I step outside, the screen door creaking as it opens and she glances over her shoulder, flashing me a wide grin as her gaze trails down my naked chest.

Shit.

I wish she would have just stayed in bed so we could start this morning off right.

"Hey, you. I didn't think you'd be up for a while."

I nod as I walk across the grass and sink into the chair next to her. "Well, those damn birds felt like I needed to be awake now."

"That just means you can watch the sunrise with me," she says, laying her head on my shoulder as I peel the paper off of my muffin and take a bite. "Isn't it gorgeous?"

I turn and look at the sun peeking over the ocean, pastel pinks coloring the few clouds dotting the expansive sky before turning back to her. I can't help but think she

228

looks better than any damn sunrise I've ever seen and I smile as she peeks over at me, waiting for my answer. I nod.

"Yeah, you sure are."

She rolls her eyes but she can't hide the faint color staining her cheeks as she fights back a smile. "God, you're so cheesy."

Yeah, but you love me anyway…

As the thought flicks through my mind, I realize that we haven't actually said those words to each other yet even though there is no doubt in my mind we both feel the same and it reminds me of the talk we need to have. Setting my muffin down, I grab her hand and look down at it, scowling when I see her bare ring finger. I rub my thumb over the spot where her rings used to be.

"Hey, do you still have your rings?"

Three months before we graduated from high school, I realized that I wanted to ask her to marry me so I started picking up more shifts at the garage where I worked part-time and putting away every cent that I could spare. I started telling Piper that we couldn't go out as much because I was saving for college but I'm pretty sure she thought I was getting ready to end things with her. A week before graduation, I finally saved enough money to go to the jewelry store in the mall and buy her solitaire diamond ring with a braided gold band as well as the matching wedding band.

Smiling, I shake my head.

God, I was such a cocky little shit but it never even occurred to me that she might say no. We were *Wyatt and Piper* and everyone knew we were going to end up together. There was no other option.

"Yeah, they're in my jewelry box at home," she says, glancing down at my thumb as I stroke over her finger again and I nod.

"You gonna put it back on?" My stomach flips as the question leaves my lips and my heart pounds as I wait for her answer. She sighs and meets my eyes as her teeth sink into her bottom lip.

Oh, fuck...

"I don't know, Wyatt. I don't want to rush into this... or make the same mistakes that I did last time."

Punching me in the gut would have been kinder and I struggle to swallow down the lump in my throat as I nod, my chest aching. It makes sense why she would want to be cautious after what happened the last time we were together but that doesn't make the pain fade away.

"Right."

"Please don't be upset, baby," she whispers, pulling her hand from my grasp and turning to me to cup my face between her hands. I meet her eyes and they beg me to understand and as much as my mind gets where she's coming from, I can't help but feel like I just got rejected. "The way I feel about you hasn't changed, at all. I just don't want to go back to that place where I can't stand on my own two feet."

"How do you feel about me? Because you haven't said the words."

Jesus Christ.

I sound like a goddamn girl right now.

She scowls and shakes her head, staring up at me like I've lost my mind. Then again, maybe I have.

"Well, you haven't said it either."

She's got a point.

"Besides, you and I... it's always been more than three little words could sum up. You know that but if you need to hear me say it, I will."

I shake my head and blow out a breath as I drop my

gaze to my lap. She's right. Our connection has always been something special and if the fact that we're back together again after ten years apart doesn't tell me how she feels then I don't know what will. She sighs and I lift my gaze to hers as she reaches down and grabs my hand, pressing it against her chest.

"You feel that?"

I nod.

"It's always been yours, Wyatt. Always. Even when we were apart and trying to move on with our lives without each other, my heart still belonged to you."

Slipping my other hand into her hair, I claim her lips, desperate to feel her and she moans as she climbs off of her chair and straddles my lap, never once breaking our connection and when she finally does pull away, she smiles down at me. The sun shines around her, illuminating her like an angel and I brush my thumb over her cheek, wondering how I got lucky enough to not only get her once but twice.

"I love you," I tell her and her eyes shine as she leans down and steals another kiss, something between a sigh and a moan slipping between us and I wrap my arms around her body, pulling her closer. When she pulls away this time, her smile is brighter.

"I love you, too." She cuddles into me, tucking her face into my neck and I take a deep breath as I stare out at the ocean and rub my hand down her back.

"You think we could talk about something else?"

She jerks up and meets my gaze again. "It's about when I left, isn't it?"

I nod and she chews on her bottom lip for a second before repeating the gesture. The last thing I want is to put that apprehensive look in her eyes and I understand why she hates talking about this stuff but we need to in order to move forward.

"Why did you write me that email?"

She deflates for a second before straightening her shoulders with a nod and that strength I'm quickly becoming very fond of flashes in her eyes. "Honestly… I don't know. I remember thinking the man who killed my parents was after me and that I had to get away… Maybe I thought I was protecting you by making sure you didn't follow me…" She shrugs. "Like I said, everything around that time is super fuzzy and I can't tell you what was real and what wasn't."

"Okay," I whisper with a nod. That makes sense, I suppose. If she thought she was trying to protect me, I don't think there is any length Piper wouldn't go to. I remember her saying she would see my dead body in the house and I scowl up at her. "Why would you need to protect me if you already thought I was dead?"

"Oh… no. The two delusions never existed together. I either saw him or I saw you but never saw both of you in the same room. I think at one point, I thought he had been the one to kill you and I felt this overwhelming hopelessness because he had taken my whole world from me again and I started thinking what was the point of even living anymore."

My heart jumps into my throat as my eyes widen. "Please tell me you didn't try to…"

"No," she says, cutting me off. "Never. I might have briefly considered the idea but by the next morning, I was seeing him again and I thought you were alive. Or, at least, I think I did. My memories are not a good indicator of the truth."

I nod, squeezing my eyes shut as I try to banish the thought from my mind. What the fuck would I do without her? My mind drifts back to the man I was just three weeks ago, before she walked back into my life and it feels like an entirely different person. I need her so I don't even want to consider the possibility that she could have ended it all...

"Why didn't you come back after you were better?" I ask, shifting gears and she chews on her bottom lip, staring down at her fingers as she twists them together.

"I did."

"What?" I nudge under her chin with my finger and force her gaze to mine. Tears swim in her eyes and she sucks in a breath. It breaks my fucking heart.

"After I got out of the hospital, I got my own apartment and started the business with Eden. When I finally felt like I was secure and I was confident that I could handle everything, I wanted to find you. I looked you up on Facebook and saw that you had joined the Devils so I went to the clubhouse to find you. When I got there, you guys were having a barbecue and there was this woman sitting in your lap. You looked happy and I..."

The tears spill down her cheeks and she clamps her mouth shut as she drops her gaze to her lap again.

"What girl, baby?"

She shrugs. "I don't know. She had blue hair and tattoos all over her body."

"Cleo," I whisper, closing my eyes and shaking my head. Jesus, what would have happened if she had talked to me that day? Where would we be now? Would I have even listened to her? I can't believe she was so close and I never even knew because I was focused on Cleo. I knew that was a bad idea from the start.

Goddamn it.

"I thought about going to talk to you but I was already nervous and when I saw you with her... I thought you were moving on with your life and I should try and do the same."

I nod, everything coming together in my head. "So you sent the divorce papers?"

"Yes."

"Pip, baby," I breathe as I grab her face and press a quick, demanding kiss to her lips before pulling back. "That girl was no one. We hooked up sometimes and she just started bartending for the club but she and I were never together. I was never able to move on from you."

She nods. "I know that now but back then, I thought I was doing the right thing. I loved you and I wanted you to be happy after everything I had put you through. You know, that whole 'if you love someone, set them free' thing."

"For the record," I tell her, stealing another kiss. "Don't set me free again. Ever."

"Okay," she whispers, a soft sob slipping out of her lips as the tears fall down her cheeks. I brush them away and pull her to me again, determined to kiss away the pain of our past. She melts into me, clinging to my shirt as she kisses me back with the same desperation I feel coursing through my veins. I want to wash it all away, make the past ten years disappear because the ache I feel thinking about everything we could have had if things had gone just a little bit differently makes my stomach turn.

I know I can't do a damn thing about the past but I will do whatever it takes to make sure the rest of our lives together are so magical that when we tell the story of our love to our grandkids, the part about when we were apart won't even matter.

Every Little Thing

Chapter Nineteen
Piper

My feet sink into the cool sand with each step and a brisk morning breeze blows through my hair, making me pull my sweater tighter around my body as I walk along the beach, thinking over the past few days of our trip. Yesterday, after our little talk, Wyatt and I spent an hour lost in each other, which is quickly becoming a common theme for us, before we went to downtown Charleston to explore. Bill, the man who owns the bakery where I grabbed breakfast yesterday, recommended we check out the market so we walked through the open sheds and browsed all the vendors selling everything from soap to sweetgrass baskets to jewelry to art before we went on a horse drawn carriage ride around the city. Charleston is absolutely gorgeous and if I wasn't "oohing" and "aching" over the scenery then I was gushing over the architecture and history. I was entranced and I really hope we can come back here often.

The sun isn't up yet and the light is soft, making

everything look and feel more peaceful but my belly flips as the nerves crash over me. I wish we didn't have to say good-bye to this beautiful place but as soon as Wyatt wakes up, we will pack everything up and drive back to Baton Rouge to go back to our regular lives. We have been in this perfect little bubble for the past three days and I hate not knowing what is going to happen when we go back. Here, it is so easy to just be us without all the pain and drama of the past and as much as I hope that will carry over to our everyday lives, I just don't know. Shit. I don't even really know where he and I stand.

Are we back together officially?
Are we taking things slow and feeling it out?

Even after our talk yesterday and me telling him I wanted to take things slow, I still got the feeling that he was trying to push the issue as we were walking around yesterday. He kept picking up various decorations and asking me if I liked them. If I said yes, he would immediately buy it so I learned pretty quick to just shrug and move along. That makes me sound cold but it's not even that I didn't want him to buy me anything, it's just that I don't know what any of it means. He would show me a piece of art and I would wonder if he was asking because he wants us to live together now or he would ask if I liked a gorgeous necklace and I would wonder if he was trying to win me over to his side.

I reach the edge of the water and sigh as the water rushes around my feet before retreating back down the beach. Backing up a few steps, I sit down and stretch my feet out until the water just barely kisses them as I stare out at the horizon. Warring emotions rip through me and I shake my head. I don't even know what I want when we get back so it is impossible to convey that to Wyatt. He wants us to be all in, I know that and there are moments when that is all I want, too, but I feel like I need to be responsible. The last thing I want is to jump in too quickly and put us in a bad place again just because I couldn't be patient. Then again, the thought of going back to my apartment alone sounds just as bad. There is no middle ground here. I either have to risk it all or tell Wyatt to wait for me and neither of those options sound ideal if I'm being honest. My heart, the always wild and unpredictable part of me, tells me to jump in, to stop wasting time when I've already wasted ten years of our lives but my head reminds me of that dark awful place I was when I left last time. I shudder as the memories flood into my mind and shake my head.

I remember walking out of the house we shared on base so clearly, like I was in my right mind but I know I wasn't because I was convinced that the man who killed my parents was coming for me and I had to run. The next thing that I can recall is pulling into Baton Rouge but I don't remember any of the fourteen hour drive from North Carolina. All I know is that I was sure Clinton Woods was right behind me, ready to finish the job he started when he killed my parents. The next year passed in a blur. I was in survival mode, both in my head and in reality, and as more of the real world slipped away from me, the more I deteriorated. By the time Dr. Brewer found me, sleeping on a park bench during her morning run, I had lost thirty-five pounds and I hadn't bathed in months.

Tears fill my eyes as I remember waking up in that hospital and being able to think clearly for the first time in over a year but that was soon taken over by fear. I had no idea where I was and all I wanted was Wyatt. Closing my eyes, I can still hear my echoed sobs as they bounced off the walls of my room late at night and the way my chest ached with the pain of his absence as I tried to deal with the trauma from my childhood. I suck in a stuttered breath, trying not to cry as my first session with Dr. Brewer comes back to me. She urged me to open up about what had happened to me but I just sat in silence, staring at the floor and wishing I could find a phone to call my husband. It was only when she told me that I needed to learn to talk about what happened and deal with the emotions associated with it before I could go back to him that I started to do the work I needed to do to get better.

"Piper?!" Wyatt's panicked voice yells from behind me and I whip my head around as I frantically wipe the tears from my face. I can't see him so he must still be back at the house, behind the dunes and I wave my hand in the air as I clear my throat.

"Over here."

I hear him before I see him, his feet slapping against the wooden walkway to the beach as he runs at full speed in my direction. He appears over the dunes in his mesh shorts and a t-shirt and as soon as his gaze lands on me, his worried expression falls away and he stops, planting his hands on his legs as he bends over and lets out a breath. Once he has recovered enough to move, he walks over to me and plops down in the sand next to me, dropping his head into his hands.

"Jesus Christ. Don't ever do that to me again."

I arch a brow. "Do what?"

"Disappear," he breathes, running his hand through his hair and my heart seizes in my chest. Reaching over, I grab his hand and wrap his arm around my shoulders as I cuddle into him.

"I'm sorry. I didn't meant to scare you."

Shaking his head, he hooks his arm around my neck and pulls me closer as he presses his lips to my head. "I thought you left me…"

"Wyatt," I whisper, trying to pull away but he doesn't let me go anywhere so I cuddle back into him and hope my presence is enough to calm his racing heart. We sit in silence for a few seconds before he reaches over and pulls me into his lap. I brace my hands on his shoulders as I straddle him and he presses his forehead to my chest as he takes another deep breath. Running my fingers through his hair, I try to get him to look at me but he just shakes his head. "Are you okay?"

He finally meets my gaze. "No, I'm not okay, Piper. I couldn't fucking find you anywhere and all of my worst fucking fears were realized."

"Baby… I'm sorry…"

He wraps both arms around me and pulls me closer as he sighs. "Just let me hold you for a minute."

"Okay."

"Why are you down here anyway?" he asks, his voice muffled by the fabric of my sweater. He pulls back to look up at me and he scowls when he gets a good look at my face. "Why have you been crying?"

I shake my head. "I was just thinking."

"About what?" He reaches up and brushes his thumb over my cheek, concern filling his hazel eyes and I can feel

239

his love surrounding me as I take a deep breath.

"The year I was homeless."

Pain flicks across his face as he nods. "Will you tell me about it?"

My teeth sink into my bottom lip and I study him for a second before nodding. As I launch into the whole story, telling him about coming back to Baton Rouge and scrounging for every ounce of food I had. I tell him about sneaking into gas stations or restaurants to try and clean myself up before I got caught and I tell him about constantly moving so the man who killed my parents wouldn't find me before explaining how bad it was when Dr. Brewer found me. His eyes are wide as he stares up at me and blows out a breath.

"God, Pip… I hate myself for not being there for you. I never should have left…"

Shaking my head, I press my hand to his cheek. "No. It wasn't your fault. It wasn't anyone's fault. It just was and yeah, it sucked but the only person we can blame is already rotting away in a jail cell."

"Or dead," he adds and I cock my head to the side as I scowl at him.

"Huh?"

"Your aunt, baby. She was a cold ass woman and she never did anything to help you deal with what had happened to you."

"Don't blame her. She was damn near fifty when she took me in and she never wanted children so to have me forced on her just sucked."

He clenches his teeth and his body tenses underneath me. "No. You were just a kid and had a horrible thing happen to you. You didn't deserve her apathy."

"Wyatt, it could have been so much worse. Besides my parents dying, I was incredibly lucky that I didn't end up with someone who wanted to hurt me more. Do you know what could have happened to me?"

"Of course, I do," he growls. "But that still doesn't make it okay. She barely even paid attention to you. Do you remember that time we both snuck out and slept in the treehouse? My parents were fucking frantic and Aunt Myra didn't even realize you were gone."

"It could have been worse," I repeat. It's the same thing I tell myself every time I think about what happened after that awful night. I got lucky with Aunt Myra.

"Whatever. I'm just glad my parents took you in after she died." I shudder as the memory of coming home from school and finding my Aunt Myra dead on the floor from a heart attack fills my mind. Shaking my head, I try to clear the image from my mind as I meet his eyes.

"I got lucky then, too."

He fights a smile as he shakes his head. "Naw, baby. That wasn't luck. That was me begging my parents for days and promising them everything under the sun if they would let you come live with us."

"What?" I ask, my jaw dropping in shock. "You did that for me? Why didn't you ever tell me?"

"I made them promise they wouldn't tell you because I wanted you to feel wanted. I wanted you to know that you were loved."

"Baby," I breathe, a smile stretching across my face as I lean down and press my lips to his. How in the hell did I get lucky enough to find this man not only once but twice?

Pulling back, I flash him the biggest smile. "I love you."

He wraps his arms around me again and steals another quick kiss before releasing me to lean back on his hands. "I love you, too, Pip. Speaking of which…"

"Yes?" I ask as I arch a brow. He sucks in a breath and my belly flips as I try to figure out what he's going to say. It has to be big to put that nervous look in his eyes.

"I got you something at the market yesterday."

I scowl as he reaches into his pocket. When in the hell did he have time to get me a present yesterday? I was always with him. My eyes widen as he pulls out a silver chain with a double infinity symbol on it and grabs my hand, dropping it into my palm.

"Wyatt," I whisper as I pick it up and study the gem encrusted charm. "This is gorgeous."

He nods. "It seemed perfect for us since we're starting over. Or, at least, I hope we are…"

"Oh, Wyatt…"

"I know it's scary for you and, baby, I'm here to support you and your recovery one hundred percent but please don't make me do it at a distance."

I chew on my bottom lip as I meet his eyes. "If we move too fast and I freak out again…"

"I won't let that happen," he says, cutting me off as he leans forward and wraps his arms around me again. "If you want me to go to therapy with you so I can learn how to help you or if you tell me you need space for a couple of hours, you got it. Whatever you need, I'll do it but I don't want to live without you anymore."

"Anything?"

He nods. "Anything, baby."

"I don't know," I whisper, my heart thundering in my chest. "What if I start leaning on you again?"

"I think it's okay to lean when you need support, sweetheart, just don't forget how to stand all on your own."

My belly flips as I stare back to him, my mind screaming for the right answer but I can't come up with anything. I want so badly to agree to this but I can't go back to that dark place, I won't survive being stalked by the man who killed my parents again.

"Please, trust me, baby. Now that I know what you went through and why, I can be here for you the way I always should have been. I don't want to take your strength. I just want to make you even stronger."

I shake my head. "I'm not strong, Wyatt."

"That's where you're wrong and I am really hoping you'll give me a chance to prove it to you." His eyes plead with me to give this a chance, trust him with not only my heart but my fragile mind and I suck in a breath as my belly flips again and my heart thuds in my chest.

"Okay."

A brilliant smile stretches across his face. "Yeah?"

"Yeah, we'll give this a real shot," I answer with a nod and he laughs as he crushes me to his chest and slams his lips down on mine. My body relaxes in an instant, melting in his lap as my eyes close and we both spill everything we're feeling into the kiss - pure joy with a little bit of fear mixed in. But I let it all go. There was a time in my life when I trusted Wyatt with every piece of me and I need to do that again. Now that he knows, now that there are no more secrets between us, he would never let me fall apart again. When he pulls away, he starts planting kisses all over my face and I giggle as I try to push him back and his answering laugh warms my very soul.

"Now that we've got that sorted out, there are two other things I wanted to talk to you about," he says and I arch a brow, as I flash him an expectant look.

"Let's hear 'em."

He stares up at me, his gaze so sure that the last of my worries disappear, ripped from me and pulled out to sea by the tide.

"First, I think we should back out of the leases on both of our apartments and find a place together."

"Okay," I agree, nodding my head. I'm not particularly attached to my apartment and I can't wait to be living with Wyatt again. "What's the second one?"

"How do you feel about having a baby?" he asks, a trace of nerves flitting across his face as my heart skips a beat. It's everything I wanted, everything I have been hoping for but is it too much too soon? It occurs to me that up to this point, we haven't used any protection and my heart start to beat a little faster as I consider the possibilities. He slips his hand into my hair and pulls my gaze to his as he offers me a reassuring smile. "Trust me, Pip. I've got you if this is what you want."

"Oh, God," I whisper, burying my face in my hands as my chest feels light as air and a smile stretches across my face. Am I really going to get everything I want? When I open my eyes again, I meet Wyatt's gaze and after searching my face, he gives an encouraging nod that makes my belly flip. "Okay. Let's do it."

He flashes me that brilliant smile again and pulls me to him, surrounding me with his arms and crushing his lips to mine as he falls back into the sand, sweeping his tongue into my mouth. I moan into his kiss as I cling to his t-shirt, wishing I could rip it away and feel him against me. One of his hands slips down to my ass as I grind against him and he groans before pulling his lips from mine.

"You better get back up to the house before I just take you right here," he growls in between desperate kisses and I shake my head, trying to climb off of him but he keeps pulling me back down.

"No way. Sand in places sand was never meant to go is *not* sexy."

He finally releases me and I stumble to my feet as he jumps up behind me and throws me over his shoulder. His hand lands on my ass with a smack and I squeal as he starts walking back up the beach with determined steps. The smile on my face makes my cheeks hurt but I can't stop it as I imagine our baby in Wyatt's arms and I slap him back as butterflies flutter through my belly.

"Hurry up, Landry. Time to put a baby in me."

A.M. Myers

Every Little Thing

Chapter Twenty
Piper

"Happy?" Wyatt asks as he walks into the living room of the adorable little farmhouse we just closed on yesterday and I force a smile to my face as I nod. Ever since we got back from our trip to Charleston, he has been amazing about checking in with me and making sure I'm feeling okay and when I'm not, giving me the reassurance I need to let the fear go. In a lot of ways, it feels like we're newlyweds again and I can't imagine being any happier than I feel now but getting back together, buying a house, and trying for a baby is a lot to take on at once and there are moments when the part of me that always remembers the dark time in my life is screaming at me to be more careful. But that part gets quieter and quieter every single day because Wyatt and this new life that we're building together makes me so damn happy that I'm running out of room to harbor that fear.

"Deliriously," I answer, my smile feeling more and more real as he sets the box in his arms down and walks over to me. His arms wrap around my waist and he pulls me closer, searching my gaze to a lie but he won't find any. It's odd to how the two polar opposite emotions can exist within me simultaneously but it's working and despite any moments of hesitation I have or any trepidation I feel, I can't remember the last time I was this happy. When Wyatt and I were together before, there was always this darkness within me that our love could never quite banish because I didn't know how to deal with what had happened to me. But now, with the new tools I've learned from Dr. Brewer, I can appreciate what we have and I can completely live in the little moments that bring me more happiness than I could have ever imagined.

"Good." He flashes me a grin before leaning down and sealing his lips over mine. I sigh into his kiss and mold my body to his as I run my hands down his arms before going back up and playing with the hair at the base of his neck. He hums against my lips and a shiver runs down my spine as he pulls away. "Shit, babe. We've got people coming over soon."

"We can be quick," I whisper, leaning for another kiss but he cuts it short as he pulls back and laughs, shaking his head.

"Later, I promise. I've got a surprise for you before everyone gets here."

I frown as I drop my hands to my sides and he chuckles again, poking my bottom lip as it juts out in a pout. The sound of laughter has me fighting back a smile of my own as he spins me around and presses up against my back, covering my eyes with his hands. His lips brush against my ear as he instructs me to start walking and a wave of desire floods my body. God, I can't get enough of this man these days and if it wasn't for work and the need to eat, I don't either of us would get out of bed.

We stop and he turns me to the side as he presses his lips just below my ear. "Ready?"

"Yes," I answer as I fidget in his arms. What the hell kind of surprise could he have planned for much in such a short amount of time? We just got the keys yesterday and he hasn't left my side since then. As he pulls his hands away, my eyes flutter open and my lips part as I gaze around the room, taking it all in. The once white walls are now a pale mint green color and there is a gorgeous mahogany crib set up on one wall with a matching changing table across from it.

"When did you have time to do all this?" I whirl around to face him and he grins as he reaches up and brushes his thumb over my cheek.

"I left the back door unlocked after we came to look at the house yesterday and I had some of the guys set this up last night. They only did a little 'cause I figured you would want to decorate yourself…"

"And because they're bikers, not interior designers?" I ask and he laughs, nodding.

"That, too. Anyway, I know it's not much but it's a start and hopefully soon, we'll have a baby to bring home to this room."

I wrap my arms around his neck and kiss him, unable to put into words how much I love what he did for me. As his tongue tangles with mine in a heated kiss, I can see the life we both want, images of babies running down the hallway, their little feet slapping against the hardwood floors and their laughter echoing off of the walls fill my mind and tears sting my eyes. That life is something I want so, so badly and I can't wait until it becomes a reality.

Wyatt's hand slips into my hair and my back hits the doorjamb as he groans and grinds his hips into me, his kiss becoming more heated. I slip my hands around his back and under his shirt, pressing them against his skin as he starts kissing down my neck. The air punches out of my lungs as I tip my head back and close my eyes, warmth spreading through my body with each press of his lips.

"Baby…" I breathe, my fingertips digging into his skin as his teeth graze my neck. "I need you."

The doorbell rings and both of our heads snap up as we struggle to catch our breaths. His eyes meet mine and I'm ready to tell all our friends to go get lost when he pulls away with a tortured look on her face.

"We're picking this up later." His voice leaves no room for argument and I barely hold back a whimper as I grip the door frame to keep myself up right. The doorbell rings again and he runs his hand through his hair. "Also, you stay here until you don't look like you want me to fuck your brains out."

I run my hand up my body as my skin tingles with need before I reach out, grabbing his hand and pulling him back to me. I steal a kiss and another. "Maybe just fuck my brains out real quick and then I won't look like that anymore."

"Baby," he groans, his eyes closing as he sucks in a breath and rolls his forehead against mine. "They're at the goddamn door."

"They can wait."

Whoever it is starts banging on the front door and the sound reverberates through the empty house as Wyatt growls. He pulls away from me again and takes a few steps back before holding his hand up when I push off of the door frame to follow him. "I was serious before. There is no way in hell I'm letting the guys see you like this. I'll fucking murder them."

"They're all married now, Wyatt."

"Doesn't matter," he growls, turning and stomping away from me. A smirk spreads across my face as I suck air into my lungs and try to get my mind off my husband's naked body and all the things I want him to be doing to me. The sound of muffled voices drift down the hallway and I take another deep breath as I smooth my hands over my maxi dress before combing my fingers through my hair. When my heart rate has finally slowed to a more acceptable pace, I walk out into the living room with a smile pasted on my face.

"Hey, sorry to hear about your mom," Wyatt says to Kodiak as I step up next to him and slip my hand into his. He glances over at me, his eyes still raging with need and my tummy does a little flip as I turn my gaze back to Kodiak and Tate. I'm glad they're the first ones to show up since I already met them a few days ago when they stopped by my apartment so Kodiak could talk to Wyatt.

"What's going on with your mom?"

Kodiak's face is somber as he sighs and Tate wraps her arm around his waist. "She passed away a couple of days ago."

"Oh my God, I'm so sorry," I whisper, pain blooming in my chest as the smile melts off my face and Wyatt gives my hand a squeeze, reminding me that he is here and I can lean if I need to. A feeling of calm washes over me as I glance up at Kodiak. "What happened?"

"They said it was an aneurysm." Tears shine in his eyes and he clears his throat. "I guess the good thing is that it happened fast and she didn't feel any pain."

I nod, my heart aching for him as memories from the day of my parents' funeral flashes through my mind and the ache I'm so used to intensifies. With all of the things going on and how happy I've been, I've been thinking about them a lot lately, wishing they could be here to see what I made of myself and the wonderful man who always has my back.

"How is your sister holding up?" Wyatt asks and Kodiak clears his throat again, nodding. He looks thankful for the distraction and I can't say that I blame him. I'm pretty fucking thankful for it, too.

"She's doing okay. As soon as she gets all Mom's stuff taken care of, I told her I want her down here with us."

I scowl.

Is he not going to go to her funeral?

"You're not going to head up to Alaska?" Wyatt asks, beating me to it and Kodiak shakes his head, glancing over at Tate, who rolls her eyes.

"Nah. Mom wanted to be cremated and have her ashes thrown into the ocean and we can do that here. Besides, I can't leave Tate right now."

"For the of God, Lincoln," she growls, pinning him with a glare. "Women have been having babies since the dawn of time. I'll be okay alone."

His gaze snaps to hers, hard and determined. "I'm not going."

"I swear to God…"

"Just keep the taser in your purse, woman," he growls and they stare at each other for a second before she rolls her eyes and turns away from him.

"I'm not going to break, you know."

He shakes his head again, completely ignoring her comment as my gaze bounces between the two of them. Wyatt told me that Smith's wife, Quinn, and Moose's wife, Juliette, we're pregnant but he never mentioned Tate.

"You're pregnant, too?" Wyatt asks like he's reading my mind, glancing between the two of them and they share a look before Tate turns to us, fighting back a smile.

"Yep. We're going to tell everyone today."

The doorbell rings again and Wyatt release my hand to go answer it as I watch Lincoln and Tate share another look full of love. When Wyatt told me he wanted to introduce me to everyone, I didn't really know what to expect but if these two are any indication, I think I'm going to like them. I was already leaning that way, though, after hearing Wyatt talk about how they gave him a purpose when he was lost and became like a second family to him.

I just hope they don't judge me too harshly for the past.

Three more couples pile into the living room and Wyatt walks back to my side and introduces me to them.

"Babe, this is Storm, his wife, Ali, and their baby girl, Magnolia." There is a hint of humor in his tone as he says the baby's name and I scowl at him but he just ignores it as he points to the second couple. "This is Chance and his wife, Carly, and this is Moose and Juliette."

"Hi, it's nice to meet all of you," I tell them as my belly flips and my heart jumps into my throat. God, why am I so nervous?

"Well, it's real nice to meet you since Fuzz here didn't even tell anyone you existed until like a month ago," Chance says and my head jerks back before I turn to look at Wyatt with a scowl.

"Fuzz?"

"Yeah, you know, 'cause he was a cop for a hot minute," Moose says and my eyes widen as I study Wyatt's face but he just shrugs. Oh, that's definitely something we will be talking about later. Actually, now that I think about it, I could see Wyatt as a cop but he would be one of those cops who straddles the line of right and wrong, the one that goes too far to find answers and put the truly bad guys away.

The doorbell rings again, pulling me out of my fantasy of Wyatt in a police uniform and he kisses my cheek as he releases my hand and walks over to the door.

"Where is my best friend?" Eden asks, her voice booming through the room and I shake my head as Wyatt stands back to let her in. She points a finger in his face. "You've been keeping her from me."

"She's my wife," he growls and I sigh as everyone else looks on in amusement. I wouldn't say that Wyatt and Eden's first meeting didn't go well but there is some definite tension between them and as hard as they are both trying to get along for me, they tend to butt heads. Eden dismisses his comment with a flippant hand wave as she turns to me and smiles.

"Pip-squeak!"

A few chuckles fill the room and I roll my eyes as she wraps me up in a hug. "Hey, Edie."

"I love the place," she says as she pulls away and glances at Wyatt as he walks up to us. "You did all right, I suppose."

"Will you be nice?"

Her eyes widen and her mouth drops open, her face the picture of innocence as she turns back to me. "What? I'm not allowed to bust his balls a little bit?"

I roll my eyes again as Wyatt shakes his head and Eden turns to look at all the people staring at her.

"Uh, you gonna introduce me to everyone?"

The doorbell rings and as Wyatt goes to answer it, I introduce her to all of the guys and their wives before doing the same when Lillian walks in. By the time I'm finished, the last group is walking through the door.

"Everyone, this is my wife, Piper," he says as he returns to my side and takes my hand. "Pip, this is Blaze, our president, Smith and his wife, Quinn, Henn and his wife, Kady, and this asshole is Streak."

Streak flashes a grin at me. "Don't believe anything these fuckers say about me."

"It's all true," Wyatt whispers in my ear and Streak pins him with a glare as he laughs. Everyone stares at Wyatt with confused looks on their faces.

"Jesus Christ, dude," Smith says, shaking his head before he motions to me. "You're like a whole new man with this one around."

I arch a brow. "Oh?"

"Oh, yeah," Streak says, nodding as he walks forward and throws his arm over my shoulders. "He was one moody son of a bitch without you."

"Get your arm off of my wife," Wyatt growls, venom in

his tone and I turn to him with wide eyes as Streak pulls his arm off my shoulders and groans.

"Oh my God, I'm so fucking sick of all the couples. We need to get some fresh blood up in this club, people that aren't already shacked up."

Blaze scoffs, crossing his arms over his chest. "Yeah, we'll put it to a vote the next time we have church."

"Perfect. Now, let's start grillin'. I'm fucking starving."

"Actually," Kodiak says and everyone turns to him. "We have somethin' to tell y'all."

They share that look again and this time, I smile with them since I'm lucky enough to be in on the secret. Tate turns to the guys, flashing them a wide smile.

"I'm pregnant!"

"Jesus fucking Christ," Streak groans before anyone can say anything else, scrubbing his hands down his face. "Why don't we just start a goddamn daycare at this point?"

"Hey, that's a good idea," Storm says with a gleam in his eyes and Ali nods, grinning as Streak continues throwing his little temper tantrum. Blaze nods.

"We'll vote on that at church, too."

Streak groans loudly, rolling his eyes. "Is there any beer in this fucking place? I can't take much more of this shit."

Everyone laughs as he trudges into the kitchen to search for liquor and I look around at the rest of the group, an unfamiliar feeling settling into my chest as they all turn to congratulate Kodiak and Tate. I know I just met most of them but as I look at their faces, I can't help but think that for the first time in a long time, I truly have a home and a family.

Every Little Thing

A.M. Myers

Chapter Twenty-One
Wyatt

I gaze out at the booths around me, full of stuffed animals and other various toys for kids to win as lights flash and sirens go off in a chaotic symphony that brings a smile to my face and reminds me of my childhood. The smell of popcorn and cotton candy drifts through the air and kids race past my booth, headed for the rides at the other end of the park. Storm and Ali are working the booth directly across from me and next to them is Smith and Quinn. On one side of my booth is Moose and Juliette and Chance and Carly are running the booth on the other side. Henn volunteered to run one of the rides and Kady is somewhere serving food with Blaze. The only ones missing are Kodiak and Tate but only because she had a doctor's appointment to make sure everything was okay with the baby - something Kodiak insisted on after she felt a little bit of pain at our housewarming barbecue last night. I glance over at Streak on the other side of the booth and frown. Piper couldn't get out of work or she would have been here with me, running the ring toss game instead of this grumpy fucker and I can't believe how much I fucking miss her.

About a month ago, the club was contacted by a few people to help work this carnival to raise money for a group of kids in a really bad bus crash. Most of them made it out okay with minor injuries but three of them are still stuck in the ICU and the community has been doing everything they can for them as well as the driver's wife after he died in the crash. Some of the guys, namely Streak, weren't too big on the idea but honestly, I loved it as soon as Blaze brought it up. It means that our neighbors are finally starting to see us as more than just a bunch of rowdy bikers and we're finally shedding more of our past reputation. Plus, this is our mission now - to help people - and that comes in many forms despite what Streak thinks.

"Thank God, this is almost over," Streak bitches, leaning back in his metal folding chair and crossing his arms over his chest. I glance back at him and shake my head.

"If you're going to be such a whiney little bitch then why did you even come?"

He scoffs. "Because Blaze made me. Said I needed some goddamn perspective."

"He's right. What the fuck is your problem lately?" I ask and he shakes his head, refusing to look in my direction.

"Nothing."

"Bullshit."

"Mama, I wanna win this one," a little voice says and I turn back to the front of the booth, smiling as I crouch down in front of a little boy with a mop of brown hair and bright blue eyes. He points to the giant penguin above my head, jumping up and down in excitement as his mom eyes us warily, Streak more than me. I resist the urge to roll my eyes. I have spent the whole day listening to his grumpy ass and picking up his slack so I'm done. He can just fucking leave for all I care. I point to the penguin.

"You want this guy?"

The little boy nods. "Yes, sir!"

"Well, you know what you got to do, right?" I ask. He can't be more than four or five and he's fucking adorable as he scowls up at me before his gaze flicks over to the game. Finally, he looks back at me and shakes his head.

"No, I dunno."

I stand up and grab four rings off of the table before showing them to him. "Don't worry, it's easy. All you gotta do is take these rings and toss them. If they land on a bottle, you win."

I'm not supposed to give a prize that big out unless they land all four rings but we're almost done for the day and I can't say no to this kid. His eyes light up as a grin stretches across his face and he nods, holding his hands out to me.

"I can do that."

"All right, bud. Let's see it," I say as I hand him the rings and his mom flashes me a more reassured smile as she steps up behind him and tries to help him toss his first ring. He shakes her off with a scowl.

"I got this, Mama."

Backing away from him, she holds her hands up in surrender. "Okay, baby."

He narrows his eyes as he focuses on the group of bottles and his little tongue pokes out of the side of his mouth. All I can think about is doing something like this with my own kid someday and I'm so lost in the fantasy, I almost miss his first toss. The ring hits the top of one bottle before sliding between another two and he sighs.

"Wow. That was so close, dude," I say, flashing him a thumbs up. "Try again. I bet you'll get it this time."

His gaze falls back to the bottles, his concentration straining his face as he lifts the next ring and it sails through the air. It's not a very graceful throw but I'm impressed for his age and when it lands on one of the bottle in the middle, his eyes pop open and he jumps up.

"I got it!"

I clap my hands and crouch down again, holding my hand up for a high-five. He slaps his little hand against mine before spinning in a circle, doing a little happy dance. Laughing, I stand up and grab the giant penguin off of the hook. The goddamn thing is almost as big as me and I have no idea how he is going to carry it.

"You want to try throwing the other two or do you just want your prize?"

He immediately drops the rings back on the counter and reaches for the penguin in my arms, his hands opening and closing in a "gimme" gesture. I chuckle as I pass the toy over to him and he almost falls back as he struggles to wrap his arms around its belly.

"Here, why don't you let Mama carry that for you?" his mom asks, trying to take it from him but he rips it out of her grasp and wobbles on his feet before righting himself.

"No. I got this."

His little voice is muffled by the toy and I laugh as she flashes me a look.

261

"Thank you."

"No problem," I reply, nodding. She turns and takes off after the kid as he struggles to carry his new friend, his steps faltering as the penguin's weight throws him off balance. Chuckling, I shake my head and turn back to Streak. The smile falls from my face when he glares at me and I grit my teeth. I'm done with this fucker.

"Hey, our shift's up," Storm calls out to all of us and Streak jumps up so fast he almost knocks the chair over.

"Thank fucking God." He stomps out of the booth and I roll my eyes as I follow behind him. Blaze walks up to us as we all meet between the rows of booths and the next shift files into the spaces we just abandoned.

"I got something I want to run by you so head to the clubhouse before y'all go home," he instructs and I nod, irritated that I'm not going to be able to get to Piper sooner but I do need to grab the folders out of my room. Since getting back together with Piper, she's stolen a lot of my attention and the cases got put on the back burner but I need to start digging into them again. Especially now that I have more to lose.

I follow the rest of the group back out to the parking lot where our bikes are parked and the roar of our engines flood the air around us as we pull out onto the street in a single file line. My mind drifts to the cases again as we drive back to the clubhouse and I hope that the time I've spent away from them will help me see things in a new light. Maybe I'll have a new perspective. Smith was right last night when he said I was a brand new man with Piper. Hell, I can't even remember that guy and I can't help but think that maybe that was the reason I couldn't come up with a lead. Maybe now, with more to fight for, I'll finally be able to see things clearly. Then again, maybe I shouldn't get my hopes up. I still can't convince anymore of my brothers that there is something going on and now that Piper is back in my life, I'm terrified of actually being right. What the fuck would I do if something happens to her? How would I survive?

Shaking my head, I push the thoughts from my mind as we pull into the clubhouse parking lot. They are too damn painful and I can't think like that or I'll go crazy. There isn't anything I wouldn't do to protect her, though. She is my whole goddamn world and I've already lived enough of my life without her. After parking in our usual spots, we all climb off our bikes and everyone jokes around as we make our way to the door. I step out ahead of everyone else, eager to get the files and get back to Piper and when I pull the door open and step into the bar, all my thoughts screech to a halt.

What. The. Fuck?

Autopsy photos of Dina, Laney, and Sammy are plastered all over the walls over and over again, so close together that you can't even see the blue paint that Ali, Carly, and Tate put on the walls a few months back. Some are in color and others are in black and white but they all stare back at me, taunting me with my inability to figure this shit out. My mind is blank, struggling to take it all in at once and process it as my heart thunders in my chest, wild and chaotic.

"Holy fuck," someone whispers behind me and I glance over my shoulder as Storm stares at the photos with wide eyes and pulls Ali closer. She gasps and a tear slips down her cheek as she looks around at all the women we lost and my stomach sinks like a stone. Not a single wall in the place isn't covered in their faces but right in the middle, written in red above the war room door is a message that confirms all my worst fears.

I AM WINNING

"Girls…" Blaze says, his voice haunted as his eyes travel around the room and I realize that everyone is standing behind me now, staring in horror at our home. "Go outside and wait for us."

"No," Chance snaps, shaking his head, his body tensing as he wraps a protective arm around Carly. "Not outside. Not out in the open."

Blaze nods and blows out a breath, almost like he's collecting himself. "Right. Upstairs, then."

Chance nods in agreement as Smith and Moose do the same before kissing their girls. The girls huddle together and file toward the stairs, whispering to each other in frantic, scared voices as they climb up and after they disappear down the hallway, I release a breath but we all are silent as we try to sort through our thoughts and this new reality we've found ourselves in.

I've never wanted to be wrong more in my goddamn life than I do right now.

Running my hand through my hair, I try to think about what this means for all of us but there is so much we need to do, so much to plan and prepare for that I don't even know where to start. I wish this was a dream or just the worst case scenario playing in my head.

I wish that I had investigated harder… been more insistent that something was going on when Kodiak challenged me.

I wish I would have been on Rodriguez's case more.

I wish I would have found anything to help us solve this.

"Streak," Blaze calls, snapping me out of my thoughts. His voice is authoritative and I think it puts us all just a little more at ease to know he's got a plan. Or, at least, I hope he does. Streak walks up to his side and they lock eyes. "Go check the security footage."

"On it." He nods and takes off up the stairs, disappearing down the hallway to his room as I turn to look at the rest of the guys as I try to force my mind to work. What the hell do we do? Where do we go from here? Storm turns and claps his hand on my shoulder as he shakes his head.

"Man… I'm sorry we didn't listen to you."

I shake my head and blow out a breath. "It doesn't matter now."

Hell, it's not their fault and I don't blame them one bit. Even I was starting to believe that it was all in my head but as I turn back around and stare up at the walls and the message left for us, my stomach twists and my heart climb up into my throat. If I close my eyes, I can see a photo of any of our girls up there with the other three and I clench my fists. He's been ahead of us at every turn, so far ahead that we didn't even realize we should be watching out for him and we're so far behind this guy, so lost that I don't even know how we're going to stop him. An image of another photo pops into my head, this time of Piper next to Dina, Laney, and Sammy and my stomach rolls again.

Fuck.

I'm going to throw up.

"What do we do?" Smith asks, echoing my thoughts and as I open my eyes and turn back to look at them, they all shake their heads.

I know what I want to do. I want to take my wife and disappear until this is all over but I can't do that. These men are my brothers and I won't abandon them.

Not now.

Not ever.

"Goddamn it!" Streak bellows from upstairs and we all turn as he comes barreling down the steps with a laptop in both hands and rage painted across his face. "I've got nothing!"

He throws one of the laptops against the wall and it smashes into several pieces as a few photos float to the floor. It's so quiet that the sound bounces off the walls, taunting us from all angles as he marches over to us. Tossing the other laptop onto the table, he spins it to face us as a video begins playing. The front door to the clubhouse opens and a man dressed in all black with a hood pulled up over his head steps inside, tucking something into his pocket.

"Who forgot to lock the fucking door?" Blaze asks and I glance over my shoulder as everyone shakes their head.

"It was locked, Blaze," Henn assures him. "Checked it myself."

We turn back to the video as the man sets a thick stack

of the photos down on one of the tables and pulls out a can of something.

"Is that glue?" I hiss, my eyes widening as he pops the top open and paints the substance inside on the back of the first photo before slapping it on the wall. We all watch in horror as he continues down the line, blanketing our clubhouse in the photos and I clench my fists as fury twists through my body. The guy is completely average, just like every other descriptions we have for him and I shake my head as I clench my teeth so hard my jaw aches.

"Please tell me you got his face," Chance hisses, his shoulders tight and his face serious. Streak slams his fist into the table before blowing out a breath.

"No. Because three of my cameras were disabled before he ever even showed up and the others never caught an image of his face. Not once during the entire two hours he was pasting these fucking things on the walls."

"How is that even possible?" Smith asks and Streak shakes his head and scrubs both of his hands over his hair.

"I don't want to give the guy props but fuck, he's good…"

My heart stops for a second and my stomach drops as we all look at each other with wide eyes and fear creeping into our gazes.

Fear for each other.

Fear for our families and fear for our club.

Holy fuck…

Who in the hell are we dealing with?

A.M. Myers

Every Little Thing

Chapter Twenty-Two
Piper

Leaning back in my chair, I stare down at the last text I sent Wyatt over an hour ago when I finished with my last client of the day that he still hasn't replied to as my leg bounces incessantly and my stomach knots with worry. It's not like him to not answer me. In fact, I would say that he is almost perfect in that regard because his responses are always so quick. If anything, I am the one that takes time to answer because I'm busy with a client or right in the middle of editing photos and I can't help but jump to all of the worst case scenarios.

Maybe I should try calling him...

My finger hovers over the phone icon for a moment before I blow out a breath and shake my head. No, he's okay and I'm just overreacting. Shaking my head, I put my phone back in my pocket, telling myself over and over again that he's okay and I need to relax as I absentmindedly nibble on the donut I grabbed off of the snack table but I can't taste it.

What if something happened to him?

What if he crashed his bike and he is lying in a ditch somewhere, injured, and I'm here at my stupid support group, eating a damn donut?

I look down at the offending pastry in my hand with disgust before getting up and trudging over to the garbage can in the corner of the room. Wyatt has been so supportive of my issues and he has been encouraging me to come back to meetings since I've been so wrapped up in us lately but on a night like tonight when I can't get ahold of him, it feels like I shouldn't be here. After tossing my food in the trash, I turn and drag myself back to my seat as I glance at the door. Maybe I should just go now, before Dr. Brewer starts the meeting so I can make sure he is okay. As I sink into my seat, still chewing over the possibility, Dr. Brewer stands up and claps her hands, commanding the attention of everyone else.

"Let's get started, everyone."

Glancing around, I look for Lillian but I can't find her anywhere and I scowl.

I wonder if she is coming tonight.

She tends to skip more meetings than I do and I get the hint that there is a big part to her story she still doesn't want to tell no matter how much Dr. Brewer pushes her. I can't say that I blame her, though. Some things are just too painful to talk about and no one understands that more than me.

As everyone finds their seats, the door bursts open and Lillian runs into the room.

"Sorry, I'm late," she says and Dr. Brewer nods. Lillian enters our little circle and sinks into the chair next to me as

I flash her a smile. She releases a breath and sets her purse on the floor, her body slumping in her seat.

"Okay?"

She nods. "Yes. Traffic was awful, though. Something about an accident on the interstate."

The haunted look in her eyes makes my heart ache for her and I shake my head but keep my mouth shut. Lillian is not as far along in her recovery as I am and she has a whole hell of a lot of walls up. I do know that three years ago, she and her fiancé were driving to dinner when something happened and he was killed. She always refers to it as an accident but the look on Dr. Brewer's face every time she does tells me there is more to it. Once, she slipped up when we were out to dinner and said that when she closed her eyes at night, she could still see that man but as soon as the words came out of her mouth, she stopped talking and I didn't want to press too hard. I know how fragile people can be and if she's not ready to talk about it, I'm not going to force it from her.

"Okay, who would like to go…"

The door opens, cutting Dr. Brewer off and I glance over my shoulder as Tate walks into the room, looking apprehensive as hell. What the hell is she doing here? My mind spins, wondering if she is here because something happened to Wyatt but then I notice how nervous she looks and I flash her a kind smile. Her gaze meets mine and she sucks in a breath before confidently walking across the room and sinking into the open chair on my other side. Dr. Brewer smiles at her and Tate shifts in her seat.

"Hi. Would you like to introduce yourself?"

Tate shakes her head and Dr. Brewer nods in

271

understanding. A lot of people like to sit through a few meetings before they feel comfortable enough to tell their own story and I was one of them. I came for an entire month before I even shared my name. As Dr. Brewer turns her attention to someone else, I nudge her arm.

"Hey."

She smiles but I can see the apprehension in her eyes. "Hey, I hope this is okay. Fuzz told Lincoln about it and he thought it might help me."

"Of course," I tell her, nodding. Things between Wyatt and me have been going really well and he knows everything now so I have nothing to hide from him, not that I think Tate would spill my secrets. "You can talk to me sometime, too, if you're not comfortable telling your deep dark secrets to the whole group."

"Thank you," she answers before chewing on her bottom lip. "I don't mean to be rude but Lincoln didn't really know your story…"

"Piper," Dr. Brewer says, cutting Tate off as we both glance up at her. "Maybe you'd like to share your story for our new members?"

She motions to Tate and a man across from me who can't seem to sit still and I nod as I take a deep breath, mentally preparing myself to relive the worst night of my life, and sit up a little straighter.

"Okay… My name is Piper and I'm here because… when I was nine years old, a man broke into my house and murdered both of my parents before trying to kill me." I can feel Tate's wide eyes boring into the side of my head but I keep going. "I never really learned how to deal with the pain of that and when my husband joined the Marines and deployed, I kind of lost it."

Dr. Brewer flashes me a look full of displeasure at my attempt to break up the tension I feel coursing through my body and I sigh.

"I lived on the streets and I honestly can't tell you what was real and what wasn't. I was found on a park bench about a year later and taken to the hospital where I started getting the help I needed."

Dr. Brewer nods. "Thank you, Piper. You have missed the last few meetings so is there anything new you would like to share?"

"Um…" I whisper, fighting back a smile as color stains my cheeks. "Yeah, actually. I reconnected with my husband after being apart for ten years and I told him the truth about what happened when I left him ten years ago."

"And how would you say things are going?"

"Really well. Back then, I told him I had fallen in love with someone else… I don't really know why… but when we saw each other again a month ago, he understandably wanted answers. Ever since I told him the truth, he's been incredibly supportive and I feel really good. I am still just trying to take it one day at a time and I'm remaining very conscious of how I'm feeling but I'm happier than I've been in a really long time."

She flashes me a wide smile, nodding in approval as she turns her focus to someone else. I know that won't be the end of it, though. At my next appointment, she will want to delve deeper but I hope she can see how strong I feel and how happy I am. Tate nudges me, keeping her voice low as another member of the group begins telling his story.

"I'm sorry about your parents."

I shake my head, never quite sure how to respond when someone says that to me.

"I know how you feel. My mother… she was murdered last year…"

Pain blooms in my chest as I reach over and grab her hand in silent support. I don't offer her the same apology she did to me because I know it doesn't make it any better.

"Anytime you want to talk, I'm available. Okay? I won't have any answers for you but sometimes it helps to just get the words out there."

She nods and I give her hand a squeeze before releasing it. The rest of the meeting passes quickly as I listen to how everyone else has been coping with their issues and when Dr. Brewer dismisses us, I pull my phone out of my pocket again, my belly flipping as I search for a message.

Still nothing.

"Hey," I say to Tate. "Is Kodiak with the guys?"

"No. He insisted on taking me to see the baby doctor today after I had that little cramp at your place last night."

"Is everything okay?"

"Yes," she answers, rolling her eyes as we stand up and grab our chairs to stack them against the wall before we leave. A huge smile stretches across her face. "Although, you should have seen his face when they said they could see two babies in there."

My eyes widen. "Twins? That must have been a shock."

"Not for me. I'm a twin and my half brother was a twin before his brother died but I think Lincoln let that little tidbit slip his mind when I told him he had knocked me up."

I laugh, imagining that big man freaking out over two little babies.

"Although, I did tell him I'm going to tase him during each contraction for doing this to me because that part is going to suck."

"You guys certainly have an interesting relationship," I answer with a laugh, remembering Kodiak's comments about tasers at my house, and she flashes me a devious grin as we walk outside.

"Oh, you have no idea. We should grab lunch sometime and I'll tell you all about it."

I nod. "Deal."

Her phone starts ringing and she rolls her eyes as she pulls it out of her pocket and checks the screen before flashing it at me.

"I gotta go before the caveman decides to ride down here to get me."

I nod as I check my phone again, my heart dropping when I still don't have any new messages. "Yeah, I gotta go find my husband."

"Good luck with that," she answers with a laugh as she walks to her car and waves good-bye. I stare at my phone for another second before dialing Wyatt's number. It rings in my ear endlessly before his voice mail picks up and tears sting my eyes as I disconnect the call and shove my phone in my pocket.

"He's okay," I whisper, squeezing my eyes shut as my heart races. "He's okay."

"Hey," a voice says and I open my eyes, glancing to my side as Lillian offers me a smile. "You feel like grabbing some coffee with me or something?"

I shake my head. "I really wish I could, Lil, but I've got to get home."

"Everything okay?"

"Yeah," I answer before shaking my head. "I don't know... It's probably nothing but Wyatt hasn't answered me back for a while now and I'm just worried."

I close my eyes again, trying not to let the panic take over but all I can see is Wyatt hurt, a mangled bike and blood everywhere before the image of Wyatt with bullet holes all over his body pops into my mind. It doesn't linger, there and gone in a flash but it's enough to make me feel like I'm going to crumble.

"Hey," Lillian says, her voice firm. "Look at me."

I open my eyes and she grabs my shoulders, holding me steady.

"Take a breath."

With my heart hammering into my ribs, I take a deep breath and keep my gaze locked with hers as a little bit of calm descends over me. She nods and I do it again, telling myself not to panic, that he is okay as my pulse starts to slow and my head feels clearer.

"You good?" she asks, eyeing me warily and I nod. Releasing me, she blows out a breath and shakes her head.

"Listen, Pip... I know you're happy being with Wyatt again but I just want you to be careful... I don't want to see you go backward because of him and if he's not taking your needs into account, maybe this isn't for the best."

I shake my head. "It's not like that, Lil. Wyatt has been amazing but I can't expect him to be at my beck and call at all times just because I worry. I'll talk to Dr. Brewer about ways to deal with it."

"Promise me you'll be careful and not rush things?" she asks and I can't help but think that it's a little too late for

276

that. My friends know about Wyatt and me being back together and buying the house together but they don't know about us trying to have a baby. I nod.

"I'll be careful. I promise."

She sighs. "Okay. Well, I guess I'm going to head home, then."

"You should call Eden. I'm sure she would love to go grab a coffee with you."

"Right," she answers with a smirk. "I think you meant to say cocktail."

I laugh because she is spot on and I give her a little shrug. "I think bars serve coffee, too, so then you'll both be happy."

"You know what, maybe I will give her a call." She turns to her car as she pulls her phone out of her bag. "Have a good night and let me know that everything is okay once you find Wyatt."

I nod as I watch her walk to her car. "I will."

As soon as she pulls out of the parking lot, my stomach twists into knots again and I grip my phone tightly as I walk to my car and unlock it. Slipping behind the wheel, I dial Wyatt's number again and it rings in my ear as my pulse picks up.

"Answer the damn phone, baby."

When his voice mail picks up again, I end the call and toss it into the passenger seat before starting the engine. I peel out of the parking lot a little too fast but I can't even bring myself to care right now. The most important thing is making sure Wyatt is okay. I'll start at the house and if he's not there, I'll go to the clubhouse.

What if he's not there either?

Shaking my head, I push the thought from my mind and focus on the road in front of me. I refuse to jump to conclusions and freak out before I know anything else. One thing is for sure, when I do find him, we need to talk. Not that I know *what* we are going to talk about but I also feel like he can't just ghost me like this. I've never seen the man go anywhere without his phone so why isn't he answering my calls? I remember what I told Lillian about not expecting Wyatt to be at my beck and call. What I told her is true and I know it's not fair to him that I freak out at the littlest sign of trouble but I also need him to be a little considerate of what I'll go through when he goes MIA. Sighing, I pull down down our street.

God, I am a fucking mess.

When I do find him, maybe I should ask him if he's sure he wants to be with someone as crazy as me. Though, I'm pretty sure I don't want to know the answer.

As I pull up in front of the house, my heart climbs into my throat. The Bronco is here but his bike isn't which means neither is Wyatt. I grip the wheel tighter and suck in a breath as I nod to myself.

"Don't freak out yet."

The roar of an engine cuts through my thoughts and I gasp. My head jerks up just as Wyatt pulls into the driveway on his bike. My body deflates and I release a breath as a wave of relief rushes through me. I put the car in park and fall back into my seat as tears well up in my eyes and all I can think about is being his arms. I don't think I'll be able to take a full breath until I can feel him. When I glance up again, Wyatt is marching over to my car, a look I can't decipher on his face but it makes my heart skip a beat.

He reaches my door and yanks it open, his eyes intense as he stares down at me.

"Turn off the car."

I reach forward and turn the key as I study his face. "What's wrong?"

As soon as the car is off, he leans in and unbuckles my seat belt before gently pulling me out of the car and into his arms. A flood of calm settles over me at his touch but there is this nagging thought in the back of my mind that something is very, very wrong. Holding me so close that it's difficult to breathe, he buries his face in my neck and releases a breath. I can feel the tension in his body and it seeps into me as my mind spins with possibilities as I wrap my arms around his neck, my chest feeling tight.

"What happened, baby?" I whisper and he shakes his head. His lips press to my neck like he needs the kiss more than I do and my stomach twists as fear snakes down my spine. "Please talk to me, Wyatt."

He pulls back and looks down the street before meeting my eyes. The haunted look dancing in his eyes makes my heart race and my hands shake as tears sting my eyes. "Let's go inside."

"Okay. Just let me grab my things."

Without another word, he releases me, grabs my hand, and reaches into the car, grabbing my purse and my phone out of the passenger seat before pulling me into his side and slamming the door shut. He holds me close as we walk up the front walk, his eyes flicking around the neighborhood like he's waiting for someone to ambush us. My heart crashes against my rib cage and tears fill my eyes as the hair on my arms raises.

I swear I can feel someone's eyes on me…

As soon as we get in the house, Wyatt shuts the door and makes sure it's locked before he runs into the kitchen. I follow him, my hands shaking and watch as he does the same to the back door.

"Wyatt," I call as he walks past me into the hallway and he holds one finger up before disappearing into our room. When he comes out again, he has a pistol in his hand and he goes to the window, pulling the new curtains I just put up yesterday back to peek outside.

"What is going on?" I yell, desperate as panic claws at my insides and the tears start slipping down my face. His head jerks to me. The need to keep watch wars with his need to comfort me on his face and after a second, he sets the gun on the dining room table before closing the distance between us and pulling me into his arms. A sob shakes my body as I grip his t-shirt and I can't tell if it's fear or comfort taking over my body as he presses his lips to the top of my head.

"I'm sorry, Pip."

I shake my head as I pull back to look up at him, wiping my face. "Don't apologize. Just tell me what is going on."

"Okay," he answers with a sigh as he runs his fingers through his hair and nods. His mind is spinning, I can see it plain as day on his face and I know something serious is going on but I can't even come up with a single reason to explain his behavior. Wyatt isn't the one who gets scared, I am. So what is it that has him so freaked? He sighs again like he's working up the courage to tell me and nods.

"The guys and I were working at the charity carnival this afternoon and when we went back to the clubhouse, someone had broken in. They plastered pictures of these girls who were killed all over the walls…"

"Wait… what the hell are you saying?" I ask as I struggle to process the words coming out of his mouth. A break-in at the clubhouse and dead girls? Why does the club have anything to do with dead girls? He grabs my shoulders and meets my gaze, keeping me steady.

"You know what the club does, right?"

I nod. He explained it to me the other night but I still don't see the connection.

"Three girls that we have helped are dead now and up until this afternoon, I was the only one who thought they were connected. Someone is coming after the club and they have been for a while now."

My knees feel weak as my heartbeat thunders in my ears. "You're scaring me, Wyatt."

"I know," he whispers, a tortured look on his face. "And I hate every second of it but I need you to be scared, baby. Fuck, I'm scared."

"Who is doing this? Are we really in that much danger?"

He shakes his head and releases me. "I don't know…"

I open my mouth to try and ask him another question but he turns and heads for the front door, unlocking it and ripping it open before marching outside.

"Wyatt?!"

Frozen in the middle of my living room, I stare at the open door, my heart racing out of control as I try to take deep breaths to calm myself but it's not working anymore.

What the hell is going on?

He runs back into the room with three folders full of

papers in his hand and slams the door behind him, locking it again before he walks over to the dining room table and slaps them down.

"These are the girls. The club helped each one of them and shortly afterward, they were murdered. At first, we thought it was their boyfriends or husband or whoever we helped them get away from until this last girl…" He flips open a folder. "…Sammy was found dead. The guy we helped her get away from is dead so he couldn't have been the one to kill her. That's when I started looking into the cases but no one else believed that it was anything more than bad luck. With the work we do, it's not impossible that a girl would go back to her man, you know? Abusive relationships and the emotions that go along with them are complicated."

I nod, my mind starting to piece it all together. "And what happened today?"

"We came back from the carnival and their autopsy pictures were blown up and pasted on every wall in the clubhouse like some kind of demented wallpaper with a note that said, 'I am winning'."

"Winning?" I breathe, the implications crashing down on me. "Winning what?"

"The game? Fuck, I don't know, Pip… Apparently we really pissed someone off and he's been planning his revenge for a while."

"Who is he?"

He throw his hands up. "I don't know, that's the problem. I have no fucking clue. For months I've been looking into these cases and I can't find any evidence for who this guy is."

"He's a ghost," I murmur, my mind reeling back to the night my parents died and the memory of the man who killed them that has been haunting me for years. Reality crashes down around my feet and I shake my head as tears well up in my eyes again. "Oh, God."

Meeting Wyatt's eyes across the room, I shake my head.

"What are we going to do?"

He abandons the files and walks over to me, pulling me close like he needs the security just as much as I do. "We are working on it, okay? The whole club is on board now and all of the guys are going to be pouring over these cases but in the meantime, we all need to be more careful. You feel me?"

I nod, trying to come to terms with everything but my mind is stuck on the fact that once again, a monster is coming for the ones I love. Only this time, I know it and I have to live everyday with that knowledge. The brothers and their wives pop into my mind as my chest starts to ache. They already feel like family to me and I can't imagine losing any of them. And if something happens to Wyatt...

"I'll drive you to work and I will pick you up at the end of the day," he says, interrupting my thoughts as my heart climbs into my throat. "I don't want you at the studio alone and I want the door locked at all times. You can let clients in and out but other than that, it needs to be locked."

"Okay," I breathe, not even bothering to argue with him. There is a part of me that wants to fall apart but there is another part that feels a little bit stronger with a plan to focus on. I'll follow his rules and I'll do what it takes to keep us safe. I meet his gaze. "Have you talked to the cops?"

He nods. "We work with one of the detectives on a regular basis and the second woman killed was his girlfriend so he's already looped in. Blaze called him after we discovered the photos."

"Good." My voice is weak and unsure as I nod my head and drop my gaze to the floor.

Oh, God, this is so crazy. How am I supposed to deal with this on top of all my other shit?

I'm not strong enough.

I'm going to fall apart and then Wyatt will see how truly weak I am.

"Hey," Wyatt says, pulling my gaze back up to his. "Lean on me, baby. I've got you and I'm not going to let anything happen to you."

I nod, feeling a little more secure in the knowledge that I'm not going through this alone. "You've already got so much on your plate. You don't need to be constantly worried about my mental state, Wyatt."

"I am your husband and I love you. None of this means anything without you so whether you let me help you or not, I'm going to worry."

I shake my head, wishing I could be a strength for him in this crazy time, too.

But could I handle it?

Sucking in a breath, I look up. "You shouldn't have to shoulder this alone. You can lean on me, too."

"No, I won't do that to you. It's my job to protect you and take care of you and I'll be damned if I let anything happen to you. No one is going to hurt you, not even yourself. Do you hear me, baby?"

"Wyatt," I whisper, shaking my head but before I can say anything else he slams his lips on mine, his kiss desperate and full of the fear coursing through his body. I wrap my arms around him, pulling him closer. I don't care what it takes or what I have to do. I'm determined to be the same unwavering support system to him that he is for me without letting my demons consume me. Wyatt and I have a life to live and I won't let this stop us.

A.M. Myers

Chapter Twenty-Three
Wyatt

Jumping in the Bronco, I slam the door behind me before leaning my head back and blowing out a breath as I scrub my hand over my face. My heart pounds hard in my chest and I focus on my breathing, trying to calm myself down but it's not working. Church just let out and despite the fact that every single one of my brothers and I have been looking into these cases for the last three days, we have absolutely nothing and I feel like I'm going to lose my goddamn mind. Right after we discovered the photos, Blaze ordered us to look into every single person we've had contact with since Dina was killed two years ago, every single guy we've rescued someone from, every single P.I. client we've had and anyone else we could think of that might have a connection to the club but we still have nothing. We're still in exactly the same spot I was and it's killing me.

"Fuzz," someone says from outside my window and I jerk up as my eyes fly open. Kodiak holds his hands up in surrender and I release a breath as I relax back into the seat. "Sorry, man. Didn't mean to scare you."

I shake my head. "What's up?"

"Fuck," he breathes, crossing his arms over his chest and dropping his eyes to the ground for a second before he meets my gaze. "I just wanted to say I'm sorry... about not believing you. I didn't want it to be true and..."

"Forget it, man. I understand. You have no fucking idea how much I wish I had been wrong right about now."

He nods as he runs a hand through his hair. "With Tate pregnant, all I can think about is the worst case scenarios..."

"Kodiak, if anyone can protect themselves, it's Tate," I tell him with a smile I don't quite feel and he nods, giving me a faux chuckle.

"Yeah, you're right."

Silence descends over us, awkward and tense, as we both struggle with something else to say but there is nothing. This situation... it's uncharted territory for us and with almost all of us in serious relationships with the women we love, we all have a hell of a lot to lose. A memory of Piper telling me to lean on her, too, pops into my mind and I sigh. She's right. This mess we've found ourselves in sucks and there is nothing we can do about that but we can lean on each other, be the family that we're supposed to be.

"Hey, why don't we plan like a big family dinner or something?"

He arches a brow. "You really think it's the best time for that?"

"It's like Blaze said," I answer with a nods. "We need

to be solid and we need to lean on each other to get through this."

Studying me for a second, he nods and reaches in the window to slap me on the shoulder. "Okay. I'll go talk to Blaze about it."

"Sounds good. I've got to go get Piper from work."

Taking a step back from the truck, he nods and I start the truck before pulling out of my parking space. As I pull out of the lot, I see him walking back to the clubhouse and I nod to myself. It will be good to get everyone together and maybe even laugh a little bit. Right now, we are all broken off into our little couples and families, silently losing our shit over what is coming. The feeling is so strong now that I can feel it in every fiber of my being, like the deadly calm just before a massive tornado strikes. Whoever this guy is, he is coming to get whatever twisted sense of revenge he thinks he is owed and we need to be ready for it.

The night of the break-in, Piper and I laid in bed talking until three in the morning. I told her all about each of the cases and explained the timeline to her, trying to make her understand how dangerous this guy is but that is not what happened. Instead, when confronted with all the evidence, she pointed out that this guy has been playing a long game since the beginning, slowly torturing us for maximum effect and she doesn't think he'll change tactics now. When I started to argue with her, she said it would make even more sense for him to go dark now that we know about him because we will all be going crazy.

As much as I didn't want to admit that she was right, it makes fucking sense. With no new crimes, we have no new evidence to look into, and we've clearly gotten no where with what we have now and all of us are feeling the tension. If it goes on much longer, we'll all start losing it. She also pointed out that he's never gone after an old lady and it would be a big escalation but I can't afford to let my guard down where she is concerned. Just because he's never gone after anyone close to us doesn't mean he won't and she needs to keep her guard up until we find this son of a bitch.

I glance behind the passenger seat where the new pistol I bought Piper is sitting. It was a spur of the moment, reacting to the crazy kind of decision and I have no idea how she will feel about it but I'm going to teach her everything I can about the weapon and teach her to shoot it so that I feel a little bit better. If Tate wasn't pregnant right now, I might even ask her to teach Piper some self-defense moves but there is no way in hell Kodiak would be okay with that. Although, I'm certain if I asked Tate first, she would tell him to suck it up. That girl doesn't like anyone telling her what to do but I can't do that to Kodiak, especially now that we're on good terms.

As I get closer to Piper's studio, I sigh. My stomach twists and my throat feels tight as I think about her and Eden there all alone. It's so dangerous and anything could happen despite what Piper thinks. On top of everything else, I am really worried about how she is handling all of this and I hate myself for bringing this down on her shoulders when she is already dealing with so much internally. I've thought of every single possibility - hiding her away somewhere, telling her to leave me, following her everywhere she goes - but none of them are ideal. This guy has obviously been watching us for a while so he already knows about Piper which means either one of the first two options will put her in even more danger and she might kill me if I try to be her personal bodyguard. I need to do something, though.

Pulling up in front of the studio, I see Piper in the doorway, waving to a cute little family of three as they get into their car and for the first time since I dropped her off this morning, I feel like I can breathe again. Her gaze flicks in my direction as I get out of the Bronco and she smiles, crossing her arms over her chest and leaning against the door frame. I flash her a smile but it feels forced.

"Hey, baby."

She smiles as I wrap my arms around her waist and pull her close, needing to feel her in my arms. Pressing her forehead to mine, she releases a breath and I feel a little bit of the tension slip out of my body.

"Hi," she whispers, stealing a quick kiss. "I missed you."

I shake my head. "I missed you way more, baby. You done for the night?"

"Yeah. Eden's still here, though."

As soon as the words leave her mouth, Eden walks into the front of the studio and when she sees me, she narrows her eyes and props her hands on her hips.

"Hey, I've got a bone to pick with you."

"What?" I growl, not in the mood to deal with Eden and her attitude. After her little scheme to get us back together, she rubs me the wrong way and I get the sense that she's jealous of the time Piper spends with me. I mean, it makes sense. Before I came back into her life, Piper spent a large amount of her time with Eden and Lillian so it will take some adjusting on her part but I really hope, for Piper's sake, she and I can work through our differences.

"All the extra security," she says, motioning to the door. "Is it really necessary?"

When I dropped Piper off at work this morning, we filled Eden in on the gist of what was happening, that someone was coming after the club and they needed to be more careful, but we didn't tell her many details about how serious the threat was. Even though it makes it hard for her to take this seriously, it's for the best. This is club business and the less people know about it, the better. I nod.

"Yeah, it is."

She rolls her eyes.

"It could be worse, you know. I could have one of the guys come babysit y'all."

A smile stretches across her face as she arches a brow. "Would it be a single guy?"

"No," I answer with a laugh and her face falls.

"Fine. Ruin all my fun."

"Honestly, Edie," Piper says, shaking her head. "As two women who stay here late at night sometimes, we should have been doing this way before now."

She sighs, reluctantly, nodding her head. "Yeah, okay."

"Are you finished for the night?" I ask her. "We'll walk out with you."

"No, sir," she replies, shaking her head with a stubborn look on her face as she pulls a pistol out of her bag and my brow shoots toward my hairline. Well, shit. "I have one more shoot tonight and I am perfectly capable of taking care of myself."

I study her for a second and consider arguing with her but there is something about the look in her eyes that tells me she has been through some shit and she is more than capable of taking care of herself. Although, judging by the shocked look on Piper's face, it seems to be something she doesn't talk about much. Finally, I nod.

"Yeah, okay. But call me if you run into any trouble." I release Piper and pull one of the club's business cards out of my wallet and scoop a pen up off of the counter before scribbling my number down on it. I hand it to her and I see a flash of vulnerability in her eyes before she covers it up and nods.

"Thanks."

"When in the hell did you get that, Eden?" Piper asks as she finally recovers enough to speak and Eden shrugs like she didn't just pull a firearm out of her purse.

"A girl's got to protect herself, Pip-Squeak."

The darkness flicks across her gaze again as Piper turns to stare at me with wide eyes. Maybe she's expecting me to say something or insist that we stay here with Eden but I'm not going to. The look in her eyes is the same one Tate gets sometimes and I have no doubt if the worst case scenario happened, Eden would handle herself just fine.

Nodding, I wrap my arm around Piper's waist. "All right, I guess we'll just get out of your hair then."

"What?"

Eden smiles her thanks as Piper bores a hole into the side of my head. "Have a good night, y'all."

"Oh, we will be talking about this later," Piper says, pointing a finger at her best friend as I pull her into my side and my body relaxes at the contact.

"Mmhmm," she calls as she stands up and grabs one of her cameras off of her desk. "Looking forward to it."

As she walks away from us, I release Piper's hips to grab her hand and lace our fingers together as I grab her purse off of the counter and hand it to her. She eyes me but before she can say anything, I flash her a smile.

"I've got a surprise for you."

She arches a brow. "What kind of a surprise?"

"Huh?" I ask, feigning innocence as we open the front door and step outside. She stops and puts her free hand on her hip as she stares me down with that "tell me now" look.

"You said there was a surprise."

"Did I?" I ask, scowling at her and shaking my head as I pull her around the passenger side door and open it. "Huh… I don't remember."

"You're a liar."

I shake my head again, fighting back a grin. "No, I swear… Are you hungry?"

She gets this cute little smile on her face and I swear I can read her mind. Memories from when we were kids flash through my mind and I mirror her expression. Right after I got the Bronco, we used to love to just drive around with the windows down and Piper cuddled into my side. After a while, we would go to the little hole in the wall burger place downtown - the kind of restaurant that only the locals know about with big greasy burgers and the best French fries you've ever had - and we'd drive down to the river, put the tailgate down, and cuddle in the back while we ate. It was part of the inspiration for the night and I hope she remembers.

She shakes her head, still stuck on demanding to know what her surprise is when her stomach growls and she lets out a surprised laugh. "Yeah, I guess I'm a little hungry."

"Jump in," I say with a nod. "And we'll go grab some food."

The defiant look on her face tells me she wants to argue but when her stomach growls again, she climbs up in the truck and I don't miss the opportunity to guide her up with my hand on her ass. As she plops down in her seat, she rolls her eyes at me, fighting back a grin and I shut the door before jogging around to my side and slipping behind the wheel. Her stomach growls again as I start the truck and I laugh as I point over my shoulder.

"I may have fibbed a little bit. Check the back."

She spins around and rises up on her knees to look behind the bench seat. She lets out a squeal that makes me laugh and when she sits down again, she has the brown paper bag in her hand with Mike's Burgers and More logo on the front. Closing her eyes, she takes a deep breath and lets out a moan that makes me sit up a little straighter.

"Oh my God, Wyatt. It smells so good."

I smile. Seeing her happy makes me happy and I just hope we take care of this threat so I get to do it for the rest of our lives. "Dig in, Pip."

She squeals again, practically wiggling with excitement as she peels open the bag and looks inside before meeting my gaze with a scowl.

"There is only one meal. Aren't you hungry?" she asks and I shake my head.

"Naw, I ate earlier and I'm still full." It's a lie. I haven't been able to eat much of anything in the last few days, too worried about Piper and too worried about my club to get anything down but I don't need her knowing that. She would just worry about me and I need all of her attention to be on making sure she is okay. After studying me for a second, she sighs and scoots across the seat until she's pressed against my side and when I glance down at her, she holds a French fry in front of my lips. Fighting back a smile, I turn back to the road and bite it in half.

"Do you want to know a secret, Wyatt?"

I nod, peeking down at her again as she eats a fry of her own. "Sure."

"You never were a very good liar."

"What are you talking about?" I ask, feigning ignorance but I know she's right. At least, when it comes to her. One look in her green eyes and I would be spilling my guts but it's always been that way. She nudges me, meeting my gaze with a no-nonsense look on her gorgeous face.

"You have to take care of yourself, too. I'm not going to let you fall apart."

I nod to her food, ignoring her comment. "Eat your dinner, baby."

We spend the rest of the drive cuddling in silence as she eats and when we pull onto the old first road that we used to take to the river back when we were kids, I see her grin out of the corner of my eye. This place holds so many damn memories for us and if I could, I would buy this land and build her a house facing the water but the old man who owns this ground has known my parents since I was a little kid and he has always said that he'll die before he sells it. The good thing is, he was always cool with letting us come down here anytime we wanted.

"Here," Piper says as I park the truck at the end of the dirt road and I glance over at her as she holds half of her burger to me. I shake my head and determination flashes in her eyes. "You need to eat and I won't get out of the truck until you do."

Rolling my eyes, I swipe the burger from her hand and take a bite. As soon as the flavor explodes across my taste buds, my stomach growls like my body is suddenly remembering how hungry it is and I inhale the rest of the food before glancing over at her. She is turned sideways in her seat, staring at me with a cocked brow and her arms crossed over her chest.

"Not hungry, huh?"

I narrow my eyes. "Watch it, Pip."

"Or what? You'll spank me?" she asks, rolling her eyes as she turns away from me and I grin. When she glances back at me, she lets out a little shriek and fumbles for the door handle but I grab her first and drag her into my lap as I press kisses up her neck. She straddles my thighs and I groan against her skin.

"That's not a bad idea."

She shakes her head and steals a kiss. "Don't even think about it, Landry."

"Why not?"

"Because I'll be very mad at you."

I grin as I thrust up into her. "Yeah, but then I'll make you very happy."

She is trying desperately to stay focused but I can see the smile threatening to break through and I thrust up again. Her lips part and she lets out my favorite sound, that sexy little sigh, so I do it again.

"Wyatt," she breathes, gripping my shoulders in both hands and my cock strains against my zipper. Shit, I love hearing her whisper my name like that. In that small fraction of a moment, nothing else exists but her and I.

There is no nosy friends poking into our business.

There is no club.

There is no threat coming for all of this.

There is just me and my woman.

She tips her head back when I do it again, grabbing two handfuls of her sexy ass and bucking my hips off of the seat, grinding up into her. I take advantage of the opportunity to lean forward and lick a path up the side of her neck.

Fuck.

She tastes so damn good and I need more.

She shudders in my arms as a moan slips past her lips and her nipples pebble against the thin fabric of her shirt. I growl as my desire for her boils over.

"Was this my surprise?" she asks, rocking her hips against my erection and I shake my head.

"No. That's going to have to wait."

Nodding, she leans down and seals her lips to mine with a moan as I try to unbutton my jeans.

Fuck.

This is going to be quick and dirty but I need her now and I don't have the patience to move to the back of the truck or wait until we get home. After the last few days, all I can think about is getting inside my wife. I need it more than the air I breathe.

Thank God, she wore a skirt today.

Once I get my jeans down and my cock springs free, she reaches down between us, wrapping her fingers around my length and bolts of pleasure zip through me as I drop my head back and groan. Her warm breath hits my neck and goose bumps race across my flesh as she pumps her hand, stroking me again and again so slowly that it's damn near torture.

"I want you so bad, Wyatt," she whispers in my ear and my entire body lights up like a bonfire. My hand skates up her spine before diving into her hair. I grab a chunk of it and pull, bringing her face away from my neck and claiming her lips again. She moans, releasing my cock to grind against me. Her panties are wet and I sink my teeth into her bottom lip as my head spins.

"You keep talking dirty to me, baby," I growl in between kisses. "And we're never going to get to the surprise."

She nods. "Fine by me."

"You want me to fuck you all night long?" I ask, hyping myself up at just the thought and her breathy little moan spurs me on, making me crazy. "Want me to put a baby inside you?"

"God, yes, Wyatt," she moans, her head falling back as she continues grinding on my lap. When she rocks back again, I can't take it anymore. Growling, I reach between us and pull her panties to the side as she grabs my cock, pressing it against her entrance as we both moan. Her lips brush over my ear and I shudder as I sink into her with a low groan. The air punches out of my lungs as I still, giving her a moment to adjust.

Shit.

She feels so goddamn good and I'm never going to last.

Why the fuck is it that the feeling of my wife wrapped around my cock turns me into a teenage boy all over again?

"Fuck me, Wyatt," she pleads before pressing a kiss to

my neck and I groan again, gripping her hips and thrusting up into her. She cries out into the cab of the truck, clinging to me like I'm a life raft and circling her hips to add to the sensations. I glance up at her and stop moving, drawing her angry eyes down to my face. "What are you doing?"

"I think I wanna watch you fuck me this time, sweetheart."

The fury fades from her gaze in an instant and a slow, devilish little smile stretches across her face as she starts rocking and circling her hips again. She plants her hands on my chest and meets my gaze as her mouth falls open in a silent moan and her body shudders.

"Goddamn, baby," I whisper, reaching up and cupping her cheek as pressure builds at the base of my spine. I slip my hand between us and grab the base of my cock, trying to hold off as long as possible but when she sinks her teeth into her bottom lip, I know I'm a goner. Her eyes flutter closed, wrapped up in the sensation as a moan tears through her and I can't hold back anymore.

I grip her hips and move with her as we both race toward completion. Smacking her hands against the roof of the truck, she moans again and again, teetering on the edge of her release. My body tenses and I wrap my hand around the back of her neck, pulling her to me and slamming her lips to mine as we both shatter around each other. Her pussy grips me, waves of pleasure milking my cock as I spill into her with a groan and we pull apart, both of us fighting for air as our eyes meet.

"Oh my God," she whispers before a giddy little giggle slips out of her mouth and I grin, pulling her to me as I lean my head back and close my eyes.

Fuck.

That was good.

"That one got me pregnant, for sure," she says into my neck and I laugh as I run my hand down her back.

"You think?"

She nods. "Oh, for sure."

We sit in silence for a moment, both of us just soaking up the quiet time with one another, before she sits up and locks eyes with me.

"Now, where is my surprise?"

Laughing, I reach behind the seat and grab the black case off of the seat before handing it to her. She scowls at it, looking so goddamn adorable I want to take her again, before she looks up at me.

"What is it?"

"Open it," I tell her, laughing as my stomach flips. I have no idea how she is going to react but I hope she'll know I'm just trying to keep her safe. She flips the lid open and stares down at the pistol inside without saying anything and my heart climbs into my throat.

"Why?" she asks, meeting my eyes and I cup her cheek in my hand.

"I just want to know you're safe, baby."

She glances down at the gun. "If I agree to this, will you let up on the whole 'you are not to be alone in the studio and I'll drive you everywhere' thing?"

"No."

"Then I don't want it," she snaps, shoving it back into my hands. I refuse to take it, sighing as I run a hand through my hair.

"What if I let up on the whole alone at the studio thing

as long as you check in with me often and I'll follow you to work and home in my truck?"

She studies me for a second before nodding her head. "Okay. If this will make you feel better, I'll carry it with me."

"Good," I answer as relief rushes through me like a tidal wave. I'll be able to breathe so much easier knowing that she has a way to defend herself when I can't be with her but I hope to God she won't ever need it.

Every Little Thing

Chapter Twenty-Four
Piper

"Smack That" by Akon spills out of the studio's speaker system and I growl as I lean back in my chair and study the photo I've been working on for the last hour. Normally, it wouldn't take me this long to edit a photo but I'm distracted today. My gaze drifts to my purse sitting on the desk where the pistol Wyatt gave me a couple of nights ago is hidden and I sigh. Honestly, I'm not even sure what is making me pre-occupied tonight but every time I try to focus on the task at hand, my mind wanders to the other night when Wyatt brought me dinner, drove me down to the river, and taught me how to shoot. Closing my eyes, I remember the way he stepped up behind me and wrapped his hands around mine, showing how to properly hold the pistol and a shiver works its way down my spine.

God, I'm hopeless lately.

It seems like all I can think about is screwing my husband every which way and it doesn't matter that he was inside me this morning as I woke up because I want it again. The memory of him whispering instructions in my ear makes my pussy clench with need and I shake my head as I lean forward and try to focus on the photo again. More than anything, I would like to just call it a night and head home but if I don't get these photos finished up, I'll be behind and I hate that.

As I start fixing something in the background, my gaze flicks to my bag again and I grit my teeth as I lean back in my chair. My mind drifts to that night again, remembering the way we came together in his truck and I smile. God, I love that man. Life would be so good right now if it wasn't for this stupid threat hanging over our heads. When Wyatt was showing me how to hold and shoot the gun, I thought I was going to hate it but it ended up being pretty fun and I do feel a little more secure now that I have something to protect myself.

Not that it seems to have helped Wyatt.

He's just as high-strung as ever and I have no clue how to help him. He won't talk to me about it but I know he's still worried, so worried that he's barely eating and not sleeping well at all. Not once has he gotten out of bed in the middle of the night but several times I've woken up to get a drink of water or pee and found him wide awake next to me. The guys still haven't found any new evidence and I feel like it's slowly driving them all crazy and so fucking overprotective that us girls can hardly breathe.

Tate and I finally grabbed lunch yesterday but Wyatt and Kodiak were lurking at a table not too far from ours the entire time so it was hard to really talk about anything. In fact, she spent a good amount of time roasting her husband, loud enough for him to hear and telling him she was going to tase him if he didn't back off. He just grinned at her, though and I'm starting to think it's some kind of foreplay for those two but who am I to judge?

To each their own and all that.

I turn back to my computer and tell myself that I'm going to buckle down but I don't even get one thing done before my gaze drifts to the bouquet of a dozen calla lilies on the counter. They are my absolute favorite and I couldn't believe it when the delivery man dropped them off today. Even in Wyatt's stressed out state, he's still thinking of me and it honestly means everything. I know enough from the few dating mishaps I had while trying to move on and Eden's exploits to know that men like Wyatt don't come along very often and I know how lucky I am to have him. Still, I wish there was something I could do to ease this burden off of his shoulder but I think the only thing that will make it better will be catching this guy and removing the threat from all of our lives.

He's taken all this on, feels responsible for the state of everyone's safety and as much as I wish he could see that it is not all on him, I love how much he cares. Seeing him like this shows me that he is going to be an amazing daddy once we get pregnant and I smile as I glance down at my belly, wondering if there is a little peanut in there already. Everything I have read says that it takes time and to just enjoy the process but Wyatt and I both want this so badly that it feels like it's taking forever. Not that I'll ever complain about a little quality time with my man.

Turning back to the computer, I sigh and shake my head as I scoop my phone off of the desk. I'm not going to get anymore done today and there is no point sitting here all night when I could be spending time with my husband. I dial his number and lean back in my chair as I press the phone to my ear.

"Hey, baby," he answers and I smile, the sound of his voice soothing all the frayed ends that a long day left in me.

"Hi. I think I'm ready to head home now."

He laughs. "That's good since I'm on my way to the studio now to drag you out if I have to."

"No dragging required."

"Good. How was your day?"

I spin back to the computer to save the edits I already made to this photo. "Long and I keep getting distracted."

"By what?"

"Oh," I murmur, grinning to myself. "Just thoughts of you and how I can convince you to reenact this morning."

He barks out a laugh. "Baby, all you gotta do is ask… no, wait… that's not true. All you gotta do is look at me."

"You're so easy," I tease and he laughs again. It's a glorious sound and one I haven't heard a whole lot this past week so I close my eyes to soak it in.

"Maybe you're the easy one. Did you ever consider that?"

I shake my head. "Never. Maybe you did some like voodoo on me or something to make me extra horny."

"You caught me," he practically groans. "And don't say the word horny when I'm still two blocks away and can't do anything about it."

There is a fluttery feeling in my belly as I lean back in my chair and press my hand to my chest. "God, baby… I'm so horny…"

"Woman!"

Every Little Thing

"You'd better hurry. I need you, Wyatt," I moan, dragging my hand across my skin and teasing myself as much as I'm teasing him. His growl on the other end of the line makes goose bumps race across my flesh and the bed in the studio that Eden and I use for boudoir sessions pops into my mind.

"Open the door."

My gaze flies to the front door and my lips part as his eyes meet mine, full of all sorts of filthy promises and a shiver races down my spine as I stand up. "Jesus Christ. How did you get here so fast?"

"I was very motivated. Now, open the door," he orders, his voice full of power as he arches a brow in warning. I stare at him and when he points to the lock, my feet start moving without any instruction from me, carrying me closer to him. As soon as the door is unlocked, he yanks it open and charges inside, pulling me into his arms and sealing his lips to mine. I moan, wrapping my arms around his neck as we stumble back into the counter and something crashes behind us. He rips his lips away and glances over my shoulder.

"Shit, baby. Your flowers fell."

I jerk back. "Oh, no."

Peeling myself out of his arms, I round the counter and grab the bundle of flowers off of the floor, shaking the water off before setting them on the counter and kneeling down to inspect the vase they came in. It was a gorgeous glass vase with little hearts blown into the sides but now it's in multiple pieces all over the floor. On one of the shelves under the counter is a roll of paper towels and I grab them as I try to mop up the water. Wyatt crouches down next to me and takes the paper towels from my hand.

"I'll do this. I don't want you cutting yourself."

I nod and stand up to inspect the flowers. They don't look too worse for wear but there is no saving the vase they were in. I thought it was so sweet when it was delivered earlier today and even thought it's just a vase, I'm kind of sad it broke. When he stands up with the pieces of glass in his hand, my bottom lip pokes out.

"Aw, baby," he whispers, dropping the pieces into the garbage can before walking over to me and wrapping me up in a hug. "I'll buy you a new one, okay?"

I point to the garbage can. "But I liked that one. It was so cute and sweet."

"Well, where did you get it? We can go right now."

Huh?

I pull back and meet his gaze with a scowl on my face. "I didn't get it anywhere…"

"So Eden did, then? Text her and ask her where we can get another one. Or was it a client?"

"What are you talking about?" I ask, taking a step back as I search his face. Is he just messing with me right now? "You sent them to me."

He shakes his head. "No… I didn't."

"But… they were delivered today… I just assumed they were from you."

"No…" he answers, his gaze flicking to the flowers on the desk before dropping to the trash can. When he meets my eyes again, his eyes are narrowed and he takes a step toward me. "Who the fuck is sending you flowers, Pip?"

I shake my head. "I don't know. I thought they were from you."

Every Little Thing

"Obviously not," he snaps, staring at the lilies again as his nostrils flare and he clenches his fist. He turns back to me, glaring daggers into my skin. "Who the fuck is sending you flowers and vases with cute little fucking hearts on it, Pip?"

"I don't know!"

"You don't know? Well, he obviously knows you well enough to know that calla lilies are your favorite fucking flower, doesn't he?"

My eyes widen. "He? Are you accusing me of something right now?"

His lips flatten into a straight line as his gaze bounces around the studio like he's looking for something and when his eyes finally land on me again, they are cold and hard. "Just tell me who sent the flowers, Piper."

"I don't know!" I scream, balling my fists up and gritting my teeth. Wyatt has been the only man to ever own my heart and I thought he knew that. I thought we were past all of this. He sighs, shoving his hand through his hair.

"Is it James? You leaving me for that fucker?"

I stare at him with wide eyes. Jesus Christ. The man has lost his goddamn mind. "Are you kidding me? I fucking love you, Wyatt, and only you. You know that."

"Then why is some other fucking man sending you flowers?" he roars, pointing to the bouquet still sitting on the counter. He glares at it for a second before scooping it up and chucking it at the wall. "Fuck this. You know what I don't need, Piper. I don't need to get my heart pulverized by you again. If you want this little pissant, then get your shit out of the house and go be with him."

He spins on his toes and walks out of the studio without

another word and I stare after him for a few seconds before pain splinters my chest and tears sting my eyes. As I stumble back to my chair, I gasp for air and try to work through the last five minutes in my mind over and over again.

Where in the hell did it go wrong?

My hands shake as I pick up my phone and dial Eden's number. I'm not leaving Wyatt and I'm not giving up on us but there is no way in hell that I'm going back to the house tonight.

"Hello?" Eden answers and I suck in a stuttered breath.

"Edie… can I come stay at your place tonight? Wyatt and I… we had a huge fight and I…"

"Of course," she says, cutting me off. I thank her and tell her I'll be there soon before hanging up and burying my head in my hands as a sob rips through me, echoing around the empty studio before being swallowed up by the upbeat pop music that only amplifies just how shitty I feel. The tears trickle down my cheeks and the pain in my chest grows as his words play on a loop through my mind. God, he was so cold, so sure that I would betray him like that I can't help but think this is my fault. I lied to him about the real reasons I left for ten years and during all that time, it is all he's known. I can't help but wonder if he is still holding onto some resentment about all of that and if we're strong enough to overcome it.

Every Little Thing

Chapter Twenty-Five
Wyatt

I clench my fists to keep my hands from shaking as I stomp out of the studio. The door slams behind me but I ignore it. Images of Piper with another man flash across my vision, fueling me as I jump behind the wheel of my truck and peel out of the parking spot. Pain blooms in my chest, pain like I haven't felt in ten goddamn years and I grit my teeth as I peel out of the parking space and press the gas pedal all the way to the floor. I'll be better once I put a little distance between me and my lying wife. My mind spins as I fly down the quiet street, going over the last ten minutes again and again in my mind and wondering where the hell I went wrong. Things have been so damn good between Piper and me but those flowers tell a different goddamn story. My knuckles turn white from gripping the steering wheel so hard and I wish I could just crack it in half as rage flows through me. I feel like my hand is attached to live wire, electricity sparking through me and making me want to crawl out of my own skin. My mind spins as I try to put it all together but it just doesn't make any sense. Who the fuck is sending my wife flowers?

And more importantly, why would she do this to me again?

Why would she do this to us?

My heart cracks in half as I think about going back to the way things were before she walked back into my life and I shake my head, fighting the urge to throw up.

Why would she do this to me again?

The thought bounces around in my head, driving me to the point of madness, before reality crashes down on me and I suck in a breath.

Oh, fuck...

Piper never cheated on me.

Almost like I'm walking through a haze, things become clearer and I run a hand over my face.

Jesus Christ.

What the hell did I just do and what was I thinking?

Piper wouldn't cheat on me. Not now that we're back together and trying to have a baby. Not when she could have had anyone she wanted only a month ago.

"Fuck!" I scream, punching the steering wheel so hard I hear a crack but I ignore it. It's not what is important right now.

Goddamn it.

I fucked up so bad.

Shaking my head, I slam my foot on the brake and as soon as the truck slows down a little bit, I yank the wheel to one side, flipping around right in the middle of the street before flooring it to head back to the studio. Maybe she will still be there and I can apologize for being such an epic

313

dumb ass.

I can't believe I yelled at her like that.

What the hell was I thinking?

My chest feels tight as I race back toward her, hoping and praying that she will hear me out long enough to make it up to her but when I get back to the studio, her car is gone.

"Goddamn it," I growl, pulling my phone out of my pocket and dialing her number as I head for home. My parting words ring in my ears and I hope to God she's not there packing.

Fuck.

I can't lose her again.

Her voice mail picks up and my heart climbs into my thorax as I toss the phone into the passenger seat.

Oh, this is so, so bad and also, perfect with all the other shit I'm dealing with. I feel like I'm losing my fucking mind and I don't know what to do with all this goddamn guilt and worry twisting itself into a poisonous little cocktail inside me. Spots flash in my vision and panic claws at my throat as I reach over and grab my phone before dialing her number again.

"Please, Piper," I whisper, my free leg shaking like crazy. Just as I pull up in front of the house and park my truck, her voice mail picks up and I grit my teeth, almost crushing the little piece of plastic. Her car isn't here either and my heart kicks against my ribs as I wonder if maybe I was right.

What if she went to him?

Shaking my head, I push the idea from my mind as I grab my phone and pull up the tracking app I put on her phone right after the break-in at the club. She doesn't know about it yet and I know she'll be pissed but I really had the best intentions. There is also a tracker on her car, in her purse, and embedded in the necklace I bought her in Charleston. Getting that one was kind of tricky, though since I had to do it in the middle of the night and hide it well enough that she wouldn't see it.

So far, it's worked.

The app loads and I stare at her car as it turns down a street not far from the studio.

Where the fuck is she going?

She stops halfway down the street and my head falls back against the seat as all of the air in my lungs rushes out of me.

Oh, thank fucking God.

I don't know why I didn't think to check Eden's place first. Sighing again, I lift my head and stare at the screen, contemplating my options. She has ignored two phone calls now and she went to Eden's instead of coming home so maybe it's best that I give her the night to cool off. The thought of spending the next almost twenty-four hours without her kills and my stomach twists at the idea. Every cell in my body is screaming at me to go to her and bring her home with me where she belongs but right now, with both of us so fucking mad, it would only makes things worse. As I look up at the house, I shake my head. The thought of going inside that house by myself is too painful and I turn back to the road and pull away from the curb.

I'll spend the night at the clubhouse and in the morning, I will think of something epic to apologize to her.

As I drive through the dark streets, my mind drifts to the flowers again and a wave of possessiveness wells up inside me. Piper isn't guilty of anything but this little fucker who sent her the flowers sure as hell is. My mind immediately flips to her recent ex, James, and the conversation we had before we went to Charleston. She said that he had wanted to get together again that night but when she said she blocked him and we never heard from him again, I forgot about it. Seems to me that James didn't, though.

I pull into the clubhouse parking lot and park my truck before jumping out. It's quiet here tonight and I glance over at the two bikes sitting near the door. Blaze and Streak are the only two people here which makes sense with all of us too consumed with protecting our families to hang out like we used to. It's actually a little sad that Blaze and Streak don't have anyone to go home to, now that I think about it.

Blaze glances up from one of the tables as I walk in and scowls as he studies my face. "What's wrong?"

"Just some little fuck sending flowers to my wife."

"Wanna go fuck him up?" he asks, nonchalant, like he didn't just suggest we go beat the shit out of a little bitch. I stare at him for a second before shrugging.

"Maybe. I'll keep you posted."

He nods and I head upstairs to grab a laptop from my room. Streak is our resident tech expert but I don't do too bad myself and for this, I'm perfectly capable of finding everything I need. Once I'm back downstairs in the bar with my computer, I set it down and grab a beer before opening it up to dig into James's past.

Fuck…

I don't even know this asshole's last name.

Shaking my head, I open my computer and after it boots up, I log into social media and go to Piper's profile. Maybe I can find a clue here. Scrolling down her page, I stop when I get a photo of them from four months ago and smile when I see that she tagged him. After opening his profile in another window, I stare at the picture for a second before I release a breath. Piper is my world and has been

316

since we were kids so I know her inside and out, better than she knows herself and all it takes is a quick glance at the picture to tell me that she wasn't ever happy with this fucker.

Reassured, I flip over to his profile and grab his birthday before opening up another search engine and typing in his full name and his birthdate. Like magic, his contact information pops up from a job search website and I look over my shoulder at Blaze, who is sipping coffee and flicking through the newspaper.

"You still feel like going to fuck someone up?"

He nods and slams his hand down on the paper. "Absolutely."

I fight back a laugh as he jumps up, looking ready to put his fist through someone's face but I can't say that I blame him. All of us are feeling antsy with everything we're dealing with and we have no way to expel that energy. As he pulls his cut on, he glances at the stairs.

"Streak!"

"What?" Streak's voice yells from the end of the hallway and Blaze just crosses his arms over his chest and waits. Sure enough a few seconds later, Streak comes storming down the hallway and leans over the balcony. "What the fuck do you want?"

"Feel like going to fuck somebody up?"

He studies me. "Who?"

"This asshole that sent flowers to Piper," I answer and his lip curls back for a second before he shrugs.

"Sure. I was getting bored anyway. Meet you outside."

He disappears back down the hallway and Blaze nods to the front door. "Let's go."

"Should I be concerned by how eager you are to go kick someone's ass?" I ask and he flicks a glare in my direction that tells me to drop the subject.

"No."

Raising my hands in surrender, I let it go as we walk outside and he stops by his bike. I walk over to the truck and tell him to just follow me before climbing behind the wheel. Once Streak jogs out of the clubhouse and swings his leg over his bike, I back out of my parking space and pull out of the lot with them hot on my heels. My knuckles turn white as I grip the steering wheel tightly again thinking about this son of a bitch thinking he has any claim to my woman. Or thinking that it's okay to send her flowers when she's cut off all contact with him.

It's assholes like this that we end up helping girls get away from and the more I think about him with Piper, the more I can't wait to put my fist in his face.

Fuck.

I don't even care if he presses charges at this point.

Although, having to call Piper and ask her to bail me out of jail might not go over so well. Then I would have to apologize for another thing.

We pull up in front of a decent looking house not from from the club and the front door opens before I can even jump out of the truck. He eyes the bikes warily as the engines cut off and steps out onto the porch.

"Can I help you?"

I look down at the paper in my hand. "James Williams?"

"Yeah, what the hell do you want?" he snaps and my brow shoots up to my hairline as I look over at Blaze and Streak. Who in the fuck does this guy think he is? If three bikers show up on your doorstep looking for you, the worst thing you can do is cop an attitude. I walk halfway up his front sidewalk and stop, crossing my arms over my chest.

"I want you to stop sending flowers to my fucking wife."

His head jerks back. "Your wife? I don't even fucking know you, douchebag."

"Sure, you do. I'm the guy you could never live up to in Piper's mind."

"Piper?" he asks, a smile curving across his face as he walks down the steps, suddenly feeling ten feet taller. Oh, I can't wait to knock this guy out. My hand twitches with the urge to throw the first punch but I wait. "How is my girl?"

Blaze throws the first punch and James crumbles to the ground with a whimper.

"Geez, guy, you gotta watch where you're going. You could really hurt yourself tripping over shit like that" Streak says, stepping up behind him and lifting him to his feet again. "Now, I think my friend here was talking to you."

"Fuck you," he growls, spitting blood at my feet but I don't move as I look down at it in disinterest. What the hell did Piper ever see in this guy? I mean, besides her desperate desire to have a baby.

"Listen up, you little bitch," I say, stepping closer to him and feeling the last week's worth of stress flowing through my veins. "You're going to stay away from my wife. You're going to stop sending her flowers and if you ever contact her again, I'll fucking kill you. She's not interested."

He meets my gaze and grins as blood trickles from his nose. "That's not what she said last night."

Before I can even think about it, I swing and land a punch right to his face, satisfied by the crunch I hear when my knuckles connect with his nose. He moans in pain but Streak holds him upright, nodding to me to go again. I remember walking into the clubhouse and finding the photos everywhere as I land the next punch and when the one after that connects, I think of the message scrawled in red above the war room. On the fourth punch, the dreams I've been having where Piper's picture is up there on those walls with Dina, Laney, and Sammy fill my mind and I land two more before Blaze grabs me and pulls me back.

"That's enough."

I shake him off and nod as Streak releases James and he falls to the ground, whimpering as he tries to crawl back up his steps.

"Dude, are you fucking crying?" Streak asks, looking down in disgust and jumping out of the way when James tries to grab his boot. A few people ride by on bikes, staring at us in horror and Streak kneels down next to James like he's checking on him. "You all right, man? You need an ambulance?"

"Streak," Blaze admonishes with a tired sigh and I glance over my shoulder as the couple on the bikes stops to see if he's okay. I wave to them and smile and they watch me for a second before pulling away.

"We've got to go," I tell Blaze, glancing around the neighborhood and he nods.

"Streak, get him back in his house."

I hold up my hand and step forward before crouching down next to James and slapping his shoulder with just enough force to make my point. "You ever even think about coming near my woman again and I'll be back. You can fucking count on that."

"I'll only stay away…" he says through clenched teeth. "If Piper wants me to."

I flash him a smile with too many teeth as I squeeze his shoulder until he whimpers again. "Then, I'll see you soon, friend."

Chapter Twenty-Six
Piper

My head pounds incessantly as I lean back in the dining room chair and close my eyes, taking a deep breath to try and fend off some of the pain. Rubbing my fingertips into my temples, I release a sigh as a wave of relief washes over me but as soon as it comes on, it's gone again. My stomach rolls and I clamp my mouth shut, fighting the urge to vomit as I shake my head. Oh, hell, I am never drinking again. When I open my eyes, my gaze locks onto our wedding photo hanging on the wall and my chest starts to ache.

I'm mad.

I'm hurt.

And I miss my husband like crazy.

We've only been apart for twelve hours but in that time, I've been a wreck of conflicting emotions, bouncing from one to the next before circling back around as I spent the night over at Eden's apartment, drinking way too much wine and bitching about Wyatt and his shitty ass behavior before I passed out on her couch. When I woke up this morning, I had three missed calls from him but there has been no contact since shortly after he left the studio last night so I have to consider the possibility that he is still mad, too. Not that he has a leg to stand on. I shake my head. He can't honestly think that I am cheating on him, can he?

Last night, when he lobbed that accusation at me and threw our past in my face with hate shining in his eyes, I was hurt but as soon as he left and I had time to process everything that had happened, that quickly changed to anger.

Does he really think so little of me?

And why the hell did I even tell him the truth if I'm going to be punished for the lie for the rest of our lives?

I assumed that once he took some time to calm down, he would realize that it wasn't true but his silence is scaring me. Tears sting my eyes as I remember him ordering me to pack my stuff and get out of the house last night but before they can slip down my face, the anger takes over again. This past week has been hell on him and I know that but I refuse to be treated this way, I refuse to allow him to use my past mistakes against me anytime something goes wrong. That is not the kind of marriage I want to have and I have a hard time believing that is what he wants either.

My heart jumps into my throat as the door handle turns and my head jerks up as Wyatt walks through the front door. We both freeze, our eyes locked, and all the pain and anger of last night arcing between us like electricity. Finally, after what feels like an eternity, he sucks in a breath and flashes me a sheepish smile. Despite my anger, it feels like I can breathe again. The man standing in front of me is the one I love with every cell in my body, not the version of him I was confronted with last night.

"How are you?" he asks and I scoff.

"Pretty fucking shitty."

He nods and sinks into the chair across from me as I grab my cup of coffee and lift it to my lips, taking a small sip. Sighing, he runs his fingers through his hair and my eyes widen at his red, swollen knuckles.

"What did you do?"

Glancing down at his hand as he sets it on the table, he shakes his head. "Nothing. Just got pissed and punched a wall."

"You're lucky you didn't break your goddamn hand," I mutter, rolling my eyes at his poor judgement.

God...

Of all the stupid things...

He nods and leans back in his chair, meeting my gaze again as he drops both of his hands into his lap. "Can we talk?"

Nodding, I arch a brow and cross my arms over my chest, waiting for his explanation. I had to keep telling myself last night that I didn't do anything wrong and I didn't deserve the treatment I got. Something Eden had to remind me of repeatedly when I tripped up and tried to rationalize his behavior with the shit that has been going on with the club.

"I'm sorry..."

"You're going to have to do better than that, Wyatt," I snap, interrupting him as I lift my coffee cup to my lips and he nods, dropping his head. He meets my gaze again and I can see the weight of the burden he insists on carrying on his shoulders. My heart aches at the strain on his face and the haunted look in his eyes. It's a face I recognize all too well and my worry for my husband grows every day. Leaning forward, I reach across the table and hold my hand out to him. He stares at it for a second before looking up at me with hope and slipping his hand into mine.

"I'm not just letting go of what happened last night. It was a shitty thing to do and we'll talk about it in a second but I'm more worried about you right now."

His head jerks back in surprise. "Me?"

"Wyatt, you're not sleeping, you're barely eating, and I can see you slowly slipping away from me. You're starting to look like I did before I left."

"It's just this shit with the club," he whispers, running his free hand through his hair. The move has always been his go-to whenever he gets stressed but I've been seeing a whole lot more of it lately. With a sigh, I abandon my seat and walk over to him before climbing into his lap and straddling his thighs so I can cup his face between my hands.

"I know it's stressful and I know how worried you are about me and everyone else but you also have to learn to deal with that instead of internalizing it and letting it eat away at you. What's happening isn't your fault and absolutely no one blames you."

He drops his forehead to my chest and releases a heavy breath as a little bit of tension seeps out of his body. I run my fingers through his hair as tears sting my eyes and my chest aches for my big strong man and his fragile heart.

"I don't know what I'll do if I lose you," he whispers and I shake my head, forcing his gaze back to mine.

"Hey. I'm not going anywhere."

Pain flashes through his eyes as he grips my hips like he's trying to keep me from floating away. "What if something happens to you? What if this guy…"

"Stop, Wyatt," I whisper, pressing my hand to his cheek as a tear slips down my face. "You're making yourself crazy and I think that's a big factor in what happened last night."

"I can't just sit here and do nothing, Pip… but there's nothing to do. We're all looking into this and we can't find anything. He's probably watching all of us and laughing as we flounder."

I shake my head. "So, why are you letting him win? You're doing all you can do and you know that. You've given me a gun to protect myself and you're still so consumed with fear and anger that you can't even enjoy the quiet moments like this where it's just you and me together."

"I don't know what else to do," he admits, his voice cracking and my heart shatters in my chest. Oh, my sweet, sweet husband. I lean down and press my lips to his. His arms wrap around me and he pulls me into his chest as he kisses me like he may never see me again and more tears slip down my face. I have to find a way to help him, a way to allow him to just breathe freely for a little while or he is going to break. An idea forms in my mind and I pull back, flashing him a smile.

"I have the best idea."

He cracks a little smile as he stares up at me but his eyes still hold an incredible amount of pain. "Why does that look on your face scare the hell out of me?"

"'Cause you're silly," I say, flashing him the biggest smile I can as I jump off his lap and slap his thigh. For me, seeing him smile is the quickest way to cheer me up and I only hope that it is the same for him. "Now, come on, let's go."

"Where are we going?"

I turn and grab my hoodie off of the couch, pulling it over my head, before glancing back at him with a grin. "It's a surprise."

He shakes his head and reluctantly follows me outside but when I stop next to the Bronco and demand the keys, he crosses his arms over his chest with a laugh.

"Oh, hell no. I'm driving."

"How are you going to drive to your own surprise, crazy?" I ask, propping one hand on my hip and holding out the other one, palm up. He sighs, studying me for a second before he digs his keys out of his pocket and plops them into my hand. Once we get in the truck, I reach over to the glovebox and pull out the bandana he always keeps in there before passing it to him.

"Put this on, please."

He shakes his head. "Absolutely not."

"Wyatt," I whine, being extra ridiculous as I cross my arms over my chest. He may be resistant but he needs this and I am not above making a fool of myself for him. When he still doesn't budge, I poke my bottom lip out and he rolls his eyes. Sighing, he shakes his head again and grabs the bandana before slipping it over his eyes. Once his vision is obscured, I start the truck and back out of the driveway.

"So, now that I have you where I want you," I say as I drive down the street. "How about we talk about last night?"

He scoffs. "Do I have a choice?"

"Nope."

"Fine," he says. "Say what you need to say, baby."

Sucking in a breath, I nod. "Obviously, I didn't cheat on you and I would never do that to you."

"I know."

"But you throwing that in my face was fucked up, Wyatt. I understand you were mad but you can't punish me for the lie I told ten years ago for the rest of our lives. That's not fair."

"I wasn't trying to throw anything in your face, Pip. I just..."

I arch a brow. "Just what?"

"I lived with that lie for ten years, you know. It was my life and there are so many goddamn ways that I could lose you that I'm fucking terrified I won't see the end coming."

"Which brings me to an important question," I whisper as my heart thunders in my chest and my heart aches. I hate that he is so certain that there is an end coming for us and I can't help but wonder if the pain of our past is too big, too powerful for us to overcome. Sucking in a breath, I shake my head. Oh, God, I'm so nervous to ask this but it needs to be done. I just don't know if I will like his answer. "Can you trust me?"

Silence descends over us, slamming into me like a brick wall and tears sting my eyes as I wait for his reply.

I wish he would have immediately said yes.

I wish he would have gasped and told me that of course he trusts me.

Anything other than this quiet that feels like it's going

to drown me.

My heart thuds in my ears and I glance over at him as my stomach twists. Finally, he sighs and I feel like I'm going to throw up.

"I don't know how to answer that."

I nod as a tear slips down my cheek and I wipe it away. "Can you explain?"

"Well, I don't think you would ever cheat on me," he says, running a hand through his hair. "But I'm terrified that you're going to walk away from me again. Especially with all this shit going on, I'm terrified that I'm going to come home one day and you're just going to be gone."

I want to tell him that it will never happen but I can't say that with one hundred percent certainty. Besides, I don't think he would believe me if I did. The past hangs heavy between us, haunting our love, something I didn't really realize until last night, and I don't know how to fix it. Right now, even with all the crazy, I feel good but something could change so quickly and I don't know how to reassure him that I'm here to stay.

"You can't tell me that will never happen, can you?"

I shake my head, my bottom lip wobbling. "No. I can tell you that, right now, I feel strong and ready to face the world with you but I can't promise it will never happen again."

His promise to me the morning after he fucked me on the kitchen counter springs to my mind and I wipe the tears from my cheeks as I look over at him.

"What happened to 'I signed up for forever, for better or worse'? This is worse, baby. I have to live with the night my parents died and the profound impact it had on me for the rest of my life. Nothing can change that. Is this something you can live with or is this something that is going to destroy us?"

"Can I take the goddamn blindfold off?" he asks, desperation in his voice as I pull to a stop at our destination. "I need to see your eyes."

"Okay," I whisper as I put the truck in park. He pulls the bandana off and his gaze meets mine as he holds his hand out. Scooting across the seat, my heart hammers, waiting for his answer and when I reach him, I melt into his arms. He presses his lips to my forehead as he releases a breath. When I look up at him, he smiles and reaches into his pocket, pulling out a ring box and my eyes widen.

Why does he have a fucking ring box?

We're already married...

"I got this for you right after we got back from Charleston and I've just been waiting for the right moment to ask you."

My eyes flick to his. "Ask me what?"

"Will you marry me again, baby?" he asks, popping the ring box open to reveal a gorgeous diamond band that matches the one he gave me when we got married the first time. "I know you can't promise me that you'll never stumble again but you were right. I did promise you forever, for better or worse so if you fall, I'll be there to pick you back up and if you completely lose your shit and run, I'll be right behind you. I love you, Piper Jayne Landry, and I want to renew our vows with this new family we've built and kick this new chapter in our lives off right."

"Wyatt," I breathe, staring at the ring as the diamond shimmers in the morning light. He cups my cheeks and directs my gaze back to his.

"But most importantly, I want you to know, beyond a shadow of a doubt, that nothing is coming between us ever again. Not another man. Not this threat to the club and definitely not your demons. I've loved you since I was ten years old and I'm gonna love you even after death rips us apart so what do you say? You wanna marry me?"

I stare down at the ring, my heart beating like crazy and butterflies fluttering around in my tummy. How the hell, after all these years, does this man still make me feel like a thirteen-year-old girl getting her first kiss? I turn and look up into his hazel eyes, feeling the strength of his love as a smile stretches across my face and I nod.

"Wyatt… I'd marry you a million times and it still wouldn't be enough."

He grins. "Is that a yes?"

"Yes," I whisper, nodding and I giggle as he grabs my left hand and slips the ring on my finger with the other two. Once it's on, he tosses the empty box onto the seat and pulls me closer, slamming his lips over mine and I'm transported again to the place were our love is the only thing that matters. In this one perfect moment, there is no drama and pain from our past and there is no threat looming over our lives. There is just us, as we were meant to be before life threw a couple of wrenches into our path.

"So," he whispers in between kisses. "What is this surprise you brought me to?"

I grin as he starts kissing down my cheek to my neck. "Take a look for yourself."

He pulls away and we both turn as the front door opens and his parents step out onto the front porch. My stomach flips. I haven't seen August or Gretchen in years and I have no idea how they will react to the news that Wyatt and I are back together but in this instance, my feelings didn't matter. This is what Wyatt needed so even if it's terrible, I will deal with it for him. Glancing over at me, he smiles.

"You brought me home?"

I nod. "I figured if you were going to feel safe anywhere, it would be here."

"Are you nervous?" he asks, brushing my hair out of my face as he studies me and I nod. He smiles. "Don't be, baby. My parents love you."

"I broke their son's heart and ran away for ten years… Fuck. They think I cheated on you."

"Come on," he replies, his grin growing as he opens his door. "Let's go tell them the good news."

"Did you not hear me?" I hiss, the realization of just how bad this is going to be crashing down on me. Why the hell didn't I think this all the way through? He jumps out of the truck, holding his hand out to me, and I release a nervous breath as I scoot to the end of the seat and step down, mentally hyping myself up. Okay, so it's going to be awful and uncomfortable and they may never forgive me but for Wyatt, I would walk through fire.

When we turn toward the house, Gretchen and August are walking toward us and Gretchen has tears in her eyes, her gaze locked on me. Before I can say anything or even start to explain, she pulls me into her arms and hugs me so tight that I can barely breathe.

"I'm so sorry," I whisper to her and she shakes her head, pulling back to look at me.

"Sweet girl, you have nothing to be sorry for and just

between us girls, I always knew you'd be back. The two of you were made for each other."

A sob bubbles out of me as I hug her back, an intense relief that can only come with being home washing over me. "I missed y'all so much."

"We missed you, too, honey," she says as she releases me. Wyatt grins as he pulls me back into his arms with a shrug.

"Oh, yeah… I guess I already told them everything. Oops."

"You son of a bitch," I growl, smacking his stomach with the back of my hand as relief rushes through me and a smile stretches across my face. August and Gretchen are the closest thing I have to parents now and I don't know what I would have done if they had hated me for what I did to Wyatt. August wraps his arms around my shoulders, sandwiching me between him and Wyatt as we all start walking back to the house and another little piece of home and family slides into place for me. It's not the same as having my own parents back but my heart still mends a little bit all the same.

A.M. Myers

Every Little Thing

Chapter Twenty-Seven
Wyatt

Walking into the house, I toss my keys on the dining room table and turn toward the kitchen to grab a beer as my mind drifts to last night at my parents' house and how nervous Piper was to see them again after all these years. Grinning, I take a beer out of the fridge and pop the top off. Right after we got back from Charleston and Piper agreed to give this relationship a shot again, I called them and told them the whole story. My mother was not pleased, at first, but after she found out the truth, her heart hurt for Piper just as much as mine did and Dad felt guilty that he didn't look for her after he went to North Carolina and found the house empty. Both echoed the sentiment that they should have known better. Piper has been a part of their lives for so long and they know what kind of person she is but more importantly, what kind of person she isn't. What we have is special and there is no way in hell she would intentionally do anything to damage it.

Releasing a breath, I smile at the sense of calm I feel

today compared to the storm of turmoil I've been walking around in for the last week. I don't think I realized just how bad it had gotten until I woke up this morning in my childhood bedroom and it didn't feel like there was a dark cloud hanging over me. Last night was exactly what I needed to clear my head and stop losing my shit at every turn and I'm so fucking grateful that Piper knew what to do to help me. I was so close to cracking up and I hate to think what could happen to her if I am not on top of my game with this maniac running around. I need to be focused no matter how nice it was to just relax yesterday.

We spent all day with my parents, sharing memories and laughing before Mom made a huge dinner to celebrate Piper and I renewing our vows. She also pestered us about when we would be giving her a grandchild but Piper doesn't want to tell anyone until she actually gets pregnant so all we could say is that it will happen when it happens as we shared a secret smile. After dessert, Piper took me out to the woods behind the house where I kissed her for the first time and we made out like a couple of teenagers before going to sleep in my old room. The full-sized mattress wasn't the greatest but it did mean I got to hold Piper all night long. When I dropped her off at the studio this morning, we both had smiles on our faces and it feels like I can breathe for the first time in a week.

Of course, I had to go to the clubhouse and temporarily ruin it. Even with all of us digging into these cases now, we're not finding anything new and I'm beginning to echo Streak's sentiment when we found the photos on the wall.

This guy is good.

But after the craziness, whoever is doing this has only

made the club's bond stronger. Where we were bickering and arguing before, we are united and ready to face down whoever this is. We won't let him win and while we can't find any evidence to go on, we have come up with a plan of attack for the next time this guy strikes and each of our women are thoroughly protected. Blaze tasked Storm and Chance with calling all of the women we've helped in the past three years also to warn them of the threat and remind them that they could reach out to us at anytime so hopefully, we won't have a new death to look into anytime soon. But it feels naive to have so much hope when we have nothing to go on.

Walking back out to the dining room, I sigh and take a sip of my beer before setting it down on the table. I turn to sit down but before I can, the phone rings on the wall behind me. I turn and pick it up.

"Hello?"

"Hi. This is Diane at the Hyatt Regency Lake Washington. I'm looking for Piper Landry."

I scowl as I turn around. "I'm sorry. Where?"

"The Hyatt Regency in Seattle, sir. May I speak to Miss Landry, please?"

Why in the hell would a hotel in Seattle be calling Piper?

"She's not here right now but this is her husband. Can I help you?"

"Oh, yes! We received your reservation this morning but there was a problem with the credit card your wife provided so we just need an updated payment method."

"What?" I ask, my thoughts screeching to a halt as I run my fingers through my hair. "What reservation?"

337

"Um… it says here that you will be getting in tomorrow night and staying for six days… oh, wait… I guess it is just your wife on the reservation… were you planning on joining her? I can add your name here in the system."

I shake my head and stumble to the table before sinking into a chair. My chest feels tight as I run my hand through my hair again. "And you said that reservation was made this morning?"

"Yes, sir."

My knee bounces. "What time?"

"Um… looks like ten-twenty-six a.m."

No.

No.

No.

This can't be right…

That was just after I dropped Piper off at work for her first session so why would she be making hotel reservations? And why all the way in Seattle? Everyone we know is here in Baton Rouge and if we're taking some kind of vacation, I have other places at the top of my list. I release a heavy sigh and drop my face into my hand as I shake my head, trying to make sense of all this. My heart feels like it's going to explode and I can't stop my damn leg from shaking.

What is happening?

Why the hell would Piper be going to Seattle?

"Sir?" the woman says on the other end of the phone and I glance up like I can somehow find the answers I need somewhere in this house. My gaze lands on our wedding picture and I shake my head again like I can somehow shake some damn answers into my head. Piper just put that photo up on the wall the other day along with a bunch of others. She said it made our house a real home.

"Yeah."

"Do you have another credit card you would like to use or is there a better number I could reach your wife on?"

I shake my head. "No. Just cancel it."

"Cancel the reservation?" she asks like I'm speaking fucking French over here and I nod, my heart hammering so hard, it's a wonder one of my ribs hasn't cracked.

"Yes. Cancel the reservation."

Silence greets me for a moment. "Are you sure? We only have a couple of rooms left and if I cancel this now, I'm not sure you'll be able to make another reservation."

"Just cancel it!" I yell, my stomach twisting as the possibilities start ticking through my mind.

Is Piper leaving me?

Did I scare her last night?

Push her too far by asking her to renew our vows?

Is the fear getting to her?

Making her see things again?

She seemed so happy all day yesterday and in the truck, cuddled up by my side this morning but maybe once she got to work, the panic started to set in and she felt like she needed to run. Maybe she is slipping away from me. The time in my life that I spent without Piper flickers through my brain and I shudder as the memory of that hollow ache in my chest haunts me. My mind drifts to that little fucker James and the shit he said the other night as I hear the woman on the other end of the line start typing.

I'll only stay away if Piper wants me to…

Is she with him? Has this all just been one big joke

since the start?

I shake my head again.

No.

There is no way she is with that little piece of shit. Right?

"No," I whisper, pulling the phone away from my ear as I shake my head and try to reassure myself that Piper wouldn't do this to me. "No, no, no. She wouldn't…"

She just told me yesterday that she would never cheat on me. Could she really lie right to my face? Is she so cold that she would string me along and agree to marry me again when all along she was planning to run away with her ex?

I press the phone to my ear again as my stomach flips.

"Okay, sir. The reservation has been canceled," Diane says, her tone guarded. It is fucking rude but I don't even care. Doesn't she realize that my whole life is falling apart right now?

"Thanks."

I hang up without waiting for her reply and toss the phone across the table before dropping my head into my hands as my vision blurs.

Fuck.

What the hell is going on? I go over the last two days in excruciating detail, looking for any sign that Piper was freaking out about anything but nothing stands out. Have I been so lost in my own shit that I just missed it? Is she fed up with me and thought it would be easier to run than confront me? God, I wouldn't fucking blame her with all this drama in our lives right now. What kind of crazy person would hang around with such a blatant threat to their lives?

Shoving the chair back, I stand up and stare into the living room, looking for a clue but there is nothing. It's the same as when we left yesterday. Running my hand through my hair, I turn and march down the hallway to our bedroom before staring at the space but everything looks exactly the same as it did the last time I was in here two days ago. I turn back to the wall and place both of my hands on it before squeezing my eyes shut and blowing out a breath.

You know what…

It doesn't matter *why* Piper is running. I made her a promise last night and there is no way in hell I'm going to let her walk away from me again. Over my dead fucking body. She is my wife and I refuse to live another second of my life without her in it. Done it before and I'll be damned if I let it happen again. Grabbing my phone out of my pocket, I pull up the GPS and release a sigh when it blinks, showing her location at the studio. With renewed determination, I walk back out to the dining room and grab my keys off of the table as I stare at the screen.

"Go ahead and run, baby," I whisper as I walk out to my truck, my mission clear to me and a wave of calm washes over me. "I'll be right behind you."

A.M. Myers

Every Little Thing

Chapter Twenty-Eight
Piper

"Okay," Dr. Brewer says, her voice chipper like we all haven't been describing the worst experiences of our lives for the past hour as she gazes around the group. Her eyes land on Lillian in the chair next to me and she smiles. "I think we have time for one more, Lillian, and it's been a while since you shared anything with the group. Why don't you go?"

Lillian shakes her head, her gaze firmly rooted to her lap. "No, I'm good."

"I know it can be hard to talk about but you'll never get better if you don't push yourself a little bit and this is a safe space. Isn't that why you come to these meetings? To overcome the trauma in your past?"

Every eye in the room is trained on Lillian, waiting for her answer and my heart aches fiercely for her. My friend is sweet and soft-spoken but I know her quiet nature harbors more pain than she knows what to do with. It's hard to get up and talk about your past under normal circumstances but when you are put on the spot like this, it feels impossible and all you want to do is go back to being invisible. When she still doesn't say anything, I nudge her arm with my elbow and as she peeks over at me, I flash her an encouraging smile.

"You've got this."

She stares at me for a second before sucking in a nervous breath and wringing her hands together in her lap. "My fiancé was killed three years ago."

"How?" Dr. Brewer asks, her face pinched in concentration as she focuses on Lillian and I'm mentally cheering her on in my mind, hoping that she can find the courage to speak her truth. I know Lillian needs to talk about this, needs get it all out, and I get the feeling that she doesn't talk much during her regular appointments with Dr. Brewer so she has no other way to try and help her.

"It was summertime and we were driving to get dinner with his parents to tell them the news. He had just proposed to me two days before."

Dr. Brewer nods. "And how did he die?"

"Someone ran us off the road," she answers, her voice cracking as tears shine in her eyes.

Come on, Lil.

You can do this.

"What do you remember from the accident?"

Lillian shakes her head. "I don't want to talk about this anymore."

"I know you can do this, Lillian," Dr. Brewer says, encouraging her with an eager expression on her face. "Is there anything you'd like to share about that night? Anything at all? It doesn't matter how little or insignificant it seems."

Lillian clamps her mouth shut, her lips pressing into a thin line as she shakes her head and refuses to look up. After a second, Dr. Brewer sighs.

"All right. I think that is all for this evening. I'll see you all next week."

As everyone else starts standing up and taking their chairs to the wall, I nudge Lillian again and she meets my eyes.

"You okay?"

She shakes her head and stands up. "I don't want to talk about it."

As she walks away from me, I turn and watch her practically run out of the building. Worry eating away at me, I stand up and gather both of our chairs before taking them over to the wall. I glance over at the door Lillian just marched out of. I can't help but remember when I was in her position and thought things would never change. It feels like an endless black hole but I just hope she will keep fighting. I prop our chairs up against the wall and turn when I hear a growl behind me. Tate is staring down at her phone with a look that honestly scares me a little but I'm quickly learning that's just Tate. She's passionate and intense but I have no doubt, she would jump in front of a bullet for the ones she loves.

"Everything okay?" I ask her and her head pops up. Her snarl falls away as her eyes land on me and she nods, glancing back down at her phone as she starts typing so fast that I swear her fingers blur.

"Yeah. I'm just about to murder my husband if he doesn't back the fuck off."

I laugh as we start walking toward the door. "Oh, him, too, huh?"

"Girl," she quips, meeting my gaze as she tucks her phone into her pocket. "All of them. Like I get it, the club is under attack and all that but Lincoln damn well knows that I'm capable of defending myself."

I nod as we step outside and stop to talk. "Yeah. Wyatt bought me a gun."

"Shit, is that all? Then, you're lucky. Storm has been following Ali around like a puppy and then, if anyone looks at her too long, he turns into a damn pit bull. She threatened to cut his junk clean off if he didn't let her breathe."

"Goddamn," I whisper with a laugh and she nods, smiling.

"You know what we should do, we should teach these damn boys a lesson."

I nod, crossing my arms over my chest. "Uh-huh and how do you suggest we do that?"

"I don't know yet. Let me think on it," she says and we turn to walk out to our cars. We reach the end of the sidewalk and she reaches out, grabbing my arm. "Hey, you feel like going to get ice cream or something? I need to calm down before I go home or I'll end up shooting that man again."

"I'm sorry… did you just say that you've shot your husband *before*?"

She shrugs. "It was a misunderstanding."

"And he forgave you?" I ask, my gaze flicking to her in disbelief. I have a hard time imagining Wyatt just letting it go if I shot him. She flashes me a grin and shakes her head.

"Oh, no, he groveled a whole hell of a lot. I was not the

one who needed forgiveness."

I shake my head, fighting back a smile. "Ah, so it was like that, then."

"It was," she says, her grin growing. "So, how 'bout it? Ice cream?"

"Ohh, you know what I've been craving for like two days? Cheesecake with cherries and chocolate syrup on top."

She arches a brow. "What are you, pregnant?"

I stop in my tracks, staring out at the parking lot with wide eyes.

Holy shit.

Could I be pregnant already?

Shaking my head, I turn to her. "No… it's too soon. Wyatt and I have only been back together…"

"For a freaking month, Piper. You totally could be pregnant… do you want to be?"

I nod, trying not to get my hopes up but my heart races as I think about the possibility. "We've been trying."

"Okay," she says, grabbing my hand and pulling me to her car. "We have more important things to do than get ice cream."

She stops next to the passenger side door and releases my hand to yank it open before bending down and digging through the glove box. When she stands up again, she has a box of pregnancy tests in her hand and I start laughing.

"Tate, why the hell do you have pregnancy tests in your car?"

She shrugs as she pulls one out of the box and hands it to me. "Because when Lincoln and I were trying, I stashed these things everywhere so that no matter where I was, I could pee on a stick and find out."

"Huh," I mutter, thinking it's actually not a bad idea. "Okay."

"Come on. Let's go back inside so you can pee."

I try to hand the test back to her. "I think it's too soon. There's no way I'm pregnant yet. I mean, it takes months to actually conceive."

"Tell that to fertile Myrtle, Juliette. Moose knocked her up *right* away. Besides, what does it matter if you waste one little test? I have no further use for them for the time being and I clearly have plenty," she says, pointing to the box sitting on her passenger seat. Sucking in a breath, I look down at the test in my hand and nod as my heart kicks in my chest.

"Okay."

She pumps her hand in the air before hooking her arm through mine and slamming her car door. "Let's go… Ooh, just think how pissed Streak is going to be if you *are* pregnant. Man might just explode."

"There will be quite a few babies hanging around the club pretty soon. Streak might not be the only one getting sick of it." I laugh as we walk back into the rec center where our meetings are held and dip into the bathroom. She shakes her head.

"If you're talking about Blaze, you're dead wrong. That man loves getting to play grandpa to Ali and Storm's kid, Mags, and I have no doubt he'll be the same way with all the rest of them."

"You know," I murmur, glancing over at her. "The club is so different than I assumed it would be when I first found out Wyatt has joined."

She nods. "Tell me about it. I had plenty of reasons not to trust them but they won me over and wormed their way into my heart. Bastards. Now, are you gonna take this damn test or not?"

"Okay, okay," I say, holding my hands up in surrender as I set my bag on the counter and step into one of the stalls. After I finish doing my business, I unlock the door and step out, my stomach rolling and my heart racing as I set the test on the counter and take a step back. Tate sets a timer on her phone and we both sigh, ready to wait for the results.

"I think I'm gonna throw up."

Tate studies me. "Morning sickness or nerves?"

"How could it be morning sickness at night?" I ask, shaking my head and she throws her head back and laughs.

"Oh, girl… you are in for a rude awakening. Morning sickness should be called all day long, constant, you don't get no break, good luck eating for the next nine months sickness. But maybe that's just me because I'm having twins."

I nod, my mind racing with the possibility that there could be a little human growing inside my belly right now, a little perfect piece of Wyatt and me. Pressing a shaky hand over my heart, I suck in a breath.

"Oh my God, I'm so nervous… I've wanted this for so long."

"Just one more minute," Tate says, trying to reassure me but as the words pour out of her mouth, it feels like an eternity. What the hell am I supposed to do for another minute?

"How did you find out you were pregnant?"

349

Tate laughs. "I threw up."

"That's it?" I ask, joining her in her laughter as she nods her head.

"Yeah. I have a freaking stomach of steel so when I threw up one morning and then felt completely fine for the rest of the day, I just knew. I took a test at the clubhouse and then I whispered the news to Lincoln as we were going home on his bike." She laughs again. "I've never seen that man pull over so fast and he insisted that someone with a car come pick me up. Not even the threat of the taser worked to change his mind."

I shake my head as a smile stretches across my face. "Y'all are something else."

"Yeah," she agrees, shrugging. "But it works for us. Lincoln likes that I'm a little crazy and I love the way he mellows me out like no one else can. And that he puts up with me 'cause you know there aren't many men who would."

The timer on her phone goes off and my stomach flips as my heart jumps into my throat. I cover my eyes with my hand and shake my head.

"Just tell me… what does it say?"

When she doesn't answer me right away, I open my eyes and look up. She flashes me a grin and my stomach does another flip. "Congrats, babe. You've got a little bun in the oven."

A giggle bubbles out of me and I slap my hand over my mouth as tears well up in my eyes and warmth radiates from my chest. Glancing down at my flat belly, I pull the hand away from my lips and place it on my tummy as I try to wrap my mind around the news.

Every Little Thing

Oh my God.

I'm pregnant.

We're a real family now.

"Shit," Tate whispers, walking over to me and wrapping her arms around me. "I'm all fucking emotional already and now you're going to make me cry."

I hug her back, feeling so incredibly blessed in so many aspects of my life. Not only do I have Wyatt back but I was also welcomed back into his family and adopted by this group of bikers, who are so close and always there for each other and the one thing I know more than anything else is that this baby will be surrounded by so much love.

"I have to go home and tell Wyatt," I whisper, shaking my head as I pull away from her and she quickly wipes a couple tears off of her cheeks as she nods.

"Yes, you do." She reaches behind her and grabs the test off of the counter. "Here. Take this. Do you know how you're going to do it?"

I shake my head. "No… I don't know."

"Luckily, I have you covered there, too. Come with me."

Taking my hand, she starts pulling me out of the bathroom and I swipe my purse off the counter as she drags me to the door. Once we get back outside, she takes me back to her car and pops the trunk, pulling out a little onesie and handing it to me. I unfold the tiny piece of fabric and laugh when I read the message on the front.

Prospect
Bayou Devils MC
Louisiana

351

"I was going to tell Lincoln with that but then I was too excited to wait and now that we're having twins, I need to get another one made so you can just have that one."

I smile as I stare at the words. "You should make these for all the kids. They're freaking adorable."

"Flip it over," she says, grinning and I do, shaking my head at the club's patch printed on the back. Oh, God, Wyatt is going to love this. "Ooh, here. I also have a gift bag you can put it in."

"Jesus, woman." I laugh as she pulls the bag out and takes the onesie from me to fold it and slips it into the bag. "Is there anything you don't have in this car?"

She shakes her head, handing me the bag. "I like to be prepared."

"Thank you," I whisper, wrapping my arms around her in another hug and she holds me tight before pulling back with a sniff.

"I swear to God, if you make me cry again…" She shakes her head. "These babies are turning *me* into a little baby."

"No, no, you're still one badass bitch."

She narrows her eyes. "Don't lie to me."

"Okay," I answer with a laugh, holding my hand up as I back away from her. "I'm just going to go now. Try not to kill your husband tonight."

Laughing, she walks around to the driver's side door as I walk backward to my car. "I make no promises."

We both slip behind the wheel and I watch her pull out of the parking lot before lowering the visor and staring at myself in the mirror as butterflies flutter through me and a huge smile stretches across my face. I can't wait to tell Wyatt the news. He's been acting weird again these past few days and I know the stress is getting to him again. Maybe we'll go back to his parents' house this weekend. It will give him a chance to relax again and we can tell them the good news about our new family member. I peek down at my stomach again and flatten my hand over my shirt.

"Hi, sweet baby… it's your mama…." Tears fills my eyes and I shake my head, wiping them away as I pull out of the parking lot. I can't wipe the smile from my face and the drive back to the house passes in a daze as I think about our baby - whether he will look like his daddy or she'll look like me. I think about bringing him home for the first time and teaching her to walk and talk. I imagine a little girl that has her daddy absolutely wrapped around her finger and by the time I pull into the driveway, it feels like my heart is going to explode.

I grab the bag out of the passenger seat and slip the pregnancy test inside before climbing out and practically skipping up the front walk. Stepping into house, I scan the living room but I can't see Wyatt.

Weird.

His truck and his bike are outside.

"Baby?" I call.

"Back in the bedroom."

Grinning, I walk down the hallway and stop just outside of the nursery Wyatt started setting it up for me before trying to wipe the smile from my face. Once I get it under control, I walk into the room.

"Hey, baby," he says, lying sideways across the bed as

he watches a baseball game on TV and I smile. His gaze drops to the bag and he scowls. "What's that for?"

"It's for you. Could you turn off the game for a second?"

He nods, sitting up and turning the TV off before turning his full attention to me, concern all over his face. "What's up?"

Without a word, I hand him the bag and my hands shake like crazy as my belly does another flip. How is he going to react? I know he wants this just as badly as I do but with all the stress going on right now, I'm not sure if he'll think it's such a good thing. Oh, God, what if he isn't happy? What if he says it's not the right time? We were so excited when we started trying but so much has changed since then. He sets the bag on the bed in front of him and reaches inside, pulling out the onesie first. His brows draw together as he unfolds it and holds it up in front of his face, reading the front. A confused gaze flicks to me and he forces a smile to his face.

"This is cute. Where did you get it?"

"Tate gave it to me."

He nods, setting it down on the bed. "That's cool. Did you tell her that we're trying?"

"Wyatt," I breathe, raising my eyebrows as I stare at him, hoping he'll get the hint. God, men are clueless. He shakes his head and I point to the bag. "There's one more thing in there."

Reaching into the bag again, he pulls out the pregnancy test and his eyes widen as he stares down at it before his eyes lock with mine and his lips part. "Are you…?"

"Yeah," I whisper, tears welling up in my eyes as I nod

my head and a huge grin spreads across his face as he jumps up and pulls me back onto the bed with him. I laugh as he plants kisses all over my face before finding his way to my lips as his hand slips into my hair. He pulls back and stares down into my eyes.

"We're having a baby?"

I nod. "We're having a baby."

"I love you," he says, his voice soft and full of love as he looks up at me and the Wyatt of the past two weeks is gone. The man staring back at me is mine, the one who vowed to always be there to catch me and follow me to the ends of the earth if I ever ran again. I nudge his nose with mine and he seizes the opportunity to claim my lips once more as his hand drifts down and grabs my ass, pulling me against him. His erection presses into my hip and in an instant, heat flushes through my body. I moan, grabbing his t-shirt and trying to pull him closer as my skin tingles with need so strong that I don't think I'll survive. His lips slip down my neck, sending a wave of goose bumps across my skin and I whisper his name.

"Fuck, baby," he growls, rolling me to my back as he looms over me, the muscles in his arms popping out as he leans down to nip at my bottom lip.

God, my husband is so fucking hot.

Gripping his t-shirt, I start pulling it over his head and he pulls back just enough to slip it off before he leans down again and presses his lips to mine. He hooks his hands around the back of my neck and brushes his thumb over my cheek, his kiss demanding but full of love and devotion. It's a perfect mix of the boy I first fell in love with under the oak trees and the man he is now.

"I need you, Wyatt. Now."

He grins and reaches between us to unbutton my jeans. "If this is going to be what you're like when you're pregnant, I wholeheartedly approve."

"Note taken. Now, fuck me." I am desperate for him and I've never gotten this turned on, this fast in my entire life. My entire body is on fire and my pussy is throbbing with need as I imagine him sinking into me. He jumps up and shoves his jeans down his legs, his cock springing free. I stare at him and lick my lips before slipping off the bed and dropping to my knees in front of him.

"Piper," he groans when I wrap my hand around his length and lick the tip. As I take him into my mouth, I glance up just in time to see him drop his head back and blow out a harsh breath. God, I want to watch him fall apart because of my touch, I want to see him lose it before he throws me back on the bed and fucks me, hard and fast, until I can't walk anymore. With those thoughts swirling around in my head, I take him to the back of my throat, massaging him with my tongue before pulling back. Before I reach the tip, I suck him back into my mouth quickly and he grabs a chunk of my hair, gripping it tightly as his groan echoes around the bedroom. When I pull back this time, I suck and graze his skin with my teeth just under the head and he pulls back sharply, grabbing me and pulling me to my feet. "You're teasing me today."

I arch a brow. "Why don't you do something about it?"

Heat flares in his eyes at the challenge and he grins as he spins me around and rips my shirt over my head. Next my bra hits the floor before he moves to my jeans and peels them down my legs. When he gets to my panties, he pulls on them until the sound of fabric ripping fills the air. He drags his lips up my neck before he places his hand against my spine and presses on my back until the top half of my body hits the mattress. Gripping my hips, he presses his cock against my entrance and applies just enough pressure to make me gasp before he pulls back.

"Wyatt," I whine and he laughs.

"Not so fun when someone else does it to you, is it?"

I try to move my hips back into him but he holds me steady and I poke my bottom lip out. "Please."

"Only 'cause you said please," he whispers, bending over me and brushing his lips over my ear. I shudder and he surges forward, piercing my core and stretching me as I grip the blanket underneath me and cry out. When he pulls back, I try to follow him and he laughs in my ear again. "You want rough tonight, babe?"

I nod. "Yes."

"You sure you'll be okay?" he asks, his voice softer than a moment ago and I realize he is worried about hurting the baby. My heart cracks wide open with my love for this incredible man and I nod. He presses a sweet kiss to my cheek before pulling back and slamming into me with a grunt of pleasure that sends a jolt of pleasure straight between my legs. Squeezing my eyes shut, I lose myself in the sensation, the drag and pull of his cock inside me, the zap of pleasure as he buries himself to the hilt and the ache when he pulls away, leaving me empty. My head swims as pressure builds in my belly and I know I'm not going to last much longer. With a firm grip on my hips, he continues his demanding pace as he presses his lips to my shoulder. A bite of pain comes next as his teeth sink into my skin and he groans, the vibrations of it making my pussy clench around him.

"Goddamn it, Pip," he groans, rolling his forehead across my back as his fingers tighten at my sides. "Fuck. I love you."

"I love you," I cry, nodding as my body barrels toward release, every inch of my skin tingling and my heart pounding in my chest.

"I want you to come all over my cock, baby. Remind us both who the hell you belong to."

I shake my head as my belly tightens and my muscles shake in anticipation. "It's always you, Wyatt."

"Do it, now," he orders, nipping at my ear and I cry out again, hands splayed out on the mattress and one slides forward like I'm reaching for my orgasm as I start falling apart beneath him. "Come for me, baby. I want to feel your tight little pussy gripping my cock."

"Wyatt!" I scream as the coil tightens to the point of breaking and just when I think it's going to snap, my release rolls through me, wave after wave of pleasure shaking my body. Wyatt groans behind me, his fingers digging into my hips as his body shudders and his release spills inside of me with another long, drawn out groan. Both of us gasp for air, dazed by the strength of it all - the sex, our connection, our love - and when he finally pulls out of me and rolls me over to my back, I smile up at him, completely sated. For the time being...

"I love you."

He drops his lips to mine, kissing me like he's desperate for something, like I might disappear at any second and my heart aches from the pain I feel rolling off of him. What is

358

going on with him and how the hell do I help him?

A.M. Myers

Every Little Thing

Chapter Twenty-Nine
Wyatt

"Piper," I call, pulling my gaze away from the baseball game on TV to lean back in the couch and glance down the hallway to our bedroom where Piper is getting ready for her first baby doctor appointment. She has been back there for damn near an hour, though and I don't know what the hell she's doing. "We've got to go, baby."

"Just a second."

Sighing, I shake my head. "We're going to miss our appointment."

"One second, Wyatt," she calls, a trace of irritation in her voice and I can't help but smile. In the two days since Piper told me she was pregnant, I have become very well aquatinted with her new dramatic mood swings, random bouts of morning sickness, and insatiable sex drive but I'm not complaining about that last part one bit. Hell, I'm not complaining about any of it because I am just so damn happy that I have my wife here and that we are finally starting our family. It's everything we have ever wanted but those dark thoughts still creep in way more than I would like since I have even more to lose now.

My mind drifts to the phone call I got a few days ago from the hotel and I scrub my hand over my face. I have spent the last three days either following Piper all around town or watching the GPS obsessively to make sure she is not running from me. She seems good, though. But that only confuses me more. Why the hell is she making hotel reservations for a city three thousand miles away if she is so damn happy? Or is she just that good at hiding that she is falling apart? I've got to stop doing this, watching her every move and overthinking every damn thing or it is going to destroy us.

"Ready," she says from behind me and I turn my head to look at her. The pale pink floral dress she is wearing hits her mid-thigh, showing off her long, sexy legs and the v-neck molds to her chest, showing everyone a peek of what is mine. I growl, shaking my head as I turn back to the TV.

"You're not wearing that."

She scoffs. "Excuse me?"

"You heard me," I say, spinning back around and meeting her heated glare. "You can't wear that."

"Just who the hell do you think you are, Wyatt Landry? I'll damn well wear whatever the hell I feel like."

Turning the TV off, I jump up from the couch and stalk across the living room to her before shaking my head as I run my fingers down her chest where the fabric ends. "I do not want every man in Baton Rouge seeing my wife like this."

"Well, we're just going to the doctor so it won't be

every man and what does it matter?" she asks, crossing her arms over her chest as she arches a brow in challenge. The move pushes her tits up even more and makes the damn neckline even more obscene. "I'm not showing anything inappropriate and at the end of the day, I'm going home with you so let them look."

Maybe I should just let it go but the thought of a bunch of guys looking at her makes me feel crazy. Does she want someone to see? Does she enjoy the attention? Shaking my head, I plant my feet and cross my arms, mirroring her pose.

"Baby, we're going to an OB's office. There will be plenty of guys there and there is no way in hell I want them seeing your tits."

She rolls her eyes. "You can't see my tits and I'm wearing this dress. Get over it.

"Absolutely not."

"Do you really think you can stop me?"

I grin down at her because, in my head, I can already see where this is going to go. She is going to challenge me and when I don't back down, we'll end up back in the bedroom, missing our appointment but ask me if I really care.

Spoiler alert, I don't.

Or hell, maybe I'll just throw her down right here on the living room floor and take her until both of us are too tired to do anything else. Either option works for me since I will have her moaning my name all damn night. She takes a step toward me and narrows her eyes but they shine with excitement, telling me all I need to know as my cock presses against my jeans.

Fuck.

This is going to be fun.

"Don't you dare give me that look, Landry. I'm horny enough as it is and we have an appointment to get to." She slips past me before I can catch her and I shake my head as I turn to see her grabbing her purse off of the table.

"I'm serious, Pip. You're not going in that dress."

She spins to face me, planting her hands on her hips as she glares. "You listen to me, I'm fucking tired all of the goddamn sudden, my boobs are fucking aching, it's ten a.m. and it's already ninety fucking degrees outside so I'm wearing this dress and if you keep arguing with me, I will chop your dick clean off and bury it in the yard. Let's. Go."

"Shit," I whisper, shaking my head. "At least put a damn sweater on."

"Ninety fucking degrees, Wyatt!" she yells, opening the front door and marching out without another word and without a sweater. Shaking my head, I run my hand through my hair.

Remember those mood swings I was talking about? *Jesus Christ.*

Swiping my keys off of the table, I grab her sweater off of the hook and follow her out. As I climb behind the wheel of the Bronco, she sulks in the passenger seat and I pass her the sweater but she just looks at it, refusing to take it. Rolling my eyes, I drop it onto the seat next to me. Her skirt rides up slightly but I ignore it as I pull the truck out of the driveway and reach across the seat, holding my hand out to her.

"You gonna be mad at me all day, baby?"

Her gaze flicks to me. "That depends. Are you

gonna be a stubborn ass all damn day?"

"No, I'm done."

Sighing, she slips her hand into mine and as I feel the tension leave her body, I pull her across the seat to me. She cuddles into my side and I press my lips to the top of her head, savoring the smell of her honeysuckle perfume. I've been acting like a maniac lately - extra possessive, over the top jealous, and not willing to let her out of my sight - and I know she doesn't deserve this but I can't shake this fear that I'm going to lose her. The worst part is, I don't know how it's going to happen so I feel like I have to cover all of my bases but it's making me lose my mind and no matter how much she reassures me that she is good and that she is here to stay, I can't help but think the worst.

"You ever been to Seattle, baby?" I ask and she looks up at me with a scowl on her face, her eyes searching mine.

"Seattle? No, why?"

I shrug. "Just wondering."

"Well, if you're planning a trip or something, pick somewhere else. I don't want to go on vacation to a place that rains all the damn time."

"Note taken," I mutter as my mind spins. Is she lying to me? All this time that I've been following her, I haven't seen anything that would make me think she is planning to leave me but that just leaves me with more questions. If she has nothing to do with the flowers at her work and the reservations in Seattle, then who could it be? As I stare out at the road in front of us, a theory pops into my mind and it's so ridiculous that I shake my head but it still nags at me.

What if it's the same person threatening the club?

"What are you thinking so hard about over there?" Piper asks and I glance down at her, forcing a smile to my face.

"Nothing, babe."

I can feel her gaze on me as I glance up at the road again. "You doing okay?"

"Yeah, baby. I'm great," I lie, hoping the smile I flash her this time is more convincing as I slow down and turn into the parking lot of the doctor's office. She sighs but doesn't say anything. I turn the truck off and get out of the truck before turning to help her down and she remains silent as she takes my hand. The silence makes me fucking nervous and I resist the urge to twitch as we walk into the doctor's office and Piper walks up to the window.

"Can I help you?"

Piper smiles. "Yes. I have an appointment at ten thirty."

"Piper Landry?"

Piper nods and the receptionist tells her she is all checked in and to have a seat in the waiting room. She doesn't even glance back at me and I follow behind her, wishing I could get my shit together but I don't see that happening anytime soon.

"Hey, babe," I say and she stops, glancing back at me. I pull my phone out of my pocket and hold it up. "I'm gonna go make a quick phone call."

"Just don't take too long."

Nodding, I turn away from her and walk back outside as I dial Streak's number and put the phone to my ear. His annoyed groan greets me.

"What?"

I laugh. "Morning, sunshine."

"Oh, shove it up your ass, Fuzz. I was up until five in the morning going over those fucking cases."

"Speaking of which, you got anything new on those?"

"What the fuck do you think?" There is a pause before something crashes on his end of the line. "Jesus fuck. I mean, this is fucking hopeless. You know that, right? I've combed through these cases, you've combed through these cases, and I'm just not seeing anything that will help us. I talked to Rodriguez again today but he's just as stumped as we are."

Blowing out a breath, I run my hand through my hair. "Yeah…"

"I mean, there is evidence but it's like only the evidence he wanted us to find. It's just enough to drive us crazy but not nearly enough to get us anywhere."

"I know what you mean."

"Like, how the fuck do we find him if all we have to go on are the breadcrumbs he wanted us to find? He's leading us in goddamn circles and I'm losing my shit over here."

I lean against the wall of the office and drop my head back. "I know what you mean. Pretty sure I'm single handedly ruining my relationship."

"That sucks, dude. I actually like Piper. She's good for you."

"Yeah…" I mutter as the idea I had in the truck pops into my mind. "Hey, do you think this guy would meddle in our lives? Like send our women flowers and make fake hotel reservations?"

He scoffs. "At this point, I don't even know how to answer that. We know about the girls but he has probably been messing with us in other ways that we don't even know about. Who knows what he's actually done."

"Right," I reply. It's the answer I wanted but it doesn't make me feel any better. "All right, man. I gotta get back inside before the doctor calls Piper back."

"Whoa. Is she okay?"

I grin, remembering his reaction to Tate's news at our housewarming party. "Yeah. We just found out she's pregnant."

"Motherfuckers. All of you," he says before hanging up the phone and I laugh as I slip it back into my pocket and walk back into the office.

"Piper," a woman in pink scrubs calls from an open door as soon as I step inside and I glance over at Piper as she stands up. Relief washes over her face when her eyes meet mine and we meet halfway across the waiting room, locking our hands together as we stop in front of the nurse. She smiles at us and turns. "Follow me, please."

We trail behind her and after she takes Piper's weight and blood pressure, she leads us back to a room with a table, two chairs, and a desk. As I sit down in the chair, she hands Piper a paper gown.

"Just put this on. The doctor will be in shortly."

Piper smiles. "Thank you."

She closes the door and Piper jumps off the table and pulls her dress over her head before slipping out of her panties and pulling the gown on. When she's covered again, she grabs her clothes off of the table and folds them, setting them in the chair next to me.

"You gonna ignore me all day, baby?" I ask as she sits up on the table and she shrugs.

"I don't know. You gonna keep acting weird?"

Leaning forward, I drop my head into my hands. "I don't know, Pip."

"I was thinking about going to your parents' house again this weekend. Tell them the good news, you know?"

"Yeah," I whisper, meeting her gaze again. "That sounds good."

"Did it help? When we went last time?"

The memories of last weekend flash through my mind and I scrub my hand over my face, unable to believe that was only a week ago when I feel like it's been months since then. Being back home did help but I'm not so sure how well it would work a second time. As I look up at my wife, I feel so much love it feels like my heart might bust open but there is also that little voice in my head, screaming all my doubts and suspicions back at me.

I'm at war, with myself, with her, and with this threat shadowing all of our lives. It's constant, teasing me, tormenting me, and it's not hard for me to understand how Piper spiraled out of control so easily when I deployed. Most days, I feel like I am one more incident away from losing it but the only thing that holds me together is the knowledge of what could happen to Piper if I'm not here to keep her safe.

"Wyatt," she whispers, tears welling up in her eyes as she stares at me. "Please talk to me."

I can't though.

I can't tell her all the awful thoughts running

through my head because she needs me to be the strong one. She needs me to hold everything together, for her.

I open my mouth to assure her everything is okay when someone knocks on the door and before we can answer, the door swings up and the doctor, a lovely older woman, walks in, flashing me a smiling.

"Hello. I'm Dr. Ward."

I nod, shaking her hand as she holds it out. "Wyatt."

"You must be Piper, then," she says, turning to my wife and glancing down at the chart in her hand. "I see you came in yesterday for the official pregnancy test so we're just going to run over a few things and take a look at your little one today. That sound good?"

Piper and I both nod as Dr. Ward sits down at the desk and starts flipping through pages, asking Piper questions about how she's feeling, her last cycle, and her medical history. When she's finally finished, she turns to us with a smile.

"Okay. Should we take a look at your little peanut? Dad, you go stand up there and hold Mom's hand."

I do as I'm instructed, positioning myself near Piper's head and grabbing her hand as her words crash down on me.

Holy shit.

I'm a dad...

Logically, I knew that and I've thought about the baby a bunch but when I think of a dad, I always think of *my* dad. It hasn't occurred to me yet that *I* am the dad now. My heart hammers in my chest and a flutter runs through my stomach as the doctor pulls the ultrasound machine to Piper's bedside and grabs a long wand. I scowl, watching her as she slips a piece of plastic over it and squirts some lube on the tip. My eyes widen and I glance down at Piper as her teeth sink into bottom lip to keep herself from laughing.

Jesus Christ…

I thought they would just move that little thing on her belly to see the baby.

Piper turns her head to the other side and covers her mouth with her free hand as her chest shakes with laughter. Dr. Ward looks up at us, takes in my expression before glancing down at Piper, and starts laughing, too.

"Oh, I know that look. When the baby is this small, we have to do a transvaginal ultrasound."

I nod, trying not to think about her shoving that wand up between my wife's legs. "Uh-huh."

"The look on your face," she says, laughing as she turns back to the ultrasound machine and Piper joins her, giving my hand a squeeze. I meet her gaze and she smiles, reaching up to pat my cheek.

"Just look at me if it bugs you."

"If you're going to pass out, pull a seat up," Dr. Ward says, pointing to the chair behind me and I scoff.

"I'm not going to pass out."

"Famous last words. Let me tell ya, I've seen it all." She turns to Piper. "Let your knees fall to the sides, honey."

Piper does as instructed and Dr. Ward inserts the wand as I glance up at Piper's face. She grimaces for a second, her muscles tensing as the probe goes in but then she sighs and smiles up at me. A grainy image appears on the screen and both of us turn to stare at it, trying to decipher the images but it honestly just looks like white

371

noise to me.

What the hell am I supposed to be seeing here?

"Ah, there is the little one," Dr. Ward says, pointing to a tiny little blob on the screen. She moves the wand, getting a few more angles before taking a few quick measurements. "Now, we may not be able to hear a heartbeat…"

A whooshing sound fills the room and my heart seizes in my chest as I stare at the little blob she pointed out to us and the flickering motion in the center.

"There is your baby."

Tears sting my eyes as I stare at the little blob, unable to wrap my head around how it will become our son or daughter but filled with so much love that I don't even know what to do with it. I glance down and meets Piper's gaze as she smiles up at me with a few tears slipping from her eyes.

"Looks like you are at four weeks and one day," Dr. Ward says as she takes a few more measurements and hits a couple of buttons on the machine. "Which makes your due date… April twenty-seventh."

The doctor pulls the probe out and I help Piper sit up and swing her legs over the edge of the bed as Dr. Ward presses a few more buttons and the machine starts printing out pictures of our baby. When they're finished, she hands them to us with a grin.

"Congrats, you two. You'll need to head downstairs and get your blood drawn, Piper, and then I want to see you back here in a month, okay?"

Piper nods, cradling the photos in her hand. "Okay."

Dr. Ward tells us to have a good day before walking

out of the room and Piper looks up at me again, fear and sadness in her eyes as a tear slips down her cheek, racing to her trembling lip. My heart seems to stop for a moment as I wrap my arms around her and pull her closer.

"Hey, what's wrong, baby?"

Her lip trembles. "I don't want to lose this, Wyatt, and everyday it feels like you're drifting further and further from me."

"No, baby," I whisper, pressing my lips to her forehead as my chest aches and my stomach twists. In my obsession to keep her safe, I've been failing her and it has to end now. "I'm not going anywhere, I promise."

A.M. Myers

Every Little Thing

Chapter Thirty
Piper

"Hey, I've got an idea," Wyatt says as we pull into the driveway after our doctor's appointment. I pull my gaze away from the ultrasound pictures to peek over at him, arching a brow.

"Oh, yeah? What's that?"

He grins and I see a tiny little glimpse of my Wyatt looking back at me, which has been rare these days. "Let's go out on a date to celebrate our new little life changer."

"Okay." I flash him a smile as butterflies flutter through my belly. It's been a while since we went out on a real date and I don't need any excuse to soak up time with my man - especially when he is actually acting like my man.

He turns to back the truck up again. "What the hell?"

"What?" I ask, glancing behind us as a man with sandy brown hair in a button up shirt and a bow-tie steps out of a little four door sedan. "Do you know him?"

"No." Wyatt turns off the truck and opens the door, stepping down before turning back to me with a serious expression on his face. "Stay in the truck."

He walks away like that is the end of the conversation and I shake my head.

Oh, hell no.

Jumping out of the truck, I set the ultrasound picture on the seat and follow behind Wyatt as he walks up to the man.

"Can I help you?" Wyatt asks as he stops right in front of the man, a little close for the other man's comfort if the look on his face is any indication, and crosses his arms over his chest. I decide to hang back, just a little, in case this visit isn't a friendly one. The guy jerks his head back before his gaze snaps to the numbers nailed to the side of the house and back to Wyatt. He scowls, looking down at his phone.

"Uh… I think I might have the wrong address. I'm looking for Piper…"

What?

"Why?" Wyatt snaps, somehow making himself seem more threatening as he stares down at him. Not that he needs it. This guys is almost a foot shorter than him and he looks like he weighs a hundred and fifty pounds on his best day. Honestly, with the clothes he's wearing, he looks like some kind of door-to-door salesman and the black framed glasses really complete the look. He can't be more than twenty-one either and with how stressed Wyatt has been, I know it will only take a tiny thing to push him over the edge.

"Is this her house? Are you her roommate?"

My roommate?

Who the hell is this guy?

Enough is enough. I have no freaking clue who this

376

guy is and I really don't care. I have a date to get to.
Walking up beside Wyatt, I put my hand on his back and he
glances down at me as the man's face lights up.

"Piper! Oh, thank God. I was so worried I had the
wrong house."

"I'm sorry… do I know you?"

He nods. "It's Colin."

"Who?" I ask, tilting my head to the side and
pursing my lips as I study him, trying to place his face but
I've got nothing.

"We met online," Colin continues and all the blood
rushes to my ears as I shake my head in confusion. "We're
going out tonight, remember?"

I step in front of Wyatt so he doesn't kill this kid
and shake my head. "I think you have me confused with
someone else."

"He'd fucking better," Wyatt growls in my ear and
my heart drops as my pulse starts to race and my belly flips.

"No, I don't. I've seen your photo and we've been
talking for like two weeks. I know it's you. We text each
other all day long and I sent you your favorite flowers last
week. Remember? You said you loved them."

Oh, fuck.

This is not good.

With how paranoid Wyatt has been lately, he will
believe this guy and it won't matter one bit how much I tell
him that I have no idea what he's talking about or that I've
never even seen him. I can feel the anger and suspicion
rolling off of him without even glancing back at his face
and I squeeze my eyes shut as I take a deep breath.

"This guy?" he hisses, grabbing my hips and I
shake my head as I spin around and plant my hands on his
chest, hoping he can see the desperation in my eyes. Wyatt
owns me, every single piece of my heart and soul. There is

377

no one else I want but will he believe that?

"I don't know who he is, Wyatt."

His nostrils flare and he releases my hips to clench his fists at his sides as my heart thunders in my ears and my stomach flips.

Please, Wyatt…

He stares down at me, searching my face for a moment before he tries to move me out of the way, but I cling to his shirt. Goddamn it, this is so, so bad. If Wyatt kills this kid, which is a real possibility, he will go to jail and I'll lose him forever. He narrows his eyes and looks down at me with disgust.

"You're protecting him? So, it's true, then? You want this little fucker?"

I shake my head. "No, baby. I'm worried about you going to jail."

"Baby?" Colin asks and I glance over my shoulder as his gaze bounces between the two of us. Wyatt flashes him a smile that makes a feeling of dread wash over me as he takes a step forward, despite my best efforts to hold him back, and nods.

"Yeah, because I'm her fucking husband, not her roommate, you little fuck."

He holds his hand up, his face going pale as he takes a step back and I roll my eyes, turning my focus back to my husband. "Uh… Piper?"

"Stop talking to me like I know you," I snap, not even bothering to glance at him as I look up at Wyatt and pray to God that he can see the truth in my eyes. His anger wavers for just a second and it gives me hope.

"You know what, I think I'm just going to go…"

Wyatt nods, his murderous glare flicking up to Colin. "That's a great fucking idea."

Peeking over my shoulder, I watch him run back to

his car and climb behind the wheel. The engine squeals, a horrible metal on metal sound filling the air as he tries to start it but it's already running. As soon as Colin whips out of the driveway and races away from our house, Wyatt's gaze drops to me, accusations swimming in his eyes.

"Inside. Now."

He doesn't even wait for me to respond or follow him as he turns and marches into the house with his fury rolling off of him in waves. Sighing, I drop my forehead into my hand and try to force my brain to work but all I can feel is this overwhelming sense of dread.

How can I make him see the truth?

How can I make him believe me when he's so certain that there is something going on?

At this point, I don't even care about finding out who Colin is or where he came from because he doesn't matter. Wyatt does. Tears sting my eyes and I shake my head as I look up at the house. Wyatt stands in the doorway, watching me but when our eyes meet, he turns and disappears inside. Sucking in a breath, I follow him and press a trembling hand to my stomach as it rolls in protest. As soon as I step inside, he glares at me, ready for a fight and I shake my head again.

"Wyatt…"

"You fucking that clown?" he asks, cutting me off and I shake my head. "Is he what you really want, Piper?"

I shake my head again. "Wyatt, I don't know who that was."

"Yeah? Well, he sure as hell seemed to know you, didn't he? All these things keep adding up and now, it's all starting to make sense to me."

"What are you talking about?"

He scoffs, shaking his head. "I'm talking about the flowers, the reservation in Seattle, and now Colin. It's all

379

coming together so how about you stop lying to me?"

Seattle?

What the hell is he talking about?

"What reservation?" I ask, scowling at him as he rolls his eyes and crosses his arms over his chest again.

"The one you made at a hotel in Seattle the morning after we came back from my parents'. The one I fucking cancelled so good luck running off with your new boy toy."

Dropping my head back, I blow out a breath, trying not to lose my temper, before meeting his gaze again. "Wyatt, I'm going to say this as plainly as I possibly can. I don't know that man. I've never seen or spoken to him before, in my life. I don't know anything about a hotel reservation in Seattle and I fucking love you with every ounce of my body. I don't want to leave you but I'm also starting to wonder if I can keep doing this."

"Doing what? Being with me?" He shakes his head, pain flashing through his eyes before he shuts it down. "Why did you even come back, Piper? Did you feel like breaking my fucking heart one more time for fun?"

Tears spring to my eyes as I shake my head. "Wyatt, I would never. I love you. You know that… we're Wyatt and Piper and you are the only man I've ever loved."

"You know, for ten years, I knew you were a cold bitch based on the way you left me last time but I've got to give you props because this is a new fucking level." His gaze drops to my belly and that pain is back. "Is the baby even mine?"

A sob rips through me as I stare at him and cover my belly with my hand like I can somehow protect our child from the hate he is flinging at me right now. Tears stream down my face as I shake my head, staring at him and trying to find a little piece of the man I love.

"How could you say that to me?"

Every Little Thing

He shrugs. "How could you cheat on me?"

"I'm not cheating on you, Wyatt!" I scream, my heart aching so bad that I don't know how I'm still standing as heat flushes through my body and I clench my teeth. "You promised you wouldn't throw my past in my face ever again."

"This isn't the past we're talking about. It's right now and I have all the evidence I need." He turns and marches down the hallway to the bedroom as I follow behind him, my heart climbing into my throat.

What is he doing?

When I step into the room, pain splinters through me and more tears slip down my cheeks as I try to take a breath but I'm crying too hard. Wyatt has a duffel bag open on the bed and he's throwing his clothes inside haphazardly. His hate filled gaze flicks to me and he stops, turning and grabbing the bag from the bed, zipping it up as he walks toward me. "I'll sign the papers in the morning."

My brows draw together as I stare up at him, wishing this was a dream or some kind of cruel joke. "The papers?"

"The divorce papers," he says before brushing past me and storming out of the house. My heart races and my mind spins as I stumble backward into the door frame and reach for the other side to keep my self upright. Another sob tears through me and I fall to the floor as pain swallows me up and spits me back out in the house that used to be my home.

A.M. Myers

Every Little Thing

Chapter Thirty-One
Wyatt

Yawning, I run a hand over my tired eyes and shake my head before grabbing my beer off of the table in front of me and taking a sip as Blaze walks into the clubhouse. He arches a brow when he sees me and motions for me to follow him back to his office. I nod and stand up, bringing my beer with me. After I stormed out of the house last night, I knew I needed to, at least, have someone keeping an eye on Piper to make sure she didn't get hurt so I asked Blaze to sit on our house all night. I would have done it myself but I couldn't go back there - not yet. My chest burns as I think about the kid that showed up yesterday and the look on Piper's face when I told her I would be signing the divorce papers in the morning. The heartbreak in her eyes looked real as hell, just like the love in her eyes when she told me she would never cheat on me but she has to be lying. There is too much evidence against her and I'm not going to be made a fool of once again.

"Sit down," Blaze instructs as I walk into his office and

I throw myself in the chair across from him as he scrubs his jaw with his hand. "She's safe, in case you were wondering."

My eyes widen. "Are you seriously throwing attitude at me when she is the one who is cheating on me?"

"Open your fucking eyes, Fuzz. That woman is completely fucking devoted to you and I know you asked Streak about this guy coming after us also finding other ways to torment us. Did you really forget about it so easily?"

"Why would he do that?" I ask, rolling my eyes as I take another sip of my beer and Blaze slams his hand on the table. I jerk forward, staring at him as he levels a glare at me.

"Pull your head out of your goddamn ass. This is an all out war on this club and you should know better than to assume anything. I watched your woman cry her eyes out all night long."

Running my hand through my hair, I release a breath. I know I entertained the thought that the man coming after the club could be behind the things going on with Piper but I'm not buying it. This guy, whoever he is, is not going to concern himself with targeting just one member of this club. Why would he?

"What would be the point of making me think my wife is cheating on me?"

"Let me ask you something," Blaze says, leaning back in his chair and crossing his arms over his chest. "You were the one spearheading the investigation in these girls' deaths. How much work have you gotten done on the cases in the last two weeks?"

"Not a lot."

He nods. "And why is that?"

"'Cause I've been too worried about Piper to focus on them," I admit, connecting the dots with where this conversation is going but I already thought through about all this and I still think it's unlikely.

"Uh-huh," he quips, nodding his head. "Would you say that you're acting sane right now? That you've got your shit together and that you've been an asset to this club and your wife lately?"

My throat feels tight as I shake my head. "No, I suppose not…"

"My thoughts exactly. So, while I was sitting in front of your house last night, I called Streak and had him dig into your wife's life. He can't find anything. The IP address of the person running the dating profile he found on her came from a restaurant that offers free wifi, the hotel reservations were also made from the same computer, and the flowers came from one Colin Owens, who was also communicating with the dating profile but there is no evidence that Piper is doing any of this. In fact, as far as Streak can tell, if she isn't at work, she is with you."

That's not exactly true. She goes to her support group, too, but I get his point. Piper isn't cheating on me and I'm an ass. All of the tension I've been carrying around for weeks rushes out of my body and I set my beer on the desk before leaning forward and dropping my head into my hands. "Oh my fucking God."

"You know the thing that confuses me the most, though? You know how to look all of this stuff up and yet, you didn't. Why the hell not?"

"I don't know…" I whisper, looking up at him and he shakes his head with a sigh.

"Seems like you don't trust her… or you're scared."

I narrow my eyes at him. "You a therapist all of the sudden?"

"Sure as hell feels like it lately," he snaps and I drop my head into my hands again as my head spins.

Piper isn't cheating on me.

The words ring through my head over and over again until the words I flung at her last night replace them, making my heart sink.

"Fuck! I've got to get back to the house and…"

"Grovel?" he supplies and I nod as I stand up and turn toward the door. "Maybe get something shiny with a four figure price tag. Just a thought."

I nod as I grab the door handle and turn back to look at him. "Yeah. Thanks for watching over her last night, Blaze."

"It's fine as long as you don't make a habit of this."

"It won't ever happen again," I assure him. Once I convince Piper to forgive me for being an epic dick, I'm going to be the best damn husband that anyone has ever seen. He nods.

"Get out of here, then."

Nodding again, I step out of the office and close the door behind me before heading for the clubhouse door with one thing on my mind. I run through our fight and the more I remember, the more my heart sinks.

Shit.

The stuff I said was so fucked up and she was so hurt. I have no idea how I'm going to explain this all to her. When we went to my parents' house, I promised her that I was going to be there through everything but it was so easy for this guy to get in my head and drive a wedge between us. I can't believe I was such an idiot about this. All I had to do was a couple of internet searches and I could have avoided hurting both of us but no, I was too damn consumed with worry and convinced that she was leaving me again.

Fuck.

Maybe I need some goddamn therapy.

The front door opens, bright morning sunlight streaming into the room and Kodiak walks in, his gaze scanning the bar before coming to a stop on me. He arches a brow as he walks over to me, shaking his head.

"Dude, you're so fucked."

"Why?" I ask as my head jerks back. How in the hell does he even know about what's going on? He glances over his shoulder and leans in.

"Tate is outside and if I were you, I would avoid her at all costs."

Before I can even ask him why, the door swings open again and Tate walks into the room with purpose, dressed in all black and her hair pulled back into a tight ponytail. She looks terrifying. Her gaze lands on me and rage rolls off her, so potent that I consider running out of the back door like a little bitch. I glance down and notice the taser in one hand and her pistol in the other.

Yep.

I definitely should have run.

"Baby, I said no gun," Kodiak hisses but she walks past him, barely flicking her eyes in his direction as she closes the gap between us and gets right in my face.

387

"What in the *fuck* do you think you're doing?"

My eyes widen and I glance at Kodiak, who closes his eyes and shakes his head, before turning back to her. "Like, right now?"

Wrong move.

She doesn't even respond, just snarls at me as she presses the taser to my skin before I can dodge out of her way. The muscles in my arm seize up before electricity rolls through my entire body, all of my muscles tightening and pain hitting every nerve ending as I crumple to the floor with a groan.

"What the fuck?" I breathe, trying to figure out what the hell I did to Tate to piss her off. That woman is ten kinds of crazy and I know better than to mess with her. Shaking my head, I open my eyes. Black boots fill my vision and I glance up at her. "Are you wearing steel toe boots?"

She grins. "Test me again and find out."

"Want to tell me why the hell you're so pissed?" I ask as my muscles begin to relax and I take a deep breath, trying to will them to release. She lifts one of her feet and presses it against my shoulder as she points the pistol at me.

"Tate," Kodiak warns, taking a step toward her and she glances back at him, halting him in his tracks.

"Shut up." She turns her gaze back to me. "Do you know what I did last night, Fuzz?"

I shake my head. "No."

"I went over to your house and held your wife as she bawled all night long, saying it hurt so bad that she was going to die so let me ask you again, what the hell kind of game are you playing with my friend?"

My heart aches as I imagine Piper sitting on the couch

and crying so hard that she can't even breathe. How many nights did I wake up to that same scene because she had a nightmare about her parents? And now, I'm the one doing it to her.

I'm such a piece of shit.

"I fucked up, okay?" I say, looking up at Tate, as Blaze's office door opens and he steps out. He takes one look at the three of us and rolls his eyes, mumbling something to himself about "fucking children".

"Tate, put the gun away."

She peeks over at him and nods. "Fine, but the taser stays out."

"Fine," he agrees with a nod and she turns her attention back to me as she slips the pistol into her ankle holster. She tosses the taser to her other hand and holds it just above my skin. "Continue."

"I was just going to go home and apologize to her."

She shakes her head. "She's not there. Eden came over this morning and took her into work to get her mind off her asshole husband."

"Okay," I say with a nod. "I'll go there, then."

"And say what to her?"

"That I'm a fucking moron and I know she didn't cheat on me."

Her eyes widen. "That's it?"

"What else would I say?" I ask and she glares at me as she pulls her foot back and presses the taser to my skin again. I yell as the jolt pierces through my body and my muscles lock up.

"How about, 'I'm a fucking idiot for ever thinking you would do that to me, baby' or 'I'm so sorry that I asked you if the baby was mine'. Honestly, just about anything is better than your plan."

"Okay," I breathe as my muscles begin to relax again and she presses her foot to my shoulder once more. "I'll tell her all that. I fucking swear."

She studies me for a long moment before she stands up and flips the taser off, removing her foot from my shoulder. When it's safe, I slowly pull myself to my feet and she points a finger in my face. "If this ever happens again, you'll get a bullet wound to match Lincoln's."

"Noted," I whisper, taking a step back from her. "Can I go find my wife now?"

Arching a brow, she studies me. "Are you going to show up empty-handed?"

Before I can answer her, the front door opens again and we all turn to look as a frail, trembling woman limps into the clubhouse. Her clothes are ripped and torn in pieces, hanging off her thin body and there is dirt smeared all over her skin mixed with what I can only assume is blood. Tear marks carve a path of clean, perfect skin down her cheeks and her hair is a wild mass as she gazes around the room in horror. Blaze steps forward cautiously.

"Are you okay, darlin'?"

She shakes her head and I scoff.

She is obviously not okay but what is she doing here?

"I.." she whispers, looking at all of us like we might jump her and Tate sets her taser down on the table before walking over to her. The woman watches her cross the room, her eyes full of fear and a whimper slips out of her mouth as Tate grabs her hands and leads her to the closest table.

"Sit down, sweetie."

"Kodiak, go call Rodriguez," Blaze orders as the girls sink into their seats and Kodiak slips into the war room as he pulls his phone out of his pocket. I turn back to the table as Tate tries to reassure her that she is okay but the woman is terrified, crying and shaking as she looks at all of us with so much fear that I don't know how she is still standing.

"Can you tell me your name?" Tate asks and the woman nods.

"Veronica Pope."

Hold up…

I know that name.

All the blood rushes to my ears as I stare at her and it feels like there is an ice block in my chest, spreading through my body with each breath. "You're Veronica Pope?"

She looks up at me and nods. Blowing out a breath, I look up and my eyes meet Blaze's across the room. Veronica Pope went missing a while back and Rodriguez asked us to help him with the case right around the time Henn was released from prison but we never found anything. Holy fuck… all this time, she's been with the guy coming after us? Pinching the bridge of his nose, Blaze releases a sigh and walks forward slowly before sitting across from her.

"Veronica, my name is Blaze and I'm the president of this club. We've been investigating your disappearance for a while now with the police so I want you to know that you are safe here, okay?"

She studies him for a second before nodding.

"Can you tell us what happened to you?"

"I… I was kidnapped… I don't know how long ago… a man… he's been holding me hostage and today… he opened the front door of the cabin he was keeping me in and he told me to run…I didn't make it far before he caught me and he made me wear a blindfold as he loaded me into his car. When he dropped me off… we were here and he told me to come inside," she says, her voice weak and my stomach flips as my heart starts racing.

"He specifically told you to come in here?"

She nods. "He said you guys would help me…"

My heart beat pounds in my ears as I stare down at her, my mind trying to catch up. Why would her kidnapper bring her here? Unless… *it's him*.

"He told me to give you," she whispers, pointing to Blaze. "A message."

Blaze runs a hand over his face as he nods. "What was the message?"

"I am just getting started."

My stomach drops like a rock and I clench my jaw as Blaze's gaze snaps to mine, the look in his eyes as grave as I feel. "Call everyone in and their families, too."

I nod. "I need to go get Piper."

"I'll call everyone," Tate says, jumping up with determination on her face. "You go get your wife."

"Thanks," I whisper as I turn and run out to the parking lot with every worst case scenario playing through my head. I pull my phone out of my pocket and dial Piper's number as Veronica's warning runs through my head again.

I am just getting started.

What does that even mean?

How does this end?

With all of us dead?

With our club destroyed?

"Wyatt?" she answers and I release a breath I didn't realize I was holding as I reach my bike and swing my leg over the seat.

"Baby... I need you to go home and I'll meet you there."

She scoffs. "That's all you have to say to me today?"

"No, Pip. We have a hell of a lot to talk about but shit is going down at the club and I need to get you to safety so can we table it for just a little bit?"

Silence greets me as I start my bike and my heart hammers in my chest. I mentally urge her to agree with the plan. Not that it will stop me from getting her and bringing her back here to keep her safe but I'd rather not apologize for another thing. Finally, she sighs. "Okay, Wyatt. I'm leaving now and I'll see you at the house."

"Thank you, baby," I say as I back out of my parking spot. "I love you."

"I love you, too, Wyatt," she replies but I don't miss the tears in her voice and I know this is nowhere near fixed for us but with the threat looming closer, everything is clear for me. Nothing is more important than my wife and our child and I'll do whatever it takes to live up to the promise I made her in my parents' driveway.

I won't let anything come between us anymore.

Chapter Thirty-Two
Piper

My hands shake, gripping the steering wheel so tightly that my knuckles turn white, as I pull up in front of the house and stare at Wyatt's bike in the driveway. I don't know what to think. Yesterday, he was telling me that he will be signing the divorce papers in the morning and then when he calls me today, he tells me he loves me and needs to get me to safety. I've got whiplash from his ever-changing moods and I don't know how much longer I can do this. Pressing my hand to my belly, I remember the ultrasound picture we saw of our baby yesterday and shake my head.

I can't believe that was only twenty-four hours ago.

Whatever happens, we are bringing a baby into this world and if he doesn't want this anymore, doesn't want me, we have to find a way to raise this little one together. Pain blooms in my chest and tears sting my eyes as I think about the possibility of being a single mother after I thought I was getting everything I've ever wanted and a sob bubbles out of me. I clamp my hand over my mouth and lean my head back as the tears start slipping down my cheeks and my chest shakes. I love him so much that I can't even explain it, can't find the words to describe the feeling I get whenever I see his face, and I don't know how I'm going to survive losing him a second time.

Opening my eyes and looking up at the house, I meet Wyatt's eyes as he stands in the doorway and gasp, my heart climbing into my throat. I wipe the tears from my cheeks and turn the car off but I can't force myself to get out. After a second, he starts walking down the stairs toward me and my heart races out of control.

Oh, God, what is he going to say?
Does he still think I'm cheating on him?
Is he leaving me?

When he reaches my door, he opens it and holds his hand out to me with a nervous smile on his face. His eyes are full of fear and uncertainty and it doesn't do anything to calm my emotions. My stomach tightens painfully as I slip my hand into his and step out of the car. Pulling me into his arms, he looks down at me, our gazes locked together as my heart feels like it's going to explode in my chest and my stomach flips. Each breath punches out of my chest, matching him and slowly, he lowers his face to mine and gently claims my lips. A sob shoots through me as I melt into him, swallowed up by our kiss and his firm touch holds me together when all I feel like doing is falling apart.

I can't lose him.

The mean, hateful words he hurled at me yesterday echo through my mind and I pull back, shoving him away from me as I shake my head and take steps back. "Stop,

Wyatt."

"Baby," he breathes, reaching for me and I shake my head again. As much as I want to fall back into his arms and believe him when he tells me that everything will be okay, I can't. Not anymore. These issues between us are bigger than either of us realized. He sighs, running his hand through his hair as he glances down the street. "Let's go inside."

I nod and ignore his outstretched hand as I pass by him to go into the house. It's not that I want to be cruel or hurt him back but I know if I let him touch me again, our connection will overwhelm me and demand that I give into him. I can't do that this time. As I step into the living room, memories of the last few weeks in this house flood my mind and a few more tears slip down my cheeks. The morning we went over to his parents' house pops into my mind and I remember his promise to always follow me anytime I run and as I turn back to face him, I know I have to do the same.

I won't give in.

I won't just forgive.

But I will fight for my man and I will fight for our love.

Wyatt runs his hand through his hair and peeks up at me, his nerves painted across his handsome face. "I don't know what to say…"

"Why don't you start with whether or not you're still planning on signing the divorce papers today?" My heart skips a beat as I wait for his answer and I cross my arms over my chest, struggling to take a full breath as he looks up at me. Until last night, I didn't even know he still had those and it kills me to think that he kept them as an insurance policy. He wanted an out from the very beginning. After what feels like an eternity, he turns and walks down the hallway to the bedroom as my heart sinks. When he comes back, he has the papers in his hand and my lip wobbles as my world crashes down around me. Stopping right in front of me, he holds his hand out to me. "Come with me."

Maybe I'm a masochist or on some level, I assume that I deserve to watch him sign our lives away but I slip my hand into his, savoring the feeling because I know this will be the last time, and let him lead me into the kitchen. We stop in front of the sink and I scowl as he digs a lighter out of his pocket and holds the flame to the corner of the papers.

"Oh," I whisper, a sob overwhelming me as I grip the counter and watch him drop the burning papers into the sink before he turns to me and cups my face between his hands.

"Blaze had Streak investigate all the things that have been happening - the flowers, the reservations, and the guy that showed up yesterday - and he found an online dating profile for you run by someone else."

Who in the hell would run a fake dating profile on me and for what reason?

"Blaze and Streak both think it is the same guy who is targeting the club…"

A bolt of fear slices through me.

"I was the one leading the charge on these cases but I haven't been doing as much lately because I've been so distracted with everything going on between us. I…" He pulls his hand away from my face and runs one through his hair. "I was tracking you and following you to make sure you didn't leave me or cheat on me and each time something new happened, it just made me feel crazier."

"Wyatt," I breathe, closing my eyes and rubbing my fingers into my forehead. I don't even know how to process all of this and I know we'll have to talk about this in more depth later but right now, I don't want to interrupt him.

"I know, baby…" His voice cracks and he shakes his head. "I don't know why I was so quick to believe the worst of you because when I look at you now… It's so crazy to me that I ever believed you could do that to me. I mean, I know you… I've known you since we were ten years old and I know you would never do that to me. It's just… I was going crazy… Fuck, Pip. I'm so fucking sorry that I've been such an ass lately. Clearly, I have some issues from our past but I promise you that I'm going to work on that."

I nod, searching his eyes and for the first time in a long time, I can see the boy I fell in love with staring back at me. "How?"

"How what?"

"How are you going to work on it?" I ask and he shakes his head, blowing out a breath.

"I don't really know yet. I hadn't really gotten that far." *That is what I was afraid of.*

I'm happy that he is identifying the problem but it's not that easy to overcome. For ten years, my betrayal became part of who he was and just because it didn't actually happen doesn't mean the trust issues disappeared. Looking down, I take a deep breath and my heart skips a beat as I meet his gaze again. "Will you go see Dr. Brewer with me?"

"What?" he asks, jerking back.

Shit.

Maybe I shouldn't have asked that.

The look on his face makes it clear that he doesn't like the idea but I remember sitting on the beach with him the morning we left Charleston and how he told me that he would do whatever it took to make this work. I just hope that still applies now.

"Wyatt, I can't fix you with my love anymore than you can fix me and if you really want to make this work, I think this is what we need to do. And I know that it's my fault that you have these trust issues but we have to find a way to move forward."

He shakes his head. "I don't know, Pip... I don't want to talk to a shrink."

"Baby," I say, reaching forward and grabbing his hand before placing it on my belly. "We have to find a way to get past this, for us and for this baby that we are bringing into the world and these past few weeks have been hell for both of us. I've been worried sick that I was losing you and you were feeling the same and it doesn't really matter who was manipulating you because the point is, you believed it. We have to fix *us* and you promised me that you would do whatever it took to make this work."

"I..." he says before sighing and running his hand through his hair again. The silence stretches between us and I can see him working through it in his mind before he looks up at me and nods. "Okay. I hate the idea so much but I'll do it for you."

I shake my head as he pulls me into his arms. "No, Wyatt. You're doing this for you."

"Let's compromise and say I'm doing it for us."

"Fine," I answer, rolling my eyes and he flashes me a grin as he pulls me closer and his gaze drops to my lips. His tongue darts out, tracing along his full bottom lip and just like that, I want him.

"Do I get to kiss you now?"

I nod. "Yes, please."

His lips crash down on mine and our bodies meld together as I grip the back of his cut and moan into his kiss. Tears sting my eyes, slipping down my cheeks as his hand slips into my hair and he massages the back of my head. Too quickly, he pulls back and brushes his thumb over my cheek, wiping away my tears.

"I love you, sweetheart, and I'm so sorry for everything I put you through."

Closing my eyes, I lay my head on his shoulder. "Pretty sure we're about even now."

Silence descends over us again but this time, it's comfortable as he holds me close and we enjoy the quiet moment together, letting go of the past twenty-four hours. When he pulls away again, there is stress lining his face.

"We've got to pack and get back to the club, baby."

I nod, blinking up at him as a chill runs through me. "What's happening?"

"A woman walked into the clubhouse this morning, saying she had been kidnapped and her abductor brought her to us and told her to pass along a message."

Sucking in a breath, my heart races as I look up at him. "It's him?"

"Yeah, baby. It's him."

"What was the message?" I ask, not really all that sure I

want to know and Wyatt presses his lips into a thin line and sighs.

"I am just getting started."

My stomach drops and the fear is so overwhelming that I feel rooted to the spot. I stare up at my husband, his eyes flash with the same dread coursing through my body right now and I shake my head, my mouth opening but no words come out. I drop my head and try to breathe through it just like Dr. Brewer taught me but my mind runs wild with the possibilities, making it impossible to calm myself.

What do we do?

No one has any clue who this guy is and he is one hundred steps ahead of us.

"Hey," he whispers, smoothing his hand over my hair and pulling my gaze back to his. "One step at a time, okay? Let's go pack."

I nod and we turn to walk out into the dining room when a loud pop comes from outside followed by the sound of glass breaking. Wyatt's wide gaze turns to me and as the second pop echoes through the neighborhood, he pulls me to the floor.

"Is someone shooting at us?" I hiss as we flatten our bodies against the dining room floor. Wyatt's hard gaze flicks to me as he pulls his gun out of his holster.

"You stay here, okay?"

I shake my head, trying to grab for him as he starts crawling away from me but he breaks free of my hold. "Wyatt!"

He disappears behind the table and I gasp for air, my pulse spiking as he pulls the curtains back to peek outside. The window breaks, raining glass down on him and I clamp my hand over my mouth to hold back my scream as tears sting my eyes again and my heart thrashes in my ears. When he appears on the side of the table, crawling toward the front door, I'm able to breathe a little easier until he opens the front door.

"Wyatt!" I hiss but he ignores me as he stands on the side of the door and takes a deep breath before stepping outside. When I don't hear another gunshot, my mind starts to run wild and I shake my head. "Fuck this."

Crawling along the floor, I move to the table and grab my bag off of the top before digging my gun out with my gaze fixed on the front door. Just as I'm standing up to move toward it, another gunshot rings out from the backyard and I spin around. Moving as quickly and quietly as possible, I cross the kitchen and stop at the back door, pulling the curtains back to peek out of the little square window at the top of the door. Someone in a black hoodie has their back to me as they point a gun at Wyatt, who has his hands up. My gaze flicks to his gun on the ground and my stomach flips.

Oh, God, I've got to help him.

Moving slowly, I turn the door handle and gently pull the door open, careful not to make any noise and when I reach the spot where the door creaks, I hold my breath and lift it up as hard as I can, relief rushing through me when I get it open without a sound. The screen on the outside door is already open and I crouch down as Wyatt's gaze flicks to me. His eyes tell me to run but there is no way in hell that is going to happen.

"Why did you have to go and ruin everything?" the person in the hoodie says and all my thoughts screech to a halt. Wait… I know that voice.

"I don't know what you're talking about."

"She was mine!" Lillian shrieks and I shake my head, trying to understand what is happening right now but no matter which way I look at it, it doesn't make sense. Why the hell is one of my best friends holding my husband at gunpoint?

Standing up, I tiptoe backward until I hit the dining room then I turn and run out of the front door before hooking around the house. Creeping along the side of the house, I hear more of her ranting at him, telling him all about her plan to make him leave me with the flowers and the dating profile and the hotel in Seattle and I breathe a sigh of relief.

As long as she's ranting, she's not shooting.

Rounding the back of the house, I raise the pistol in my hand, holding it just the way Wyatt showed me as I stop a few feet behind her. "What are you doing, Lil?"

"Piper," she gasps, wheeling around as she lowers her gun but when she sees the gun in my hand, she lifts it again, pointing it at me.

"No! Point that back at me," Wyatt urges her, pointing to himself and I narrow my eyes and shake my head as she glances between the two of us before backing up until we form a triangle in the yard. She trains her gun on Wyatt and my heart sinks.

No.

No.

No.

"Lillian, what are you doing?"

She shakes her head as her gaze turns to me but she still

keeps the gun pointed at my husband. "I'm fixing this mess."

"What mess is that?" I ask, eyeing her warily and waiting for her to make her move. Images from the night my parents died flick through my mind but instead of reducing me to a bubbling mess like they usually do, this time I use them to fuel me. As much as I don't want to, I will protect my husband at all costs. She shakes her head again and when her eyes meet mine, they fill with tears.

"You're not supposed to be with him."

I scowl. "He's my husband, Lil. Of course I'm supposed to be with him."

"No!" she screams, shaking her head again. The blank look in her eyes scares me and the tired look on her face tells me just how close she is to snapping and I know from all my time with Dr. Brewer and in the group that I have to be careful. "Stop saying that. Don't you see, Pippy? I love you…"

"I do see that," I answer, remembering what Dr. Brewer said about people lost in a delusion before I remember Wyatt admitting to me in the kitchen that he was tracking me to make sure I didn't cheat on him. Where did he put it? In my car? My phone? Sucking in a breath, I meet his eyes and hope that he will understand my plan. "I can't believe I didn't see it before, Lil. I'm so sorry."

"It's okay," she whispers and I shake my head.

"No, it's not. You've always been there for me. Do you want to get out of here? Just you and me?"

She gasps, her eyes widening and hope flickering in her eyes. "Really?"

"Yeah. Let's go right now."

404

Every Little Thing

Wyatt grits his teeth and shakes his head. "Piper. No."

"Shut up," she hisses, turning back to him and raising the gun to his head. My heart jumps into my throat and my mind screams but on the outside, I remain calm.

"Lillian? Please don't do that. If you kill him, they'll come after us and rip us apart."

Her eyes widen and she shakes her head. "No… they can't take you away from me."

"Then let's just go," I whisper, lowering my gun and holding my hand out to her as my heart hammers against my ribs. Wyatt's face is tortured but he doesn't say anything and I just hope he will understand what I'm doing and go along with my plan. Her gaze flicks between Wyatt and me before she starts walking over to me, still pointing the gun at my man. When she reaches me, she takes my hand and I resist the urge to shudder at the fear racing through my veins as we start backing up toward the side of the house as she continues aiming the gun at Wyatt.

"Don't follow us," she warns him, flashing him a glare and I shake my head, mouthing the words "I love you" to him just before we disappear around the side of the house. Once we're in the clear, she starts running, pulling me along with her. "Come on. We have to go."

We step into the front yard and she turns to me. "Do you have your keys?"

"Yes. They're in my pocket."

She grins and nods. "Okay. Let's go."

"But wait, I don't have my wallet or anything," I tell her, suddenly doubting my plan. Her gaze flicks to the side of the house and she shakes her head, pulling me along.

"I've got plenty of money for us and I'll drive."

405

I nod, trying to think but my brain won't work. My gaze drops to the gun in her hand and I suck in a breath. "Can we leave the guns here?"

"Sure," she answers cheerily as she drops his pistol into the grass and I do the same. Maybe it's a bad idea but I feel a whole hell of a lot better knowing there's not two firearms in the car I'm about to get into.

My stomach flips as we reach the car and she pulls open the passenger side door.

Oh, fuck, this is such a bad idea.

Why the hell am I doing this?

Slipping into my seat, I buckle up and pull the keys out of my pocket as she runs around the front of the car.

Okay, just breathe, Piper.

I just need to keep her distracted long enough for Wyatt to call reinforcements and track us down. Reaching down, I feel the phone in my back pocket and pray that he put the tracker in there or on the car... otherwise I'm screwed. My hands shake and my stomach does another flip as Lillian slides behind the wheel and reaches for the keys. As she starts the car, Wyatt runs around the house and stops when he sees me sitting in the passenger seat. I wish I could press my hand to the glass or anything to let him know how much I love him in case I don't make it back from this but I can't let Lillian get suspicious of me.

"So, where to?" Lillian asks, flashing me a wide grin as she pulls away from the curb. I shake my head as my chest aches and my shoulders feel tight. I wrap both of my arms around my body and hug myself as I look over at her.

"I'm open to anywhere."

She scowls. "Are you cold?"

Every Little Thing

I shake my head and release my arms as I lean back in the seat and my stomach twists. Oh, God, I'm going to throw up.

"You know, I got scared there for a minute... thinking you were like everyone else but now you're here." Her smile is wide and happy as she looks over at me. "I never should have doubted you."

"What do you mean, like the other ones?"

She rolls her eyes. "My ex..."

"Your fiancé?" I ask, remembering the story she told in group not that long ago and she nods, tears filling her eyes.

"You know, he asked me to marry him and then that night, as we were going to his parents' to share the news, he tells me he's having second thoughts and maybe we shouldn't say anything just yet."

I drop my gaze to my lap and scowl as I try to put all the pieces together. What exactly is she saying? "I'm sorry. That must have been hard."

"I begged him to just give us a chance, you know? But the more I begged, the more he stood his ground and then he said that he wanted to break up instead so I did what I had to do."

"What did you do, Lil?" I ask, my eyes snapping up to hers and she shrugs.

"I couldn't let him leave me."

Oh my God...

Jesus fucking Christ.

In the three years that I've known her, I never would have guessed that she was this unbalanced and I shake my head, wondering how the hell I never saw it. How I never picked up on the fact that, at some point, she fell in love with me?

"You killed him?" I ask as I struggle to draw a breath into my lungs and she shrugs again, her grip on the steering wheel tightening.

"I couldn't let him just leave me, Piper. Not after everything. Don't you judge me."

Holding my hands up in surrender, I shake my head. "I'm not. Just surprised is all."

"Oh, okay…" Her gaze flicks to the rearview mirror and she hisses a curse. I glance in the side mirror and my heart jumps when I see the Bronco right on our heels.

Oh, fuck, Wyatt, what the hell are you doing?

She glances over at me and I turn, meeting her eyes. Her grip on the steering wheel tightens and she blows out a breath.

"This was all a trick?"

I shake my head. "No, Lil… it's not a trick but he's not just going to let me go."

"I shouldn't have left the gun," she growls and I'm suddenly very glad for my quick thinking as I glance at the truck in the side mirror again. When I glance back at her, her eyes are sad and she shakes her head as a tear slips down her cheek.

"I don't want to do it…"

My brows knit together and my heart sinks as I try to decipher her words. "You don't want to do what?"

"I won't let him take you from me…"

My eyes widen and I open my mouth to scream, beg her to rethink her plan but before I can get the words out, she jerks the wheel to the side and the car flies off the road. My head smashes against the window and everything flips upside down just before my world fades to black.

Chapter Thirty-Three
Wyatt

"What the fuck were you thinking, Piper?" I hiss to myself as I press my foot harder against the gas pedal as my chest feels tight and I struggle to pull air into my lungs.

Fuck.

I can't lose her.

"Where are they headed?" Rodriguez ask over speakerphone and I relay our location to him. As soon as Lillian and Piper walked out of the backyard, I called Detective Rodriguez and told him what was going down. He urged me to just wait for him to get there but there was no way in hell that I was leaving my wife.

Hell no.

"We're almost there."

I nod. "Okay."

The car jerks to the side out of nowhere, flying off of the road and I slam on the brakes, my whole world screeching to a halt as Piper's car begins flipping through the air. I throw the truck in park, gasping for breath, and jump out as

410

it comes to a stop on the roof, my heart pounding in my ears. Running my fingers through my hair, I stare at it for a second, unable to move before I start running toward it, toward her.

Shaking my head, I pull myself from the memory and stare up at the monitor as Piper's heart rate steadily tracks across the screen. My knee bounces like crazy as I prop my chin on my hands and stare at it like at any moment, she could crash despite all the doctors telling me she looks good and it's just a waiting game now. She's been unconscious for thirty-six hours and while that might not seem like a lot to most people, it has felt like an eternity to me. Although, I suppose it's better than the total dread that swarmed me as I watched the car fly off the highway.

I shake my head to clear the memory as I turn to look at her bruised face. When I got to the car, it was clear that Lillian had died in the crash but Piper was in and out of consciousness until the ambulance showed up along with Rodriguez and two other patrol cars.

"Hey," someone says and I glance over at Chance and Storm as they walk into the room and sit in the chairs along the wall. I nod my greeting. "How is she holding up?"

I shrug. "Same."

"She'll wake up, man," Storm assures me and I nod. I know he's been exactly where I am now but he can't promise me anything. Chance stands up and walks over to me, clapping my shoulder.

"You need anything?"

"No."

He sighs. "All right. Call us if you do, okay? Moose and Henn are taking over guard duty for us."

"I'll be fine. Go see your wives."

They walk back out of the room and I release breath as I run my hand through my hair. Blaze ordered everyone to the clubhouse after Veronica showed up and that is all where we're hunkering down while we try to figure all of this out. I can't wait to get Piper there, where I know she will be safe.

"Mr. Landry?" someone says and my heart jumps into my throat. Fuck, is it one of the doctors? Do they have more information on her condition? I spin around and scowl at the woman I don't recognize. She forces a smile to her face. "I'm Dr. Brewer, your wife's therapist."

I nod, eyeing her. "And Lillian's doctor."

"Ah, yes… that's why I'm here, actually. I wanted to tell you… well, both of you, how sorry I am. I knew Lillian had some deep seeded trauma but she was reluctant to open up to me and I had no idea that she was so…"

"Unhinged?" I hiss, glaring up at her and she nods.

"Yes. She… hell, I probably shouldn't be saying this… but she was in another car crash when she was very young and she lost her sister. It… manifested itself with this fear that she would lose everyone she loved and so, she took matters into her own hands. I thought… I thought we were getting somewhere with her but if I had known about her developing feelings for Piper… I would have…"

"It's not your fault."

My head whips to Piper and relief rushes over me when I see her green eyes staring back at me and I don't know how I don't collapse on the floor.

"Baby," I whisper, standing and leaning over her, pressing a soft kiss to her lips. She closes her eyes and

412

when she opens them again, she flashes me a smile.

"Hey, you."

I shake my head, cupping her face as softly as I can so I don't hurt her. "Don't you ever do that to me again, you hear?"

"Yes, sir," she answers, her voice scratchy and a dreamy smile on her face for a second before her eyes widen as she reaches up and grips my shirt in her hand. "The baby?"

I smile. "The baby is just fine, sweetheart."

"I'm just going to give you two a little time," Dr. Brewer says and Piper shakes her head, glancing over at her.

"No, wait… I wanted to thank you."

Dr. Brewer's eyes widen. "Why? You were in that situation because of me."

"No, I wasn't. But I knew what to do and how to handle Lillian in her fragile state because of you. You saved all of our lives."

"Oh," she whispers, tears welling up in her eyes.

"And there is something I wanted to ask you."

Nodding, Dr. Brewer takes a step forward. "Okay…"

"Do you offer couples counseling?" Piper asks, looking up at me with a grin and I roll my eyes. Leave it to my wife to get shot at, kidnapped, and put in a coma for a day and half and still remember the promise I made her about counseling. Dr. Brewer glances between the two of us and nods.

"I do… but are you sure you wouldn't prefer someone else?"

I shake my head. "Nah. Piper was right. This wasn't

your fault and honestly, you already know all about our past and you're probably the best person to help us."

"Okay, then," she answers with a smile. "Call me when you're feeling a little bit better and we'll schedule something, okay?"

We agree and she tells us good-bye before stepping out of the room, leaving us alone. I turn to look at my wife, wishing I could pull her into my arms but I don't want to hurt her and she is bruised everywhere.

"Lillian?" she asks with a sigh, looking up at me and I shake my head. Tears well up in her eyes and she nods. "Oh."

"I'm sorry, baby. I know she was your friend before all of this happened but I can't be sad that she's dead. You're my everything and I don't know what I would have done if I had lost you."

She nods. "I can't believe I never saw it…"

"It sounds like she did a very good job of hiding how she really was," I say and she nods with another heavy sigh.

"I know you're right. I just wish I could have helped her."

I flash her a grin and her eyebrows knit together as she stares up at me. "Well, look on the bright side, we can talk about it in therapy."

"If I didn't love you so much," she growls, shaking her head and I laugh.

"Yeah, but you do and now… you're stuck with me forever."

Her green eyes meet mine again and fear flashes through her gaze for just a moment. My heart stalls. "You promise? Even with all the shit going on with the club?"

"Yeah, I do, baby. I know I've said this before but I'm not letting anything come between us and this time, I'm going to prove it to you - every single day, for the rest of our lives."

She and I have a lot of work to do and I'm not under the impression that it will be easy but if I've learned anything in the past two months, it's that my life is better with her in it and I will do whatever I have to do to make this work. Piper is my whole fucking world and I am never going back to the man I was before she walked into my life again.

Epilogue

I take a drag of my cigarette, the smoke burning my lungs, as I scan the clubhouse parking lot but it is nothing compared to the rage burning through my chest as I watch them all gather to celebrate Fuzz and Piper renewing their vows.

How fucking sweet.

When I first heard of this impromptu wedding, a part of me hated the idea of letting them take a break from the panic and paranoia I've instilled in all of their hearts and minds but after taking some time to think about it, I decided this was better. It's my little gift to them, the only small instance of charity they'll see from me. So, let them celebrate and be happy for this one day before I rip it all away.

Brutally.

Violently.

In a pool of blood.

It's what they deserve. I clench my teeth so hard that

my jaw aches as I watch Fuzz step up to the end of the aisle in his cut with Streak and Smith on his side. He rubs his hands together, waiting for his bride to join him as all of his brothers and their wives look on with smiles on their faces.

Not for long, though.

God, what I wouldn't give to carve those grins from their faces.

I am so close to ending this, so close to getting the one thing I have wanted more than anything else in the world for as long as I can remember - justice. There is a pounding in my ears and my hands shake, rage coursing through my veins as I think about everything they did to me, everything they took from me. I used to fucking be somebody and then they came into my life. My thoughts drift to the plans I have laid out for them and I smile. It's taken me a hell of a long time to put all of this together and most days, I hated how long I had to draw this all out. I wanted action and I wanted it now but I also wanted to inflict the most pain, the most suffering possible and that takes time. Now, this is almost over and when I'm done, they'll be left with the same thing I have.

Nothing.

Can't get enough of the Devils?
Pre-order the next book in the series, Wicked Games,

now!
https://www.amazon.com/dp/B07YL8NFQR

Note from the Author:
I've stated many times on my author page and in my reader group that from the very beginning of this series, there has been something going on in the background. I've dropped hints and left clues in each book and now in these last two books, they are all coming together. Everything will be wrapped up and all of your questions will be answered in Wicked Games, Streak's book, due out Feb. 2020.
Click the link above to pre-order your copy!

Every Little Thing

Want to stay up to date on A.M. Myers and all things Bayou Devils MC?

Follow me on Facebook!

https://www.facebook.com/authorammyers/

Or

Join my reader group

https://www.facebook.com/groups/585884704893900/

A.M. Myers

Other Books by A.M. Myers

The Hidden Scars Series

Hidden Scars:
https://www.amazon.com/dp/B014B6KFJE

Collateral Damage:
https://www.amazon.com/gp/product/B01G9FOS20

Evading Fate:
https://www.amazon.com/gp/product/B01L0GKMU0

Bayou Devils MC Series

Hopelessly Devoted:
https://www.amazon.com/dp/B01MY5XQFW

Addicted To Love:
https://www.amazon.com/dp/B07B6RPPPV

Every Breath You Take:
https://www.amazon.com/dp/B07DPNTV2G

It Ends Tonight:
https://www.amazon.com/dp/B07JL4FJ18

Little Do You Know:
https://www.amazon.com/dp/B07M812N1T

Every Little Thing

Never Let Me Go:
https://www.amazon.com/dp/B07NWWN2VJ

Every Little Thing:
https://www.amazon.com/dp/B07XFGC82J

Wicked Games:
Releasing February 2020
https://www.amazon.com/dp/B07YL8NFQR

A.M. Myers

About the Author

A.M. Myers lives in Cody, Wyoming – a little town about an hour away from Yellowstone National Park – with her husband and their two boys. She has been writing for most of her life and even had a poem nationally published in the sixth grade but the idea of writing an entire book always seemed so daunting until a certain story got stuck in her head and wouldn't leave her alone until she started typing. Now, she can't imagine a time when she won't be letting all of the stories in her head spill out onto paper.

A.M. Myers writes emotional, gripping romantic suspense novels that will leave you swooning and hanging off the edge of your seat from start until finish. When she is not writing, you can usually find her up in the mountains with her boys, camping, fishing and taking photos of the beautiful landscape she is lucky enough to call home.

Made in the USA
Middletown, DE
14 October 2021